The Schumann Proof

For Sylvia –
Enjoy!

The Schumann Proof

Peter Schaffter

RENDEZVOUS PRESS

Front cover art and design by Résolutique Globale

LE CONSEIL DES ARTS
DU CANADA
DEPUIS 1957

THE CANADA COUNCIL
FOR THE ARTS
SINCE 1957

We acknowledge the support of the Canada Council for the Arts for our publishing program.

Napoleon Publishing/RendezVous Press
Toronto, Ontario, Canada

Printed in Canada

08 07 06 05 04   5 4 3 2 1

National Library of Canada Cataloguing in Publication

Schaffter, Peter, 1957-
        The Schumann proof / Peter Schaffter.

ISBN 1-894917-06-5

I. Title.

PS8637.C42S4 2004   C813'.6   C2004-903194-5

For James C. Potter, Esq., in memoriam
Antiqui milites non moriuntur

PART I

Ich kann wohl manchmal singen
Als ob ich fröhlich sei.
"Though troubled in my heart I sing
With gladness seeming true..."
—*Liederkreis*, Opus 39, VII

One

Und keiner kennt mich mehr hier.
("Unknown here, no kin shall I find.")
   —*Liederkreis*, Opus 39, I

I released the Steinway's pedal slowly. It creaked a bit, but I doubted anyone could hear. The autumnal harmonies of Strauss's "Allerseelen" lingered in the taut, steel strings, then faded like the song's All-Saints-Day asters. I turned the page quietly, careful not to break the spell. "Zueignung"—the final number of our set.

Poised in the bow of the piano, Ulrike Vogel spun out the pause before she sang again. Slender arms in long white gloves hung motionless at her side. The cobalt satin of her gown shimmered gently with her breath. I put my fingers on the keys and waited for her nod telling me she was ready.

Beyond the margin of the stage, bodies shifted, seeking a position more comfortable than the last they'd tried. As they soughed and settled into silence, a slim grey-suited man rose from his aisle seat and slipped to the back of the hall. A few necks craned, but by and large, the well-heeled crowd affected not to notice.

Recital audiences are seldom as respectful as they seem. Even frozen into attitudes of rapt appreciation, they betray a curious indifference to the music they have come to hear. Fluttering programs used as fans skirl discordant eddies of

1

aftershave and perfume through the room. Cough drops slip from crinkling sheaths, the sound as hard to pinpoint as a rustling in the grass. Watches beep and heads swivel, down to check the time, or sideways in reproach.

And inevitably, an Important Man gets up, lured away mid-concert by the promptings of his phone or pager.

At one time, cell phones and pagers used to chirp their bearers into action. Nowadays, they have a switch to silence them. Technology borrowed from women's erotic hardware heralds urgent business with an insistent buzzing sensation on the skin. It's a futile advance in courtesy. Important Men still vacate their seats the moment a call comes in.

No remote communications device had roused tonight's Important Man, however. His own participation in the evening required that he leave. The retreating form in made-to-measure worsted flannel belonged to Nils Janssen, president of Toronto's Royal Conservatory of Music, the institution in whose concert hall I was performing. Punctilious as always, Janssen had chosen to withdraw by the rear exit, the one that gives onto Bloor Street, instead of by the double doors at the front of the auditorium that lead directly to the lobby.

Less obligingly, he had not timed his departure to fall at what programs the world over call "a suitable break in the performance."

Ulrike stiffened. Indignation rippled up the back of her gown and lodged between her shoulders. Turning toward me, she raised a gloved arm and rested her hand lightly on the rim of the piano. Abruptly, a frown snaked across her brow, while her index finger rapped irritably just inside the case. I tried hard not to smile. Strict professionalism had characterized our one and only rehearsal the day before, and her display of pique, artfully concealed from the audience, caught me unawares. For a brief moment, the misgivings I'd had since agreeing to this job subsided.

My name is Vikkan Lantry, and if you haven't guessed, I'm a pianist. Or, more accurately, I play the piano. The distinction is important. The stage and I have never had an easy friendship. I dislike the minute scrutiny of the musical cognoscenti and distrust the fulsome praise of the less discerning. My playing must bring real pleasure to a few, though, and the assessments of my peers cannot all be bad, otherwise I would not have found myself accompanying Ulrike Vogel—*das Vöglein,* the little bird (to her acolytes); *die Krähe,* the crow (to her detractors)—on a warm evening in early May.

The occasion was the launching of the new Conservatory Alumni Gallery. After generations of gazing from the lobby walls, portraits of the school's past principals—the same staidly framed oils that had surveyed my teenage years—were being taken down. In their place, images of former students who'd gone on to glorious international careers would now provide inspiration for young musicians. What's more, visitors to "the Con" would have a constant reminder of the school's world-class stature. Three paintings had been commissioned to seed the Gallery: heldentenor Jon Vickers, fiery and unpredictable opera star Teresa Stratas, and, of course, the incomparable keyboard wizard, Glenn Gould.

None of the honorees was in attendance that night. Vickers, still nursing a grudge against Canadian parochialism, could not be coaxed from his farm north of Toronto. Stratas was "recovering". Gould, even had he not died in '82, would never have consented to appear in public. To offset the absences, Janssen had convened an impressive roster of Conservatory staff and associates for a gala performance marking the Gallery's inauguration.

3

Janssen himself would take part in the proceedings, but not as a performer. Although the CBC still aired his recordings of Grieg, the school's former registrar had not concertized since taking on the mantle of president two years earlier. Tonight, his sole contribution would be to unveil the three canvases waiting on crepe-hung easels behind my back. This duty and its accompanying prefatory remarks were what obliged him to leave. In all likelihood, the ever-efficient Janssen had clocked himself against Ulrike's final song, and found it gave him just the right amount of time to walk outside along Bloor Street, re-enter through the main doors, tour past the front desk and lobby and enter the greenroom, which gives the only access to the stage short of vaulting from the parterre.

Ulrike didn't actually leave me much time to speculate on Janssen's forethought. Having telegraphed her irritation at his departure, she nodded gravely and faced the audience again. A goad of adrenaline nudged me in the ribs as she drew a singer's well-supported breath, and we began.

> *Ja, du weißt es teu're Seele*
> *Daß ich fern von dir mich quäle*
> *Liebe macht die Herzen krank*
> *Habe Dank...*

Yes, dear soul, thou know'st it truly / Far from thee my heart's unruly / Love inflicts such misery / Grateful be...

"Zueignung" is a crowd-pleaser, but its artless verses—a few lines about love's turmoil followed by an exhortation to give thanks—transformed playing for Ulrike from an equivocal pleasure into a manifest nightmare. The conceit demands more skill from the singer than Strauss exercised when setting it to music. Ulrike rose to the challenge, urging

4

the tempo passionately forward here, teasing it out for languid emphasis there. If we'd had more rehearsal, I might have enjoyed some of her tricks. As it was, I was too involved with guessing when, and by how much, she'd be speeding up and slowing down.

Worse, moments before we stepped on stage, she'd murmured: "I am not happy with "Zueignung". It falls badly in the voice today. You will play it a semitone higher?" Her rich German accent turned the request into a command.

For a pianist, transposing—playing music in a key other than the one that appears on the page—requires a sort of voluntary schizophrenia, like reading aloud in English from a book that's written in French. Singers rarely appreciate the mental, not to mention digital, gymnastics demanded by their ongoing search for flattering tessituras. My fingers grew slick as I grappled with Strauss's restless triplets, while love's sweet turmoil took a back seat to the inartistic task of converting flats to naturals and naturals to sharps.

> *Heilig, heilig, an's Herz dir sank*
> *Habe Dank!*

A deafening ovation assaulted the ultimate thanksgiving, which, miraculously, we'd arrived at simultaneously, and in the same key. The barrage seemed out of place—we'd performed Strauss, not sunk a killing sword into the neck of a Spanish bull—but Ulrike drank it in like a parched flower in heavy rain. Utterly still, she bathed in the sound until a sixth sense told her it would momentarily abate. Only then did she acknowledge her audience, tilting her chin modestly and dipping her shoulders.

The clamour continued. Ulrike waited, then extended her

arm in my direction. The din grew fractionally louder when I rose and took her proffered hand. Bowing from the waist, I concocted a smile while Ulrike nodded once more and dipped her shoulders. The gesture reminded me of Glenn Close doing the Marquise de Merteuil in *Dangerous Liaisons*. *Bravas!* peppered the applause as we descended the narrow steps into the greenroom.

Janssen stood to one side to let us pass, then mounted the steps and waited for the commotion to subside. It took over a minute, giving him time to check the set of his half-Windsor, adjust his lapels, consult his watch and study a small notecard. Ulrike regarded his movements without expression. At length, the accolade thinned to a sporadic staccato and died out. Janssen squared his already perfect posture and stepped onto the platform.

There'd been no question of an encore. Janssen had made that perfectly clear during the run-through. No one was to divert attention from the concert's real stars, the Gallery portraits. Given the restriction, Ulrike had prolonged her ovation with considerable skill. There's a knack to keeping people clapping when no showy tidbit will reward their perseverance. After more than a decade out of the public eye, she evidently hadn't forgotten how.

I wanted a cigarette, but the concert's participants had to remain in the greenroom until final bows. Eleven musicians milled about in the inadequate space. In one corner, backed by a full-length mirror, a flautist in slinky red confided something to her accompanist. The members of a string quartet flanked an antique practice keyboard. A brawny tenor with hockey-player eyebrows idly depressed its silenced keys. The unrecycled air smelled of soap and shampoo. No colognes. It wouldn't do to have the cellist sneezing at the oboe's Karl Lagerfeld.

The stress of waiting settled in my shoulders. I flexed them and leaned against the wall. Hard plaster cooled my skin through the back of my suit. The jacket no longer fit; the black serge tugged uncomfortably through my chest and arms. I'd grown some muscle in the past four years. When I'd stowed the outfit away, I thought I'd never need an all-purpose concert black again. The last ten months had proved me wrong. I'd have to buy a replacement.

Undoing a button, I took a deep breath. Across the room, a gnome-ish, grey-haired man looked up from the book he'd brought to kill time. *Pierre Sabourin.* I wondered if he still taught in three-sixteen, the studio next to Zoltan Berényi. Sabourin's requests for boiling water from my former teacher's electric kettle had been a regular feature of my lessons.

Beyond the stage door, now closed, Janssen was warming to his speech. Crisp consonants and fluid vowels conveyed his theme authoritatively.

"...our reputation is unquestioned. The excellence of our program is admired throughout the world. Our teachers, gifted artists in their own right, are gathered from around the globe. The seeds of genius flourish in the fertile soil we provide."

Beside me, Ulrike smoothed her gloves. One by one, she pulled the fingers tight, then massaged loose material over her hands and up her arms. The movement attracted glances that strayed to me and lingered. *Should I know him? What's his connection with her?*

"And while not every student is destined for greatness, the Gallery seeks to inspire all, paying tribute to those whose fame will not be forgotten in the passage of time."

The passage of time. My eyes wandered to a schoolroom clock over the door to the greenroom's small washroom. A quarter to ten. Add fifteen minutes, subtract thirty-six hours, and an early morning call from Elly Gardiner was waking me from sound sleep...

"You do know about tomorrow night's concert?" she'd begun, as usual without preliminaries. Her voice held the customary undertone of reproach as well: *you should pay more attention to the goings-on at the Con.* Understandable, I suppose, from someone who's taught voice there longer than I've known how to speak.

I mumbled yes, and rolled onto my back. Elly likes to call when I'm still in bed. She knows I'll agree to anything then, too dopey to invent a reason for turning her down.

"Ulrike Vogel will be singing."

I pulled the sheets up over my legs. "Is that supposed to mean something?" I knew the name: a reclusive voice teacher who taught from her home on Castle Frank instead of using a Conservatory studio. Periodically, I came across CDs of hers at HMV. The covers featured out-of-date glamour shots with heavy makeup and airbrushed skin. Listening to the CBC, I'd sometimes hear her name in connection with this or that rising vocal star. Opinion about her had been divided when I was at the Con. Her pupils, a tight-knit lot, worshipped her. Those not in the clique tended to be skeptical.

"She hasn't sung in public in over ten years," Elly said.

"Are you saying I should go?"

"In a manner of speaking. She needs an accompanist."

I sat up. "What? She doesn't have one?"

"He had to cancel."

Elly sets me up with two kinds of jobs: busywork, like voice exams and student recitals, and engagements no one else will

8

agree to. It's her way of chastising me for the time I spent away from Toronto.

"What's she singing?" Bad question—it sounded as if I were interested. What had I been thinking, installing a phone up here in my loft?

"Strauss."

"Not Johann, I hope."

She greeted the sarcasm with a moment of silence. "Five songs," she said finally. "You know them all, I imagine."

"I wouldn't be so sure."

"Pitching bales of hay for three years can't have left that many holes in your repertoire."

"It wasn't hay. I worked at a co-op." Feed sacks and salt licks were more like it. "Which songs?"

"You'll do it, then?"

"It's pretty short notice."

"You'll manage."

"Can I call you back?"

"After you make arrangements. I have Ulrike's number here."

I wasn't being given a choice. Nothing new there. I kicked off the sheets, climbed down from the loft and picked up the phone by the piano. "Shoot."

I scribbled the number she gave on a scrap of manuscript paper. "I'm in the studio with a pupil," she concluded. "If you need to call me back, wait till eleven."

I hung up both phones, then ducked into the compact kitchen underneath the loft. Fifteen minutes later, synapses reamed by two mugs of Kenyan and a cigarette, I dialed Ulrike's number. She recognized my name immediately. Yes, she'd been expecting my call; did I know the material well? and could I come by her home that afternoon? I bent the truth a little on the first, and demurred on the second. She sounded put out but agreed to meet at the Conservatory concert hall. Our conversation ended with an abrupt "Till this afternoon, then." In German.

I started hunting around for my volume of Strauss songs as soon as she rang off. Much of my music was still in boxes. As I went through them, I began to wonder what had prompted *das Vöglein* to call Elly Gardiner for an accompanist. Elly was a minor player at the Con, more interested in teaching music than training stars. Ulrike, to judge from the success of her students, was big league.

"I thought it was odd, too," Elly said when I phoned her back. "I hardly know the woman. I was quite surprised when she called. Even more so to find out for sure she'd be singing. There's been talk for a while now."

"Talk?"

"That she's planning a comeback." Elly made the very notion sound tawdry. "And since you ask, it wasn't me who gave her your name. She had it already. She merely wanted to know the best way to get in touch with you."

"How did she even know about me?"

"From a mutual acquaintance."

Elly being coy with intelligence—always a bad sign. I waited for her to fill me in. "Dieter Mann," she said at last.

"You can't be serious."

If I were a physicist and Stephen Hawking had just nominated me for the Nobel Prize, I couldn't have been more surprised. Mann was possibly the greatest piano teacher alive. Octogenarian son of the twentieth century's most revered interpreter of Beethoven, he visited Toronto once a year, sharing his prodigious knowledge of piano and art-song repertoire through a week's worth of master classes and lessons.

Elly let the name sink in, then added, almost as an afterthought: "Whom, by the way, I hope you haven't forgotten you're to pick up at the airport on Tuesday."

❧   ❧   ❧

A gesture to my right, a flash of cobalt satin in the corner of my eye, and I was back in the Conservatory greenroom. Ulrike was adjusting a shoulder of her gown. Elsewhere, the bustle of jackets donned, dresses straightened and hair patted into place told me Janssen was nearing the end of his speech.

"Therefore, in closing, I think it not immodest to suggest that were it not for the Conservatory, those whom we honour tonight might never have become the celebrated figures they are today, recognized around the globe for their unique contributions to the world of music."

Polite clapping and the thrum of an audience soon to be released from their seats. Janssen would be moving over to the shrouded easels, preparing to uncover them one by one.

"Jon Vickers."

The applause grew, continued for a seemly length of time, then died down.

"Teresa Stratas."

Further courteous approbation.

"And finally, Glenn Gould."

Utter silence, then a noisy and protracted ovation. Janssen must have saved the best for last. I couldn't help wondering how Gould would have felt having his portrait so publicly applauded, given his notorious boycott of the concert stage.

The unveiling finished, Ulrike and I led the other performers out for final bows. Afterward came the reception, an event I would happily have missed if Elly hadn't asked me to stick around for final instructions concerning Mann's arrival the next day.

I was shouldering through the Harry Rosen suits and Holt

Renfrew dresses in the lobby, hoping to grab a cigarette outside, when she caught up with me. She'd made no sartorial concessions to the evening, I noticed. A tweed skirt, fraying cardigan and serviceable brown shoes mutely disdained the toniness of Janssen's affair.

"Dieter's plane comes in at eleven-thirty," she said, not bothering with frivolous compliments on my playing. "You won't have to worry about traffic either way. And you do know where he's staying?"

An apartment-hotel on Church Street. The suites there had kitchenettes. Mann, a vegetarian, prepared his own meals. So Elly had told me, more than once.

"He's known at the desk," she went on, "but I want you to go in with him."

"Don't worry. I'll deliver him without a scratch. Promise." I held up three fingers, Boy Scout style.

She tilted her face up, checking to see if I was making fun. It was hard not to smile. Strands of salt-and-pepper hair escaped from a bun at the back of her head, making her look every inch a mother hen. The problem was, she was fussing over a man nearly thirty years her senior.

"You're really fond of him, aren't you?" I said.

"Of course. Dieter's been coming to Toronto for nine years now."

"That tells me a lot."

"There was something else you wanted to know?"

"Just curious about you two."

Despite his age, "the Great Mann" still travelled the globe, giving lessons in London, New York, Sydney. Elly Gardiner taught from a cozy, plant-infested studio on Bloor Street.

"I'm not sure what you mean by 'you two.' We met in New York when I paid to attend one of his master classes. Piano

12

teachers who give instruction in lieder accompaniment are so rare I wanted to see what he had to say. We spoke afterwards. I asked if he'd consider adding Toronto to his itinerary."

"And he agreed? Just like that?"

"Why not? We're both teachers. Music is music. And we discovered we have something in common." She forestalled further probing by taking a sudden interest in the baroque trio setting up near the front desk. "He'll only be here for four days this time," she said after the group launched into a Corelli sonata. "Laura Erskine will be singing in Wednesday's master class. That's the Schumann—" a look to see that I hadn't forgotten "—and I've decided to have a lesson with him myself on Thursday. I'll need you at one o'clock."

"Did it ever occur to you that I might not be available?"

I might as well have asked in Chinese. "Don't be ridiculous," she said.

"Do I get to sleep sometime this week?"

"It's not that much work. Besides, I know you're looking forward to Wednesday. Laura says your get-togethers are going extremely well."

"They are. She has an incredible voice."

"I thought you'd feel that way." Elly permitted herself a smile of prim satisfaction. The informal weekly sessions had been her idea. "There's one other thing. I've paid for an extra lesson on Friday, and I'd like you to have it. Dieter says he wants to work with you." She paused significantly. "Alone."

"Dare I ask how he even knows I'm back in Toronto?"

"Your name came up when we spoke in March."

"I'm surprised he remembers me." I'd only played for him twice, both times as Elly's accompanist.

"He thinks very highly of you. Why else do you suppose he gave your name to Ulrike Vogel?"

"I was meaning to ask about that. What's the connection between them?"

"His daughter, Anna. She and Ulrike are old friends. They went to school together, I believe, in Vienna. And Dieter helped launch Ulrike's career. He was her coach when she started singing professionally."

"That's a lot of information about a woman you hardly know."

"It's no secret," she said, the gossip's first line of defence.

"You wouldn't also happen to know why her pianist backed out? I wanted to ask her myself, but I got the feeling the only question she'd allow was 'Am I playing too loud?'"

"I gather he's sick. And whatever he's come down with," she added, her voice rich with irony, "it must be near-fatal."

"Why?"

"Her accompanist is David Bryce."

"Ah."

I knew Bryce from our student days. He taught history classes at the Con now, as well as giving private lessons in music theory. Too handsome by half, he'd always shown a remarkable talent for insinuating his Ken-doll good looks into other people's limelight. Elly was right: it would have taken something life-threatening to tear him away from accompanying *das Vöglein's* comeback performance.

My yearning for a cigarette, forgotten while we talked, suddenly resurfaced. Elly must have seen it in my face. "Go," she said, making shooing motions with her hands. "I'm keeping you from your habit. I'll be here when you come back."

꙳   ꙳   ꙳

I lit up and leaned against a low iron rail separating the

Conservatory lawn from its parking lot. Humidity in the air sharpened the bite of tobacco in my throat. I looked up, exhaling. Only a few stars were visible, even though the night was clear. Across the street, dance music thudded from an upstairs bar, joining with the idle and rev of slow-moving traffic. Over on Queen's Park, a siren wailed and dopplered into the distance. *City sounds, traitorously familiar.* I straightened up and started pacing, taking long hauls on my cigarette, getting the most out of it.

I wonder if non-smokers grasp the syntactic role of cigarettes in a smoker's life? Between the clauses of existence, they act like punctuation—emberous commas, periods and semicolons that provide an interval in which to pause, reflect, assimilate.

Ten months now I'd been back in Toronto, ten months of Elly's peremptory strategies to draw me back into the world of serious music. Hadn't she understood? I didn't re-contact her because I wanted to resume what I'd abandoned three years earlier. I'd picked up the phone and called her because I needed to hear a familiar voice, one that would be happy to hear mine. Perhaps she had understood, and thought what I needed was the distracting balm of work.

It was difficult to fault her meddling. Arranging a lesson for me with Mann would cost her upwards of two hundred dollars. And her belief in my talent wasn't unfounded if Mann himself remembered me from four years ago. The problem was, I didn't want her faith, nor her generosity. I wasn't ungrateful; I simply had no desire to go where she was steering me.

My cigarette started to give off the sweetish smell of burning cellulose. I crushed it underfoot and went back inside.

The caterers had done a good job decorating for the reception. Cream-coloured swags adorned hand-lettered, wooden scholarship plaques, normally relegated to the Con's

15

administrative tower but trotted out for the occasion. Seating had been removed, a trade-off between gaining space and exposing pristine patches of dark varnish on the scuffed hardwood floor. A snowy linen cloth covered the lobby's low library table. Atop it, plates of sushi and carved crudités surrounded a vase of peonies. Hot house, I decided. It was too early for the shaggy pink-and-white blooms.

The trio of musicians had moved into Telemann. I silently complimented Janssen's choice of acoustic wallpaper. Nothing matches the conversational bouquets of a genteel party like the cool pulsation of a harpsichord under strings.

I looked around for Elly but couldn't see her. My Strauss was still in the greenroom, but the lobby-side door was locked. Since I wanted to check out the Gallery portraits anyway, I decided to try my luck through the concert hall.

The sounds of the reception faded as soon as I stepped inside. A church-like stillness permeated the room. To me, empty halls are numinous with the solitude that music loves best. I examined the paintings. They'd been moved forward on the stage, screening the piano. Vickers glowered manfully out of his, every inch a Siegfried or a Tristan. Stratas looked dark and Greekly tragic. Gould's picture was by far the best. Three quarters of the canvas—painted horizontally, like a landscape —was filled with the black mass of a piano. At the far left, a silhouette hunched over the keyboard, its posture unmistakably, reverentially, Gould's.

A sibilance in the auditorium, a whisper of fabric on fabric, caused me to break off my inspection. I turned around, my vision partially obscured by a spotlight. I was just able to make out a figure in one of the side aisles, moving slowly toward the stage. Ulrike Vogel. She appeared to be studying something on the wall.

"There used to be paintings here," she said, sparing me the

decision of whether to speak. "Abstracts." A singer's artful knowledge of projection carried her voice without effort.

"Yes, I remember."

"I never liked them. They lacked...*Leidenschaft.* Passion. I'm glad they're gone."

She entered the apron of light around the stage. An aureate glow suffused her hair. In CD photographs, she wore it long, falling across her brow like Veronica Lake. It was shorter now, flattering her features, but adding some years to her face.

"*This* is very good," she said, indicating the rightmost of the three portraits.

"Gould?"

"Yes." She moved in for a closer look. "I knew him, you know. We spoke many times. On the telephone. He wanted me to record *Das Buch der Hängenden Gärten*. He loved Schönberg. In the end, he did it with Vanni."

Friends with Dieter Mann? On speaking terms with Glenn Gould? The enigmatic *Vöglein* was becoming more intriguing by the minute.

"You play well—Vikkan, isn't it?" she asked. I nodded, unoffended. Singers often forget the names of stand-in accompanists. "I should have thanked you earlier. Such short notice. You will be paid?"

"Yes. It's all taken care of." Elly had said I could pick up a cheque from Janssen's office in a few days.

"It was fortunate Dieter knew someone who could play for me. I can only work with talented people." She looked from Gould to me. "Have you studied long with Dieter?"

"A few lessons, that's all."

"You studied here, then? Or at the Faculty?" She meant the Faculty of Music at the University of Toronto, the Con's sister—and sometimes rival—institution of musical learning.

The two schools eye each other from a distance of not more than a quarter mile, share staff, use each other's facilities, and every once in a while engage in bouts of sibling hair-pulling as they jockey for preeminence. By tradition, budding musicians in Toronto attend the Conservatory first, then repeat a large portion of their studies at the Faculty.

"Both," I said. "I majored in composition at the Faculty."

"Who was your piano teacher, then?"

"Zoltan Berényi."

"Ah. Poor man." It was hard to tell if she meant me or Berényi, who had died the previous year.

She seemed distracted, quite unlike the woman whose demands had guided our rehearsal the day before. Stratas held her attention for a while, then Vickers. At length, she turned back to me. "Vikkan?" Once more, the hesitation over my name. "I may need you again. I have a young man already," — Bryce— "but..." She let the sentence hang.

"If I'm available."

"Natürlich."

She went to a seat over which she'd folded a beige trench coat. Slipping into it without fuss, she began to walk away.

"Do you need a lift?" I called out, more from courtesy than a desire to make good on the offer. Our conversation seemed to have ended inconclusively.

"Thank you, no," came the faintly amused reply. "I have a car. Good night. *Und vielen Dank.*"

"Bitte schön."

I waited till she was gone before hoisting myself onto the stage and retrieving my music from the greenroom.

𝄞   𝄞   𝄞

Back in the lobby, I looked again for Elly. I still couldn't find her. Waiters in evening dress were conveying champagne to the guests, so I snared a glass from a passing tray and waited near the library table. She could have been anywhere. Elly barely surpasses five feet, making her difficult to spot in a crowd.

Nils Janssen, on the other hand, stands nearly as tall as my six-foot-two. I spotted him over by the scholarship plaques, bent deep in conversation with a short, fat man whose girth nearly equalled Janssen's height.

Elly came up beside me. "Doug Rawlings," she said at my elbow, startling me into almost spilling my champagne.

"I'm sorry?"

"The man with Janssen. His name is Doug Rawlings."

"Should I know him?"

"You would if you weren't such a hermit. Rawlings is the reason for all this." She gestured around the lobby.

"I was under the impression Janssen arranged it for the Alumni Gallery."

"He did, but haven't you noticed the money being spent? Hardly what you'd expect from the Con."

She had a point. The Conservatory I remembered from my teens was a stodgy institution, the sort of place that made do with greasy mimeographs long after photocopiers had become the norm.

"Haven't you told me Janssen wants to breathe life into the place?"

"Oh, yes. It's why we appointed him. With Ludlow at the helm, we were turning into a mausoleum."

Ludlow—Sir Geoffrey—had run the Con for twenty-five years from a musty office in which the Queen's portrait figured prominently. He'd been in his eighties when he finally stepped down.

"But you're saying there's more to this shindig than meets the eye?"

There was. Elly took hold of my arm and drew me closer. A faint smell of sour wool emanated from her cardigan. "Rawlings owns a company called Bovitech. They manufacture livestock feeding systems, or some such. A few years ago, he finagled a contract with the government. Aid to developing countries, I think. The deal made him filthy rich, and now he wants to join the Old Boys club. Problem is, his blood's not blue enough for them. He's hoping he can thaw them out with a splashy donation somewhere, and he's settled on the arts. That would be his wife's doing. She's quite the snob."

If there's rumour, Elly's sure to have it. "This is all general knowledge, of course," I said.

She had her excuse close to hand. "I teach his daughter, Siobhan."

I glanced over at Rawlings. He seemed an unlikely candidate for the rarefied world of arts patronage: glistening moon face, thick lips, black hair pasted ineffectually over a visible pate. Next to Janssen, silver-maned and patrician, he looked like Oliver Hardy in conversation with Peter Cushing.

"He's let it be known he intends to make 'a significant contribution to the musical community of Toronto.' The *Globe's* words, by the way, not mine. Or his, I should imagine. His choice of lucky recipients has come down to either us or the Faculty."

"How significant a contribution are we talking about?"

"Several million."

"And you're suggesting Janssen arranged this whole affair, Gallery and all, to woo him into making the right decision?"

I set my champagne glass on the table, next to a plate of zucchini whose skins had been incised with delicate meanders. Nearby, cornets of sushi fanned out on a lacquer tray, interspersed with tiny marigolds.

Elly reached in front of me and took a stick of intaglioed vegetable. "Hard to say who's wooing whom. Rawlings' financial charms are considerable. Janssen wants to move the Conservatory ahead, put us up there with Juilliard, Moscow and Paris. That'll take a lot more money than we generate at present."

"Heady stuff."

"Indeed." She popped the zucchini in her mouth. "And now, Vikkan, if you don't mind, I have to be going. Don't be late for Dieter's plane. And call me once he's at the hotel."

"Yessir." I sketched a salute.

She tsk-ed and walked away, her no-nonsense tweed disappearing quickly in a sea of designer fashions.

No one came up to me after she left. Janssen, who might have remembered me from his years as registrar, was introducing Rawlings to "name" teachers. Of those who'd actually taught me, none approached. Even the Rosedale and Forest Hill ladies stayed away, which surprised me since tall, dark-haired, and blue-eyed usually acts as a magnet for critical effusion.

The sushi looked appealing. I took a piece, even though I wasn't hungry. Japanese wasabi detonated in my mouth, blasted into my sinuses, and dissipated near the corners of my eyes. When the shock passed, I helped myself to more. No one else appeared to be touching it.

I felt adrift, not wanting to stay, unwilling to leave. After ten minutes, I decided solitude at home was preferable to isolation in a crowd, and edged my way to the front door.

Outside, a breeze had come up. Spring odours softened the city tang of gasoline and asphalt. I'd parked half a block away. My yellow Land Rover (Series IIA88, circa 1970; "Vintage", its former owner had assured me) looked shabbier than usual behind a sleek teal Acura. As I walked toward it, I noticed a dense, sweet smell cutting through the night air. Hard by the vine-covered brick of the Conservatory, a horse chestnut was coming into bloom. Cone-shaped clusters of white blossoms protruded from a mantle of gently stirring leaves. The fragrance beckoned, brought me to a halt, refused to let me move. The city dimmed. A remembered country chill brushed my face...

One year ago. Ruthless stars glittered over the Caledon Hills, north of Toronto. Other leaves whispered in a fitful breeze. Lights from a cedar Pan Abode cottage cast elongated ochre rhomboids on the ground. In the faint illumination, facedown and still, a pale body—arms crooked, one hand curling round the pruning knife he'd used against himself.

And all around, indifferent to the passing of his life, our life, the careless siren-scent of chestnut flowers.

wo

Und mich schauert's im Herzensgrunde.
("And my heart's deepest suff'ring wakens.")
    —*Liederkreis*, Opus 39, XI

I got to Pearson International at eleven o'clock the next morning. A quick check of the arrivals board revealed that Mann's flight from Vienna would be delayed fifteen minutes. With three quarters of an hour to kill, I bought a coffee and looked for somewhere to smoke. Eldorado in the cigarette-free wasteland of the terminal showed up as a row of chairs unaccountably furnished with an ashtray, one of those meter-high chrome cylinders with a hole in the side for garbage. I took it as dispensation from the nearby no-smoking sign.

I'd brought a Dick Francis with me, then gone and left it in the Rover. The book's horsey hero probably felt quite at home on the British jeep's Naugahyde bench, so I left him there and killed time with coffee and illicit cigarettes. A crew-cut ticket agent glanced over from time to time, disapproving or flirtatious, I couldn't tell.

Lufthansa flight 609 was announced at eleven-forty. I took my place at the debarkation gate. Nearby, a gaggle of elderly women were chattering excitedly in German. I fancied they'd be welcoming an Onkel Heinz or Tante Katerina back from the old country, but when the passengers emerged, they swarmed a stick-thin, blue-haired girl, crying: *"Judith! Liebling! Du bist so groß geworden."* Not exactly the lederhosened *Landsmann* or jolly *Hausfrau* I'd been expecting.

I spotted Mann behind a couple of pinstripes who were hogging the corridor. I wasn't sure he'd recognize me after four years, but his broad smile and big wave set my doubts to rest.

"Vikkan!" He put down his briefcase. "So nice to see you again. Eleanor told me she'd pressed you into service. No inconvenience, I hope?"

"Always happy to do Elly a favour," I lied smoothly.

He gripped my shoulder with his right hand. The gesture surprised me, coming from a man I'd only met twice before. "You're looking well," he said, assessing me from head to toe. "You've filled out, if I remember. Life in the country will do that."

Thanks, Elly. What else have you told him?

"How is Eleanor?" he asked, reading my thoughts.

"Same as always, as I'm sure you already know."

"True," he conceded. "We do speak often. It's how I knew you had resurfaced." He removed his hand and regarded me warmly. "It was time, Vikkan. At your age, I, too, ran away. Three years in the Apennines, and not a single letter to Father." He bent down and picked up his briefcase. "Which way to your car, then?"

"You don't have luggage?"

"I had it sent ahead. I don't like to wait at Customs. It makes me feel like a criminal. Herr Doktor Freud would have had something to say about that, I'm sure." Mann pulled at an imaginary beard and parodied his own Austrian accent: "Ze adult displaying his suitcase to ze authorities is reminded of ze infant who has soiled himself and hopes his parents vill not notice.'"

I had to laugh. "True enough. I always resent it when the government's minions are pawing through my underwear. All that testosterone-charged moral certitude."

"Some of them are women, too."

"The comment still stands."

We headed toward the parking lot. For a person in his eighties, Mann was exceptionally fit. I had trouble matching his vigorous strides. "The joke's on them," he said, glancing back as if the terminal were crawling with customs agents. "Whatever questionable possessions I have are in my briefcase. The good gentlemen who serve the country inspected it and said nothing." He shook his head. "Such respect for paper and ink. They will ask about a bottle of aspirin or a nail file, but never about what is printed on the page."

The Rover stood out like an unwashed country cousin between two rental-agency sedans. I let Mann in and went round to the driver's side, fiddling and tugging with a door latch that seldom worked. I prayed the engine wouldn't give me trouble, too. The last thing I needed was to crank-start it with Mann waiting.

When Elly asked me to pick him up, she'd also asked—pointedly—if I still drove "that truck", clearly unimpressed by its power takeout and ancient get-out-of-the-cab-and-unlock-the-hubs four wheel drive. Mann himself took it in stride. "A good vehicle, this," he observed, moving Dick Francis to one side. "My friend in Cape Town owned one. I used to give classes there, you know, until the trouble started. She said it was remarkable. You could go anywhere—anywhere at all. Repairs were so easy to improvise."

Luckily, it started right away so I didn't have to test the theory. I eased out of the parking space and headed for the ramp.

The engine roared off concrete walls as we spiralled down, providing a reprieve from conversation. Driving Mann downtown put me in the awkward position of playing both chauffeur and host, and I wasn't sure of my ability to small-talk.

I wanted to stay away from the subject of music. My years with Zoltan Berényi had left their mark: I'd probably never shake the apprehension that a teacher of Mann's stature would berate me for aspiring to play the piano at all.

The parking attendant took his time making change. As he counted loonies and quarters, I noticed a small, yellowing card taped to the side of his cash register. A Caucasian Christ gazed heavenward over a Biblical quotation, surrounded by gold curlicues and roses. The Hallmark border made me think of an incident during one of Elly's lessons with Mann. "Sentimental, Vikkan," he'd called out in the middle of "Frühlingsglaube". "Not schmaltz. Put some smelling salts in your playing, or poor Eleanor's going to faint from all the hearts and flowers." He swooned, holding his wrist to his forehead.

No—Berényi and Mann were as unlike as a tiger and a teddy bear.

"I played for Ulrike Vogel last night," I essayed, once we were on the road, heading south on the 427. "Elly tells me you had something to do with that."

"Indeed. And how did little Ulrike do?"

"Hard to say. She bumped one of her songs up half a tone before we went on stage. I didn't have much time to listen."

"Ah—so you transposed at sight. I used to do that too, back when I was a young man."

He made it sound like a pissing contest. I sidestepped the compliment and asked him about Ulrike. "I don't know much about her. I gather she used to be quite famous."

"I do not think she would thank you for that 'used to be.'"

"Probably not."

He rearranged himself on the seat, getting comfortable. I glanced over. With his grey fedora, round gold spectacles, and crumpled brown suit, he looked more like a homesteader dressed for a day in town than a globetrotting music teacher. I couldn't help noticing his hands, resting loosely on his briefcase. The left one was maimed, the thumb and top joint of the index missing. Decades-old scar tissue blended into age-spotted skin. I wondered if he ever resented the injury that had kept him from joining the ranks of the great performers.

"Ulrike may well have been the best lieder singer of her generation," he began. "Critics were already calling her the heir to Schwarzkopf. Some even nicknamed her *das Vöglein*. Personally, I never liked that. It made her sound like a second-rate Piaf."

"Around here, she's also called *die Krähe*."

"You don't become known without offending some lesser egos."

"True."

"Like so many performers, she was...needy, even from the start." He cleared his throat. "You understand, I say this because I know her well. She and my daughter have been friends since before forever."

"Elly mentioned that."

"She practically grew up in our house. Her parents' garden adjoined our own, you see, and her father was a magistrate. Our music salon offered more enchantment than his library of statutes, I imagine. Even then, though, she was...fragile." Another discreet cough. "She craved attention, devotion, from everyone. It wasn't vanity. She simply never felt secure in herself."

"Common enough in people with talent."

"Oh, yes. Certainly. Perhaps even you are not exempt?" He questioned me with his eyes. "But in Ulrike's case, it was *rehaussé*, as the French say. Exaggerated. She needed constant reassurance. And everyone gave it to her—her schoolmates, her friends at the *Gymnasium*, later on her colleagues. No one wanted to see her hurt. She had that effect, you see. One felt she would crumble without our support."

Lulled by Mann's voice, his cultured English overlaid with the accents of his native tongue, I nearly missed the turnoff for the QEW. A Miata beeped ineffectually beside us when I swerved sharply across two lanes.

"Sorry," I said. "Not paying attention."

"Oh, that's quite all right. The advantage to driving this" —he put his good hand on the metal dash— "is that you can insult lesser vehicles without fear of reprisal."

I navigated onto the QEW and stayed in the slow lane. Anything over eighty, and I risked drowning him out. Even so, Mann's narrative was periodically interrupted by the roar of impatient eighteen-wheelers.

Ulrike's story, as he told it, seemed like a too-perfect match for her "I vant to be alone" demeanour. At the moment that her career was about to break out of Germany and Austria, she fell in love. I recognized her lover's name immediately. His symphonic poem *Isolde und Brangäne* had turned the musical world on its ear and launched the neo-Romantic school of composition.

Some years earlier, he'd written a huge work for soprano and orchestra on texts by Rilke. Until Ulrike, he claimed no singer was up to its demands. She convinced him otherwise. After negotiations with the Vienna Philharmonic, he announced that the piece would finally be heard, in a concert devoted exclusively to its premiere. Ulrike, of course, would sing, and all Vienna knew it.

A few weeks into rehearsal, the composer suddenly withdrew the work, ostensibly for revisions. A ruse, as it turned out. He'd started seeing someone else—another singer.

I knew the piece Mann was talking about. The liner notes

of my Deutsche Gramophon recording mentioned that the composer and soprano were husband and wife.

"At first, Ulrike took it remarkably well," Mann said. "'With equanimity'—that's an English expression I like. Or so it seemed. Then, one night, in the midst of a performance, she tried to take her life."

"You don't mean on stage?"

Mann nodded.

"You're kidding. How?"

"She slit her wrists."

I had a sudden mental image of Ulrike the night before, dark stains spattering her gown, her white gloves blossoming crimson. At the same instant, another picture formed: a pale, unclothed body, motionless beneath a canopy of leaves. There'd been no audience that night, unless it had been the ground imbibing blood from a gash across the throat. Across *Christian's* throat. He'd been kneeling, fallen forward—an intimate, exclusionary act that called out for no witnesses.

A passing GO bus farted out a cloud of diesel, shattering the image.

We'd reached the highway no-man's land where the QEW feeds onto the Gardiner Expressway. To the right, Lake Ontario shimmered in the May sunlight. Sailboats moved briskly beyond the breakwater at Sunnyside. Willows swept the shore with peridot leaves and mustard-coloured branches.

Mann stared out the window. "I don't know which was worse for Ulrike: the humiliation of losing the premiere—everyone in Vienna knew the whole story—or the shame of her own futile dramatics. She began treatment after the incident, of course, but could never bring herself to sing in public again."

"And fled in shame to Canada with the remnants of her

reputation?" Ulrike may have specialized in lieder, but her story sounded like grand opera.

Mann grew silent. A wall of condominiums abruptly cut off our view of the lake. I exited at Jarvis Street and headed back toward Church.

"I hear from Elly she's planning a comeback."

"Quite so."

"Well, for whatever it's worth, she seemed comfortable enough on stage last night."

"I'm glad to hear it." He patted the briefcase in his lap. "I've brought something with me, something that will put her, as they say, front and centre again. She may have lost one premiere, but she will get the chance at another."

I looked over for an explanation, but none came.

We inched up Church Street, past Dundas and Carleton, and came to a stop at Wellesley. "What will you be playing on Friday?" Mann asked.

Friday? Oh, yes—the lesson Elly had arranged for me.

"I'm not sure. The Haydn F-minor Variations, maybe?"

"Marvellous. Hardly anyone plays those nowadays. A good choice."

I didn't mention that the selection had more to do with pragmatism than preference. There weren't many works left in my classical repertoire that I could whip into shape on such short notice. I wondered if Elly had told him what I'd been doing for a living since returning to Toronto.

He read my thoughts a second time that day. "I understand you've been playing at a bar."

I made a sour face. "I suppose Elly's told you my brand of toothpaste, too?"

"Don't be hard on her, Vikkan. She recognizes your talent. And she likes to gossip. As, I'm afraid, do I."

The light changed. I pulled forward slowly, checking for parking even though Mann's hotel was still several blocks away.

"Father worked in a cabaret once, you know. That was after the war—the *first* war. He said it taught him how to play tremolo without freezing the wrist. And Brahms is said to have taken a job in a brothel. How you play is more important than where. There are only two kinds of music: that which sings, and that which does not. If it sings, it will do so anywhere."

A car pulling into traffic ahead of us distracted me, and I lost the chance to say how much I agreed. He started asking questions related to his stay in Toronto. Was Noah's Health Foods near Spadina still open? Would the convenience store across the street carry his preferred mineral water? Had taxi fares gone up? I answered as best I could, and toyed with the idea of inviting him to hear me play some evening.

I had a feeling he'd accept, with pleasure.

✻ ✻ ✻

After seeing Mann into the hotel as per Elly's instructions, I drove over to the University. My destination was the Faculty library. In the transition from Caledon to Toronto, I'd misplaced the music I was going to need during his stay. Laura would be singing four songs from Schumann's *Liederkreis*, opus 39 in the Wednesday class. I couldn't find it anywhere. The Schubert for Elly's lesson on Thursday I had, but in all the wrong keys.

I parked on Hoskin across from Wycliffe College at the bottom of Philosopher's Walk, the paved pathway that cuts through Taddle Creek ravine up to Bloor Street. The Conservatory looms over its north end, and Trinity, a venerable Anglican college, verges on its southernmost terminus. Midway, a narrow bridge links Philosopher's Walk to the back of the Edward Johnson Building, home of the University of Toronto's Faculty of Music. Set into a steep slope beside the law library, EJB's austere brick-and-glass exterior is offset by a modest peristyle of unfluted concrete columns. The classical conceit lends itself well to the art served inside.

Once through the doors, though, the architectural aptness disappeared. Institutional-looking linoleum hallways and a stainless steel elevator carried me down to the library, where I located the music I needed and settled in for a wait by the photocopiers. Ten minutes passed before one became available. Too late, I remembered that I needed a Xerox card, purchased at the desk, to make it work. I surrendered my machine to a goateed student laden with an orchestral score so studded with notes it looked as if it had been blasted by a shotgun.

The line at the desk wasn't long, but when I caught sight of the figure pulling up the rear, I had second thoughts about joining in. Calf-high boots in oxblood red, a mauve poncho, and brassy orange hair demarcated the personal space of Bernice Morris-Jones, Professor of Music History. I hoped she wouldn't turn around, but as luck would have it, the musk she wore like olfactory barbed wire caught in my nose and brought on a violent sneeze.

She whirled around. "Wot the..." she began. Then, recognizing me: "Lantry. What the fuck do you think you're doin' 'ere?" A belligerent North English accent carried her question over to the library assistant, who looked up.

"Professor Morris-Jones," I said civilly. "Excuse me." For what? Getting snagged on her appalling perfume?

"You've got no business bein' 'ere," she said, unmollified. "You know this library's only for staff and students."

Behind her, the library assistant winked.

"I realize," I said, "but I have a small emergency."

"Well, wot is it?"

"What is what?"

"Your emergency. Wot's so bloody important you can just waltz in 'ere like you own the place?"

I had half a mind to say it was none of her business. It wouldn't have mattered if I had. Provocation and diplomacy had approximately the same effect on Bernice Morris-Jones.

"Dieter Mann's in Toronto," I explained, "and I'll be doing some accompanying. I need copies of the music."

"Mann? Bloody pig."

"I beg your pardon?"

"You 'eard me. Fuckin' reactionary pig." Her voice went up a notch. "It's no wonder the Faculty and the Con won't have anything to do with 'im."

"That's not entirely accurate," I said, speaking softly, hoping to remind her we were in a library. "As I understand it, Herr Mann prefers to remain independent of any school, no matter what city he's teaching in."

"Roight, so nobody'll notice 'e's got muck for brains. Think's 'e can set 'imself up like a little demi-god because 'is father was Karl-almighty-Mann. Makes 'is students play Bach like Chopin, and Scarlatti like Debussy. If you ask me, 'is father wasn't all that hot shit anyway. And you know what that prick did last year?" She took a step forward, planting a platform heel dangerously close to my foot. Musk emanated from her like a force field. "'E criticized my paper on Fanny Mendelssohn-Hensel. Took me seven bloody years to research that, and 'e goes and trashes it in *Piano Quarterly*. 'What's important is not that Fanny Mendelssohn published music under her brother's name, but that Felix's fondness and generosity toward his sister ensured that these remarkable works survived,'" she quoted in a travesty of uppercrust English. "Bleedin' Kraut wanker defending a patriarchal Jewish bastard." She glared at me as if I were personally responsible.

Without knowing the whole story, I suspected Mann had merely offered a pianist's perspective on her work, but I knew better than to argue. Accent and vocabulary notwithstanding— it's difficult to take seriously someone who swallows the t's in Scarlatti—Morris-Jones could be a formidable adversary. Her academic reputation rested largely on research into misattributions of music composed by women. We'd butted heads once, in a third-year course on Late Romantic Cadential Ambiguity. The subject had been Mahler, and I'd committed heresy by suggesting we focus on his symphonies themselves, not the putative role his wife played in their inspiration. My marks had plummeted, leading to a nasty dispute before the Faculty arbiter. The final decision, unpardonably rendered by a woman, had come down in my favour.

She kept up her defiant stare, daring me to defend Mann, or Mendelssohn, or maybe the entire male sex. I held my peace. Antagonism seethed beneath her hennaed bangs, then slaked to a frustrated simmer. She turned abruptly and stormed the desk, barking out demands for course materials to be kept on hold. I waited till she'd clomped out of the library before buying my Xerox card. The library assistant took my money with the ghost of another wink. She looked familiar. Violin—no, viola. We'd taken keyboard harmony together. Her hair had been shorter then.

I intended to go directly to the Con when I finished. Elly needed to know that all had gone well at the airport, and the niceties of assuring her I'd delivered Mann safely promised some relief from Morris-Jones. A palliative not forthcoming, as it turned out. Like the aural analog to acid reflux, glottalized invective echoed down the hallway to the left of the elevator when I got off on the main floor.

"...and you know fuckin' well what I mean. That money will not be used for your ruddy opera school. You've already kiss-arsed more from the dean than you deserve."

I rounded a corner and found my way blocked by a quivering Morris-Jones and the target of her rant, the Faculty's Head of Performance and almighty starmaker, Russell Spiers. A few feet behind, to my surprise, stood Laura Erskine. She wiggled her fingers at me in greeting.

Spiers folded his arms. "Bernice, dear, really," he egged her on. "There'll be oodles to go around. I was merely pointing out that something more obviously prestigious like the Opera School stood a better chance than your Centre For Women's Studies In Music. It just sounds so drea—" The flow of words halted mid-taunt. "Well, well, if it isn't the lovely Vikkan Lantry. *Quelle surprise.* Don't see much of you around here these days. Still tickling the ivories?" He fluttered his fingers over an imaginary keyboard.

"I keep my hand in," I said evenly.

He eyed me up and down, pausing at the region below my belt. "Pity. You never did know where your real talents lie."

"And you never got a chance to find out."

Laura glanced at me, then Spiers. "Vikkan will be accompanying me in Dieter Mann's class on Wednesday," she put in.

"Really?" His eyebrows shot up. "You're filling in for someone, of course." He turned to Laura. "You know, dear, it's not doing your career any good wasting time with hacks. You should find someone whose talents lie in music, not ingratitude. Mind you, a class with Mann will look good on your résumé."

Laura opened her mouth, but Morris-Jones harumphed loudly before she could say anything.

"Now, now, Bernice," Spiers said. "I agree Mann's a bit unorthodox, but you can't deny lessons with him give artists a leg up in the profession. He's quite useful."

"Useful? Roight—like pimples on an 'emorrhoid."

"Bernice, dear, really—"

"Don't you 'Bernice, dear' me, Spiers," she snarled. "And don't give me that muck about 'the Great Mann'. You'd suck up to Genghis Khan if you thought 'e'd make one of your students look good."

Spiers lifted his hand to his mouth. "My, such language. And from a lady." He aimed the comment like oil at an open flame, then dodged the conflagration by returning his attention to Laura. "Now where were we? Oh, yes—Howard Snelling. I spoke to him about representing you. He was very impressed by the tape you made last year. It would be quite the little coup if his agency took you on so soon after graduation."

"Should I call him?" Laura asked.

"No, let me handle it."

"Why?" Morris-Jones shrilled. "So you can claim 'er as your own? If I remember rightly, you didn't even want 'er in the voice program in the first place."

There must have been some truth in what she said. Spiers blanched. "Laura," I broke in, "I was just on my way to the Con. You're not headed over there by any chance?"

She looked relieved. "As a matter of fact, yes. I'll go with you."

I braved crossfire between Spiers and Morris-Jones and followed her down the hall. "Thanks," she said when we were out of earshot. "I'm not really going to the Con."

"I didn't figure you were."

"But I was going to have lunch. Care to join me? We could eat outside."

I looked at my watch. One-thirty. Elly could wait.

"Sounds good. I'm starving."

≈ ≈ ≈

We picked up subs and coffee from vending machines in the Faculty common room and took them outside. "Where do you want to sit?" I asked.

Laura scanned Philosopher's Walk. "Over there?" She pointed to a stretch of grass behind the ROM, the Royal Ontario Museum, facing the Conservatory.

"Fine by me."

We strolled over. Laura knelt and tested the ground with splayed fingers. "Dry," she announced, settling down tailor-style, brushing off her jeans.

"Hardly surprising. We haven't had much rain this year."

She squinted up. "Ya reckon it's gonna be a hard summer for the crops?"

"Huh?"

"You sounded like a farmer." Out of nowhere, she began to sing: "You picked a fine time to leave me Lucille / Six hungry kids and a crop in the field..." The sound was throaty and glorious.

"With a voice like that, you could make millions," I said.

"I intend to."

I hunkered down to join her. The sweet smell of sun-warmed grass hovered near the ground. Over by the Conservatory, hedges of forsythia had already lost their canary-yellow flowers. Spring in Toronto is a fickle season, in some years lenient and precocious, in others, reluctant to let loose of winter's grip.

"What was that all about?" I asked, unravelling my sub from yards of plastic.

"You mean back there? Rawlings' Riches. You must have heard about it."

"Elly told me. Last night, after the concert."

"How was that?"

"Okay. A lot of mortgage-free types patting themselves on the back for having two hundred dollars to blow on something they didn't give a damn about."

"Talk is Janssen set the whole thing up to impress Rawlings." Laura tore a bite from her sub.

"Elly said as much."

She chewed hard, swallowed and took a gulp of coffee. "I won't be surprised if the Con gets the money. Janssen's going after it aggressively, and when he wants something, there's not much stands in his way."

"Tell me about it. We practically goose-stepped our way through the concert rehearsal."

"The feeling over at the Faculty is that Dean Simmons isn't trying hard enough. The departments have all started approaching Rawlings separately."

"And that's what Spiers and Morris-Jones were going on about?"

"Everybody's got their pet project: education, composition, history, the works. The dean called a meeting this morning— I got this from Spiers—and told them to lay off. Let him go after the cash cow. Nobody listened. It ended up being a free-for-all."

"Morris-Jones wants the Hildegaard of Bingen Centre for Music's Mislaid Maids, and Spiers wants fancy fencing foils for the opera school?" The alliterations came out garbled through a mouthful of tuna sub.

"You got it."

We finished eating in silence, washing down the doughy buns with weak coffee. I lit a cigarette. Laura stretched out on the grass. Our outfits made us look like twins: jeans, thick white cotton shirts, canvas running shoes. Her sneakers were worn where her little toes pushed up against the fabric.

"Why was Spiers so nasty to you?" she asked, her eyes closed.

"Ancient history now. He wanted me to be one of his golden boys. Darling of the Performance Department and all that. He courted me all through first year, but when it came time to choose a major, I went for composition. I couldn't see myself as one of those trained monkeys who spend their whole lives playing the same concerto. He turned vicious when he found out. You'd think I'd jilted him. In a way, I suppose I did."

"He had the hots for you?"

"I could be wrong."

"I doubt it. The man's a slimeball. What Professor Morris-Jones said is true. When I went to him at the end of second year about switching from Education to Performance, he flat out refused. But then I won the du Maurier competition, and all of a sudden, it had been his idea to have me in the vocal program all along."

"So how come you're still hanging around with him? You graduated—what?—two years ago?"

"He keeps setting things up—contacts, auditions, stuff like that. I think he's still hoping for reflected glory. It really pissed him off when I started working with Elly."

"Because she's Con?"

"Exactly."

"Who were you with before that?"

"Ulrike Vogel."

"You're kidding. Elly never told me that."

"You probably never asked."

"Ulrike's Con, too, though."

"Not entirely. She accepts a few Faculty students every year, so technically she's in Spiers' department."

"What was she like as a teacher?"

"Brilliant. Demanding. And neurotic. I made the right decision leaving her when I did."

Lunch and the balmy weather were beginning to take their toll. I felt drowsiness settling on my eyelids and in the back of my neck. A westerly breeze sprang up, soft on the skin, but overlaid with an out-of-place, throat-catching smell of heating tar.

Laura made a moue of distaste and opened her eyes. "Yuck. That's even less appetizing than lunch." She sat up and brushed herself off. "I've got to get going. Are we still on for tonight?"

"Come by around seven. With any luck, I'll know your music by then."

"As if. Elly says you could sight-read a symphony if you had to."

"Elly is a meddlesome little teller of tales."

"And you love her." She stood up, flipping grass from her long dark hair. "Ciao. Thanks for having lunch."

"See you later."

I watched her head up to Bloor Street, then crushed out my cigarette and leaned back on my elbows. I didn't know Laura well, but the more time I spent with her, the more I enjoyed her company. It had been Elly's suggestion, several months earlier, that we work together. I'd been hesitant at first. During the barren period after my return from Caledon, I'd holed up in my apartment-to-be and sunk myself into repairs and renovation. When a last coat of sticky latex covered the raw spruce of loft, kitchen and postage-stamp bathroom, I'd hoped to find another project—something, anything—to keep me from getting out, meeting people, making friends. I didn't want to fill the crater left by Christian's death. Elly's informal sessions with Laura "just to look at repertoire" sounded like she wanted them to do just that. For once, I was glad Elly is so hard to refuse.

I lit another cigarette and fought down the urge to nap. Since coming back to Toronto, I'd turned into a creature of the night. Getting up that morning to meet Mann had disrupted my schedule, but if I slept now, I'd end up feeling logy the rest of the day. I finished my cigarette, then reluctantly stood and crossed over to the Conservatory.

Elly's second-floor studio was dark. Mrs. Wigrell, a motherly woman who teaches preliminary piano across the hall, was hugging one of her little charges goodbye. Her cotton print dress and cap of curly white hair made her look as if she would smell of apple pie and fresh-baked rolls. "Are you looking for Miss Gardiner?" she asked, waving to her departing pupil.

"Yes. Is she on lunch?"

"No. She has an ear-training class till three-thirty. I can give her a message if you like."

I said no thanks and walked to the end of the hall, feeling her eyes on me as I went through the door. Elly had told me some studios had been vandalized recently. Perhaps Mrs. Wigrell was being properly cautious. Then again, maybe she was just being nosey.

I took the northeast staircase down and exited at a shady corner of the building. Sunlight bounced off the back of the ROM, momentarily blinding me. I waited for my eyes to adjust, then set off back toward Hoskin Avenue.

Just south of the Conservatory, Philosopher's Walk splits in two. A small spur curves up to join the parking lot shared by the Con and Varsity Arena. A few metres past the fork, a tow-headed cyclist swept by, taking the slope at breakneck speed, all muscles and focus in thigh-hugging Spandex. I spun around to watch him, and in so doing, discovered the source of the tar smell I'd noticed earlier. On the flat roof that covers a section of the Conservatory basement where it rises eccentrically one-half storey at the back of the building, two men were doing repairs. One of them was bent over, his back to me, but in the split second before I turned away, he straightened up and turned.

A jolt like fire and ice kicked me in the sternum. *Christian—the man looked just like Christian.* Heart pounding, I felt myself being pulled back.

It wasn't him. I knew that. The corded arms straining to lift a bucket, the damp curls spilling over tilde-shaped eyebrows, these belonged to a man who still lived and breathed and sweated. Christian was gone. His body had been lifted from the ground, scrutinized, adjudged "suicide", and rendered to a handful of gritty ash. But the physical memory of him still held sway, its absurd concomitant of hope provoking a conditioned response no less real for its stimulus having been imagined.

I willed myself away, feeling weak as the adrenaline subsided. The aftermath would endure, but not for long days, not like it had before. The unbearable had become something I could live with. *On ne guérit jamais—on s'habitue.* Jacques Brel: you never heal, you just get used to it.

A ticket was flapping on the windscreen when I reached the Rover. I tore the flimsy paper from the wipers and jammed it in my pocket. The engine wouldn't start but finally kicked over when I gave the key a punishing twist and held it in place.

The stream of cars feeding in off Queen's Park Crescent thinned, and I eased into traffic, heading west. A half hour later, my tires crunched to a halt on the gravel drive beside the old stone carriage house, over near High Park, that I call home.

⚜   ⚜   ⚜

I waited until three-thirty before calling Elly. She sounded miffed I hadn't phoned immediately once Mann was safely downtown. Her irritation evaporated when I confirmed I'd be taking the Friday lesson with him.

"What will you be playing?"

I told her the same thing I'd told Mann, the Haydn F-minor Variations. "I suppose I ought to thank you," I added. "And I don't just mean for the lesson. You've been doing a lot lately."

"Well, don't get it in your head I've only been trying to keep you busy."

"It feels that way sometimes." All those exams and sparsely attended student recitals.

"Consider it paying your dues. You can't go on forever playing only for yourself."

"I'm not."

"Surely you don't mean working at that bar?"

"Don't pretend you don't know what it's called." Evelyn— gallantly named after his wife by the owner, Léo St-Onge.

"It's hardly what I'd call living up to your potential. You have obligations to your talent."

"The way I see it, I'm meeting them, and some others, too. Léo's helped a lot, you know." He owned the carriage house and let me have it rent-free. "He pays well, I have a job, and it's in music. You should be pleased."

43

How many times had we been through this—Elly going on about obligations and responsibilities, me defending my choices? We sounded like an old married couple. For once, she decided to drop it. "Ulrike Vogel called this morning," she said.

"What did she want?"

"Bryce is still indisposed."

"Did she say what's the matter?"

"No. What she wanted was to know if—and I'm quoting— 'that young man who played so well last night' was still available."

"Elly, you didn't—"

"No, I merely told her you'd call."

"Did she say when, or for how long?"

"No."

"Does she have a lot of students?"

"Why do you ask?"

"You know how I hate sight-reading. I'd have to learn all that material."

"You misunderstand. She already has an accompanist to cover her lessons. What she wants is someone to practise with. Alone. Just until Bryce is back."

"I don't know, Elly—"

"You can not-know as much as you like, but call her. This evening. She needs someone right away."

"I'm working tonight."

"Vikkan..."

"All right, all right."

I glared at the phone after she hung up, wanting to take a hammer to it. I could understand why ancient Greeks used to kill the bearer of bad tidings.

Laura wasn't due to arrive until seven, which gave me three hours to look over her music, the Schumann *Liederkreis*. Elly's

Schubert would need some work, too.

Pianists have different ways of settling in to practise. Some study their scores in silence from the comfort of an easy chair. Others sharpen pencils for marking fingerings and phrasing. Still others limber up, yoga-style. Not a few uncork a bottle of wine.

I went to the kitchen and got out a Gripstand bowl, two bread pans and a dough-cutter.

There isn't much by way of counters in the little space under the loft, but as I jockeyed around bags of flour, oatmeal and flax, I heard a dry, familiar voice in the back of my head instructing, "Good cooks work wonders even in the smallest kitchens, provided they clean up as they go along." Uncle Charles: Bertrand Russell professor emeritus at McMaster University, baker of his own bread ("instills patience and discipline") and the closest thing I'd had to a parent after mine died on Highway 403 when I was six.

It took ten minutes to get everything ready—warming the Gripstand with hot water, ripping open bright red-and-yellow packages of yeast, sifting the dry ingredients, stirring in scalded milk. I tussled with the embryonic dough for another five minutes, beating it with a wooden spoon, then covered it with a damp dishtowel and moved on to a second pre-practice activity.

The roofer I'd spotted earlier had left a bruise on my memory, and I found myself thinking of Christian again, how he used to sit at our kitchen table, entranced, whenever I started in on rounds of baking, practising and whatever other project took my fancy at the time. "Discipline through avoidance," I'd tell him. "If doing something makes me feel like I'm putting off doing something else, everything turns into a guilty pleasure." His ghost didn't understand any better than the living man.

Curtained off at the back of the carriage house, I'd set up a workspace—pressboard shelves, a lightbox, metal filing cabinet, a draughting table. I sat down on an office chair, rescued from the curb on Queen Street, and twisted around to the shelves, taking down a botany text, a copy of Euell Gibbons' *Stalking the Wild Asparagus*, Culpeper's *Compleat Herbal*, and a translation of the Greek physician, Galen. From the filing cabinet, I extracted a folder labelled *Indian Pipe—Jack in the Pulpit*, and, scooting over a couple of inches, laid the contents on the lightbox. Rows of photographic transparencies glowed to life like stained glass miniatures when I flipped a toggle switch on the side.

In the centre of the draughting table was a single, thick sheet of vellum paper, held in place by strips of acid-free tape. I pried the page free of its moorings and held it up for inspection. *Herb Robert*, uncials proclaimed at the top, *Geranium Robertianum*. Underneath, in cursive: *Glanduliferous stem...pinnate or pinnatifid leaflets...styptic, exanthematous...against erysipelas*. The arcana of plants—words to ensorcel leaves and roots, and turn age-old, homely physics into esoteric science.

As a child, I loved to know what plants were called. For reasons I still don't understand, I wanted to be able to greet them correctly, by name. Uncle Charles had helped. With the books he bought, Devil's Paintbrush became Orange Hawkweed, and later, *Hieracium aurantiacum*. The interest had faded when I entered my teens—there'd been very little time for anything but music—but up in Caledon, it had resurfaced, in force.

After Christian's death, I couldn't face the project I was now working on. But like a blade of grass that pushes up through concrete to reach the light, it had poked its head through layers of grief and was once again a flourishing source of fascination and distraction.

I filed the *Herb Robert* page between onion skins in a

shallow wooden box and set out nibs and a small jar of ink. Preparing another sheet of vellum and dog-earing entries in the reference books occupied just enough time for my dough to have finished resting and be ready for kneading.

"Six hundred strokes," a spectral Uncle Charles lectured. "Bread becomes jaded if you lavish too much attention on it." I sprinkled water on the counter and sank my hands into the sticky mass. At first, it clung with every stroke, but after ten minutes, it was stretching and shrinking smoothly under the heels of my hands. I stopped, sweating, and unbuttoned my shirt. Another ten minutes, and Uncle Charles' requirements had been satisfied. I tucked the flesh-warm dough back into its bowl and set it in the oven to rise in its own heat.

Fingers and arms limbered, thoughts neatly ranged like paper, pen and ink, I got a beer from the fridge and went to the piano. The gleaming August-Förster had been a gift from Uncle Charles, bought with money from my parents' estate. It fills most of the front room. The only other piece of furniture is a throw-covered Sally-Ann couch that sulks beneath the window like a disenfranchised relation.

I spread photocopies out across the music rack—down flat, a habit I'd picked up playing at Evelyn—and started in on Elly's Schubert. She'd selected "teaching" repertoire: "Gretchen am Spinnrade", "An die Musik", "Du bist die Ruh'". Gretchen's spinning wheel sounded a bit creaky when I set it into motion. The hypnotic up-and-down rotation of sixteenth notes lurched instead of whirling smoothly. I dislodged dust and cobwebs from the mechanism by banging out the whole song *fortissimo prestissimo,* then tried again. This time, the sound came out just right, spindly and mesmerizing, a perfect accompaniment to Gretchen's anxious reveries. "An die Musik" got only a cursory run-through; the simple repeated chords offer no special challenge. I spent longer on "Du bist die Ruh'", sending shivers up my spine with Schubert's aching harmonic suspensions.

An hour and a half, a bottle of beer, and four cigarettes later, I broke off and checked my dough, punching it down and returning it to the oven. In the back room, I picked up a loupe and inspected my transparencies. Eleven close-ups of Indian Pipe came into focus as I moved the lens across the celluloid. The photos came from Léo St-Onge's Caledon estate. My folio, consisting of the pictures and hand-lettered pages, would be a gift to his wife if ever I got it finished.

I spent fifteen minutes choosing which shot of Indian Pipe to use. The ghostly white plant had been difficult to capture. A little overexposure yielded just the right shade of pearly luminosity, but bleached definition from the scaly stems. Underexposure turned the waxy blossoms an unpleasant shade of pewter. Of the three where colour and definition were perfect, I selected one where two plants nodded up against each other, looking intimate and dejected at the same time.

My afternoon alone was having what the old herbals call "a soverein effect". An effortless flow of notes whispered out of the piano when I started in on "In der Fremde", the first of Laura's Schumann. The voice that sings in my head when I practise accompaniments floated plaintively overtop:

> *Aus der Heimat hinter den Blitzen rot*
> *Da kommen die Wolken her...*

"From my homeland, red lightening stains the sky / And clouds loom not far behind." An equivocal image, blurred by Schumann's veiled, minor mode setting. War, or hallucination? Recollection, or oneiric landscape?

The simple melody came around again:

Aber Vater und Mutter sind lange tot
Es kennt mich dort keiner mehr.

Straightforward statements replaced the vague imagery, but ambiguous harmonies underneath robbed them of clear meaning. "But father and mother in graves do lie / Unknown there, no kin shall I find."

Suddenly, the music switched to an ardent, major tonality. Soaring vocal leaps replaced the guarded intervals of the song's first two phrases.

Wie bald, ach wie bald kommt die stille Zeit
Da ruhe ich auch, da ruhe ich auch...

"How soon, oh, how soon comes that silent time / when I too, shall rest..."

When I, too, shall rest. Unanticipated, the voice of remembrance began a duet with the one already in my head. My playing faltered. A single word in the next phrase caught my eye. *Waldeinsamkeit.* Fervidly drawn out, its four syllables revealed the object of the song's cryptic longing—forest solitude, sylvan isolation. A serene, indifferent place, secluded from the world, sheltered by overhanging trees. Christian—remote, solitary Christian—had tried to share a place like that with me in life. I'd never have it back. I swallowed hard against a tightness in my throat and turned to another song.

❦   ❦   ❦

Laura arrived at a quarter after seven. "Sorry I'm late," she said, shrugging out of a windbreaker. "I got confused between Indian Grove and Indian Road." She laid her jacket on the couch. "This is terrific. Nice piano."

It was the first time she'd been to my place. Up until then, we'd always practised at her apartment over by the Don Valley. The August-Förster would make a nice change from her old Mason & Risch.

She insisted on looking around, climbing up to the loft ("...like a tree fort up here..."), checking out the bathroom ("A sink in the shower? That's clever..."), inspecting the kitchen ("Roll top counters?" "So I don't have to look at dirty dishes."). It felt strange having someone exclaim over the renovations. I really hadn't planned on the results appealing to anyone but me.

"And you bake?" She peered at the loaves arching over their pans in the oven. "Every woman's dream."

We rehearsed for an hour and a half. If my playing seemed mechanical, distracted even, she chose to ignore it. When we finished, I offered her a ride home. She declined, which left me an hour to clean up the kitchen, shower, bully my hair into submission, and put on a tux. I have two; the other one's at work, in case some days I don't make it home to change.

I left the apartment at nine-thirty and by ten o'clock was sitting at an overlarge Yamaha, adorning the opulent dimness of Evelyn with strains of "Moonlight In Vermont".

Three

Alte Wunder wieder scheinen.
("Wond'rous things of old appearing")
 —*Liederkreis,* Opus 39, XII

I'd been hoping to see Léo at Evelyn Tuesday night, but he hadn't come in. "At a wine and food show," Toby Ryan, the weeknight bartender, told me. "Porking out with the rich and shameless."

"I need to remind him that I might be starting late tomorrow."

"You want me to leave a note?"

"Will he be in in the morning?"

"Around eleven."

"Just say I'll drop by then."

Playing at the lounge keeps me busy four nights a week: Sunday, then Tuesday through Thursday. Mondays, it's closed. Fridays and Saturdays, a trio dispenses cool jazz to quench the patrons' musical thirst. I try to restrict extracurricular engagements to my nights off, but every once in a while, conflicts do arise. Léo never objects, although more than once I've used him as an excuse to get out of doing things for Elly.

I drove back Wednesday morning and spent fifteen minutes looking for parking. A space finally showed up five blocks north of Evelyn, on Bedford Road. Clear skies and a summer-warm breeze mitigated the annoyance of walking back to Prince Arthur. I wondered how long the weather would hold. A suggestion of haze high up in the atmosphere hinted at change.

Léo St-Onge's contribution to the good life in Toronto sits on a gracious lot at an exemplary address in an exorbitantly pricey part of town. Architects' studios, lawyers' offices and tasteful little art galleries rub shoulders with the refurbished former manse. Léo had assessed the lie of the land unerringly. A scion of old Montreal money, now in his sixties, he'd wanted an establishment that captured something of his home city's savoir-faire, the sort of place where the oil-and-water of lucre and learning could commingle. He'd succeeded. Evelyn's gleaming rosewood dining room and baize-coddled, second-floor lounge stood at a nexus of affluence and erudition. The former streamed down from residential streets north of Prince Arthur; the latter came up from the university. The two met and regularly flowed in and out of Evelyn's gleaming doors, leaving behind a rich silt of profit and prestige.

Rosemary Dickens, Léo's restaurant manager, greeted me at the service entrance and offered her cheek for a kiss. "I've been expecting you," she said.

"Is Léo in?"

"He's down at Queen's Quay getting a wine shipment."

"How long will he be?"

"An hour, maybe, depending on traffic. Come in and have a coffee."

She led me through the kitchen, past rows of stainless steel shelves and dangling copper pots. Her patent-leather pumps clicked smartly on the tile floor. Many clients imagine that Rosemary is Evelyn's eponym. A slender woman with large brown eyes and russet hair, her make-up is flawless, her clothes expensive and her shoes always tastefully seductive. Léo couldn't have found a better incarnation of urbane sophistication.

"Do you mind waiting here?" she asked when we reached her office, a tiny room off the passage between the kitchen and the dining room. "They're setting up for lunch." Behind her, busboys were spreading linen and polishing glasses.

"This is fine."

While she went in search of coffee, I made myself comfortable on a love seat pushed against one wall of her office. Léo had repeatedly offered her a larger space, but she always turned him down. "I can see everything from here," she said. "Keeps the staff on their toes."

When she came back, steaming cappuccino in hand, I asked to use the phone. I'd forgotten to call *das Vöglein* the night before; Elly was going to kill me.

An answering machine kicked in after three rings. I left the number at Evelyn, hoping Ulrike was with a student and would call back shortly.

"Who was that?" Rosemary asked, never shy with questions.

"Someone I'll be turning down."

She raised an eyebrow.

"A teacher who wants me to do some work. Accompanying."

"Teacher?"

"Voice. At the Conservatory."

"The Conservatory? I didn't know you played classical music."

"Léo never told you?"

"No. Is there anything else about you he neglected to mention?"

The phone rang before I could think up a smart reply. Rosemary answered and handed me the receiver, her head tilted quizzically. Maybe it was the Marlene Dietrich accent on the other end.

Ulrike went straight to the point. "I have spoken with Eleanor Gardiner," she said. "She has explained to you that I need someone?"

"Yes."

"So you are available? This afternoon?"

Her abruptness caught me off guard. I'd been planning to turn her down, but suddenly, I couldn't muster a single excuse.

"What time?" I asked, feeling like I do when Elly calls first thing in the morning.

"Two-thirty. Herr Professor Dieter Mann will be here. You are aware that he is in town?"

"Ja, gewiß," I answered, slipping into German so I wouldn't get annoyed with her Teutonic habit of making questions sound like accusations. "Of course. *Ich habe ihn gestern am Flughafen mitgenommen. Wird dies dann eine Unterrichtsstunde sein?"* I asked, curious why Mann would be present.

"No," she said, sounding faintly amused. "It will not be a lesson." Perhaps she found the idea of needing instruction impertinent.

I still had time to offer excuses: short notice, I didn't know what she was singing, I'd have to sight read—the whole litany. It never worked with Elly, but I was ready to give it a shot when Ulrike announced: "Herr Professor will be bringing the music. I would have preferred my own accompanist, of course, since he already knows the work, but Fräulein Gardiner assures me you are competent."

I bit back the urge to ask why she herself hadn't noticed. "Your accompanist," I temporized, still hoping an excuse would spring to mind, "that would be David Bryce?"

"That is correct."

"What will you be singing?"

"It is difficult to explain. Please just come by at two-thirty."

It looked as if I'd be taking the job whether I wanted it or not. She gave me directions to her home—not on Castle Frank as I'd heard, but north of the subway station with the same name—and finished off with a curt *"Bis später."* Till later.

I'd scarcely put the phone down when it rang again. Rosemary picked it up and spoke briefly, glancing at me. "Léo," she said, hanging up. "He's been delayed. He won't be here till one."

"I'll come back."

"Stay and finish your coffee. I have to go check tables."

I could have left a message with her, but I wanted to see Léo in person. He'd been in Montreal the previous week, taking care of the family fortune, and I needed to ask a favour, in addition to reminding him that I might be late coming in that evening. I knew he'd agree; asking was a matter of form, to remind us both that he was now my employer, as well as a friend.

I took the front way out after I'd finished my cappuccino. A big mulberry tree on Evelyn's lawn shades the entrance. At that time of year, its nearly translucent leaves made a glowing backdrop to the tiny clusters of immature drupes that would later ripen into sidewalk-staining fruit. I stood there awhile, debating whether to go back for the Rover. My next stop was the Conservatory, to see if my cheque for Monday night was ready. The fine weather—and the fact that the Conservatory was only a couple of blocks away—clinched my decision.

A police cruiser was doubled-parked in front of the building when I arrived. I didn't give it much thought until I passed two uniformed constables on the way up to the second floor. A third, loutish in his heavy uniform, loomed over

Janssen in the secretary's office at the top of the main stairs. It didn't look like a good time to enquire about my cheque, so I turned to leave.

"Mr. Lantry?" Janssen called out. "Would you mind waiting in the hall? I'd like to have a word with you."

I nodded and pushed through double safety doors into the corridor from which his office had a private entrance. Janssen's predecessors, the ones formerly displayed in the lobby, stared at me from the walls. I was inspecting the brushwork on Sir Geoffrey's eyebrows when Janssen opened up, hailed me.

"Vikkan? Thank you for waiting. Please—come in."

I mentally bade the former principals goodbye and entered a room so changed from the time of their reigns that they'd scarcely have recognized it. Every piece of solid, old furniture had been removed. Luxurious new carpeting covered the floor, pale blue and thickly padded. Donnish, mahogany bookshelves had given way to Danish-modern cabinetry. A stylish executive desk of some damson-coloured wood basked in the light of unadorned windows. Hyperrealist paintings hung in brushed chrome frames. The Queen's portrait was gone. Even the fine old Baldwin had been replaced by a glossy new Kawai. Clearly, Janssen wanted his President's office—even the title had changed—to reflect his aspirations for a Conservatory entering the new millennium.

"First things first," he said, motioning me to a wooden chair, himself settling behind the desk in highbacked cordovan leather. "I'd like to thank you for stepping in on Monday. I was counting on Ulrike's presence to make our concert a significant event."

"Glad I could be of assistance."

Before I sat down, I couldn't help noticing the music open on his Kawai— "The Rustle of Spring", a parlour piece that no one played anymore.

"The SM5000 people have asked me to record an anthology of Scandinavian composers," he explained, seeing my interest. "You'd be surprised. Some of the music's actually quite good."

I took my seat and nodded toward his secretary's office. "What did the police want?"

"We've had another incident of vandalism. I don't know if you've heard, but it's happened before. Minor things. This time it was serious. One of the studios was completely ransacked."

"Anything stolen?"

"Thankfully, no, but the damage was considerable. Someone with a key got in. The teacher whose studio it is is one of those who doesn't always sign out at the front desk." He shook his head over the common breach of regulations. "Her key has gone missing. I've ordered all the studio locks changed, and I'm setting in motion less informal measures to track the keys' whereabouts. It won't happen again." A modest tugging of shirt-cuffs under grey suit accompanied the prolepsis. "But I mustn't go on. You're here to be paid." He plucked a cheque off the top of his desk. *Snakker du norsk?* he enquired, scrutinizing it.

"No, I'm sorry, I don't." It was the only Norwegian I knew: *Do you speak...?*

"I wondered because of your name."

"My mother's family."

"The spelling's a bit odd." He frowned. "Two Ks. It could be Finnish, I suppose. No matter." He handed me the cheque. "Are you free right now?"

"I have a few minutes."

"Good. I was hoping to speak to you Monday night, but I had other duties." I remembered him glued to Doug Rawlings.

"You play very well. A student of Berényi's, is that right?"

I nodded, surprised he remembered.

"May I ask what you're doing now? I checked our exam records. It seems you were one of his best pupils."

"I do a little work for Miss Gardiner's studio and play at a lounge over on Prince Arthur."

"To be perfectly honest, I already know," he said, smiling apologetically. "I made inquiries with Miss Gardiner, after hearing you on Monday. I trust you'll forgive me."

"At least you went to a good source."

"I gather you absented yourself from Toronto for several years. I'm wondering if you're up to date on the changes taking place at your alma mater?"

"In what sense?"

His eyes strayed around the office. "The Conservatory is undergoing a period of transition. As you know, the emphasis here has always been on teaching, which it goes without saying is of the highest calibre. But something has always been missing. Too often, musicians spend their formative years here, then go on to become what? Office managers, hairdressers, mechanics, school teachers... It's a shameful waste, and the reason is that we don't give our students enough support once their training is finished. Talent alone is not sufficient to carve out a career. There are practical matters to be considered as well, especially the business of promotion. We've neglected that far too long. Our brightest and best can no longer be allowed to fall through the cracks."

"I fail to see how this pertains to me." The phantom voice of Uncle Charles muttered something about being disingenuous.

"According to Miss Gardiner, and to others who've heard you, you're very gifted. Your work with Ulrike Vogel confirms that. It's unconscionable that someone of your abilities should be playing at a bar." He paused, giving me time to wonder if he'd been infected with Elly's biases when he pumped her for my *curriculum vitae.* "I have a proposal."

"Yes?"

"Would you consider returning to the Conservatory? As a member of staff?"

I couldn't think what to say. I should have felt flattered; any normal person would. Instead, something like the little prickles of fight-or-flight brushed my skin. It seemed that no matter what I did, I couldn't avoid being drawn into music. Elly and Léo. Now Janssen. It was as if there were a conspiracy of Fate, or a cabal of well-wishers, all pulling me in a direction I didn't want to go. I didn't want to be a pianist; I merely wanted to play the piano. I was sure Janssen wouldn't understand the distinction, so I took a deep breath and said: "No."

I wasn't sure he'd heard. "We need a full-time accompanist to work with our singers. They need to perform more, compete more, get more exposure. To do that, they must have access to a pianist of your skills. Someone to work with them, closely, helping prepare the high-calibre programs needed for international recognition. The position would involve a great deal of concert work. Presently, no one on staff is quite right to fill the position. It requires not only a gifted pianist, but someone who looks good on stage as well. Such things cannot be overlooked."

"What about David Bryce?" I asked. "I understand he already works with Ulrike Vogel, and I'm sure he'd jump at an opportunity like this. He certainly fills the cosmetic requirements."

For a moment, Janssen looked nonplussed. "Mr. Bryce is not a suitable candidate," he said, picking an invisible thread from his lapel. "True, he does play for Ulrike's pupils, but primarily, he is a teacher of history and theory. It is there he will make his mark."

I couldn't tell whether he was being discreet, or merely pragmatic. It couldn't have escaped his notice that Bryce embodied the adage that ambition succeeds where talent fails. As a student, his playing had impressed no one, although rumour had it he could sight read just about anything. Unfazed by his lack of pianistic distinction, he had parlayed moderate academic skills into a burgeoning career by the simple expedient of seducing the Con's most brilliant theoretician. His name now cuddled next to hers on the jackets of the indispensable texts and workbooks she wrote on history, harmony and counterpoint.

"I only ask that you consider my offer," Janssen concluded. "This is an exciting time for the Conservatory. We plan to expand, build a second concert hall, add recording facilities. I intend to make this institution a major force in the music world. It could be worth your while to be here when that happens."

He didn't seem too perturbed when I didn't respond. If he'd talked to Elly, he already knew I'd likely turn him down. He leaned back and contemplated me over steepled fingers, then stood up. "Well, at least let me thank you again for helping out." His suit brushed frictionlessly on the polished wood of his desk as he leaned over and shook my hand. "Perhaps we'll be seeing more of you in the future."

❧   ❧   ❧

Elly and I needed to arrange a time to go over her Schubert, so I went round to her studio after leaving Janssen. Outside her door, I could hear the muffled sounds of inexpert vocalizing. *Ee-ay-ah-oh, ee-ay-ah-oh...* Rising tonic chord, descending dominant seventh, same thing at double speed, a short modulating cadence on the piano, then the whole exercise up a semitone. *Ee-ay-ah-oh...* The thin soprano voice strained for the high notes like a mountaineer grasping for an out-of-reach handhold.

I peered in through a small pane of glass at eye level in the door. All I could make out was the back of a big club chair—Elly's throne—and a section of piano. Every studio is fitted with a viewing window, but Elly, like most gossips, takes a dim view of other people snooping. Her arrangement of furniture frustrates all attempts. I waited until the singer squawked a final assault on her exercise, then knocked gently.

It wasn't brown tweed and fraying wool that greeted me when the door opened, but jeans and a pair of worn sneakers.

"Laura! What are you doing here? Where's Elly?"

"Having lunch with Dieter Mann. I'm using the studio while she's out."

Behind her, a girl in baggy pants and a t-shirt down to her knees gathered up music. A tangle of frizzy hair surrounded a face that might have been pretty, had she not kept it averted. I put her age at about sixteen.

"Come on in," Laura said. "We're just finished. I'll introduce you. Vikkan, this is Janice Cleary. Janice, Vikkan."

Janice mumbled something that might have been "hello," then crammed music into a shapeless purple satchel and gave Laura a beseeching look.

"You did well today," Laura said. "We'll get together at my place next week, as usual."

Janice ducked her head and fled out the door.

"Quiet girl," I observed, shutting it behind her.

"One of Elly's. We have an arrangement. I work off lessons by coaching some of her students."

"I think you're getting the short end of the stick."

Laura dropped down on the Victorian *récamier* that scrolled elegantly along the studio's north wall. "It's not so bad," she said, stretching out, "and it does remind me how glad I am I'm not sixteen any more." She let her head loll back on the velvet roll cushion.

"Were you like that?"

"God, no. The horror of sixteen was being around girls who were. Every man they met made them mute, or turned them into simpering idiots."

"You think I scared her?"

"Hardly. Don't worry about it. You should see her with her best friend, Siobhan. A real pair of mallflowers. Everything and everyone is beneath contempt, unless it's the *beauhunk du jour* on *The Young and the Restless.*"

"Siobhan?" The name rang a bell. "Rawlings' daughter?"

"The same."

"Elly said something about her being a pupil."

"Ward's more like it."

"What do you mean?"

Laura sat up. "The girl has no talent, and unlike Janice, no real interest. But her father wants her to study music, so here she is. He probably thinks it's what genteel young ladies do." She got off the *récamier* and crossed over to Elly's desk. Her sneakers squeaked on the parts of the floor not covered by a threadbare Turkish carpet. "She takes voice with Elly and does her theory with Bryce. I'm stuck coaching her. It's a real pain. Janssen's always breathing down our necks."

"I can't imagine why."

She made a sour face, went to say something, then thought better of it. "Are you looking forward to tonight?" she asked.

"The master class? You bet. You've never worked with Mann, have you?"

She shook her head. "No. Why?"

"It's special. You're going to enjoy it."

"You and Elly should form a fan club. Are you doing anything beforehand?"

"Nope."

"Want to have dinner?"

"Sounds like fun. How about Evelyn?"

"I was thinking more along the lines of cheap Hungarian."

"Go on—splurge. How's six o'clock?"

"That should give me enough time to take out a loan."

We chatted a few minutes more, then she scooted me out the door, saying she wanted to get in some practising before Elly returned.

My watch said twelve-thirty, and my stomach said "Feed me!" A strip of fast-food restaurants across from the Conservatory does brisk business malnourishing students from the north end of the university. I chose the McDonald's; man does not live by homemade bread alone.

I purchased a burger and fries, and along with it, the ill-considered indulgence of a chocolate shake. I was trying to suck the unyielding liquid through a straw, thinking a spoon would make more sense, when I happened to look up and see the girl Laura had just introduced me to. She was sitting near the front of the restaurant, elbows resting on the table, her chin supported by her fists. A nervous foot vibrated close to her satchel, tucked underneath the seat. Like me, she was drinking through a straw.

Slouched back across from her was an anorexic-looking redhead, languidly shredding a napkin. Bits of paper floated like confetti to the floor around her. Something about the girls' respective postures said they spent a lot of time together. From what Laura had told me, I wondered if Janice's companion was Siobhan, Doug Rawlings' daughter. If so, it was obviously her mother who had supplied the dominant genes. Her hair, an intense shade of copper, plumbed perfectly straight over painfully thin shoulders. Nearly blond eyebrows surmounted eyes the colour of faded Levi's. Shockingly pink lips emphasized a wan, freckled complexion.

She must have felt me staring, because she stopped tearing up her napkin and turned. Her look, at first merely curious, grew overtly appraising. She said something to Janice, who looked over and dissolved in a fit of giggles.

The exertion of sucking up cold sludge defeated me. My cheeks were sore; stars were swimming at the edge of my vision. I left the shake unfinished, gathered up the detritus of my meal and deposited it in a garbage can. I could feel the girls watching me as I walked out. I resisted the urge to turn around and say Boo!

☆   ☆   ☆

Back at Evelyn, a substantial post-lunch crowd of well-dressed professionals lingered in the lounge, loathe to leave its cozy semi-darkness. A susurrus of conversation rose from the banquettes scalloped around the piano, accompanied by the rich tinkle of ice cubes. The daytime bartender saw me coming and stopped skewering martini olives long enough to let me behind the bar. I squeezed in and made my way past shelves of aristocratic intoxicants to Léo's office at the end.

"Vikkan! Come in. Have a seat. Drink?"

"Thanks, no." I sank into my favourite chair, a big wing-backed monstrosity.

"But you will have one of these?" He pushed a silver box of slender, brown cigarettes across his desk. Shermans, from New

York. As if smoking weren't already expensive enough.

I lit up, exhaling smoke more blue than grey. "I'm just here to remind you that I might be late tonight."

"Yes. Your class with the famous teacher."

"He knows I have to be early in the program, but if he gets inspired with someone ahead of me..."

"...the customers will have to wait." An indulgent smile put some creases on his already lined face. "You hardly needed to drop by for that. My memory's not going."

"Just being professional. Treating this like a real job."

"You don't still imagine I hired you as a favour?" His smile tapered off, but the humour remained in his eyes, magnified behind thick, square bifocals. "You're supposed to have gotten over that by now."

"It never hurts to keep things straight."

"You wouldn't be here if it didn't attract clientele."

"But you didn't know that when I started."

"No," he drew out the syllable, "I didn't. But I had a pretty good idea. At any rate, does it matter now?"

"Truth?"

He nodded.

"I like working here, but the spectre of charity's a hard one to get rid of."

Léo's gaze shifted to a brass-framed photo on his desk, identical to one on my piano at home. When he looked up, his expression had turned sombre. "Nothing will make me happier than when you exorcise that phantom once and for all. You're family, Vikkan. You were from the start. The last thing you should ever feel is indebted."

"But I do. And besides, isn't that what families are supposed to be all about?"

I meant it as a joke, but it didn't come out that way. Léo

didn't say anything. I took a pull at my cigarette and released the smoke in a long, steady stream. He and Evelyn were like family—the one everyone dreams of having: loving, supportive, generous. Uncle Charles, unstinting when it came to life's instruction, had never provided much by way of warmth. I could scarcely blame him; he'd done what he thought right for the unexpected child who'd obtruded on his bachelor's life. But after Christian's death—long before, in fact—Léo and Evelyn had shown me consideration as close to parental fondness as anyone could hope for. I owed it to their kindness, and the enormity of their own loss, not to sound resentful.

"What's really bothering you?" he asked.

"I didn't know anything was, until now."

"Whenever you turn acerbic, I know something's wrong. What is it?"

"Too many helping hands, I think."

"In general, or are you talking about music?"

"Music, mostly. Would you believe the president of the Conservatory offered me a job today?"

"Which you refused." His smile returned. "Do you want to talk about it?"

I took another drag on my cigarette and shrugged. "Not really."

Léo didn't take offence. We seldom discussed my ambivalence about working in music. For the most part, he acknowledged it unspoken, like an unadmitted countercurrent troubling a close friend's love affair. Even when he'd first suggested I play at Evelyn, he'd put forth the matter diffidently, worried I might bite his head off.

A knock on the door interrupted us. He answered and held a brief conference on the other side. When he returned to his desk, I addressed the other matter I'd come to see him about.

"Do you think I could go up to Caledon this weekend?"

"Of course."

"It's for Evelyn's book," I explained. "The marsh marigolds are coming on. The shots I have aren't good enough. The saturation's terrible. The yellow hardly shows at all. I'm hoping it'll be overcast on Friday or Saturday so I can try again."

Léo straightened a pen against the edge of a leather-sided blotter. "You know, Vikkan," he said, not looking up, "I get the feeling you could have spared yourself the trouble of coming by today. You didn't have to remind me about tomorrow night. You hardly need my permission to go to Caledon for a visit. And you certainly don't have to invent excuses." His eyes strayed to the photo on his desk again. "There's nothing wrong with wanting to go back. Evelyn's up there now."

"I thought she was in Montreal."

"She flew into Pearson International yesterday."

I had planned on spending a day or two alone on Léo's property, but on second thought, I realized Evelyn's company would be welcome, someone to help take the sting out of memories. "Thank you, Léo," I said. "Thanks to both of you."

In the silence that followed, he needlessly tidied a stack of invoices. I finished my cigarette and crushed it gently in an onyx ashtray.

"How is Evelyn's book going?" he asked.

"Fine. I found a photographer who specializes in printing onto unusual materials, everything from canvas to Formica. He says there'll be no problem treating vellum to receive an image. But it's going to be expensive. There could be well over a hundred and fifty plates."

"Let me worry about that. How's the rest progressing?"

"The written stuff? Slow but sure. It's hard keeping the descriptions down to a single page the way I want. Words like acuminate, verruculose and galactogogue take up a lot of space."

"Whatever they mean." He shook his head. "Evelyn's so excited about this, you know."

"It's a hell of a gift. For me, as well as her."

A small clock on Léo's desk said it was nearly two, reminding me that I had an appointment with Ulrike in half an hour. Something told me she wouldn't take kindly to my showing up late, so I made apologies and got up to leave. Léo walked me to the door, his arm across my shoulders.

Downstairs, I went in search of Rosemary.

"A table for two at six?" she said, opening a maroon-bound ledger. "No problem." I could tell from the careful way she pencilled in my name that she wanted details.

"It's just a friend, Rosemary."

"Of course," she said sweetly. "Anything special from the kitchen?"

Why not? "Orange roughy in lemongrass. Rice with chive flowers. Steamed asparagus. A small radicchio salad."

"Something light, in other words. A female friend?"

"A singer. She's performing afterward. Hard to do that on a full stomach."

※   ※   ※

I had some difficulty finding Ulrike's, since the streets in her part of lower Rosedale had been laid out with an eye to whimsy, not ease of access. The address she'd given was on a keyhole-shaped cul-de-sac with a raised, circular flowerbed at the end. I drove around the gracious planting of salmon-coloured tulips and pulled up in front of a narrow brick house. An asphalt driveway, too short to park in, sloped down to a one-car basement garage. Beside it, three very tall and slender cypresses separated her property from the one on the left. To the right, trimmed yews and junipers formalized an expensively green front lawn.

Ulrike answered the door herself, mannishly elegant in tailored slacks and a long-sleeved blouse. I was a bit surprised; I'd expected her to have a maid or servant, someone to act as a buffer between her and her callers.

"This way," she murmured, leading me down a parqueted hallway with rooms on either side. At the far end, a kitchen done entirely in black and white gave onto a landing, from which a half-flight of stairs descended into a long sitting room. Generous French doors at the far end admitted sunlight from a spruce-bordered back yard.

Mann was already there, sitting in a chair that looked as if it might be Biedermeier. "So, Vikkan," he said, getting up, "once again you are called in to help on short notice. My fault, this time, I'm afraid. I trust you'll forgive me when you see what we'll be doing."

He motioned me to a Bösendorfer hulking imperially in front of the French doors. I went over, confused. I'd been under the impression I was there at Ulrike's request.

"You'll have to sight-read, of course, but I promise, no transposition this time." He winked. "I've spoken to Ulrike and told her she should thank you for being so accommodating on Monday night."

His teasing brought forth a tight smile from Ulrike. "Herr Professor speaks very highly of you," she said. "I trust you can appreciate the compliment."

"Thank you," I said—to Mann. "So, what are we doing?"

He gestured to a sheaf of music on the rack. "Have a look."

I pulled out the bench and sat down. A title page in ornate

Fraktur script lay on top. *Robert Schumann,* it said, *Liederkreis über Texten von Ebert. Als Geschenk seiner geliebten Braut zugeeignet.* The name of the publisher appeared at the bottom, along with a date in Roman numerals.

I began leafing through the sheets, pivoting them aside between my thumb and forefinger. The paper was yellowed and had a furrowed, sturdy texture that told me it came from a time before the brittling use of chlorine and alum. There were fifteen songs in all. I gave each a cursory glance, just enough to establish how difficult they'd be to play.

"I don't know them," I said, turning the stack over, thinking it would have been easier to work from a bound copy. "But I shouldn't have too much trouble."

Mann chuckled. "But I didn't expect you to know them. In fact, I'd have been very surprised if you did." He leaned over my shoulder. "Perhaps you should look at them again." The expression on his face made me think of a grandfather encouraging his grandson to open a special Christmas gift. "Go on," he nodded.

The title page was on top, so I reread: Robert Schumann. *Liederkreis*—Song Cycle—on texts by Ebert. Dedicated as a gift to his beloved fiancée.

"I was under the impression Schumann only wrote two *Liederkreise,"* I said. "Opus twenty-four and thirty-nine. He gave his other cycles descriptive titles, like *Dichterliebe* and *Frauenliebe und Leben.* At any rate, this one's new to me."

Mann's look transformed into one of comical disappointment. "Really, Vikkan, you're not paying attention. Check the date."

I hadn't bothered with the Roman numerals at the bottom of the page: MDCCCXXXIX. I started deciphering: M for one thousand, three C's after the D for eight hundred, three X's for thirty... Something clicked. Eighteen hundred plus thirty plus nine—a few too many X's and one L short of a date known to every student of music history: eighteen-forty, the year Schumann first turned to writing lieder.

Mann saw my look of comprehension. "You paid attention in school after all," he commented drily.

"You mean this isn't what it says it is?" Unknown works resurface from time to time, but usually as manuscripts, not fully printed editions. Schumann couldn't have published a *Liederkreis* prior to his famous "year of song" without there being some record. "Is it a fraud?"

"You're still missing something," he said, wagging his finger, his eyes twinkling. "Something obvious."

What was he getting at? One by one, I turned the loose sheets over again, exasperated that he wouldn't just tell me what was going on. The pages were all of slightly different dimensions, making it difficult to lift them individually. I was prising one of the narrower ones up with a fingernail when it dawned on me. The pages themselves—they'd all been cut and trimmed by hand. No trace of binding showed along the edges. The publication had no cover. And when I turned back to the title page, I saw that it had no opus number.

"These are publisher's proofs, aren't they?" I said, turning to Mann. "Galleys for making corrections."

He patted my shoulder. "Very good. That is indeed what they are."

I recalled his comment at the airport, the one about "questionable possessions" in his briefcase. Was this what he'd been talking about?

"Are you saying this is an undiscovered work?" It didn't seem possible. A song cycle by Schumann in pre-publication form that had never made it to the history books? The composer's writings and correspondence were amongst the best-documented of the nineteenth century. "Where did it come from? Why hasn't anyone heard of it?"

Mann stepped back from the piano. "Later, Vikkan, later. Enough mystery and surprises for now. What I need from you is not questions, but an accompaniment. One that is complete. Ulrike and I have been over the songs, but sadly, the bass was missing a few notes." He held up his left hand, minus its thumb and index joint.

Ulrike, who'd been seated while we spoke, rose and put a hand on his arm. "Are you sure this is right, Dieter? David knows the music already, from the copies you sent. Would it not be better to wait? I sing so much better if the pianist is…secure. *Wenn es keine Fehler gibt."* When there are no mistakes.

"Ulrike, Schätzi," he chided, *"du hast schon mit Vikkan gearbeitet. Du weißt, er ist sehr begabt."* He looked over to see if I'd understood: You've already worked with Vikkan; you know he's very gifted.

She carried on as if I weren't present. *"Ja, gewiß. Aber…"* Yes, of course, but…

"No buts. I will be here only a few days. We may not get another chance."

She looked extremely unhappy, but capitulated by going over to her music stand and arranging pages. It struck me as odd that Mann had provided her with copies, but was expecting me to play from the original. It seemed risky. Pages get torn being flipped one-handed in the heat of a performance.

"Begin when you like," Mann directed, settling back in his chair. "And Ulrike—relax the tempo in the songs marked *bewegt.* Also where it says *ziemlich rasch."*

I wondered if they'd discussed this before, or whether he was obliquely telling her to go easy on me. *Bewegt* and *rasch* are the German for *allegro.* Lickety-split. Hell to play at sight.

72

She took her time getting ready, rolling her neck and massaging her jaw, then going through facial contortions to relax her throat. Finally, she squared her shoulders and nodded. I placed my fingers on the keys and stroked out the opening chords. Four bars later, she entered:

> *Dämm'rung ist mir ach! so leise*
> *Murmeln Bäume Abendweise...*

❧   ❧   ❧

The songs were beautiful. Exquisite preludes set the mood; haunting postludes whispered wordless paraphrases at the end. Seamless piano lines wove around melodies that rose and fell in perfect concord with the text. Yearning dissonances pierced the lush, poignant harmonies. Whoever the composer, he'd been touched by genius.

The poetry told a simple narrative of love—found, lost and recovered—through customary Romantic metaphors. Cypresses and lindens, forests and glades, twilight, mountains and castles abounded. But the music spoke where the clichés could not, distilling essence from the words, alchemizing them into pure gold.

Mann said nothing during the run-through. He sat perfectly still, only once shifting his weight from one side of the chair to the other during a break between songs.

Ulrike's mastery of style and phrasing was superb. I could well understand the comparisons to Schwarzkopf; her upper notes had a similar breathtaking, maternal warmth. Just the same, I noticed some roughness in her tone, especially in the lower register. She shot small, nervous glances toward Mann whenever it showed up.

It took over an hour to go through the cycle. When we

finished, I felt completely drained. Ulrike's expressive rubato, tough enough to follow even when I wasn't sightreading, had kept me on my toes. Mann's intense focus on us had brought on an unaccustomed bout of nerves. I let my head slump forward, then glanced at him. He appeared lost in thought, his earlier excitement attenuated.

"Well done," he said finally, clearing his throat. "Very well done. Excellent work, Vikkan. Eleanor's confidence in you is not misplaced. You must be exhausted." He looked at Ulrike, who seemed lost in her own reverie. "Ulrike? Perhaps you could offer Vikkan something to drink?"

She shook her head to clear it. "Yes. Of course. What will you have?"

"Would coffee be too much trouble?"

"How do you take it?"

"Just with milk."

She turned to Mann. "Dieter?"

He reached into his jacket and pulled out what looked like a package of teabags wrapped in plastic film. "Just bring me some hot water in a cup, please."

Ulrike crossed the long room and mounted the steps into the kitchen. Mann unwrapped his package, sniffed the contents, and made a selection. "A tonic," he explained. "Woodruff and blackberry leaves. Revitalizes the system. You do not get to my age without some assistance."

"Sorry to say, I'm addicted to coffee."

"Coffee is not good for you."

"So I've been told."

I'd been expecting him to comment on the *Liederkreis,* or at least tell me what was going on, and here we were discussing beverages. "Thyme and strawberry leaves with chamomile make a good tonic, too," I offered in what sounded like a variation on *nice weather we're having.*

He looked amused. "It would appear that Eleanor is right. There is no subject on which you cannot converse intelligently."

"She's exaggerating. It's just that I'm working on a project these days that keeps that sort of information close to hand."

He listened with more than polite interest while I told him about the folio I was putting together for Evelyn St-Onge.

"So there's a touch of the mediaeval scholar about you," he said, nodding thoughtfully. "I think I understand. It's not unheard of for musicians to become fascinated with the natural world. Father loved birds, for example. Painted them remarkably well. I wonder if it has to do with the abstractness of our art. Nothing in the natural world resembles music. We need to be reminded of things concrete, tangible, so we don't lose our way. Ah, here are our refreshments."

Ulrike came down into the room with a tray holding Mann's hot water, my coffee and a tumbler inverted over a bottle of Evian.

"Well?" she asked, serving us, pouring herself some water. "Shall we go on?"

Mann spent a long time dunking his teabag in his cup. "I think, Ulrike," he said at last, "that once through is enough, don't you agree? For now, at any rate."

"But I am not satisfied. There were problems in several of the songs. I was...unaccustomed...to the playing." She turned to me and issued a command. "We will do them again."

"Not now, Ulrike." Mann spoke firmly. "It won't be necessary. And besides," he consulted a pocket watch, "it's getting on. I have students between five and seven."

She looked very displeased and answered him stiffly. "Of course. I understand. I, too, have students. But we will have an opportunity again before you return to Vienna?"

"Natürlich." He sipped his tisane of blackberry leaves and woodruff. "I do not leave until Saturday."

She still wasn't happy and began speaking to him in rapid German, which I took as a sign she didn't want me in the conversation. I obligingly tuned her out, sipped coffee and longed for a cigarette.

Finally, Mann made a show of drinking up. "I really must be going," he said, setting down his cup. "I don't want to be late for my students."

"Do you need a ride?" I asked.

"I don't want to be a burden, but, yes, I would be most grateful." He stood up, stooping slightly from having sat so long. "Do you know where?"

"Yes." A friend of Elly's over on Palmerston donated her salon and pristine Bechstein to Mann whenever he was in town.

"Do you wish to be paid, Vikkan?" Ulrike asked suddenly. "It is unlikely that I will require your services again. I have spoken with David, and his ailment appears to be healing. For which he thanks you, Dieter," she added with a little nod to Mann.

"Maybe we should wait," I said. "That way, if you need me again, you'll only have to write one cheque. And may I say," I added, growing tired of her lack of recognition for the work I'd already done, "it's been a pleasure working with you."

She accepted the compliment, oblivious to any sarcasm.

Mann collected the *Liederkreis* from the piano, wrapped it in what looked like a chamois, and placed it in his briefcase. Ulrike accompanied us to the front door and bid him a supplication-tinged *Auf Wiedersehen*.

Heading for the Rover, I asked him what she'd meant by attributing Bryce's recovery to him.

"Oh, that," he said, waving it away. "You know—we amateur naturopaths are always full of good advice."

The automotive gods appeared to be on my side that day. The motor started without difficulty, the spindly stick shift didn't grind when I eased into reverse, and the loose front tie rod didn't clunk when I twisted the wheel to head us down the street. Normally, I wouldn't have done anything to disrupt my good fortune. Instead, I drove only as far as the stop sign, pulled over to the curb and shut off the engine. *"Herr Professor,"* I said, formally addressing an impishly grinning Mann, *"ich habe keine Lust, unhöflich zu erscheinen,"*—I have no wish to appear impolite—*"aber was zum Teufel passiert?"*

What the hell is going on?

Four

Als wollten sie was sagen
Von der alten, schönen Zeit.
("As if to tell the romance
Of a golden age gone by.")
  —*Liederkreis*, Opus 39, VII

Mann convinced me to restart the Rover, assuring me he'd talk as we drove. "Unless, of course, you wish to extort the information from me with threats of tardiness," he said, "in which case, I shall clam up like a captured spy." He mimed zipping up his lips and tossed the imaginary key out the window.

"Hard to believe," he began when we were moving again, "that Beethoven had been dead scarcely a year when Robert Schumann first set eyes upon little Clara..."

I drove on autopilot. Mann related his story like a fireside tale told by someone who'd witnessed the events. The stop-and-go Bloor Street traffic seemed to fade, giving way to horse-drawn carriages on Old World cobblestone. Toronto's glass office towers morphed into gracious stone buildings, history and heritage evident in their careful masonry.

In 1828, Schumann, still two years shy of his twentieth birthday, entered the home of Friederich Wieck to give piano lessons to Wieck's nine-year-old daughter, Clara. The girl showed exceptional promise, and teacher and pupil grew close in the years that saw her talent unfold and blossom. As Clara matured, physically and artistically, affection between the two of them turned ineluctably to love.

In time, Schumann approached Wieck and asked for his daughter's hand in marriage. Wieck refused; any marriage, he felt, would distract Clara from the brilliant and profitable concert career he no doubt hoped to manage for her. But his forbiddance only strengthened the passion and resolve of the lovers. A court battle ensued, in which Wieck tried to forestall the possibility of marriage by secessional manoeuvring.

In the end, though, he relented and, yielding to the superior power of love, gave Robert and Clara permission to marry. Their engagement took place in 1839, and in 1840, they became man and wife.

In a frenzy of inspiration occasioned by his triumphal marriage, Schumann, who had hitherto considered vocal music beneath his notice, suddenly devoted his entire fervid genius to composing lieder. A hundred and twenty-seven masterpieces flowed from his pen in the course of one astoundingly fertile, song-filled year.

"You know," Mann interrupted himself, "most history books aren't one hundred percent reliable on the matter of when Schumann wrote his first lieder. Most of them overlook a collection of eleven songs from 1827, composed when he was only seventeen years old."

"I've never heard of them."

"Not surprising. I don't think he tried to publish them, although that didn't prevent him from proudly inscribing the manuscript 'Opus Two.'" He chuckled. "However, much more interesting—and troubling, at least for those whose careers rest on fixing dates—is a mature song cycle bearing his name, but dated 1839."

Jubilant over his engagement, and in anticipation of the forthcoming nuptials, Schumann decided to make his bride-to-be an extraordinary musical offering: the *Liederkreis* I had just played.

Although the distinguished Leipzig firm of Breitkopf and Härtel usually handled Schumann's music at the time, he chose to have Clara's gift published by a smaller company, Gottlieb and Schranz, possibly to protect the larger concern's reputation in case the song cycle wasn't well received.

In those days, preparing music for printing was a laborious process. Unlike a poem or novel, where rows of letters march in orderly fashion down the page, music is made up of fluid signs and symbols that can't be fixed so neatly. A sheet of music is closer to a picture than a page of words. Until the advent of the computer, the composer's manuscript had to be etched—drawn by hand onto copper plates—rather than typeset.

The finishing touches had just been put on the plates for Schumann's *Liederkreis* when disaster struck. On the evening of August thirteenth, a fire broke out on the premises of Gottlieb and Schranz. Jakob Schranz, the firm's junior partner, was summoned from a cosy supper with his bride of scarcely three weeks, Greta, arriving at a blaze which, he learned, had trapped Gottlieb in their second-floor offices. Jakob braved the inferno to rescue his associate, but his heroism proved futile; both men perished, as did the building along with its contents.

"However," Mann intoned with a storyteller's flourish, "it just so happens..."

...that that very day, a first set of proofs had been pulled and given to Jakob for delivery to Schumann. Expecting to call on the composer the next morning, Jakob had taken the proofs home with him, and thus, miraculously, they'd escaped the conflagration.

"So what happened to them?" I broke in. "How come nobody's ever heard of this *Liederkreis*? Shouldn't there be some reference to it in Schumann's writings? And where did you find it?"

Mann held up his hand. "Too many questions, Vikkan. Don't you know your own proverb about curiosity and the cat? Let me finish."

What followed seemed at first like a detour. Mann began detailing his own genealogy, starting with his famous father and equally renowned mother, Käthe Lemper, a soprano revered for her interpretation of Mozart's Queen of the Night. The side trip ended at one Wolfgang Mann, his thrice great-grandfather, and second husband to Jakob Schranz's tragically widowed Greta.

"It would seem," he said, "that when Jakob and his partner died, there was no hope of rebuilding the business. Neither was there much of an inheritance for poor great-great-great-grandmother Greta. What little there was went into settling her husband's accounts. Bereft, she packed everything of Jakob's into cartons and returned to her family. The proofs of the *Liederkreis* went with her.

"You know the way of it, I'm sure. Boxes with papers get moved upstairs and gather dust. Succeeding generations move them farther and farther into the attic.

"Fortunately, my family is like those little mice who collect things; we hate to throw anything away. When my grandfather decided to purchase the summer house in Piedmont, grandmother Maria cleaned out the attic in Vienna and shipped everything down there.

"Sadly, I had to part with the summer house last year. No one can afford such an extravagance these days. But before the sale, my daughter, Anna, went through everything. I intended to sell the house with all its contents, you see, and she didn't want me parting with anything whose value I'd accidentally overlooked.

81

She was thinking mainly of things like the Gallé vases and some furniture by Guimard. At any rate, it was she who came across the *Liederkreis*. She brought it back to Vienna thinking it was simply an old edition I might want to keep as a curio." He sighed. "Anna's knowledge of music history is at best rudimentary. She prefers the courtroom to the concert hall, I'm afraid."

"She had no idea of its significance?"

He shook his head and sighed again. "I had to explain it all to her. Since that time, though, we have often discussed her little 'find.' Not all the conversations have been *freundlich*—amicable. We don't always see eye-to-eye, Anna and I."

"What's the problem?"

"We have differing views on what to do with it. However, I will say this: it was Anna who thought of Ulrike for the first performance. In that, I agreed with her."

We were half a block from Palmerston, and I was about to ask again how the songs' very existence had gone unsuspected for so long when the ever-willful Rover chose to stall. When I tried to get it going again, the engine flooded. I apologized to Mann and got out.

A miasma of gasoline vapor rose to greet me when I lifted the hood. Holding my breath, I wedged one of the carburetor's butterfly valves open with an empty ballpoint I keep taped to the battery for just such emergencies. Mann tried the ignition when I called out to him, and after a couple of turns, it roared to life. An impatient soul started honking as I came around the side. I gave him the finger and climbed back in.

"A man of many talents," Mann observed wryly.

With only a block and a half to Elly's friend's house, there wasn't time to ask anything further. Mann was silent until I pulled up to the oak-shaded curb, gunning the engine to keep it going.

"There is one thing, Vikkan," he said, getting out. "The *Liederkreis* is not yet public knowledge. I would appreciate..."

"Say no more." I had to raise my voice to make myself heard. "I'll see you this evening."

He lifted his arm in an informal gesture of parting, then headed up a petunia-lined walk toward the house. I waited until the door opened before driving off in a cloud of blue exhaust.

≈ ≈ ≈

It was a quarter after five when I got to Evelyn. Léo and Rosemary were in a meeting, and Laura wasn't due to arrive until six, so I went up upstairs and ordered a Glenfiddich, taking a seat at the only unoccupied banquette in the lounge. A waiter I didn't recognize brought my Scotch. Rather than claim special privileges as an employee, I paid the listed price. It was suitably steep.

I sat by myself for fifteen minutes, savouring Scotland's finest and reflecting on Mann's discovery. The way he'd related the details, I got the feeling he was putting on a show, as much for my entertainment as his own. There'd been an element of private amusement in the way he characterized the players, a sort of fond indulgence that I couldn't reconcile with the magnitude of his find.

I'd probably have gone on wondering about it if Russell Spiers hadn't shown up, accompanied by a big bear of a man in loose corduroys and a turtleneck: Dean Norbert Simmons, head of the Faculty of Music. "The dean," as everyone simply called him, had probably worn the same pants and sweater under his academic gown when he intoned *Ego te admisso ad gradum* at my convocation. Spiers, lilliputed by his companion and dressed in a shiny suit of uncertain colour, looked for all the world like a middle-aged functionary. Standing at the top of the stairs and scanning the room, his eyes held the same ferrety look of move-up-the-ladder eagerness.

Spotting the expanse of Léo's floral print upholstery beside me, he headed over. "Taking a liquid break, I see," he said, sitting down without asking. "You should watch that. Alcohol will make your looks slip, and the patrons might find out your playing's not as scintillating as they thought."

I would have liked to tell him to take a hike or, better yet, to throw my drink in his face, but innate civility and the cost of the Scotch held me back. "I'm waiting for someone," I said coolly. "Laura Erskine. I only play here later in the evening."

"Of course—when everyone's too far gone to listen," he shot back.

Until yesterday, I'd had no contact with Spiers for several years. I couldn't believe he still nursed a grudge because I'd refused to be a jewel in his crown. I was preparing a reply to that effect when the Dean intervened.

"Lantry, isn't it?" he said, holding out a huge, friendly paw. "You were in Composition."

"That's right." I had to reach in front of Spiers to shake hands. "It's Vikkan, by the way."

"Right. Vikkan."

Spiers snagged my waiter. He and the Dean placed their orders: a vodka and tonic for Spiers, a Sleeman for the Dean. When the drinks arrived, Spiers asked to run up a tab.

"Whatever happened to you, anyway?" the Dean asked, pouring his ale. "You were pretty good, as I recall." It sounded like something he said to all alumni when he couldn't quite place them.

"I left Toronto for a couple of years."

He nodded, as if this explained everything. "Still keeping your hand in?"

"I've been doing some work for Eleanor Gardiner over at the Con."

He turned to Spiers. "Elly Gardiner? Isn't Laura Erskine with her now?"

"Yes." Spiers squeezed a wedge of lime and dropped it in his drink. "I told her to stay with Ulrike after graduation, but apparently she doesn't feel quite the allegiance to the Faculty she should." He sipped his drink and pursed his lips critically.

"Laura and I will be in a master class with Dieter Mann tonight," I told the Dean. "It's his yearly visit to Toronto."

"Yes, I know. We had a meeting yesterday afternoon."

"Really? He'd only just arrived. I collected him from the airport."

"You?" Spiers interjected. "Mann's a bit out of your league, isn't he? Or is driving a limo the closest you can get to real talent any more?"

It took no special insight on the Dean's part to discern Spiers' antagonism. "Russell," he said, pleasantly enough, "if you have something against Vikkan here..."

It was obvious Spiers knew who stood where in the Faculty pecking order. He heeded the admonishment and returned to his vodka and tonic.

"As I was saying," the Dean went on, "I saw Mann Tuesday afternoon. An interesting character. Full of surprises."

"As I'm beginning to realize. Do you know him well?"

"First time we've met. I was surprised when he asked to see me. Couldn't imagine what he wanted. Has quite the reputation for avoiding academic types, doesn't he?"

"Not entirely without justification," I said.

The Dean smiled, unoffended.

I wanted to ask what he and Mann had talked about, but I knew it wouldn't be long before Spiers pulled himself away from his drink and found something nasty to say again. I checked my watch: a quarter to six—I could wait for Laura downstairs. I stood up and said goodbye to the Dean, offering him my hand again. Spiers mugged a wounded puppy look when I didn't do the same for him.

As I walked away from the table, the two started in on a heated conversation, as if they'd been waiting for me to leave.

"—me handle it, Russell."

"—biggest publicity bang for his buck."

"—forgotten, I make the decisions..."

❧   ❧   ❧

Laura arrived right at six. I was pleased to see she'd dressed casually: cotton slacks and a jersey pullover. My own attire was less than formal. I also noticed she hadn't worn make-up. Her squarish face and wide, frank eyes looked better for it.

"So this is where you work," she said, appraising the room.

"Upstairs, actually. In the lounge. You've never been here before?"

"Only ogled it from outside."

"Lovely, isn't it? Léo did a good job."

"Léo?"

"The owner."

She nodded and sat down. "I'm famished. What's good to eat?"

"Everything, but you should know I put in a request with the kitchen. If it meets with your approval, all you have to choose is an appetizer." I told her what I'd ordered.

"Is that why you work here? To get an in with the chef?"

"Membership has its privileges."

"Maybe I should reconsider the direction of my career, if

this is what lounge work gets you."

"Barry Manilow isn't your style."

She grimaced. "Tell me that isn't what you play."

"Once in a while. "Could It Be Magic" is pretty good. He borrowed it from Chopin."

"Could be that's why it's the only song of his I like."

She turned her attention to the handwritten menu. A minute later, our waiter—Robert, according to the gold pin on his vest—arrived with bread. Both of us ordered consommé to start. I wanted an apéritif, but followed Laura's lead and stuck with water. Robert already knew what we'd be having for dinner, and said I was to tell him when the chef should start the orange roughy.

Laura broke one of the small, pale loaves and bit in, uttering a muffled exclamation of delight.

"Good, isn't it?" I said.

"Mmm."

"Sourdough, made the old-fashioned way. No yeast in the starter, just flour and water left to sit until some errant little beasty floating in the air dives in and starts excreting alcohol and other tangy stuff. It doesn't always work. Sometimes, you end up with smelly pink glop. This one turned out pretty well."

"This one?"

"I got the mixture going a couple of years ago when I was out in the country. Léo passed it on to his baker."

"Impressive. You're seriously into bread making? What I saw at your apartment looked amazing."

"Legacy of the uncle who raised me. He had some odd notions about what I needed to know in life. Good thing he wasn't into butchering his own meat."

The consommé arrived in gold-edged Limoges cups. It looked wonderful: a clear veal broth with tiny dumplings drifting on top, wild mushrooms skulking at the bottom. Laura sampled it, her face melting. "Don't tell me you had a hand in this, too, or I'll have to marry you on the spot."

"Don't worry. Your marital status won't be changing on account of the soup."

We finished rapidly—too rapidly for something so good. If fine cooking is an art, then it's an ephemeral one, and its appreciation should be slow, so as to prolong its fleeting existence. Thus spake Uncle Charles, who also maintained that the only fitting response to beauty, especially in music, should be utter silence, not applause.

Robert came and removed our cups. Should the kitchen begin the main course, or did we want to wait? I said they could start right away. Laura eyed the last of the bread. "Go ahead," I said. "Evelyn doesn't do doggy bags."

She popped it in her mouth with a Cheshire Cat grin, then leaned forward, elbows on the table. "So," she asked, "what else do you do, aside from baking, carpentry, photography, and playing the piano?"

One of my childhood guardian's most frequently enunciated proscriptions dealt with talking about myself. "Thy modesty's a candle to thy merit," he'd remind me, quoting Fielding, but Laura had posed her question with such humour that for once I didn't feel self-conscious. "I ride sometimes," I said, "and build kites. I also dabble in watercolours, and occasionally spend hours making insects out of little squares of paper. Oh, and I try to keep my jeep running, which is nearly a full-time occupation."

"That's all?" she laughed. "You know what Elly says, don't you?"

"Do I want to hear this?"

"She says that you're a dilettante. Your true talent lies in music, and you hide from it with all the other stuff you do. She maintains it's Berényi's fault."

"Elly says all that?"

Laura shrugged. "She's very fond of you."

"So people keep telling me."

"Is it true? What she says about Berényi?"

I didn't have to ask what she meant. Berényi's reputation preceded him. Still, I thought carefully before answering. "Yes and no. My years with him weren't easy. Sometimes I wonder how different I'd be if I'd studied with someone else. You know he used to boast that not one of his students *hadn't* broken down and cried during at least one lesson? His favourite pedagogical tool was abuse. His rages were unpredictable. It didn't matter how much practising you put in, you never knew from week to week if it would be enough to satisfy him. Sometimes it was, which only made it worse when it wasn't. I remember once he threw a mug of coffee at me from across the room just because I'd played a Chopin Ballade perfectly. He was livid. If I could play like that, why didn't I do it all the time?"

"Sounds like a psycho."

"His favourite line was: 'I have no patience!' He'd say it over and over with this weird Hungarian accent. Scared the hell out of me, because the more he said it, the angrier he'd get. Sooner or later, he'd start screaming and throwing music around. Then he'd shove me out the door. The worst of that was when someone else was in the hallway. He'd keep on yelling even when I was outside."

Laura's eyes crinkled in a funny way, as if she didn't want to believe me. "And you put up with it? For how long?"

"Nearly ten years. From the time I was eleven."

"But why?"

"It sounds incredible now, but would you believe I just

didn't know any better? He was supposed to be the best. It was an honour to study with him. I didn't want to tell my uncle about it because I assumed a man of Berényi's reputation had to be right: I just wasn't working hard enough. I didn't want my uncle to think that the money he spent on lessons wasn't justified. I owed him a lot. He'd never planned on raising a child. I wanted to excel at everything by way of gratitude."

She nodded slowly, understanding, making me wonder how much of love and a desire to please had fueled her own studies.

"Funny thing is, I still can't say for sure whether Berényi's methods were wrong. I did learn to play the piano, and I can't help wondering if I'd have learned so thoroughly if he'd been different. I read somewhere that humiliation is the best teacher."

"But when you finished with him, you went on to study music at the Faculty?" She shook her head. "It sounds sick."

"Lots of Berényi's students stayed in music. Mind you, a fair number had nervous breakdowns, too. And none went on to become super-successful. Maybe we were all just suckers for punishment, although in my case, I think it was more a question of the path of greatest resistance. I hate admitting defeat."

Robert arrived just then with our *plats principaux.* I disliked talking about Berényi. My time with him sounded like a catalogue of horrors, and any analysis of it made me sound like a weak-willed masochist. I suspected the real dynamic between us had been like the intimacy that's supposed to spring up between interrogator and interrogee, captor and hostage.

The restaurant was filling up. Muted voices and the clinking of cutlery filled the lull in our conversation. Laura sampled her fish, then attacked it with gusto. The way she dug in, I wondered if I shouldn't have had the chef whip up something more substantial.

I went at my asparagus first: emerald green spears glistening with sesame oil. Next, the rice and chive flowers. Last of all, the orange roughy. An ultra thin coating—chestnut flour? arrowroot?—crisped into shards in my mouth, forming a kind of tactile staccato to the buttery flesh inside. The radicchio salad afterward added a pleasantly bitter counterpoint.

"Su-*perb*," Laura announced, laying down her fork. "Definitely better than stuffed chicken at the Budapest."

She sat back and watched me polish off my salad. I popped a last pink leaf into my mouth with my fingers and pushed the plate away. When I looked up, she had an odd expression on her face.

"What?" I asked.

"I'm just wondering who he is."

"Who who is?"

"The man in the photograph on your piano. I couldn't help noticing when I was there. He looks a lot like you. Your brother?"

"No. His name is Christian."

"And?"

"And what?"

"And who is he?"

"Not is—was. A lover. For four years."

Laura's eyes widened a fraction. I realized with a start that she didn't know I was gay. The subject hadn't come up in the months we'd been working together. The easy rapport I had with her from the piano had tricked me into thinking she knew.

"Handsome," she said, with only the barest flicker of hesitation. "Looks like you pick boyfriends as well as you do everything else. Do you still see each other?"

God, Elly, with all the talking you do, why couldn't you have told Laura this?

"He's dead," I said simply, nearly adding: "I'm sorry." News of death, no matter how much time has passed, puts the onus on the teller to absolve the asker of any pain accruing from the question. Laura, for her part—and to her credit—neither apologized nor retreated with hasty, futile sympathy.

"Coffee?" I suggested, not very subtly.

"Good idea."

I flagged Robert and tried to think up another subject of conversation. Laura beat me to it. "Tell me about that book you're working on. The slides were beautiful."

"The folio? Léo's wife—Evelyn, in case you're interested—owns a shop in Montreal that specializes in rare books. First editions, author printings, that sort of thing. She came up with this idea of creating a 'botanical' for Léo's property in Caledon. You know, like those old-time natural history books: a picture of the plant on one page with a description and commentary on the other."

"Sounds like a big undertaking."

"You have no idea. Léo owns a hundred hectares on the Credit River. Lots of different ecosystems. There's an incredible variety of flowers."

"Sounds beautiful. Must be nice to be rich."

"*Very* rich. His family's been in mining and lumber in Quebec since Wolfe and Montcalm had their tiff on the Plains of Abraham."

"Are you going to publish it?"

"No. That's the whole point. It's a one-of-a-kind. Léo is paying for it. A friend of Evelyn's will do the binding."

Robert returned with our coffee, and I asked Laura if she minded if I smoked.

"Not if you let me light up for you." She meant it literally, holding out her hand for the du Maurier I was about to put in my mouth. "I used to smoke," she explained, extracting a wooden match from the little gold-embossed box supplied by the restaurant, "but I had to give it up. One of the hells of being a singer. I deal with it by lighting other people's cigarettes if they'll let me."

"Clever."

She struck the match and touched the flame to the tip of the cigarette. After one long slow puff, she passed it back to me.

"How did you land the job here?" she asked. "Elly says getting you to play in public is like pulling teeth."

"It was Léo's idea, when I moved back to Toronto last year. He thought I needed the routine of work. Anyway, I like it. It's not like being the centre of attention the way you are on stage. More like playing in the comfort of your living room."

"The apartment where you live, that belongs to Léo, too?"

"That's right. He lets me stay there for free. Well, not quite. He rents out the main house. There are two flats. I keep an eye on it and do maintenance."

"He seems to do a lot for you." She tilted her head to one side. "Is there something going on between you?"

"Léo and me?" My surprise must have gone over the top, because Laura asked "What?" in that wounded tone people use when what they mean is: Did I say something wrong?

"Sorry," I said. "Of course you wouldn't know. Léo is Christian's father."

Out of nowhere, Robert appeared at her elbow with a pot of coffee. One could almost suspect he'd been following the conversation and sensed the need for intervention. Laura looked up at him and shook her head, flustered. I asked for the bill. Neither of us spoke until he returned.

"My treat," I said.

"No way."

We both reached for the leather bound *présentoire,* hoping

for a pre-emptive strike in the battle over payment. I got to it first, but Laura snatched the bill from inside. She studied it, then handed it back with a smile. "You've got friends," she said.

I took a look. The total had been scratched out. In its place were Rosemary's signature and a smiley-face with the word "Gratis" in tiny letters on the curve of its silly grin.

❧ ❧ ❧

Mann was holding his class at the Heliconian Hall, a couple of blocks east of Evelyn on Hazelton Avenue. We decided to walk over instead of taking the Rover. The sun had already dipped behind the city's west end high-rises, but stored-up heat in the streets and sidewalks warmed the evening air. The sky in front of us had deepened to a rich cerulean blue. Street lamps were coming on, making globes of melon-coloured light against the dusk.

Laura took my arm, a gesture that, while it had no precedent between us, felt unaffected and comfortable. I reflected on the irony of sexual orientation, that part of human nature that decrees the gender of our mates. For most people, myself included, it is an unshakable constant. Had Laura been a man, her gesture might have signalled something more than the acknowledgment of a growing friendship.

"What's your story with Elly?" she asked as we neared Avenue Road. "Did you used to study with her?"

"No. We didn't actually meet until I was at the Faculty. One of her former students was singing something I'd written. I was playing, and Elly came to the recital. We got introduced afterward. She didn't like the songs—she never likes anything I write—but she wanted to know if I'd be available to accompany some of her students. If I'd known then what I know now, I'd probably have said no. For the next three years, she just expected me to be free every time she called. Somehow, I always was. You know Elly.

"I left the city for a couple of years after that, which pissed her off, even though she'll never admit it, but I guess she's forgiven me now, because we're right back where we left off. She calls; I jump."

"Why *did* you leave Toronto?"

"Long story. And aren't you inquisitive tonight?"

"Striking while the iron's hot."

"Meaning?"

"Meaning you don't usually talk much about yourself."

"Must be the Scotch I had before you showed up for dinner."

She poked me in the ribs, then let go of my arm so we could cross Avenue Road during a break in the traffic.

Heliconian Hall, home of a women's cultural club, sits in the heart of Toronto's trendy Yorkville district. Across the road, an upscale promenade presents its thoroughbred backside to the modest former church. From outside, the building's vertical wooden siding and countrified gingerbread trim make it look like a frump at a chi-chi ball. Only inside does its breeding show: wood-only acoustics make it one of the best recital venues in the city.

Mann was already on stage, sitting at one of the two Steinways that crowded the platform. The class hadn't started yet. A young woman stood beside him, watching him pencil something in her music. Fingerings, most likely. Ninety percent of playing the piano involves little more than getting your fingers in the right place at the right time.

I didn't see Elly right away. I did, however, catch sight of Spiers—minus the Dean—and Nils Janssen. I recognized almost no one else. Mann's predilection for staying away from music schools had the reciprocal effect of discouraging their staffs from attending his classes.

Laura spotted Elly near the middle of the hall. She'd saved two places on the aisle—thoughtful, since Laura and I would have to get out later on—but her location left something to be desired. Waves of musk billowed back from the mauve poncho and fulgently hennaed hair in the row in front.

"What do you suppose *she's* doing here?" I whispered to Elly. "When I ran into her yesterday and mentioned Mann's name, the air turned a marked shade of azure."

Elly clucked. "I have no idea," she said, "but I wish she'd sit somewhere else. I can hardly breathe."

Because the audience was made up in part of students who would also be performing in the class, a nervous hum buzzed through the hall. Mann's classes put considerable strain on those who took the stage. First came a performance of their chosen piece; afterward, criticism and instruction from Mann. For those not participating, it was an edifying look into the art of interpretation. For those who had to do the work, it could be nerve-wracking.

Mann, alone now, signalled the start of his class by playing a ferocious scale in double thirds from bottom to top of the piano, one hand only. It was more impressive, and more effective, than any fanfare.

"We have an interesting class tonight," he said into the startled silence. "Some Debussy, some Bach. A singer doing Schumann. And the Berg Opus 1. It should prove most challenging. We'll begin with the Debussy."

He gestured to a teenager in the front row, East Indian or Pakistani, with wide, dark eyes and a tawny complexion that looked as if it had yet to know a razor. He mounted the stage and handed his music to Mann, then sat down to play without ceremony. Mann leaned over and whispered in his ear. Doe-brown eyes turned from the keyboard. " 'Reflets dans l'eau' from Debussy's *Images,*" he said, his voice cracking mid-sentence. "Book One."

Mann settled back and held a finger to his lips, admonishing the audience to special silence. His student waited until the quiet was complete, then dropped his opening notes into the stillness like pebbles in a pond. Sonic ripples coursed through the piano, building to a quasi cadenza that sent a fountain of notes skittering out into the hall.

Debussy's synaesthesia of light, colour and sound demanded utter concentration from the player, whose brow furrowed as the piece progressed. Halfway through, it became apparent that while he'd mastered the technical difficulties, he had a way to go before his interpretation lost a certain hard-edged quality. It was too precise, like an inked page awaiting the softening touch of watercolours.

Just the same, Mann beamed with pleasure when he finished. "Most impressive," he said, prompting the student to take a well-earned bow. "Debussy is never easy on the performer. So many traps. But I couldn't help noticing—you never once used the left pedal. So much of the piece is marked pianissimo.*"* He leaned over and stage-whispered, "Did you take a pledge or something?"

Laughter swept the room, a good indication of how many in the crowd were pianists. The left pedal—the *una corda*—softens a piano's loudness by half, but precisely because of its ease in creating pianissimo effects, some players think it's cheating.

"The difficulty with this piece," Mann continued, touching the boy's arm to reassure him, "is that the reflections it conjures up do not come from water that is merely still. Every once in a while, a light breeze blows up, clouding the surface. At other times, a current moves underneath, creating waves and ripples. And while it's true that there is an overall wash of colour, there is also brilliance. This is not just a placid millpond painted by Maxfield Parrish, but neither is it Monet's little stream at Giverny."

In front of us, Morris-Jones snorted and muttered something that sounded like "friggin' hart 'istory lesson."

Mann grew specific. "Use the left pedal throughout, even in the forte passages...firm fingers here, so it sounds like a skipping stone...and here, just the opposite; stroke the keys so the chords have no beginning...put in an eighth rest, even though it's not marked...events need silence to give them meaning, you know...playing all the notes too loud is a worse mistake than missing a few...this is pianissimo; one is not supposed to hear everything...even with the sustaining pedal, this won't sound over four bars...repeat it, I'm sure Debussy wouldn't mind."

Hesitantly at first, then with growing confidence, the young pianist experimented with Mann's suggestions. Diffidence turned to confidence and finally delight when an iridescent waterscape began to emerge where before there'd been only notes.

My enjoyment of the lesson was somewhat dampened by audible and churlish grumblings coming from Morris-Jones. Every one of Mann's textual revisions brought on a fit of arm- and leg-crossing. Beside me, Laura sat rapt and undisturbed, but Elly tsk-ed several times. People in seats next to Morris-Jones shifted uneasily.

Mann summed up. "Interpreting, you see, is not about obeying orders. Written music is a shorthand. The composer can only convey what he wants with the symbols he has. I have found, for example, that the more dynamic markings in a score, the more likely it is the composer is trying to *suggest* what he wants, not specify it."

Morris-Jones sat with her arms folded defiantly during the

warm applause that followed.

Next up was a long-haired blond in his twenties. Unlike the previous performer, he exuded confidence—too much of it.

"The Prelude and Fugue in D-major from *Das Wohltemperierte Klavier*. Also Book One," he added, mocking the student who'd gone before.

No doubt about it, the guy had fingers. His Prelude sped by in a flurry of sixteenth notes. After the briefest of pauses, he attacked the fugue with a dry muscularity that made it sound like a volley of gun fire. At the final cadence, bashed out like an axe splitting wood, his expression challenged Mann to say anything but "Bravo!"

Which he did not do.

"You know," he said casually, speaking to the audience, "there is a common misconception about playing Bach on the piano, that one must at all costs avoid availing oneself of the instrument's full resources. That one should try to imitate the harpsichord. Personally, I think this is a terrible mistake. Bach himself was not averse to transcribing music for instruments quite different from what was originally intended. My feeling is that we, as pianists, have an instrument unknown to Bach, and so we should, in effect, feel free to 'transcribe' his music when we play it."

Elly nudged me, nodding with her chin at Morris-Jones. Under the mauve poncho, her shoulders were twitching indignantly, and her orange hair looked as if it might burst into flames. I'd have known without looking the incendiary effect of Mann's comments. Morris-Jones had devoted her life to music history; her knowledge of Baroque performance practice probably exceeded his own, and I'd have wagered a lot that she was a card-carrying member of the faction who believes Bach shouldn't be played on the piano at all.

"Now, to the Prelude," Mann said to his student, who was running his fingers distractedly through his hair. "I want you to play the whole thing with the pedal down."

"With pedal?" He looked as if Mann had asked him to eat a plate of raw liver. "But this is Bach!"

"Indeed. Which is why I'm not asking you to pedal it as if it were Chopin. I mean something quite different. Are you familiar with a technique called quarter-pedal?"

A frown of incomprehension allowed Mann to explain. "Begin by placing your foot on the pedal. Don't depress it. Just let it rest there, and play me a D-major triad. Good. Now, what I'd like you to do is repeat the triad, and gradually put more weight on the pedal until just a little resonance remains."

It took about ten tries before a faint trace of sound clung to the strings. "Excellent," Mann encouraged. "Now, I want you to play the whole Prelude, holding the pedal in precisely that position, and never once let it go."

A hoot of derision from Morris-Jones caused all eyes to turn our way. Mann looked out into the audience. "Someone wishes to challenge?" he asked politely.

"You're bleedin' roight I want to challenge." Her broad diphthongs compared badly to Mann's refined, Germanic English. "You can't play Bach like that. This is eighteenth-century counterpoint, for chrissake, not cheap salon music. We're past the age of Busoni, in case you hadn't noticed."

It was highly irregular to speak out in a master class this way, but Mann replied calmly. "Of course, madame," he said, "you're quite right. Performance styles *have* changed. But please, be patient. The playing may convince you of the point I wish to make." He addressed his student: "Whenever you're ready."

The difference was astounding. Instead of rapid notes punched out with mechanical precision, Bach's fleet, sinuous melody dipped and wheeled and soared. It sounded like a page of doodles might sound—if the hand that had sketched them belonged to da Vinci. In the silence following the spirited applause, Morris-Jones offered no comment.

Mann moved on to the Fugue. When it was finally to his liking ("This is a noble subject; play it as a lion among lions, not as a lion among lambs..."), the blond pianist, arrogance chastened, held out his hand and thanked Mann profusely.

Laura and I were up next. Mann greeted me on stage with a clap on the shoulder. "I know Vikkan here," he announced. "I believe we're in for a treat." I ducked my head, then formally presented Laura. It said much about Elly's relationship with Mann that he'd accepted Laura into the class without an audition.

Of the twelve songs in Schumann's Opus 39 *Liederkreis,* Laura had chosen to sing the four slowest and moodiest. We started with the eerie forest solitude of "In der Fremde", then moved on to "Mondnacht". The title only imperfectly translates as "moonlit night". The German word encapsulates a wealth of Romantic associations English can't begin to convey. Laura wrapped Schumann's dappled harmonies around her dusky mezzo voice and let the ecstatic poetry sing itself.

Next came "Auf einer Burg"—In a Castle—one of Schumann's starkest lieder, a piercing musical evocation of desuetude, decay and tragic love. Last of all, "Wehmut"—Melancholy—a song whose rich sonorities and placid melody underscore the text's ironic theme: the dissembling of grief in music. *"Ich kann wohl manchmal singen,"* Laura sang, and everyone believed her, *"als ob ich fröhlich sei..."* Though troubled in my heart, I sing / with gladness seeming true.

We'd never performed together in public, and I wasn't ready for how a roomful of listeners inspired her. With every song, her voice took on a different colour: now despairing, now warm with fervor, now cold, hollow, ghostly. My fingers followed on their own, the muscles responding without effort to the breath and pulse of every phrase she sang.

Even Mann looked taken aback during the tremendous ovation that followed. Laura acknowledged it simply, then smiled in my direction. I raised an eyebrow to indicate her artistry had not been lost on me either.

"It would be a sin," Mann said when things finally calmed down, "to criticize anything so lovely. However, this is a class, and you have all paid to be instructed. I shall have to be pedantic and attempt to find fault where really none exists."

He began with Laura, fastidiously correcting her diction in three or four places, asking her to approach several phrases a little differently "to make them truer to the spirit of the German language," making insignificant suggestions about breathing. For the most part, he focused on the songs themselves, not Laura's interpretation, helping the crowd to understand the genius of Schumann's music.

Finally, he turned to me. "You know, Vikkan," he said, "when you begin a song, I have the strangest feeling, as if the ghost of Schumann himself has entered the room. It's eerie. But I find I have to strain to hear the music. You're playing is too intimate, too private. You mustn't be afraid to communicate to your listeners. After all, that's what music's all about." He sat down at the second piano. "You don't mind singing again, do you, Miss Erskine? I want to show Vikkan a few things." To the audience he added: "I'm merely being indulgent, you understand. I want to enjoy this a second time."

We started from the top. Taking Mann's suggestion, I worked on coaxing more substantial sounds from the piano. I let my forearm and wrist relax deeper into the keys, drawing out a fuller tone, vaguely aware that Mann was using his left hand to reinforce occasional bass notes.

As we progressed, Mann's support became more insistent. Laura had no difficulty making herself heard over the two pianos. In fact, she seemed to enjoy the full-throated challenge. I gave myself over to the playing and let it speak without restraint.

By the time we reached "Auf einer Burg", Mann had joined in fully. In the final verse, a rising sequence of dissonant chords marches in stately progression toward the song's anguished conclusion. Mann played what he could with his left hand, and with his right, stretched and filled in the tortured harmonies. Laura's voice soared over the duet to a magnificent climax, vastly more dramatic than what Schumann intended, but utterly, soul-quenchingly liberating.

A grating voice broke the astonished silence that followed.

"What the *hell* was that?" Morris-Jones rose from her seat. "This is Schumann, not bloody Tchaikovsky. Where do you get off raping a composer that way? It's fucking obscene."

"Madame, please," Mann said, struggling to keep his composure, "if you wish to argue with my methods, then speak to me after the class. This is very disruptive."

"You're damned right!" Morris-Jones moved into the aisle, advancing on the stage. "Somebody's got to stop this. It's a travesty. Have some bleedin' respect for the composer. You may be famous, you may be 'the Great Mann,' but there's some things even you can't get away with."

It was Laura who intervened. "Professor Morris-Jones, *please*. Couldn't this wait? You're embarrassing everyone. This is Herr Mann's class, not yours."

Morris-Jones stopped, glaring at Laura as if only then aware that someone other than Mann held the stage. For a moment, I thought she was going to flare up further, including Laura and maybe even me in her tirade. Her eyes slewed over to Mann, then back to Laura. Abruptly, she whirled and stomped out of the hall. The wood acoustics picked up every quivering nuance of her exit.

"Well," Mann said into the stunned vacuum left by her departure, "it isn't often we get to hear dissenting opinions expressed so...colourfully." Uneasy laughter rippled through the hall. "And, as I have in fact finished with this portion of the class, I suspect now would be as good a time as any to take a break. About fifteen minutes, and we'll start again."

He stood and removed his spectacles, rubbing his right eye with the heel of his hand. He looked pale all of a sudden, and I wondered if Morris-Jones had bothered him more than he let on. I asked, but he said everything was fine, not to worry.

I would have liked to stay, especially since the Berg Piano Sonata was on the program, but I had to get back to Evelyn for work. I thanked Mann, said goodbye to Laura, spoke with Elly ("...now don't forget, my lesson's at one o'clock tomorrow...") and left.

I chuckled a couple of times on the way back to Prince Arthur, thinking about Morris-Jones' outbursts. They seemed so over the top. What had brought them on? Some sort of payback for Mann's article about her work in *Piano Quarterly?* Or did she have other reasons for wanting to denounce him?

Donning my back-up tux in Léo's office, I contemplated asking Elly if she had any dirt, but by the time I'd ripped into an uptempo version of "The Days of Wine and Roses" to start my first set, I'd decided against it. No sense in encouraging a gossip.

Five

Und mich schauert's im Herzensgrunde.
("And my heart trembles with foreboding.")
  —*Liederkreis*, Opus 39, XI

Thursday morning, I woke up on my back. I'd thrown off my top sheet sometime in the night, but when I reached for it, it wasn't there. Rolling on my side, I looked from the loft and saw it, eight feet down on the floor. I wasn't chilly—just feeling the need for something over me—so I left it there and turned on my back again.

For most of the past year, waking up had been the hardest part of my day. I'd have thirty seconds of feeling exactly as I'd felt every morning of my life until Christian died—pleasantly aware of my surroundings, drifting peaceably into consciousness. Then, like a switch being thrown, memory would snap into place. A paralyzing emptiness would settle in my chest, my throat, my stomach. Part of me would feel as if it were sinking, while another stayed behind and helplessly witnessed the descent.

That morning, the sensation should have struck like a sledgehammer. One year ago, to the day, I'd woken for the last time with Christian's arm flung morning-careless over my chest. But sometime in the last month or so—whoever remembers the precise moment pain fades into memory?—the feeling, when it came, was more like a mirage than the thing itself. It took longer to set in, and even when I called it up deliberately, probing the ache the way one tongues a sore tooth, it didn't have the power to make each day an Everest.

I stayed in bed for half an hour, staring at a water stain on the ceiling. I'd have to check out the roof. But not today, not this one-year-after.

Christian seldom came to Toronto. The noise—the conflicting mental eddies coursing up and down a crowded sidewalk—disrupted the order he only just maintained over his thoughts and feelings. The city held few memories for us. It was only by chance that, one fall day five years earlier, I'd been walking in High Park when he'd been there. This day of recollection, I'd pay a visit to the hillside where, a total stranger, he'd first approached me. And Kew Beach—I'd go there, too, later in the day, when the sun had set. The boardwalk, with its calm horizontals of lake and sky and sand, had had the power to soothe the inner discord that in the end had snared him. One night, hidden by the eastern pier, we'd made love against the rocks.

I climbed down from the loft to an apartment cooler than I thought. I threw on a flannel shirt and knelt on the couch to have a look outside. The weather seemed nice enough. Patches of blue showed through the green-gold tangle of unpruned sumacs screening the window.

I brewed up coffee, toasted two slices of the bread from Tuesday's loaves, and carried my breakfast to the piano. I needed to go over the Haydn I'd be playing for Mann on Friday and wanted to work out some new arrangements for use at Evelyn.

It's an odd thing about working at the piano, in private at any rate, that it opens up vast mental space for thoughts unrelated to the task at hand. Logically, watching every finger move, listening to every note, using every faculty of memory—these shouldn't leave much room for cogitation, yet they do.

Between the graceful double trills of Haydn and the extravagant nostalgia of Carmichael and Ellington, I started turning over Laura's question from the night before.

Why did you leave the city? Long story, I'd said—the stock reply to a question you'd rather not answer, or can't. I could have said it was because of Christian, and on the face of it, that would have been true. But no one entices a person to change his life, unless the urge to do so is already strong. I'd left because I ached to get away—from the city, from the world of music. Studying piano since the age of four, practising so many long hours every day, had consumed my childhood and adolescence. The average professional—doctor, lawyer, chartered accountant—has scarcely started training for his or her vocation by the age at which I'd already been at mine for eighteen years. So much adult work so young had robbed me of experiences that other people take for granted. I'd never even been in love. Christian's eyes-wide, guileless suggestion—"Move with me, up to Caledon"—so simply put, so unexpected (was it only the third time we'd slept together? the fourth?), had overwhelmed emotions newly made defenceless by the liberating rush of romance. To be something other, to live a life freed of obligations imposed by years of training, to love and be loved.

Haydn's trills were giving me trouble. As anyone who's ever whisked meringues by hand knows, prolonged rotation of the wrist leads to cramps. Trills use the same muscles, but in order for the rapid-fire alternation of two adjacent notes to sparkle as one, the wrist has to remain supple. Unfortunately, the very act of practising trills freezes it up. I was zenning my way out of this pianistic Catch-22 when I heard a warbling that had nothing to do with Haydn. It took a moment to realize it was the phone. Elly, no doubt, with last-minute instructions about her lesson with Mann that afternoon.

"I'd better warn you," she said. "I won't be singing today."

"Don't tell me—you've succumbed to one of those mysterious throat ailments that are always plaguing prima donnas at the last minute."

"No, and I wish you wouldn't be so flippant."

"What is the problem?"

"There isn't one. It's just that I won't be singing. Laura will. Dieter asked last night, after the class."

"I guess it's too much to hope for that she'll be doing the Schubert I got ready for you."

"Yes, it would. But don't worry. You won't be sightreading. Dieter says you know the music. He'll bring it with him."

A little warning bell sounded in the back of my brain. Ulrike, the day before, our phone conversation in Rosemary Dickens' tiny office at Evelyn: *Herr Professor will be bringing the music.*

"Elly, tell me this isn't what I think it is." It never even crossed my mind that she might not know about the *Liederkreis.*

"Dieter's Schumann?"

Shit. It didn't take a genius to see that yesterday's runthrough with Ulrike had been as much an audition as a rehearsal, and that Mann hadn't been completely happy with her singing. Now he was showing the *Liederkreis*—supposedly a secret, and Ulrike's chance to revive her career—to Laura. I could see trouble coming, and me right in the middle of it. "I don't suppose I can bow out of this," I said.

Elly didn't reply.

"Maybe you could play?" I suggested.

More silence, followed by a deep breath. "Dieter wants you."

"Elly—"

"If you don't want to do it, I'll understand."

I waited for a "but," but it never came—worse than if it had because it made me feel like a recalcitrant six-year-old for trying to back out. With Elly, I sometimes had trouble believing I was twenty-seven. "All right, I'll be there," I said, none too happily. "It's still at one o'clock?"

"Yes. And Vikkan...thank you." She sounded relieved. Maybe she'd already told Mann I'd be there.

I didn't feel like going back to the Haydn after she rang off. I hadn't wanted anything to disrupt this day, but her call had done it. I lay down on the couch and lit a cigarette. Little tendrils of smoke drifted through the window, twined around the sumac leaves, and vanished. If only getting out of doing things for Elly were so easy.

I finished the cigarette and took my breakfast dishes back to the kitchen. There was still some sludge in the bottom of coffee pot. I poured it in my mug and added milk. The result was worse than even I could bear.

The only way I was going to restore the day to its proper mood was by getting out. I took my Pentax from the back room, loaded it with film from the fridge, and stuffed some extension tubes in the pocket of a nylon jacket.

Weather very like the day before greeted me outside, although wisps of stratospheric clouds leached some blue from the sky. The shady, settled streets of my neighbourhood carried me westward in roundabout fashion to Parkside, where I crossed over and took a little-used service road into High Park.

Almost as soon as I entered, the sounds of the city dimmed. The winy smell of spring-damp leaves replaced the metropolitan odour of car fumes. I made my way along the service road, turning at an unmarked trail that branched imperceptibly off to the left. A few metres into the trees, the temperature dropped, making me glad I'd worn a jacket. The remnants of city noise and smell faded entirely as I penetrated deeper.

Fifteen minutes later, I came to a cleared hillside where

some clever soul with a sense of mystery and mischief had rescued the gargoyles from a demolished bank and buried them deep into the ground. Only their faces peered out of the short grass, making them all but invisible until you were right on top of them. For some reason, the effect called to mind Druidic groves and solstice revels.

I stopped dead centre of the leering circle and hunkered down, noticing a dusting of tiny white flowers in the grass: chickweed, a plant so shy that it thrives unnoticed in even the best-kept lawns. Its five petals, so deeply cleft they look like ten, virtually disappear at a distance of more than four feet. I took the extension tubes out of my pocket, screwed them onto the camera, and knelt down for a closer look. Focusing proved difficult, so I lowered myself onto the ground, stretching out on my stomach. It wasn't until I had the camera supported on one hand, turning the focus ring with the other, that I realized I'd adopted, unconsciously, the same posture I'd been in on a fall afternoon five years earlier when a voice off to my left had spoken, without preface: "There are asters over by the deer."

The sentence, so odd that I assumed the speaker had mistaken me for someone else—a friend perhaps, with whom an earlier conversation gave the statement context—caused me to look up. A rangy figure stood nearby, clad in jeans and a dirty work shirt. Some trick of breeze blew a rich smell of soil from his clothes, mixed with something faintly chemical that made me think of Uncle Charles' garage in summer filled with sacks of seed and fertilizer.

When I didn't say anything, he crouched down to study the lithic grimaces I'd been photographing, then sat on the ground with his knees up. It was then that I noticed his eyes, or rather, his eyebrows: two thick, curving lines like sine waves the colour and texture of sable. His proximity, the scent coming off him, and the peculiar familiarity with which he'd spoken flustered me. I felt an urge to reach out and trace the line of his brows with my thumbs. Unable to think of a sane rejoinder—"I'm sorry, what did you say?" or, less amicably, "Do I know you?"—I found myself struggling to make sense of what he'd said so I could frame a suitable reply.

I guessed he'd been talking about the small High Park zoo, which includes a herd of fallow deer. And somewhere nearby, there must be asters growing. Suitable for photographing? Had that been what he meant? I turned over. "I'd like to see."

He stood and offered me a hand up.

The pattern of cryptic statements, followed by unhurried silence while I sought the referential underpinnings, continued throughout the afternoon. "Christian," he said as we approached the zoo. Without a proffered hand, I had to think it through before I realized he'd given me his name. And later, after watching me take pictures of the maroon and gold flowers near the deer pen: "You could edge while I feed the juniper," which was his way of asking my assistance with some lawn work—at the house beside which, five years later, I would live—and an invitation to spend more time together.

Even with medication that, in the end, did not stave off chaos's final onslaught, Christian could mistake a thought conceived for one expressed. I didn't know that then. What I felt in his elliptic speech was a presupposed closeness, an intimate emanation—tangible, sexual—vibrating in the handsome air around him. Mind and hormones sympathetically alert, I worked at entering a stranger's world and fell in love.

The recondite chickweed flowers were playing coy, refusing to arrange themselves in artful patterns in the Pentax's prism. I took a few shots anyway, then stood up, stretched, and looked around. Surprisingly, the sun-warmed hillside held no visitors but me.

Following the same path Christian and I had taken, I made for the zoo, which is really nothing more than a stretch of paved road with pens on either side for a lackadaisical collection of unexotic animals. The fallow deer, ghostly white and miniature, had herded together at the far end of their enclosure. I stood very still—the best way to arouse an animal's curiosity—and whistled snippets of *Finlandia* at them. They remained where they were, unmoved to nationalistic fervor by Sibelius's gloomy, Nordic tunes. After fifteen minutes I gave up, and circled around the park to Grenadier Pond, where I discovered some early bullhead lilies in the marsh at its north end. The knobby, yellow flowers were too far away for me to photograph without a longer lens, so I merely congratulated them silently for showing up so early in the year, and retraced my course around the park.

I returned home invigorated, not melancholy, the way logic would dictate. The forthcoming lesson with Mann and Laura didn't seem as bad as it had when Elly dumped it in my lap. The only thing troubling me was a slight headache, probably the result of all the fresh air. I brewed up some wintergreen tea; the methyl salicylate it contains works just like aspirin, but tastes much better. I drank it with a lunch cobbled together out of mashed avocados and toast.

Afterward, I decked myself out in a loose summer shirt and lightweight trousers and left for the lesson. Driving over, I tried to remember Elly's friend's name, the one whose house I'd dropped Mann off at yesterday. Munrow? Morrow? She had one of those private-school nicknames that stick with society women all their lives: Snoopy or Bunny, something like that.

It came to me just as I rang. Cece—Cece Moore.

❧   ❧   ❧

It was Elly who answered and showed me into Cece Moore's salon, a fussily formal room done entirely in shades of purple: mauve carpet, lilac walls, frothy lavender sheers. The effect was overwhelming. A person with seasickness might dream in these colours. Laura, in soothing shades of denim blue and dark green cotton, stood behind Mann at the piano. The Bechstein, mirror-bright and probably polished by a maid, was about one metre too long for the proportions of the room.

Elly waited for Mann to finish explaining something to Laura, then coughed discreetly.

"Vikkan," he said, turning. "Good to see you again. I am starting to think I should hire you full time whenever I work with singers. Before I leave, you must let me take you to dinner. It will be small recompense for the trouble I'm putting you through." He stood. "Please, have a seat."

He spoke jovially enough, but I didn't think he looked well. There was more of effort and less of energy in his movements. His complexion seemed pale. I may have imagined it; with all that purple around, anyone would have looked like death warmed over.

"Hi, there," Laura said quietly as I sat down.

I nodded at the Schumann. "So, what do you think?"

"Beautiful." She looked over at Mann and Elly, holding a conference at the other end of the room. "I hope he doesn't think I'm mangling it."

"I doubt it. Did he give you the low-down?"

"Briefly. It's an incredible find."

The yellowing pages were spread out at the third song. I ran my fingers over the tune. Laura joined in.

Als Waldesblumen sah ich
Durch Schatten tief und kühl...

I saw as woodland flowers / through shadows deep and cool...

Presently, Mann and Elly broke off their conversation. "We only have a little time this afternoon," Mann said, coming over. "I have another student at two. However, Eleanor has just offered us her studio for this evening."

"Six-fifteen," Elly put in, to me. "You'll be there?"

Did I have a choice? "I can only stay for an hour or so," I said. "I have another commitment."

She narrowed her eyes as if she didn't quite believe me. She had every right. There was only the visit I planned to Kew Beach—important to me, but hardly a commitment.

"With the time we have now, an hour should be enough," Mann said. "I want to hear Miss Erskine sing all the songs at least once, with full accompaniment. Afterward, we can work alone."

"Well then, I'd best be going," Elly said. "Otherwise you'll never get started."

"You're not staying?" I asked.

"I have some student records to catch up on, and a pupil at two-thirty."

It was my turn to look dubious. Elly, passing up a chance to hear this mysterious new work? She'd admitted to knowing about it this morning, and if I knew her, she'd been privy to Mann's discovery a long time before that.

"I'd stay," she said, discerning my thoughts, "but I imagine things will go more smoothly if there's only one set of critical ears present."

She gathered up her cardigan from a phlox-coloured settee and left the room. Did I detect Mann's hand in her circumspect departure? She'd have to defer to him if he'd asked her to scram.

"So," Mann said, positioning himself on the settee, "did you enjoy last night's class?"

"Very much," I replied on top of Laura's "It was great."

"The audience participation was…*unerwartet.*" He pressed his lips together good-humouredly. "Quite unexpected."

"Indeed."

"Do you happen to know who that woman was?"

"No one told you? Her name is Morris-Jones. She's a professor at the university."

"Ah, so that is the redoubtable defender of composers female. We've been carrying on a dispute in print for some time. I'd like to speak with her sometime, but under less antagonistic circumstances. I suspect we agree rather more than she thinks. But enough chit-chat. We have work to do. Whenever you are ready…"

I doubt that had I been in Laura's place—sight-reading a recently discovered masterpiece in front of a world-renowned teacher—I could have sung with so much confidence. An accompanist can, if necessary, hide nerves and apprehension behind the main performer. Laura didn't have that option, but if anything, her singing sounded more assured, her voice more vibrantly electrifying, than I'd ever heard before. A couple of times, it raised the hair on the back of my neck.

She had questions about each song: where to breathe in long phrases, the meaning of some obscure directions in the score, translations of the poetry. Mann's interaction with her and his evident pleasure in her singing restored him to his usual vigour. The colour returned to his face; his movements became charged with enthusiasm.

Between the fourth and fifth songs, Laura noticed something that had escaped my attention. "This line here," she said, requesting a translation, *"Eine Rehgeiß stand allein.* What's a *Rehgeiß?"*

"I believe the English word for Reh is *'roe',* a kind of deer. *Rehgeiß* refers to the female."

"A doe, in other words."

115

"Yes, that would be it."

She reached over my shoulder and flipped back one song, then another. "This is a woman's set, isn't it?" she asked, straightening up. "Like *Frauenliebe und Leben?* My German's not great—I guess you figured that out—but it seems like most of the imagery is from a woman's perspective."

Mann nodded. "Just so. The cycle is about a woman recalling the love of her life. Happily, she gets her man, not like the poor poet in *Dichterliebe*. You're very percept—" His left eye squinted suddenly, as if a cinder had blown into it. He winced and unwound his spectacles from his ears. "So sorry," he said, massaging the left side of his face. "I seem to have slept in a bad position. One should be more careful at my age." He put his glasses on again and took a breath. "Please, go on."

Before we started, I flipped quickly to the title page. *Über Texten von Ebert.* Words by Ebert. I didn't recognise the name. A *nom de plume,* maybe? For a woman poet? I didn't want to waste time with questions of my own, so I made a mental note to check at the Faculty library, and turned back to the fifth song. A foreboding harmonic cloud, dark and eerie, rose from the bass strings as I played the opening chords. Laura's voice entered, seeming to come out of nowhere:

> *Eine Rehgeiß stand allein*
> *Unvorsichtig in der Au*
> *Es rauschten leis' die Bäume*
> *In dem finster'n Dämm'rungblau...*

She sang without colour, as if she were reciting, simply letting the narrative unfold itself. A doe, carelessly alone, grazes in a twilit meadow. The trees around, in dark blue shadow, rustle in the breeze. A snap of branch disturbs the evening calm, but the creature pays no heed. The trees begin to whisper, but the sound they make is more than just the rustling of innocent leaves. Still the deer is unconcerned. Suddenly, a twang of bow splits the air, and too late, she awakens to her peril.

The story telegraphed itself through simplistic metaphors. Its warning that young maidens should be wary probably occasioned a few giggles even at the time the poem was written. But the music cut through the naïveté to an emotional core that the words could only hint at: a truly menacing anxiety, an unshakeable feeling of impending doom.

We still had a few bars to go when the doorbell sounded in the distance, out of tune with the song, adding to its unsettling mood. The front door opened, and hushed voices came from the hallway. A quiet knock followed.

"Excuse me, Mr. Mann? There's someone here to see you."

A fiftyish women in a pleated skirt and silk blouse hovered in the archway to the room. Beside her, decked out in olive chinos and a form-fitting polo shirt, stood Ulrike's delinquent accompanist, David Bryce. The illness that had kept him down for the last few days had evidently passed. He appeared trim and healthy, from his thatch of artfully casual blond hair down to the tips of his polished collegiate loafers.

"I'm so sorry to interrupt, Herr Professor," he said, approaching Mann and holding out his hand, two actions I've never seen combined except in movies. "David Bryce." He flashed an easy smile full of even, white teeth. I'd forgotten that about Bryce: he had a grin like a Hammond organ.

"Ah, so at last we meet." Mann lifted himself up off the settee. "Ulrike has spoken your name often."

Bryce unslung a glossy leather knapsack from one shoulder and pulled a piece of paper from inside. "I'll only be a minute. Ulrike wants you to call. She doesn't have the number here, so she asked me to come by. I live only a few blocks away. Here's her number, in case you need it."

"Thank you," Mann said. "I'll call her when I'm finished at two."

"I'll be on my way, then. So sorry about barging in." He hoisted up his knapsack, sounding genuinely apologetic but making no move to leave, regarding Mann instead with wide, green eyes. "Such an honour to meet you."

I half-expected him to kneel and kiss Mann's ring. Finally, I tinkled a few notes on the piano to remind him that he was, in fact, interrupting. He broke off his gaze. "Vikkan. Long time, no see. I didn't realize you'd be here. I should thank you for filling in on Monday night. I feel just awful about letting Ulrike down. I really wanted to be there."

For her sake or yours? I wondered. His doleful expression looked sincere enough, but following so hard on equally convincing displays of courteous apology and respectful awe, it came across as bogus.

"I trust she wasn't too put off by the last-minute change in accompanists," I said.

"Well, you know...." He shrugged away the rest of the sentence. "Anyway, thanks again. I'd better get going. By the way, what are you two looking at?"

I played a few notes of the Schumann, figuring he'd recognize it if he'd been practising with Ulrike. His eyes went wide. "Really?" He looked from me to Laura, and back again. "That's interesting. Well, like I said, I'd better get going."

He spent another moment paying ocular homage to Mann, then shook his hand effusively and left. Laura glared at his departing back. There was no disguising her look of distaste.

"Not a fan, either?" I asked, *sotto voce.*

She shook her head.

We had time for only one more song before the doorbell rang again. Mann checked his watch. "My next student, I'm afraid," he announced. "We'll have to break off. Miss Erskine, your singing is remarkable. Christa Ludwig in her prime never sounded better. I shall be counting the hours till we get together this evening."

Laura beamed. "Thank you. I don't suppose you'd let me take the music this afternoon so I can study it?"

"I'd rather not. Not that I'd worry anything would happen, you understand, but..."

I still wondered why he hadn't brought copies. Aside from the inconvenience of not having them—Laura had to read over my shoulder—it seemed risky to be carrying the original in his briefcase. I knew that old paper needed to be copied under special light, but he could have had that done in Germany. Had, in fact, since Ulrike had been singing from reproductions the day before.

"It's okay," Laura said, "as long as you can put up with my sight-reading."

"If only all singers had your skill. And the same goes for you, Vikkan. I think, sometimes, that my greatest pleasure in teaching comes from finding those who don't need to be taught."

I gathered up the music and handed it to Mann. On the way out, we passed the doyenne of the house, Cece Moore. Etiquette seemed to require that I say something to her, so I complimented her on her salon.

"Why, thank you," she said, beaming. "I chose the colours myself."

Outside on Palmerston, I asked Laura where she was headed.

"I have an appointment with the toad who would be God."

"You mean Spiers? That's not a nice thing to say about the Faculty's Head of Performance. Want a lift over?"

"If you're headed that way."

"I want to look something up at the library."

The Rover had been sitting on the unshaded side of the street and smelled of warm upholstery. "What are you seeing Spiers about?" I asked, starting the engine.

"The meeting he set up with that agent, Howard Snelling. I'm not exactly sure why he thinks we have to talk about it."

"He'll want to make sure you say something nice about him. How he discovered you, and all that."

"As if."

Laura fiddled with the latch of her window, trying to get open it. "There's a trick," I said, reaching across. "Remember I told you keeping this thing running was a full-time occupation?"

I slid the window back. A breath of nearby flowering crab blew through the jeep. I took in a lungful, then pulled into the street.

"Speaking of Spiers," I said, once we were on Harbord heading toward the university, "I ran into him yesterday. Upstairs at Evelyn, while I was waiting for you. He and Dean Simmons came in for a drink. They ended up sitting with me."

"Lucky you."

"Well, I enjoyed seeing the Dean."

"But not Spiers."

"When I left, I heard them—not exactly having an argument—but obviously disagreeing over something. I'm pretty sure it was the Rawlings endowment."

"No surprise there. Spiers wants it, and bad. He's convinced the Dean isn't doing enough. He's mentioned it several times."

"But as I understand it, there's no guarantee it'd go to the Performance Department anyway."

"As far as he's concerned, the Faculty *is* his department."

"Good point. By the way, I think I saw Rawlings' daughter yesterday. Emaciated, long red hair, kind of washed out eyes?

She was with that girl, Janice. The one you said she was best friends with."

"Sounds right."

"Brazen little thing, isn't she? You should have seen the look she gave me."

"What do you mean?"

"Let's just say I have a much better understanding now of how women feel when construction workers whistle at their tits. Is she always like that?"

"Not when her father's around."

I looked over in surprise. "You'd expect her to be? She's what—sixteen? seventeen? Teenagers aren't noted for sexual eloquence when their parents are nearby."

"It isn't that."

"What then?"

"She's two-faced. What you wouldn't know is that she's the apple of Rawlings' eye. Daddy's little girl. Nothing too good for his little darling. You should see her with him. The sweet and innocent act is enough to make me puke. She out-lollipops Shirley Temple. But once he's out of range..."

"'Debbie Does Dallas'?"

"Something like that."

"Sounds like she's acting out, pardon the psycho-babble."

"You might act out, too, if you had Rawlings for a father. But the thing about Siobhan isn't what she's doing, it's how she does it. Rebellion I can understand, but with her, it's so calculated..." She shook her head. "Gives me the whim-whams."

"Whim-whams?"

"You know what I mean."

We reached the sharp curve where Harbord turns into Hoskin just past Spadina. I started looking for parking, and spotted a place on St. George, across from the Robarts Library.

"My, aren't we the outlaw," Laura said as I made an illegal left turn and pulled in.

"If you don't like the ride, get off the horse."

"I'll take my chances. It's cheaper than the subway."

I joined her on the sidewalk and offered my elbow with a flourish. "Shall I escort you to your destination, madame?"

"Certainly, sir." She twined her arm through mine. "Are you sure you're gay? Gallantry like that always gives a girl's heart a little flutter."

"A sexist comment if ever I heard one."

"Shoot me."

We strolled along Hoskin, past the brilliant green of University College playing field. A middle-aged jock in sweatpants was haranguing a soccer team. The players seemed to thrive on his verbal abuse, running faster and kicking harder with every insult. We turned onto Philosopher's Walk at Trinity College, walking slowly up toward the Faculty.

"Why didn't you stay with Ulrike after graduation?" I asked.

"She's a soprano, and I wanted to work with a mezzo. With Elly, I'm doing repertoire better suited to my voice. And I was feeling suffocated. Stay with Ulrike too long, and she expects you to join her coterie of doting students. It only gets worse when your career takes off. She refused to speak to me after I told her I was changing teachers. Mind you, Mr. David Bryce had a few holier-than-thou words on the subject."

"I forgot—you'd have had to work with him while you were with her. What did he say?"

"He accused me of betraying her."

"Is that why I detected a certain, shall we say, animosity on your part back there?"

"Smarmy little shit. I wouldn't trust him farther than I could throw him. His own loyalties are as fickle as the wind."

"Ah, yes, but in Bryce's world, there's always a strong prevailing breeze of self-interest."

"I see you know him as well as I do."

"Remember when I told you Spiers wanted me to be his golden boy? Well, after I had the bad grace to decline, guess who slid in to take up the slack? For my last couple of years at the Faculty, I never saw the one without the other. I never did figure that out. Spiers wanted more than a protegé, but unless I'm severely mistaken, Bryce is straight."

"Oh, he is," she said darkly.

"Thereby hangs a tale?"

"Yes, but not the way you're probably thinking."

We'd reached the Faculty of Music, and I held the door for her. "Do tell."

"Can't," she said, heading for the stairs just inside. "I've got to run, or I'll be late. See you at Elly's tonight."

I waited until she was out of sight, then cautiously made for the library, alert to traces of Morris-Jones' perfume. A cloud of musk hung ominously around the stacks, but luckily my research took very little time. I tracked down a reference to Ebert, the *Liederkreis's* poet, and escaped without running into her. In fact, I nearly got out of the building without seeing anyone I knew at all. Nearly. I was pushing open the doors when a voice hailed me from behind.

"Vikkan—would you wait up a minute?"

Nils Janssen was making his way neatly down the stairs. I couldn't imagine what the Conservatory's president was doing at the Faculty, but he answered the puzzle when he caught up. "I've just been with Dean Simmons," he said, "doing my diplomatic duty to ensure cordial relations between our schools."

"Admirable, given your competition over the Rawlings endowment."

He blinked. "You've heard about it?"

"It's no secret."

"No, of course not. I just thought perhaps you might not be up to date."

"Elly keeps me posted."

"Miss Gardiner? Yes, she is one to talk. And on that subject, there's something I'd like to ask you. Do you have a minute? I'm walking back to the Conservatory."

"I'm going the other way."

"In that case, just let me ask you this. I understand that when Dieter Mann arrived in town, he had with him a rather unusual acquisition. I know Miss Gardiner's close to him. Did she mention anything about it to you?"

I thought over his question and realized I could truthfully answer in the negative. Elly hadn't told me about it; Mann had. And he'd asked me not to say anything. "No," I said. "Why do you ask?"

"It came up in my meeting with Dean Simmons, that's all. I was curious."

I remembered the Dean saying he'd seen Mann on Tuesday. Had Mann told him about the *Liederkreis* at that time? For something that wasn't supposed to be general knowledge, the number of people who knew about it seemed to be growing.

Janssen didn't say anything further, and I didn't ask, lest he realize I'd stretched the truth when I answered his question. We walked together out to Philosopher's Walk, where he reminded me to think over his offer of a job. Little lies lead to big ones; I promised faithfully I'd give it my full consideration.

The weather was holding, but only just. The sun had begun to pale behind the filmy clouds I'd noticed earlier. In an hour or two, it would be completely overcast.

Having nothing else to do for the next couple of hours, I

drove home, threw on some old jeans, and spent an hour puttering about in the Rover's motor, changing plugs and oil. While I was at it, I fixed the window latch Laura had had trouble with earlier. I tried to do the same for the handle on the driver's side door, with no luck.

True to my forecast, the sky clouded over. By the time I'd shucked off my jeans and T-shirt inside the carriage house, a light drizzle had started. I didn't bother getting dressed again. The sumacs up front prevent anyone from seeing in, as good a reason as any to put off pruning them.

I scrubbed grease from my hands, then settled in to do some work on Evelyn's wildflower folio. My textbooks were still open at the Indian Pipe entries, so I fanned them out and started making notes. *Indian Pipe...Monotropa uniflora... brittle roots...waxy, ivory-white stem with scaly bracts...single nodding fleshy flower, usu. white, sometimes pinkish; turns black when bruised.* It sounded like something that would give you a nasty scare if you came upon it by accident in the woods, like a dead snake or a severed limb. I consulted several herbals, all of which had unusually short entries, and jotted down *antispasmodic, nervine, sedative.* My trusty Peterson's said the plant's habitat was "throughout," so I wouldn't be marking *M. uniflora* as a rare or unusual find.

About an hour later, my thighs started itching from the chair's twill covering. I stood up and scratched, feeling little crosshatches all the way from my glutei maximi down to my knees. I needed a shower and shave before going back to the Con, so I put my books away and grabbed a fresh towel from milk crates stacked beside the bathroom.

Trying without success to do something about my hair afterward with a blow drier, I found myself thinking about the hornet's nest Mann was stirring up by showing the *Liederkreis* to Laura. Good thing Bryce was feeling better so I wouldn't be

125

doing any more work for *das Vöglein*. I didn't want to be around if—or when—she found out.

⚹   ⚹   ⚹

Every time I walked into Elly's studio, I had the feeling I was stepping back in time.

Over the course of her three-plus decades at the Con, she'd moved in a lot of antiques. On the south wall was a desk that wouldn't have looked out of place in a Hudson's Bay outpost. Beside it stood a carved armoire on stumpy pineapple legs, stuffed with music. On the north wall, towering next to her *récamier*, was a glass-fronted floor-to-ceiling bookcase holding her collection of Busts of the Great Composers. Scattered throughout, cachepots on extravagantly lathed pedestals supported an assortment of aspidistras, ferns and dieffenbachias. Nearly everything was oak—dark-stained, massive and proudly bourgeois. Only the baby grand and her club chair—low, deep, and comfy—had saved an entire Quercus grove from extinction. The piano, an old Eaton's Heintzman, was done in honey-coloured maple. The chair glowed with well-oiled leather, richly red against the Turkish rug hiding some of the dingy floor.

Elly was watering flowers when I arrived. Her thriving, if staid, congregation of violets, begonias and gloxinias sat on a generous window sill to the left of the piano. Nearby, jammed in a corner beside the armoire, a tangle of philodendrons reared triffidically over her.

"Mildred and Chastity taking strong waters again?" I asked.

"They're quite happy, thank you," she said primly. "This is a perfect spot for them. Violets don't like too much sun."

Laura, seated at the piano, was picking out notes and humming softly. She acknowledged my arrival with a nod,

126

concentrating on mastering a difficult interval. Mann stood in front of the bookcase, admiring the rogues' gallery of Great Composers within. He looked better than he had that afternoon, even in the fluorescent light that irradiated the studio with a sallow, all-too-modern glow.

"Some interesting choices, don't you think?" I said, going over to him. The twenty-centimetre-high solid bronze heads had been cast in England at the turn of the century. In a number of cases, the choice of what constituted a "great composer" bespoke the tastes of an era more than any real claim to fame. Cheek by jowl with Beethoven and Brahms were Delius, Massenet and Gottschalk.

"*Sic transit,* Vikkan," Mann replied. "But you know, some of these lesser composers were talented. I would miss them if they were not here." He turned from the bookcase and went to the club chair.

Elly finished tending her flowers just as clouds of steam began rising from an electric kettle on her desk. She unplugged it and filled a Styrofoam cup.

"Dieter?"

"Thank you." He took the cup and set it on the carpet, then rifled through his pockets and brought out the little packet of teabags I'd seen at Ulrike's. He sniffed at the contents, selected one, and dropped it in the water.

"I'd offer you something, Vikkan," Elly said, "but I'm out of instant coffee."

"That's okay. It was decaf anyway, if I remember."

Mann repocketed his teas. "Shall we begin, then? After this afternoon, I'm quite impatient to hear Miss Erskine again."

Laura stood and went behind the piano bench, brushing an errant philodendron leaf out of her face. Elly moved over to the *récamier* and plumped up the roll cushion.

"You're staying this time?" I asked.

"Curiosity has overcome my inclination to be considerate. But I promise, I shan't interfere." She glanced at Mann, who winked.

True to her word, she turned silent the moment Laura announced, "Any time you're ready, Vikkan," and stayed that way throughout the remainder of the *Liederkreis*. Her non-interference became nerve-wracking after a while. I started wishing she *would* contribute something to the dialogue between songs.

As earlier, Laura sang with breathtaking assurance—caressing *Meine Thränen (My Tears)* with innocent sensuality, injecting a troubling note of doubt into *Gewißheit (Certainty)*, achieving a tone of ethereal ecstasy in *Schicksalsfügung (Providence)*. How could anyone sing unfamiliar music with such artistry? If I didn't know better, I'd have sworn the songs had been composed with her in mind.

We finished at a quarter after seven. Laura slumped down beside me, exhausted. "God, that's hard work. Is it just me, or is it hot in here?"

It *was* quite warm. I got up to open the window.

"I wouldn't, Vikkan," Elly said from the other side of the room. "They're patching the roof down there. The tar smell is awful."

I peered over Mildred and Chastity and their friends to the flat roof below. "Nothing going on now," I said. It had been raining off and on for the past couple of hours, but the workmen would have broken off at five anyway. All I could see were a wooden extension ladder and some empty buckets.

"It's okay," Laura said. "I'll be fine."

I left the window and sat down. Mann leaned back in the club chair, resting his head on a snowy white antimacassar. The crocheted linen framed his face like a halo. He turned his eyes toward Elly and steepled his fingers. It seemed a peculiar gesture. I would have thought he'd avoid it, given his missing thumb and index joint. "Well?" he asked. "What do you think?"

Elly stood up and fussed with the roll cushion again, snugging it against the *récamier's* curved end. "It's impressive, Dieter. For some reason, I didn't expect it to be so good. The writing's extraordinary. I had no idea." She made it sound as if the *Liederkreis* had been composed by an aspiring Conservatory student, not a full-fledged master. "And as to what we talked about before," she continued, going over to her desk, "that's entirely up to you. More hot water?"

"Please."

She crouched down to plug in the kettle. Mann watched her, then took off his spectacles. "Miss Erskine," he said, rubbing the bridge of his nose, "I find myself in an extremely awkward position. Perhaps Vikkan has told you?"

Laura shook her head, puzzled. Mann sat forward. "Ever since I, or rather, my daughter, Anna, first came across this work, I have given Ulrike Vogel—your former teacher, so Eleanor tells me—to understand that she will have the honour of singing its first performance. As you can well imagine, the event will be of no small significance. Unfortunately, now, having heard you, I find myself questioning my hastiness in approaching her.

"I've come to feel a proprietary interest in this *Liederkreis,* like a father who wants the best for his child. I knew after last night that you and the songs belonged together. But how can I bring myself to disappoint Ulrike? Sadly, I am caught in a war of loyalties, between what is right for friendship and what is right for this remarkable music. Perhaps I should not have indulged myself so, asking you to sing it."

Elly's kettle started to boil. She unplugged it and refilled Mann's cup, returning to her desk.

"What to do, what to do?" he asked, selecting another tisane. "I suppose I should put it to you first, Miss Erskine—"

"Laura, please."

"—Laura, whether you would be willing to premier the songs. Perhaps your answer will solve my dilemma for me."

"It'd be the chance of a lifetime," she said without hesitating. "I'd be an idiot to turn it down."

I looked over at Elly, wanting to see her reaction. There was none. She sat demurely at her desk, fingering the massive glass paperweight that holds down her correspondence.

"There is one thing, though," Laura added. "I'd want to have Vikkan play."

I felt a stab of anxiety, just like the one I'd experienced when Janssen unexpectedly offered me a job. "No way, Laura," I said. "Absolutely not. I wouldn't do it."

She turned to me. "How come?"

"Yes," Mann echoed. "Why ever not?"

Elly continued to study her paperweight, but a tiny smile pulled at the corners of her mouth.

"Well, for one thing," I said, coming up with the first excuse that popped into my head, "there's Ulrike."

"Ulrike?" Laura repeated. "Why should that bother you? I'm already *persona non grata* as far as she's concerned. I can't see how that would make any difference."

What else could I say? That taking part in an important premiere was dangerously close to a brink from which I'd been recoiling for years? That it would simply be too public? That for all my love of playing the piano and working with talent like Laura's, I never wanted to be that close to the spotlight? "I just don't want to do it," I said lamely. "Sorry, Laura."

Mann sensed that some intervention was required. Perhaps he understood my ambivalence and realized now was not a good time to delve into it. "Well, perhaps you'll change your mind," he said conversationally. "Meantime, Laura, if you were to sing, would you consider using this man of Ulrike's?"

"Bryce?" Laura looked sceptical.

"You don't feel he's good? Or is it that there might be a conflict because he plays for Ulrike? Yes, of course, that's it. Silly of me to have suggested it. No matter; this is all very hypothetical at the moment. The premiere will not in any case be for some time."

They continued to discuss the matter back and forth, a lot less hypothetically than Mann claimed, until Elly, mostly silent at her desk, stood up and announced it was time for her to go.

"I'll leave you the key," she told Mann, "even though I'm not supposed to. Just be sure to drop it off at the front desk on your way out."

I got up to join her.

"Are you sure you can't stay?" Laura asked. "Herr Mann and I are going to do some Mahler afterward. The *Kindertotenlieder.*"

The offer was tempting. Of all Mahler's songs, the five comprising the *Kindertotenlieder*—Songs on the Death of Children—are my favourites. For such a painful subject, the emotional range is staggering. One day, Laura would be known for her interpretation, the way Kathleen Ferrier and Dietrich Fischer-Dieskau were in preceding generations.

She saw me waver and went to say something, but I shook my head. "Sorry. Gotta go." I didn't want Elly to see I'd lied about having a prior commitment. Moreover, I had the feeling that the longer I stuck around, the harder I'd find it to defend not getting involved with the *Liederkreis* premiere. I said goodbye to Mann, sketched a wave to Laura, and held the door for Elly. She made her own farewells and went ahead of me into the hall.

Downstairs, we encountered resistance to leaving her key with Mann. The ever-efficient Nils Janssen had already instituted new regulations following yesterday's vandalism. No one was allowed in a studio unless they'd signed for the key themselves, their names duly inscribed on a big ledger sheet provided for that purpose.

"I'm really sorry, Miss Gardiner," the girl minding the front desk told her, "the memo came down yesterday." She slid a typewritten page over the counter. "You see, it says right here..." She pointed to a line highlighted with yellow marker.

"The person up there is Dieter Mann," Elly countered starchily, "and he's working with Laura Erskine, who is one of my students. If you have an ounce of sense, you won't make me drag an eighty-year-old man down here to sign his name on a sheet. It should be enough that I've told you he's up there. Just remember to buzz the studio before the building closes so they'll know when to clear out."

"I don't know—"

A voice from behind broke in. "I'm sure it'll be fine, Karen."

Elly and I turned around, coming face to face with the blond hair and catalogue model figure of David Bryce. Ulrike Vogel stood a few paces behind, fetchingly belted into her Ingrid Bergman trench coat. "Miss Gardiner's a teacher," Bryce explained, sidling up to the desk. "The president only means the new procedure for students renting out the studios."

Karen looked doubtful, but he crinkled his eyes and showed just enough capped teeth to reassure her.

Ulrike moved closer. "Vikkan," she said stiffly, "it is good that I run into you. Dieter told me you would be here, when I spoke to him this afternoon. I would pay you now. As you can see, David is quite recovered. I shall not be needing you again." She handed me a folded cheque from a pocketbook. "I trust the amount is correct?"

I took it without looking. "It's fine, I'm sure. Thank you."

Bryce stepped between us. "If you don't mind, Ulrike," he

said, "I'll leave you here. I have some things to catch up on upstairs." He took her hand and cocktail-kissed one of her cheeks. "I'll see you tomorrow."

Ulrike followed him with her eyes as he went back to the counter and requested his key, then she nodded, murmured "Miss Gardiner," and walked off.

Elly and I took the long corridor that runs past the Conservatory Music Store to get to the parking lot. Outside, the rain had let up, but the air was still thick and soft.

"Do you need a ride?" I asked.

"No, thanks. I have my car. Vikkan..."

"Yes?"

"Are you free tomorrow morning? I know you're busy just now,"—her tone implied otherwise—"but I think we need to talk."

"What time?"

"Nine o'clock?"

"Here?"

"Yes."

I walked her to her car, a nice practical little Hyundai and said goodnight. I didn't ask what she wanted to discuss; Mann's discovery, and his plans for it, were as much on my mind as on hers.

Six

Ist's mir doch, als könnt nicht sein!
("T'is as if it cannot be!")
    —*Liederkreis*, Opus 39, XII

I enjoy my job at Evelyn. Most of the time, it feels as if there's just me and the Yamaha on a spotlit island of parquet in the middle of the room. The lights make it difficult to see the patrons at the banquettes, and I tend to forget they're there. The level of conversation rarely rises above a civilized hum, and I almost never get requests.

Thursday night was an exception. Around ten-thirty, a gang of Bay Street suits came in to celebrate some blood-soaked victory on the battlefield of high finance. Vestigial propriety kept their jubilation shy of toss-'em-out rowdy, but alcoholic guffaws still erupted periodically into the lounge's cushioned ambiance.

And during my second set, the requests started coming in.

"Play something faster," a florid-faced pin-striper asked. "You know, something with a beat." I did my best with "Take the 'A' Train" and "It Don't Mean a Thing If It Ain't Got That Swing", but Ellington proved either unknown to him or too refined for his taste. As the evening wore on, his dissatisfaction grew. I finally suggested that if he wanted uptempo, he should try a dance club on Maitland Street. I guess he knew the place catered to gay men; his response impugned my parentage, my masculinity and my talent all in one fell swoop.

The unpleasantness set me on edge, so that when I got home, I couldn't fall asleep. I tossed and turned until nearly five, cursing every Bay Street bozo who ever thought gambling with other people's money made him master of the universe. When I climbed down from the loft three hours later, I was feeling grungy, wired and out of sorts. A quick look outside did nothing to improve my mood. A disheartening drizzle oozed out of low, charcoal clouds.

I checked the key sheet when I got to the Con at nine, but Elly hadn't signed in. I took a seat on a leather couch in the lobby and stared gritty-eyed at the newly hung Alumni Gallery portraits.

Elly showed up at ten after, dressed in a sou'wester and carrying a flowered umbrella. It must have started raining hard after I'd got there; little puddles formed around her shoes as she signed for her key. I got up and joined her at the desk.

"Here, take this," she said, giving me the umbrella. "There's some music in boxes in my car. I want you carry them upstairs for me." She handed me her car keys. "You'll need these."

There were three cartons, covered with a plastic drop sheet. Any one of them was heavy enough that Elly would have had trouble on her own. I wondered if she'd saved them for a day when I happened to be handy. I had to forego the umbrella in order to balance them in my arms, getting thoroughly soaked while she waited inside.

"I hear Morris-Jones got dressed down for her behaviour on Wednesday night," she told me as we mounted the east wing staircase.

"By whom?"

"Russell Spiers. Laura had a meeting with him yesterday. She heard the two of them going at it while she was waiting outside his office. Here, let me get that." She held the door at the top of the stairs. "I suppose we could have taken the elevator," she said belatedly, a little out of breath.

"We'd still be waiting." The Con elevator could hoist several grand pianos at once, but an elephant on Valium would move faster. "What else did Laura say?"

"She didn't hear everything—Spiers had his door closed—but she did catch Dieter's name a number of times. And when Morris-Jones came out, she was hopping mad, yelling something about how 'that man can't be allowed to get away with it.' Spiers accused her of overreacting," Elly unlocked her door, "and added a comment about her female monthly cycle."

"Ouch."

"Ouch, indeed. I know she deserved the reprimand, but honestly, Vikkan, the way men—"

Elly came to a halt. With my arms full, I didn't see her. I kept on walking and collided into her. The top carton tipped and fell to the floor, spilling its contents. "Shit. Sorry," I muttered, hunkering down. "I hope this stuff wasn't in any kind of order."

"Vikkan..." Her voice sounded funny.

I looked up. "What's the ma—?"

Her studio looked as if a hurricane had blasted through, scattering papers, hurling objects, overturning furniture. Her ungainly club chair rested on its side on the carpet. The arms of a fallen coat-tree protruded from behind the door. Wastepaper baskets spewed Styrofoam cups and balled-up Kleenex. The doors of the armoire behind the piano hung open. Music from the empty shelves littered the room. Her sturdy cachepots lay like toppled soldiers. The plants had been torn out, the potting soil dumped and spread on the floor. Gloxinias, violets and begonias wilted in a heap of shattered terra cotta and loam beneath the window. A wet breeze blew in through javelins of glass clinging to the frame around the upper pane.

Elly reached for my shoulder, missed, seemed not to notice. "Oh, no..." Her hand remained suspended as she gazed toward her desk.

Face down, her long dark hair snarled with blood and splintered bone, Laura Erskine sprawled beside the upended chair. A few metres away, limbs crooked in unnatural repose, Dieter Mann crumpled around the front of the piano.

An overlay of time and images: Christian, sleeping/not sleeping on a night-darkened lawn. Then, as now, my brain refused the evidence of my senses. My psyche folded in upon itself, contorting to accommodate the scene before me. Perspective flattened. I looked at Mann and Laura, knowing they would never move or speak again, and what I saw came to me through a glass wall. A movie, I thought. That's it. I'm watching a movie. But not the right one. Someone had made a mistake. I waited for the error to fix itself: the bodies to get up, the room to restore itself, Elly to go on with...what had she been saying?

"Vikkan..." She began to teeter. I rose instinctively to steady her. Was she in the same unreal place as I? We stood, waiting for the scene to go away. An intimate odour like faeces seeped into my consciousness. My mind rejected the implied indignity out of hand. It could not—did not—emanate from the bodies on the floor.

"What do we do?" she asked, her head weaving back and forth in stunned slow motion.

My answer came back from a great distance. "Call the police?"

"The police?" She shook her head, clearing it, like someone shooing off a blackfly. "Of course. That's it." She seized on the idea like a drowning person thrown a lifebuoy. "We have to call the police."

Again, my perspective shifted. Objective became subjective. This wasn't a movie anymore. It was a detective novel. I was one of the characters. But what was I supposed to do? I couldn't remember. Check the bodies for signs of life? Step carefully? Avoid disturbing evidence?

"Outside," she said. "Not here. Outside."

What was she talking about? Oh, yes, the telephone. She was saying to use the public phone beside her studio. I started to leave.

"Elly?" She didn't seem to grasp that I wanted her to come with me. I touched her arm. "We should both go."

The phone was in a converted utility closet. I forgot there was a low bench mounted between the walls, and barked my shins. The pain registered in a dull, disembodied way. "Nine-one-one," Elly prompted through the door. "Call nine-one-one."

My hand seemed disconnected from my brain. The distance from the 9- to the metal stopper of the old rotary dial took forever. Then 1-1 slipped by before I noticed. A brisk voice answered: "Which service, please?"

"Police." I couldn't think of the words I needed. "There's been an accident..." What was the formula? I'd like to report a murder? That couldn't be right; two people were dead. I'd like to report some murders? That wasn't it, either. "I'm at the Royal Conservatory," I tried. "There, uh...there's been a break-in." Shit. I took a deep breath. "Murder," I said. "Two people have been murdered."

The word galvanized me, or maybe it was the voice on the other end that instantly clicked into high, proper gear. A stream of questions followed, easy to answer, each coming like a sturdy pylon in the soft subsoil of shock. In what seemed like no time, I was replacing the receiver. Relief spread through me like a dose of morphine. Wheels were turning, the police would arrive shortly, everything would be taken care of.

"We have to stay here," I said to Elly.

She looked toward her studio in alarm. "In there?"

"I don't think so." Two metal chairs flanked her door. "Here?"

She frowned as if affronted by the idea of waiting outside her own studio like a student. "Downstairs," she announced, squaring her shoulders. "The police will almost certainly come to the front door. We'll meet them there." It sounded as if she were planning to receive dinner guests. I choked off an hysterical urge to giggle.

She set off down the hall without waiting. I caught up halfway and took her arm. "I can manage on my own," she snapped, shaking me off.

She turned right at the doors at the end, heading for the stairs. "Shouldn't we tell Janssen?" I said. His office lay in the other direction. She kept on as if she hadn't heard me.

I thought her determined march—downstairs, through the twisting first floor corridors and past the front desk—was going to carry her all the way out to the street. The screaming of sirens brought her up short. On Bloor Street, four officers leapt from flashered cars, loped up the sidewalk, took the stairs two at a time, and pushed their way into the building.

It was only much later that I could see humour in what happened next. Clearly, none of the officers had been in the Con before. Faced with its daunting main staircase, and the choice of three hallways—left to the front desk, right toward the parking lot, and straight ahead to the administrative tower—the bravado of their entry faltered. The four of them looked left and right and bumped—one, two, three, four—into each other.

The officer in charge, a heavyset woman made even bulkier

by her uniform, headed for the staircase. Had I told them where to go when they arrived? I couldn't remember. The others followed, charging the steps two at a time again.

"Excuse me," I said tentatively, and when they failed to stop, shouted: "Hey! Wait up!" The loudness of my own voice surprised me.

"Name?" the female officer demanded when Elly and I reached them on the landing.

"Vikkan Lantry. I was with Elly here when we..." Another phrase from cinema and fiction refused to come forward. *Found the bodies?* There had to be a better way to accommodate what was in her studio.

She turned to Elly. "And you?"

"Eleanor Gardiner. It's my studio where—"

"Which way?"

They parted ranks and let us through. At the top of the stairs outside Janssen's secretary's office, one of the constables, a young linebacker-type with breath like garlic sausage, moved up beside me. Another took position beside Elly.

"We do need to tell him," Elly said, more to me than the surrounding uniforms.

"The president," I clarified. "Janssen. This is his office." I nodded to my left.

The officer in charge barked out orders. "Marshall, Giotti—take care of it. Get him to act as liaison. Have the floor cleared. Meet the others downstairs. Move!"

Her take-charge manner sounded like a TV script, but apparently Marshall and Giotti didn't think so. They peeled off at Janssen's office while the rest of us carried on to Elly's studio.

We weren't allowed to enter. The pungent-breathed constable blocked the door while his superior took preliminary reconnaissance of the room. A walkie-talkie crackled at his belt, informing him reinforcements were on the scene. He turned aside and mumbled into it as if he didn't want us to hear.

Shortly afterward, a battalion of police erupted into the corridor. The relief I'd felt earlier when I'd known they were coming evaporated. The invasion of uniformed brawn struck me as a violation of the Conservatory's genteel corridors.

When I went to say something about it to Elly, I saw that her face had gone ashen. Under the wary eyes of the sentry constable, I helped her to a chair, but when we sat, it was I who slouched forward, head between my knees, warding off the reeling, bright darkness that heralds fainting.

I straightened up when the spell passed. Elly offered no assistance. She stayed motionless in her chair, ramrod straight, her hands clasped white-knuckled in her lap.

⚜　⚜　⚜

In shock or crisis, expected emotions and reactions go on hold. The mind and body conspire together to wall off trauma in unforeseen and selfish ways.

For me, the hell of the next few hours wasn't remembering the horror in Elly's studio, or confronting outrage, or giving in to grief. It was lack of sleep. I craved to take back the hours I'd lost the night before. My eyes burned with fatigue, my surroundings shimmered, and my skin chafed unnaturally against my shirt.

And I wanted a smoke. Badly. Every time I thought about it, the ache for nicotine hurt so much I nearly groaned out loud.

The police held us in the teachers' lounge. Elly and I, Janssen, the woman who oversees the front desk, and all the teachers with studios in Elly's wing waited to be called to the president's office. Janssen, capable and efficient as ever, had turned his sanctum over to the authorities.

Elly and I were questioned early on, then asked to stay and wait. A coffeemaker by the windows provided me with regular hits of caffeine. I was pouring a fifth cup and staring outside when Janssen approached and asked how I was holding up.

"Well enough, I guess."

"And Miss Gardiner?"

I looked over at Elly. Whenever I left her side, curious staff members descended like vultures in the guise of mother hens. "We're both all right, thanks," I told him.

"The police said it looked like a break-in."

I wasn't supposed to discuss what we'd seen, but Janssen had already been interviewed, and I couldn't see the harm of talking to him. "It looked that way to me, too," I said, glancing over at the east wing, which extends back along Philosopher's Walk. The shattered pane of Elly's second-storey window was all too visible. "They must have used that ladder."

Janssen peered down to the partially repaired section of flat roof covering the Conservatory basement's eccentric incursion above ground. The workmen's ladder lay on its side, along with the empty buckets I'd seen the night before. Two men in orange rain capes were inspecting the tarred surface.

"I never imagined someone might break in," Janssen said. "I thought that by being more careful with security *inside...*"

"It's hardly your fault."

"Everything that happens here is my responsibility." He turned from the window. "I'll need to speak with you after this is over. The press will be involved. I'm concerned what might be said to them. Once the police are finished, do you think I could have a moment?"

"After this is over, I'm going straight home."

"Of course." He nodded. "I understand. Tomorrow?"

"We'll see."

I could tell he wanted a firmer commitment, but when it didn't come, he moved off. I added creamer to my coffee and went back to Elly.

"This room is getting to me," she said. "I've never liked it. I only come here for faculty meetings. So dreary." She waved her hand listlessly at the beige walls, murky Group-of-Seven knock-offs, the conference table hemmed by stacking chairs. The overcast light from outside only added to the drabness.

"Do you think they'll let us go soon?" I asked.

"I hope so. I can't think why they're keeping us. I would have thought they'd want me at the studio." A look of anguish took hold of her features. "You don't suppose I'll have to go in there again with the...the..."

So far, we hadn't spoken about the bodies lying on her floor. I tried to suppress a nauseating eidetic image of the ruin done to Laura's head. An equally vivid mental picture slipped into place: Mann's skull. One side had been battered in. An arm of his gold spectacles protruded from the bloody declivity. I set my coffee down, afraid I'd be sick if I tried to swallow.

A constable entered the room and approached Elly, asking her to come with him. She stood stiffly. Her eyes caught mine as she ritually straightened her skirt. "Don't worry," I said, trying for a smile, "I'll be here when you're finished. I'm not going anywhere."

I tilted my chair back on two legs and watched her leave. All at once, I couldn't keep my eyes open. The chair sank slowly forward. My head snapped back against the wall. Sounds of conversation turned into echoes from a well. The cheerless room with its sombre paintings and institutional furniture slid into double image and faded out.

What seemed like only seconds later, I felt my shoulder being prodded. "Mr. Lantry," said a voice outside the dark

143

place I'd descended to, "Mr. Lantry...Inspector March would like to see you again." I floundered awake with the self-conscious animation of someone caught napping. When I checked my watch, more than an hour had gone by. There was no one else in the lounge.

I followed my escort across the hall. A uniformed woman— not the one who'd headed the morning's vanguard—stood to the right of Janssen's desk. Behind the expanse of plum-coloured wood sat the same man who'd interviewed me four hours earlier. I hadn't formed much of an impression then, just brush-cut and dark-suited, with all the warmth of a bank manager turning down a loan. He'd shed his jacket now and loosened his tie. The top button of his shirt was undone, the sleeves rolled back over muscular forearms. His broad shoulders nearly exceeded the width of Janssen's chair. This was one cop who clearly preferred dumbbells to doughnuts.

I waited inside the door while he talked with the uniform. Their conference went on long enough for me to wonder if the holdup was intentional. Finally, the woman officer retreated around Janssen's Kawai to the secretary's office and closed the door. Inspector March sat back, and with all the unconscious arrogance of one who knows he serves the law, asked me to take a seat.

He wasted no breath apologizing for the delay. "I just want to confirm a few details," he said, flipping through a notepad. "We'll prepare a statement for you to sign later."

He could have at least looked up while he spoke. "If you want," I said, "I could write it myself. If you think that would help." The offer sounded ridiculous, but I couldn't help myself. Uncle Charles, ever-present in difficult situations, had been prompting from the wings: "Always parry rudeness with a counterthrust of courtesy—it both disarms and inflames your opponent."

"I'm sure you could," March said drily, "but I wouldn't bother. We know what we're doing. Now, correct me if I'm wrong: you were acquainted with both of the victims?"

"Yes."

"And you saw them on two separate occasions yesterday?"

"Yes."

"For rehearsals?"

"Not precisely."

He glanced up, revealing grey eyes that held no compromise to blue or hazel. "No? What were you doing, then?"

"Looking at music. 'Rehearsing' suggests we were preparing for a concert. We weren't."

He shook his head, unimpressed by the distinction. "And that was your reason for being together on both occasions?"

"Yes."

He jotted something on his pad, holding the cover so I couldn't see. The way he did it looked contrived, as if he wanted me to wonder what he'd written. Still writing, he asked: "Would you mind going over your last meeting with the victims, Mr. Lantry?"

I didn't like the way he said my name. Too polite, too slick. The emphasis on "Mister" sounded bogus. I bet he talked to pimps and low-life scum the same way. "They had names, you know," I said testily.

"I'm sorry?"

"The victims. They had names."

He put down his pen and looked squarely at me—the first time he'd done so since I entered the room. His face, all lines and planes in the blond-and-crew-cut military mould, wore a puzzled expression, as if I were a lab rat who'd decided to go on strike.

"As you wish, Mr. Lantry," he conceded, "Laura Margaret

Erskine and Dieter Wilhelm Friederich Mann." He pronounced Mann's names perfectly, like a CBC announcer slipping into German for the title of a Bach cantata. "Is that better?" His fluency surprised me, and he knew it. "Now, do you want to tell me what happened?"

I summed up. Laura, Mann and I had been together in the afternoon to go over music; we'd met at Elly's studio in the evening to continue; we'd worked for about an hour; Elly and I had left at seven-thirty. Since March hadn't cared for the precise distinction between rehearsing and merely going over music, I skipped the details of what we'd been looking at.

"And no one else was with you in the studio? Aside from—" he consulted his notebook "—Eleanor Gardiner?"

"No."

"What did you do afterward?"

"Elly and I came downstairs. We spoke with two staff members at the front desk, then went out to the parking lot. She asked me to meet her here this morning. We said goodbye. That's all."

"And then you went to work? Over on Prince Arthur?"

I hesitated. Hadn't I told him I drove out to the Beaches first? I must have, but given the shape I was in during my first interview, I might have forgotten. Perhaps he was testing me, omitting things on purpose. "I didn't start work until ten o'clock," I said carefully. "Before that, I drove over to the Beaches."

His eyebrows rose a fraction. Lips pursed, he riffled back through his notes, then pushed away from the desk. "Will you excuse me a moment?"

He stood up and went over to the secretary's office. For the first time, I registered how tall he was, probably six-four. His shirt was creased at the back and stuck to his skin. I could see a ripple of muscle when he opened the door. "Gabrielle," he called out, "will you come in here? Bring your pad." He returned to the desk. "Perhaps now you can see why it's better for us to prepare your statement," he said smoothly. "Here's something you might have left out."

I knew I shouldn't let the sarcasm get to me, but I was worn down from the long wait in the teachers' lounge. "Maybe you haven't noticed," I shot back, "but I happen to have the triple misfortune not only of knowing the 'victims', but also of being one of the last people to see them alive and having found them dead. Does it occur to you that I wasn't thinking too clearly before? I'm sorry if I left something out, but being snide isn't going to jog my memory. In fact, I think it's fucking inconsiderate."

He stared at me, his rainy-day coloured eyes holding mine for the longest time. "Why not just tell me where you were?" he said at length. "That way, we'll get through this faster." As Gabrielle entered, he added: "I know it's been rough."

"After I left Elly," I said, calming down, "I gassed up at a station on Yonge Street, near Davenport. From there I drove to the Beaches and spent an hour and a half walking around. At nine-thirty, I came back downtown. I got to Evelyn shortly before ten."

"Did you meet anyone?"

"No."

"Would you care to explain then, Mr. Lantry, why Miss Gardiner has the impression that you were off to something more pressing than a stroll on the boardwalk when you left her?"

Why would Elly think that? Oh, yes—it's what I'd wanted her to believe. "I needed an excuse," I said lamely, "to get out of something."

Suddenly it occurred to me: what would have happened if I hadn't lied to Elly? If I hadn't made it sound as if I couldn't stay with Laura and Mann past seven-thirty? Would the events in her studio never have taken place? Or, if they had, with very different issue? I felt the blood drain from my face as a wave of what-ifs crashed over me like a North Atlantic breaker.

"For her?" I heard March ask and realized he was repeating his question.

I wrenched myself back. "Yes. In a manner of speaking."

A muscle flickered on his jaw. "In a manner of speaking?" he mimicked.

"I've been doing Elly a lot of favours recently. I simply wanted to remind her that I have a life of my own."

He gave me a long, assessing look. I began to wish he'd go back to his notepad. Finally he nodded, satisfied with whatever he'd read in my face. "What kind of vehicle do you drive, Mr. Lantry?"

"A Land Rover. Light yellow. Why?"

"We'll have to check your movements."

"That should be easy. The gas station attendant knows me, and I parked in full view of umpteen dozen stores in the Beaches. The Rover's bound to have attracted notice."

March looked over at Gabrielle, who nodded and flipped her pad shut. It wasn't hard to guess who'd be doing the legwork on this case.

"Now, Mr. Lantry," he said as she left, "I'd like you to go over what you saw in Miss Gardiner's studio this morning."

There it was again: that too-polite way of saying my name. And hadn't we covered this before? Did he think I was lying?

"The room had been vandalized," I said evenly, controlling my irritation. "The top pane of the window was shattered, presumably so the lower one could be unlocked. The flowers Elly keeps on the sill were on the floor, probably knocked over when the intruder climbed in. The other plants in the studio were on their sides, too. The soil was everywhere. Anything and everything that could be overturned or tossed around had been: chairs, wastepaper baskets, knick-knacks, the coat-tree. Elly's music cupboard had been ransacked. The books were ripped up and thrown all over the place."

"Anything else?"

"Of course. Silly of me to forget. There were two dead people, one by the piano, and the other by the desk."

He gave me a *that's all?* look. "What else do you want?" I asked. "A description of the bodies? I didn't exactly stick around."

"Another studio was vandalized a few days ago; is that correct?"

"So I heard."

"Do you think this might be connected?"

"It could be."

"You don't find it strange that someone would vandalize an occupied studio?"

"How would I know? If you'd been this thorough when it happened before, maybe you wouldn't have to ask."

His lips twitched in a tight smile. "I don't want to shatter your faith in the police, Mr. Lantry, but you should know we generally take homicide a bit more seriously than vandalism." I guess he'd picked up that I didn't think much of the cruller-and-chocolate-glazed set. "I have a few more questions; then you'll be free to go. Who, besides you and Miss Gardiner, knew Laura Erskine and Dieter Mann were in her studio? I understand neither of them taught here in any official capacity."

"I'm not sure. I didn't discuss it with anyone. Elly may have."

"You didn't meet or speak to anyone on your way out of the building?"

"Just the two teachers I told you about before."

He checked his notes. "That would be David Bryce and Ulrike Vogel?" Again, the perfect German: *Ool-ree-kuh Foh-gh'l.*

"Yes."

"Did you mention it to either one of them?"

"Not directly. The girl at the front desk, Karen, was giving Elly a hard time because Elly had left her key upstairs with Mann. The president's gotten very strict about that. No one is supposed to be in a studio unless they've signed the key sheet themselves. Bryce overheard and stepped in on Elly's behalf."

March made a few notes, then straightened up, flexing his shoulders. "That'll be all then, Mr. Lantry," he said, rolling his neck. "Come by Fifty-two Division some time tomorrow to sign your statement."

"Down on Dundas?"

"Yes. Ask for me when you get there. Oh, and by the way, do you have any objection to being fingerprinted?"

"Fingerprinted?" The feeling of being caught in a detective novel visited me again. "I suppose not."

I would rather have said no. I didn't relish having my fingerprints on file. The less the authorities know about me, the safer I feel. Maybe Uncle Charles shouldn't have read me *1984* as a bedtime story.

March leaned forward and began writing again. I sat for nearly a minute, wondering if he'd at least have the decency to thank me for my time. Finally, he looked up. "That'll be *all,* Mr. Lantry."

"Vikkan," I said.

"I beg your pardon?"

"My name. It's Vikkan. I don't like being called—" it was my turn to mimic "— 'Mr. Lantry'."

He laid down his pen and stared. "If you say so. My name's

Andrew, but it doesn't change anything. You're still free to go."

※   ※   ※

I checked for Elly in the teachers' lounge, but she wasn't there. The coffeemaker was still on. A smell like burnt rubber came from the empty carafe. I went over and shut it off.

Outside Elly's hall, a policeman told me Miss Gardiner had left ten minutes ago. I walked downstairs, trying to remember where I'd parked the Rover. Bloor Street, the other side of Avenue Road, ticketed if not towed by now. Could I fight the citation because I'd been with the police? *But Your Honour, how much money are you supposed to put in the meter when you're going to find two dead bodies?*

I left by the front doors and immediately regretted not going out by way of Philosopher's Walk. A mob of reporters crowded around, assaulting me with microphones, cameras and questions. "Mr. Lantry... Mr. Lantry..." I couldn't figure out how they knew who I was; I might have been the guy who refills the Coke machine. I said nothing, experiencing the same vague guilt I get from not answering the phone.

The onslaught continued until I reached Avenue Road, by which time even the thickest reporter could see I was not going to be seduced, urged, bullied, or cajoled into speaking. They retreated like a pack of dogs outsmarted by their quarry.

The jeep hadn't been towed, but a ticket flopped damply on the windscreen. I got in and started the motor, only then realizing I didn't have a clue what to do next. I considered calling on Léo, but what would be the point? Giving into the I-need-to-be-with-someone urge never did much good. The empty feeling always came back. I lit a long-delayed cigarette, smoked it to the end, then U-turned and headed home.

The answering machine was flashing when I got in. Elly. Her

voice lacked its usual confidence. I didn't recognize the number she gave and grabbed a book from the piano to jot it down.

"Is this Vikkan?" The voice on the other end sounded higher and older than Elly's. "Elly said you'd call. I'll go get her."

When Elly came on, she told me she was at her sister's in Willowdale. "I couldn't stand to be alone. Do you have someone with you? Someone to stay with?"

"I'm okay."

Neither of us wanted to discuss the murders, but the need to talk hung heavy. It was Elly who broached the subject.

"They took me back to the studio, you know."

"Yes. I went looking for you. The police wouldn't even let me in the hallway."

"Dieter and Laura were...gone, but the room was just the way we found it. All my plants, my flowers..." Her voice cracked at the mention of her lost violets and begonias. The mind deals with what it can.

"I'm sorry," I said helplessly.

A rustling sound told me she was taking a hankie from the sleeve of her cardigan. "It's all right," she said at length. "They can be replaced. The police asked me to look around without touching anything. It'll be a few days before I can clean up."

"I'll help when the time comes."

"They'd taped these outlines around where Dieter and Laura had been. I don't know, Vikkan—somehow, that made everything worse. And I could see where they'd been hit. There were still...traces...on the floor."

"Maybe we'd better leave the cleaning to someone else. I'm sure Janssen will pay."

"I want to do it myself." She spoke firmly. I could only guess at her reasons.

"Was anything missing from the studio?" I asked. "Anything valuable destroyed?"

"As far as I could tell, no. The piano was untouched, but then it's hard to do anything to a piano short of going at it with an axe." She gave a weak laugh. "And what would anyone steal? There's nothing of value in there except the furniture."

"What about Mann's stuff? The Schumann?"

"I thought of that. His case was open. I could see the Schumann lying on top."

"That's a relief, I guess." We were running out of conversation. I began doodling on the cover of the book where I'd written Elly's sister's phone number. Haydn, *Klavierstücke*, The F-minor Variations. "I was supposed to have a lesson with him today."

"I know."

"What do you think happened?"

She sighed—a small, weary exhalation. "I have no idea. Someone chose to vandalize my studio. I can't imagine why. Dieter and Laura must have been out of the room and come back. It couldn't have been anything else. The police will likely piece it together."

I heard her sister's voice in the distance. "I have to go now," she said. "Winnie's made supper. I don't feel much like eating. Do you have to work tonight?"

"No, I'm off Fridays."

"I wish you had someone with you."

"I'll be all right."

After she rang off, I went to the kitchen, thinking I should get something to eat myself. I hadn't seen food since breakfast. I fixed an indifferent tuna sandwich and took it to the front room. My appetite deserted me after the first bite. I set the plate on the window sill and looked outside. The clouds still hung low and grey, but at least the drizzle had let up. I stared at the gloom for a while, then lay down on the couch. Tired as I was, I knew I wouldn't sleep.

It was going to be a long evening.

Seven

Kein Mensch es sonst wissen soll.
("None other need ever know.")
—*Liederkreis,* Opus 39, IV

T he call that woke me from the heavy sleep I did finally
fall into came at ten the next morning. Nils Janssen,
wanting to know when I'd be available to meet with him.
When, not *if.* I massaged the small of my back, stiff from a
night on the couch and agreed to come by around noon. I had
to go out to sign my police statement anyway.

"The secretary won't be in," he told me. "Just knock on the
hall door."

The mood at the Conservatory was subdued. Walking up
to the second floor, I wondered if the east wing were still off
limits. I hoped so. Death hallows the places that it visits. It
would be wrong to restore that part of the building to
mundane use too quickly.

I heard voices through the door, so I knocked quietly and
prepared for a wait. Not a long one, as it turned out. Unlike
Detective Inspector March, Janssen didn't play the summon-
and-delay game.

"Thank you for coming," he said, opening up. "We're just
finished. Let me introduce you. Vikkan, this is Doug
Rawlings. Doug, Vikkan."

The overweight man I'd seen at the reception on Monday

night sat in the wooden chair in front of the desk, his thighs overflowing the seat. Struggling up, he offered a hand that, on contact, proved unpleasantly moist. "Pleased to meet you, Vik. You played for that woman Monday night, right?"

"Yes. Ulrike Vogel."

"You were pretty good. So was she."

"I'm sure she'll be pleased to hear it."

I kept my expression neutral, but he heard something in my voice he didn't like. His eyes ranged over me like a wary bulldog's. Janssen sensed trouble. "Vikkan's extremely talented," he put in. "In fact, I'm hoping to get him on staff here."

"Yes, well," I said, still looking at Rawlings, "that's very much up in the air."

"Why's that?" Rawlings asked.

Janssen shot me a cautionary look. "We've only had a chance to discuss the matter briefly," I hedged, feeling trapped between the two men's stares.

The suspicion cleared from Rawlings' face. Janssen relaxed. "Holding out till he makes a better offer, eh?" Rawlings asked. "Smart man." He all but winked, then turned to Janssen. "Now, Nils, hope you don't mind, but I've got to run."

"Of course not. You're a busy man. I hope I haven't taken too much of your time already. It's just that with your interest in the Conservatory, I felt you deserved to hear what happened from me directly."

The only thing worse than someone laying it on thick is someone lapping it up. Rawlings preened, running a fleshy hand over his remaining hair. "I appreciate that, Nils, but don't think I can't see through you. Don't worry, I still haven't made up my mind. I won't be holding bad luck against you." He chortled, an unpleasant phlegmy sound. "Good to meet you, Vik. If Nils here wants you, you must be good. Take my advice:

don't agree to anything until he puts his money on the table."

Janssen ushered him out with the impartial decorum of an English butler. Rawlings paused at the door. "That woman," he said, "what's her name—?"

"Ulrike Vogel?"

"That's it. She surprised me. I thought only fat ladies could sing like that."

Janssen closed the door and went to his desk. I expected some acknowledgment of the fat-lady comment—a wry smile, a raised eyebrow—but none came. "He's very important to us," he said, sitting down, indicating with an upturned palm that I should do the same. "His endowment will have a profound effect on the Conservatory's future."

"If you get it."

"We will. Doug Rawlings wants his money where it will look best."

"Which means your ugly stepsisters over at the Faculty don't stand a chance?"

Janssen studied his nails. "Miss Gardiner warned me about your sarcasm."

"No doubt. But I assume we're not here to discuss Rawlings' donation?"

He looked up. "On the contrary. It's the very reason I asked to see you. Yesterday's events were a terrible misfortune. The loss of one of music's greatest teachers, and the more immediate tragedy of a student's death." He sounded like a funeral director called on to eulogize people he'd never met. "You knew Laura Erskine, I believe?"

"We were friends."

"I'm very sorry." He allowed a moment of silence. "However, to be blunt, my own position as president does not afford me time to grieve. Not now. My first concern must be our reputation, our image, especially now that so much depends on it."

"You're worried that what happened will scare off Rawlings?"

"Not precisely. You heard him—he won't hold bad luck against us." A note of distaste finally crept into his voice.

"What, then?"

He leaned forward. "Like it or not, yesterday's affair will put us in the limelight. Possibly for some time. I believe it would be foolish not to take advantage of that."

"You mean since Rawlings hasn't made up his mind, you'd like to see this get the right spin? Something to sway him in your favour? A nice headline? 'Tragedy at the Royal Conservatory' in the *Globe and Mail* instead of 'Music School Mayhem' in the *Sun?*"

He looked seriously annoyed. "I'm only asking that you be circumspect in anything you say to the press."

"I wasn't planning to say anything at all."

He nodded, appeased. "Good. I hoped you'd feel that way."

I got the feeling what he really hoped for was that I'd sympathize with his ever-so-delicate position between expedience and outright opportunism.

"While you're here," he went on, "there is one other thing. I spoke with Miss Gardiner last night. It seems you weren't quite honest with me."

"About what?"

"The Schumann song cycle Dieter Mann brought with him from Vienna."

"You asked whether Elly had said anything, not whether I knew about it."

He favoured me with a tight-lipped smile. "Then perhaps I should have been more precise. Let me try again. Were you aware that Herr Mann was considering donating the manuscript to the Faculty library?"

The Faculty? Why would he want to do that? Janssen read my expression. "You didn't know, then?" he asked.

I shook my head.

"Dean Simmons told me about it on Thursday."

Was that why Mann had brought the proofs to Toronto? Not as a copy to work from, but because he intended to leave them behind?

"It's not a manuscript," I corrected. "What Mann had were publisher's proofs. The manuscript was destroyed by fire."

"I gather you've seen the work?"

"Yes. Played through it a couple of times."

"Really? I had no idea you and Herr Mann were so well acquainted."

"More a question of availability than friendship."

"I see." He paused, choosing his next words. "The reason I brought this up is that when I talked with Dean Simmons, he implied that Herr Mann's intentions were far from settled. They discussed the *possibility* of a donation, nothing more. What I'm thinking is, would it be too far off the mark to suppose that he might not in the end have gone through with it?"

"Why would you want to suppose that?"

Janssen's look suggested I was a six-year-old who'd just asked why the sky is blue. Or why Mommy and Daddy sometimes lock the bedroom door. "Doug Rawlings. Imagine if he found out that someone of Mann's stature were honouring the Faculty with such a gift."

"You're saying you'd rather the information didn't get around."

"Precisely. I knew you'd understand. Mann's discovery will come to light, of course. After all, it was with him when he died. That alone gives it a certain significance. But I see no reason for this...plan of his to become general knowledge."

No reason, indeed. The morning after a brutal double murder at the Conservatory, its president had stated his concerns pellucidly.

≷   ≷   ≷

I left a relieved Janssen and drove down to Dundas Street to sign my police statement.

From outside, Fifty-two Division could pass for a small, ultra-modern hospital—all clean white lines and aquamarine glass bricks. The health-care image stayed with me when I went to be fingerprinted. The constable donned medical-looking latex gloves, then rolled my fingers on an ink pad with the gentle firmness of a lab nurse tapping for a vein. He even kept up a line of reassuring patter. Upstairs, outside Inspector March's door, I expected to find magazines.

He called me in after twenty minutes. His office was a cramped, windowless affair. Beige walls enclosed a metal desk, computer workstation, wooden chairs and a bank of filing cabinets. No personal touches individualized the space, other than two framed eight-by-tens of a lacrosse team.

With a gesture that reminded me of Janssen, he waved me to a seat. His dress was Saturday-overtime casual: faded jeans and a grey sweatshirt. The sweatshirt sported a flaking University of Waterloo logo and brought out the colour of his eyes. He looked like a gym instructor—a very tall gym instructor.

"You'll be happy to know we confirmed your movements Thursday night," he began, opening a manila folder. "The gas jockey remembers you, and one of our own officers spotted your vehicle over in the Beaches."

160

"I'm so relieved."

"I wouldn't be." He flipped a page. "It says here you have fifteen unpaid parking violations."

"Seventeen, at last count, including the one I got while you were holding me in the lounge."

"Life's a bitch." He handed me a typewritten sheet. "Your statement. Read it over. If everything's in order, I'll have someone witness while you sign."

I studied the page, fascinated by the way the legalese made it sound as if I had something to hide. No one's life could possibly be that itemized, that accounted for. "It seems accurate," I said.

He picked up his phone and punched a button. "Beltrane, can you come in here a minute?"

A paunchy man stepped in, dark-suited the way March had been the day before. He looked on while I wrote my name, then appended his own with an aggressive flourish. March examined my signature before adding his own. "Nice handwriting," he commented, nodding Beltrane out of the office.

"Thank you. Is there anything else?"

"That's about it."

"Do you mind if I ask whether you have any idea what happened yet?"

"You can ask."

I waited. He wrote in the manila folder, closed it, got up, and opened a filing drawer.

"Well?" I asked his back.

He shut the drawer and turned around, resting his elbow on top of the cabinet. He was tall enough to do it easily. "Right now," he said, somewhere between bored and testy, "we know as much as you. Someone broke into the room your friends were in and beat them to death."

"Only Laura was my friend," I amended. "Mann, well…" I didn't know how to qualify the warmth I'd felt for him on such short acquaintance.

"Were you lovers?"

"Mann and I? Of course not. He was over eighty."

March looked down, hiding a smile.

"You find that funny?"

"I was asking about you and the girl. I wanted to know if you and Laura Erskine had been lovers."

"Friends."

"I realize that now."

"And that's amusing?"

"Differing assumptions, that's all. I thought you were straight. You thought I knew you weren't."

"I'm still not laughing."

He looked up. His smile was gone. "You don't like me much, do you?"

"Your interpersonal skills could use a little work."

"Sue me. I'm investigating a double homicide."

"That excuses being rude? Treating me like a suspect?"

"How do I know you're not?"

"You said you verified my whereabouts."

He took a deep breath and blew it out slowly. "We confirmed your vehicle was where you said it was. If necessary, we can probably find someone who saw you. You're not an easy man to miss." I wasn't sure what he meant, but let the comment pass. "We've established that your friends were killed sometime between eight-thirty and nine. I doubt you could have driven to Kew Beach, left your car, gone back to the Conservatory, killed someone, returned to the Beaches, and made it over to Prince Arthur by ten."

"And now you want me to like you just because you don't *think* I'm lying?"

162

His eyes darkened a shade or two. "In case you hadn't noticed, I'm in charge of finding out who killed your friends." He spoke evenly enough, but I could sense him holding back not exactly temper, but something equally perilous if unloosed.

"Is there some point to all this?" I asked.

He didn't answer right away, but stared at me instead as if coming to a decision. Finally, he straightened up. The new posture signalled a deft bit of quick-change artistry. Implacable Mr. Hyde turned into understanding Doctor Jekyll as he came around the desk and sat on the right corner, friendly-like. This close, his sweatshirt smelled of bleach and Sunlight.

"I need your cooperation. This isn't going to be an easy case. What I'm hoping is, you'll get over whatever problem you have with me—maybe it's the police in general—and help me do my job. These murders weren't just the result of a nasty prank gone wrong."

"You implied as much yesterday. Why are you so sure?"

"Those other incidents at the Conservatory were small-time, most likely a kid with a screw loose. Thursday, someone went to a lot of trouble—setting up a ladder, smashing a window, climbing in. It wasn't late at night. Anyone could have seen them. That's a lot of chances to take for petty vandalism."

"You're saying the profile doesn't fit."

He gave me a funny look. "You read a lot of mysteries?"

"Some."

"Sounds like it. But here's the kicker: why would a vandal, petty or otherwise, target an occupied studio? Doesn't it make more sense they'd go after one that wasn't being used?"

"Obviously they thought it wasn't. Come to that, it had to have been empty, or they'd never have gotten past breaking the window. Mann and Laura must have left for a while, turned the lights off."

"A teacher across the hall says no. The lights were on until at least nine. But you're right; the studio was empty. We found a bag there from a doughnut shop over on Bedford Road. The guy at the counter remembers Laura coming in somewhere between eight-thirty and eight-forty-five."

"And Mann?"

"The Conservatory janitor saw him near the washroom earlier, around eight o'clock. He was an old man, his bladder wouldn't be that strong. He probably took another pee while Laura was out."

March got off the desk and rolled first one shoulder, then the other. I could make out a flex of deltoids beneath his sweatshirt. He'd made a similar stretch the day before, signalling the end of our interview. I wondered if it meant the same thing today.

"What I think, Vikkan," he said, massaging a kink, "and what you should start considering, is that someone was watching the studio, waiting for an opportunity to break in. They could see it was occupied and knew who was in it. Nothing was stolen, nothing seriously damaged. Two people are dead. Doesn't that suggest an intent rather more malicious than vandalism?"

Now who sounded as if he read too many mysteries? The wording came easily. Perhaps it was standard phrasing in police-inspector argot.

"But why?" I said, more to myself than expecting an answer. "And who were they after? Laura or Mann?"

"Like I said, Vikkan—I'll be needing your cooperation."

☆   ☆   ☆

It was raining when I left Fifty-two Division, a sluicing downpour that washed cigarette butts and gum wrappers into the gutter. I was drenched by the time I reached the Rover. The door wouldn't shut, and the engine wouldn't start. Rovers are supposed to do well in any climate, but I suspect they prefer the Sahara to the Amazon.

I wasn't sure where to go next. Saturdays I usually make the trek to St. Lawrence Market, but I didn't feel like facing bright stalls filled with produce and delicatessen. A peculiar apathy follows on death, a lethargic protest against life-supporting tasks like procuring food. I sat in the Rover with the heater on, clearing steam from the windows, thinking about what March had said. Death by random violence is said to be the hardest to accept, but for me, it was preferable to believe that chance or fate had simply placed Mann and Laura in the wrong place at the wrong time. To know they were intended victims, deliberately sought out for murder, seemed to implicate them, in some twisted fashion, in their own demise.

I wondered if March realized that I didn't want to think this way, that I wouldn't easily accept that someone had had reason to batter Mann's and Laura's skulls until that reason vanished with the passing of their memories, their personalities, their lives. If not, what was the point of his asking for my cooperation? A palliative? A cheap way of making me feel I could do something pro-active?

While the last of the condensation crept up and off the windscreen, I considered that maybe he'd been trying to help, forcing me to see things as they were.

If so, I hoped he didn't want gratitude in return.

꙰   ꙰   ꙰

"One year ago Thursday night," I said to Léo. He was sitting across from me on an off-white linen couch, feet up on the coffee table. I was nursing the bottom finger of the Scotch he'd poured when I arrived, unannounced, at his condominium on Glen Road. "One year to the day. I wasn't going to say anything, you know."

"Why not?"

"To prove something, I guess."

He took a sip of his brandy and tonic. "Like you'd gotten over it?"

"Not exactly. More like not wanting to let you down. Wanting you to see you'd made a difference. You and Evelyn both. I can't imagine what it must have been like, dealing with your own grief, helping me through mine."

"We had each other. That helps, a little. And we had some inkling. Christian was our son, after all. In a way, we'd been given time to prepare."

"For his suicide? I don't think so."

Léo studied the frozen strawberry at the bottom of his drink. "We knew he was troubled."

"I didn't see it, Léo. I honestly thought it was something else."

He pressed his lips together as if he would say something, then thought better of it. I finished my drink. "Have I ever thanked you for not interfering?" I asked. "For letting me know Christian the way I did? Not as..."

"Schizophrenic? You've got it backwards, Vikkan. You loved our son. We're the ones with a debt of gratitude." He stood up and went to a highboy, taking out a bottle of Talisker.

"I don't want to get drunk, you know," I said.

He sat and poured, ignoring me. "It might do you some good."

I swirled the amber liquid around in my glass, inhaling peat-iodine-apricots-peaches. "Thursday night," I said, taking a sip, "I drove out to the Beaches. There aren't many places in the city we ever went together, but that was one of them. It seemed right, somehow, to give in, to remember..."

Léo nodded.

"And while I was out there, someone was killing Laura and Mann."

Léo had read about the murders but hadn't known about my connection to the victims. Nor that I'd been one of the two "Conservatory teachers" who had found them. The papers, as always, had compressed the facts to fit their columns.

"It must seem like a ghastly practical joke."

I took a deeper swallow of Scotch. "I know it's vanity to think there's an intelligence out there interested enough in any one human being to inflict this sort of misfortune deliberately, but, yes, that's exactly what it feels like."

"Coincidence happens."

He was right, of course, but that didn't stop my brain from seeing a connection between Christian's suicide and Thursday's murders, if only as an imaginary line of pain joining two dots of sorrow in some complex, abstruse puzzle.

"Have the police got any leads?" he asked, steering me away from metaphysical reflection. "The papers said something about other incidents at the Conservatory."

"The detective in charge doesn't think this is related. He thinks whoever broke into the studio meant to kill Laura or Mann."

"Premeditated, in other words."

"That's the assumption he's working from." I outlined what March had said earlier about the unlikelihood of someone targeting an occupied studio for hooliganism.

Léo concurred. "It's true. A delinquent wouldn't take those kinds of risks."

"I know, but I'm having trouble believing it. And I can't figure out how he thinks I can help if this is more than just a case of interrupted vandalism. Twice today he said he'd be needing my 'cooperation'."

"Sounds like a veiled threat. Does he suspect you're involved somehow?"

"Hard to say. He's not the easiest man to read. Mostly, I get the impression he thinks I know more than I'm telling him. No, correct that—it's more as if he thinks he knows more about me than I'm telling him."

"Have you been completely open with him?"

"It's not easy. He's like something out of a TV show—the beefed-up detective who's a little too full of himself."

"So there are things you haven't told him." Léo didn't even bother to make it a question.

I took another mouthful of Scotch and set my glass on the table. Léo watched patiently. "Three things," I said finally. "One of them...how can I put this?...its significance might be lost on March, or misconstrued. The other two, well, one is speculation, and the other's something that happened on Wednesday night."

I told Léo first about the *Liederkreis,* pointing out before he drew any conclusions that the proofs had neither been harmed or stolen. "Getting at the thing itself wasn't behind the break-in, which is why I didn't mention it to March. Now I'm worried that if I tell him, he'll ascribe some sort of sinister importance to my not having said something before."

"Is he really so bad?"

"What can I say? He's a policeman."

"Meaning?"

"I couldn't like someone who'd even want to be in the police, let alone someone who already was."

"That's a bit harsh, don't you think?" He held up his hand. "Don't answer. It's not important. What else is there?"

"This woman, Ulrike Vogel? The one I played for on Monday? Originally, Mann had asked her to premiere the *Liederkreis*. She hasn't performed in years, and she's planning a comeback. He wanted to help out. Trouble is, and I know this firsthand, he was having second thoughts."

"Shall I venture a guess? He was considering your friend Laura instead?"

"You're quick."

"No, Vikkan, I know you. Well enough to figure out what you wouldn't tell this man, March." He got up to replenish his drink. "Ambition makes you uneasy, whether it's your own—and I can't believe you don't have any—or other people's. I think you have this idea it sullies your art, which is romantic, and foolish, and utterly you. I'd expect you to insulate yourself from even considering that your friends had been murdered because of someone else's hopes for glory."

His comment got my back up. "You're wrong there, Léo. The only reason I didn't tell him was because I thought some sicko had broken into the studio, not someone out to get Laura and Mann. Besides, Elly will have said something already."

"That doesn't remove your own obligations."

"But I don't even know whether Ulrike was aware of what Mann was doing."

"That's not the point." Léo cracked ice cubes sharply out of a tray. I lit a cigarette and waited while he took longer than usual to fix his brandy and tonic. When he turned around, I could see he was upset, worried that he'd spoken out of turn. "How are you feeling?" he asked gently. "I mean, really?"

"I don't know. I'm having trouble sorting things out. I didn't know Mann well. Laura and I...we were only just starting to get close. We had dinner on Wednesday." I shook my head.

"Do you need some time off? You were planning to go up to Caledon. Evelyn would still love to see you."

"I imagine I'm supposed to stay in town. As long as I'm here, I might as well work."

We sat again without speaking, Léo content to let me drink his single malt for as long as I needed.

"The other thing," I said, finishing my cigarette, "was this woman who used to be a professor of mine, Bernice Morris-Jones. Mann wrote a critique of her research in *Piano Quarterly,* and she had a mammoth hate-on for him."

Léo couldn't help smiling while I described Morris-Jones' antics during Wednesday's master class. "She sounds like quite the character," he said afterward, "but somehow, I can't imagine anyone so unhinged they'd kill over a magazine article."

"Me either."

"You said she's a historian. Did she by any chance know about this Schumann piece?"

"I can't see how. Mann's not likely to have told her, and the number of people who know about it is pretty small. Why?"

"Oh, I was just thinking if it weren't genuine, or she'd been tracking it down, and he beat her to it..."

"Somehow, I don't think so."

My words came out listless. The drinks were starting to have an effect. I didn't have the energy or the will for this kind of speculation. Léo saw it and dropped the matter. After a moment, he asked if I wanted something to eat.

"What have you got?"

"I'll check."

He left and came back with a plate of *cretons*—coarse québécois pâté loaded with pork fat—sliced French bread, a jar of mustard, and some dill pickles. "Comfort food," he said.

"Only in Québec."

The afternoon stretched on into evening. Léo's company was like a balm to the past two days. It felt good just to sit, relax, let someone take care of me. Our conversation petered out, but he gave no indication of wanting me to leave.

Finally, I drank the watery remains of a last Scotch and picked crumbs off the plate.

"Don't forget," he said as I stood up, "you can take time off if you need it."

"Thanks, but I'll be in tomorrow night."

"The show must go on?"

"Something like that."

⚜ ⚜ ⚜

The Rover was in a visitors' lot off to one side of the drive circling up to Léo's condo. Pink granite boulders and a few low shrubs embellished the half-moon centre. The arrangement brought to mind Christian's work in Caledon. A landscaper, an artist of the earth, his paint and canvas had been rock and tree, slope and plain, light and shade. He'd done Léo's property first, then some of Léo's acquaintances, then others. His creations were austere, beautiful and very much in demand. Who was tending them now that he was gone?

The rain had let up. A breeze from the south carried green, decaying odours from the lake. On a whim, I left the Rover where it was and walked to Craigleigh Gardens, four blocks away. The greyness of the evening, the early streetlamps shimmering off the rain-dark pavement, put me in a mood to sit by myself, out of doors, in the humid dusk.

After rain, Christian used to sit—often for hours, unmoving, impossible to speak to—beside a stretch of the Credit River running through Léo's property. I never knew what transfixed

171

him so completely in the spooling currents and doubted I could ever muster the intensity of sadness or peace that kept him rooted in one place for so long, but surely my frame of mind just then was something similar, however diluted.

The park wasn't deserted, as I'd hoped. Some dog owners had brought their wards to frolic on the grass. The animals ran and skidded while their guardians conversed in a tight little clique. Periodically, a raincoated figure would break away from the group and zero in on a squatting mutt, plastic bag in hand.

I found a bench away from the activity, swiped water from the back, and sat with my shoes on the seat. The city's background murmur, cotton-wooled by venerable oaks and maples, had a lulling effect. Without meaning to, I started turning over my conversation with Léo.

Ambition makes you uneasy.

He'd hit the nail on the head with that. In a world of my own making, the urge for fame would never outweigh the desire simply to do what you loved, and do it well. But I wasn't as naïve as he imagined. I did understand that talent and ambition had to be allied, otherwise a person's gifts frittered into—what had Elly called it?—dilettantism. The problem was, I couldn't make the nexus in myself. I was indifferent about getting ahead, jockeying for my share of the spotlight. Worse, my apathy didn't even have the decency to cloak itself in lofty moral precepts. Regardless of Léo's crack about sullying my art, I didn't judge people who were ambitious. I merely shied away from them.

"I'd expect you to insulate yourself from even considering that your friends might have been murdered because of someone else's hopes for glory," he'd said, and he'd gotten that right, too. Now that he'd planted the idea in my head, I couldn't just ignore it. What if Ulrike had discovered that

Mann was considering Laura for the *Liederkreis* premiere? Had she staked so much on her comeback ticket that she'd kill to hold onto it? I found it hard to believe. The scenario sounded too much like something out of opera: Ulrike, betrayed, wreaking vengeance on Mann and Laura, he for his treachery, she for the perfidious usurping of a second chance at fame.

Still, something niggled—a stirring of anger, the need for answers. Someone had killed a friend I had every right to have gone on knowing longer and robbed the world of a great man whose affection and respect I'd only just begun to enjoy. Ulrike's house wasn't far from Léo's. I could drive over before heading home.

I got off my bench and started back to Glen Road. Along the way, I recalled Mann telling me about Ulrike's public suicide attempt a decade before. What had happened that evening in Vienna? Had she been wearing long gloves? Did she remove them one finger at a time, like a burlesque dancer, or draw a razor and slice through silk or satin before anyone could stop her?

And did violence to herself make her capable of murder?

❧   ❧   ❧

Ulrike wasn't in when I drove by—a relief, since I hadn't figured out how to ask what I wanted to know. It wasn't my place to be making enquiries. Questions like that were better left to the police.

Just the same, when I got home, I debated leaving her a message to call. I made it as far as picking up the phone.

Sunday crept in still overcast and damp, inspiring me to further procrastination. Midafternoon had arrived before I drove back to Rosedale.

Fog shrouded the cypresses beside Ulrike's driveway, turning them into gloomy spires worthy of a canvas by Kaspar David Friederich. The house itself was completely dark. A rumour of chimes echoed within when I rang, but no footsteps sounded down the hall. I waited a few minutes, then gave up.

"Do you want to see the lady who lives there?"

I looked around for the voice that had addressed me. It seemed to have come from a gap between Ulrike's house and the one on the left. "Yes," I called out. "I don't suppose you know when she'll be back?"

A small figure emerged from the shadows: a girl of about seven or eight, dressed like Paddington Bear in yellow boots and a rain hat to match. "Are you her friend?"

"Not really, but I would like to see her."

"If you're not her friend, why do you want to see her?"

"I want to ask her something." I have this idea it's best to answer children's questions candidly. It's a notion I should lose; their literal inquisitiveness gets tedious quickly.

"She's in her back yard. Sitting. I was watching her. She's all alone. Is that yours?" She pointed to the Rover.

"Yes."

"My name's Tessa. What's yours?" Tessa seemed to have difficulty concentrating on one thing at a time.

"Vikkan."

She furrowed her brow in that winsome way only the very young can get away with. "How come your parents called you that?"

"How come yours called you Tessa?"

Never answer a question with a question, especially around children. "That's easy," she giggled. "I have an aunt, well, not really my aunt because she and Uncle Brian aren't married the way they're supposed to be, but Mommy says..."

"And you're named after her?" I cut in.

She nodded, wide-eyed. My powers of deduction must have impressed her. Her attention went back to the Rover. "Can you take me for a drive in your truck?"

So much for never accept rides from a stranger. "You'll have to ask your parents. And not today. I need to talk to the lady in the back yard. Do you think it's all right if I go around?"

"I guess so."

I said thank you—something else I have the idea you should always do with children, even when it's not really called for—and walked round to the back.

Ulrike was there, as Tessa had promised, sitting alone on her flagstone patio. A vine-covered pergola provided shade on a day when no sun shone. Her gaze was directed at a linden tree, dimly visible at the far end of the lawn.

I let myself in through the gate. She turned at the sound of the latch. The movement was slow, dreamlike.

"I hope I'm not disturbing you," I said, approaching from in front so she could see me better.

"Vikkan," she said, her voice spectral. "How thoughtful."

It took a moment to fathom her meaning: she thought I'd come to offer condolences. "I'm very sorry," I temporized, not sure what to say. "I know you were close to Herr Mann."

"Ja. Very close."

She sank back and looked beyond me to the linden. I sat down beside her at a low, wrought-iron table and turned my gaze in what I hoped was respectful silence toward the tree. After a few minutes, taking my cue from the object of our contemplation, I recited from Schubert: *"Die Lindendufte sind erwacht..."*

"...Sie seufzen und weben Tag und Nacht," she finished. "Yes. I cannot look at that tree without thinking of Schubert." She smiled weakly. "I have been staring at it all day. As yesterday.

I have no will for anything else."

"I understand."

She gestured to an empty glass on the table. "If you wouldn't mind, some water. I'm sorry, I should be doing this for you. So...*rücksichtsvoll*...considerate of you to come by."

I remembered from my previous visit that she drank mineral water. I went in through the French doors, traversed her long studio, and climbed the stairs up to the kitchen. The refrigerator held several bottles of Evian and a lemon with a wedge notched out. I found a knife in one of the drawers and cut the rest of the lemon, arranging it on a clean plate from the dishrack. I checked the cupboards and located a small serving tray. Ulrike struck me as someone who'd appreciate the niceties.

"The police came by," she said when I came back outside. She was still staring straight ahead.

"When?"

"*Gestern.* Yesterday. In the morning."

"Did you know then what had happened?"

"Yes. Anna called, on Friday. From Vienna. You know of Anna?"

"Herr Mann's daughter? Yes. He told me that you and she are friends."

"Since we were children." Ulrike unscrewed the bottle and poured half a glass, ignoring the lemon. Her hands trembled slightly. A parchment thinness of skin at the knuckles betrayed years not evident in her face. "The police must have gotten Anna's name from someone. Miss Gardiner, *vielleicht?* Anna telephoned me. She thought I knew."

"An unfortunate way to find out."

"*Ja.*" She took a sip of water.

I wished I knew her well enough to make condoling small talk. In the presence of her grief, I felt like an intruder. After a period of silence, I asked what the police had wanted.

"To know my whereabouts on Thursday night."

"Why?"

"Because I knew where Dieter was."

So March had acted quickly on his supposition that the break-in wasn't random. "That's my fault," I said. "I told them you and David Bryce knew he was in Elly's studio. You remember—you gave me a cheque? When Elly was signing out?"

"I remember. But I was at home when...it happened. Alone."

"I was by myself, too."

Ulrike rewarded me with a furtive smile, as if the fact of our two solitary natures formed a momentary bond. I decided to approach the question I'd come to ask. "You don't suppose the Schumann has anything to do with this?"

She turned her head sharply, the first sudden movement she'd made since I arrived. "The *Liederkreis?* But I thought what happened was a—" she sought the word "—*Vandalismus.* That the deaths were *ohne Sinn und Verstand.* Without reason."

"I thought so, too," I said, "but the police believe otherwise. The man in charge thinks the murders were intentional."

"But the proofs? They weren't stolen? Or damaged?"

"Not as far as I know."

"Then why...?"

I looked out over the expanse of lawn before us. In the pearly grey light, the cropped grass glowed lambent green. A birdbath off to one side had attracted two sparrows. I watched them jockey for position in the shallow water.

"Were you aware that Laura Erskine had seen the *Liederkreis?*" I asked. "Had sung it?"

She either missed the implications of my question, or chose to ignore them. "I did not," she replied simply. "Laura Erskine's doings ceased to be my concern the day she chose to leave me."

It was clear from her statement that whatever sorrow she felt, it encompassed only Mann. Laura had forsaken her, and ceased to exist some time before. I can't say I found her attitude odd. Grief is selfish; even murder is no cause for forgiveness.

We sat silent again, surveying the day's gloom. "Will you go ahead with the *Liederkreis* premiere?" I asked at length.

"Dieter wanted me to sing it. As does Anna."

"It's a beautiful work. I've always loved Schumann. I wish you the best with it."

"Thank you."

I had no further reason to stay. I had found out what I wanted and sensed that Ulrike would prefer to be alone. I got up and said goodbye. I was almost at the gate when she called out: "Vikkan, what did Dieter tell you of the *Liederkreis?*"

I looked back. She'd half-risen from her chair. "A bit about its history, not much more. Why?"

"You didn't know, then." She sank down into her chair. "I suppose it doesn't matter now."

"Know what?"

She hesitated. I stood where I was, my hand on the gate.

"It's not Schumann," she said finally.

"I don't understand."

"The *Liederkreis*. It's not by Schumann. It was written by his wife, Clara."

PART II

Eight

Es weiß und rät es doch keiner.
("But none can guess or explain it.")
   —*Liederkreis*, Opus 39, VI

I couldn't get the plastic pail—$2.99 on special at Zellers—
to fit under the antique faucets. I resigned myself to filling
it halfway. An enervated stream of water bled down the sides
and met with Pine Sol in the bottom. The resulting liquid had
the milky quality of Pernod over ice.

I carried the pungent solution from the women's washroom
on the second floor of the Conservatory back to Elly's studio,
knocked and waited. The devastation inside was scarcely
visible. The most noticeable object, the glassed-in bookcase
with Elly's Great Composers, hadn't been touched. A passerby
wouldn't have given the studio a second glance.

Presently, Elly's face appeared at the window, or rather, her
salt-and-pepper bun, looking wispier than usual. "I forgot to
tell you," she said, opening up, "the men's is out of order."

"I know. I went up there first. So, how shall we do this? You
straighten up while I play charwoman?"

Her mouth tightened at the cross-gender quip. "Why don't
you start on the window?" she said. A more manly task.

I set the pail down next to a scrub brush and a pile of
rags and picked up the plywood, hammer and nails I'd left
on her desk. "You're sure this is okay? Don't the police need

things left undisturbed?"

"I spoke to Inspector March earlier today. He said it would be all right. They've been over everything thoroughly."

It wasn't hard to believe. Aside from the general shambles, fingerprint powder bloomed like mildew everywhere.

"You're certain you want to teach in here again so soon?" I asked.

"I wouldn't have called you otherwise," she replied. "I hope you didn't have anything planned."

Truth was, I'd wanted to do some practising before I started at Evelyn.

I picked my way through the scattered music, avoiding the Turkish rug so I wouldn't grind soil into the nap. "Did you bring garbage bags? We should clear up this mess under the window first."

She came over with some plastic grocery sacks—what did people do for garbage before them?—along with a broom and dustpan. I crouched down and started picking glass off the shattered remains of her potted flowers.

"Too bad about these," I said. "Can any of them be saved?"

Elly bent over, studying them, lips pursed. "No." She removed a lethal-looking shard from a limp gloxinia. "They'll never recover from the shock."

"Seems a shame to throw them out."

"It can't be helped."

Once we'd dealt with the bigger pieces of glass, I held the dustpan while she resolutely swept up. Afterward, she went to work salvaging music from the floor while I started peeling duct tape off the cardboard covering the window.

"I paid a visit to Ulrike today," I said over my shoulder.

"That was thoughtful," she said, echoing Ulrike's sentiments. "How did she seem?"

"Pretty out of it." I tore off a long strip of tape, taking some paint with it. "Understandable, I guess, given her history with Mann."

"She had a history with Laura, too, you know."

"You'd never have guessed it." I removed the cardboard, folded it in half and hoisted up my plywood. "Actually, it was more than a sympathy call. I had something I wanted to ask her. Whether she knew Mann had had Laura sing through the *Liederkreis*."

"Why?"

"You do know the police think that what happened in here wasn't just a break-in gone wrong?"

"Surely you're not suggesting Ulrike—"

"Not really, and in any case, she didn't know." I toed in a first nail. "However, she did tell me something interesting."

"Oh, what's that?"

"Were you aware that the *Liederkreis* wasn't composed by Schumann?"

Had I thought I could surprise Elly? "You didn't know, then?" she asked, again echoing Ulrike's words.

"No, I didn't. Why the hell didn't someone tell me?" I hammered in another nail in two exasperated blows. "Well?"

"Well, what?"

I stopped and turned around. Elly had cleared a little circle on the floor and was sitting cross-legged in the middle, skirt over her knees like a wool-clad Buddha. "Why didn't you or Mann tell me the *Liederkreis* was by Clara?"

She blew some dirt off a sheet of music. "It wasn't my place. If Dieter wanted you to know, I'm sure he'd have said something. Perhaps he hoped you'd work it out for yourself."

"How was I supposed to do that? All I saw were the proofs. The title page says Schumann. The story Mann told me sounded convincing. What was I supposed to think? That he wasn't telling the truth?"

She sighed and looked up. "To be honest, Vikkan, I don't know. Dieter only said he had some sort of document proving it had been written by Clara. He never told me what."

"And of course you didn't ask."

"I assumed he'd show it to me when I saw him. Besides, he asked me not to say anything."

"But musicologists have been arguing for over a century whether Clara published under her husband's name. A chance to settle the debate isn't just something you keep under your hat!"

"That's always been an interesting speculation, hasn't it?" she responded. I could have throttled her. "Robert and Clara did write those Rückert songs together in 1841. You really can't tell which is by whom."

I turned back to the window, feeling like the butt of a private joke. "Morris-Jones might not have raised such a stink in Mann's class if she'd heard about this, you know."

All I got for an answer was a noncommittal "Mmm."

I finished hammering in the plywood. Elly came over to the armoire with a load of music. I got out of her way and addressed myself to the overturned cachepots on the other side of the room. Unlike the potted flowers, the larger plants had survived three days of horizontal neglect.

"You might be interested to know," I said, uprighting an aspidistra, "that I did at least a little research on the songs."

"Oh?" she said distractedly. "What?"

"I tracked down the poet. Ebert. Did you recognize the name?"

"No. I wondered about that."

"It's actually Schumann."

She stopped what she was doing. "Really?"

"According to Fischer-Dieskau's *Words and Music,* anyway.

It's a *nom de plume* he used on occasion when he wrote words for his own songs."

"How conscientious of you to have looked it up."

The faint praise told me she didn't like being one-upped in the *you didn't know, then?* department.

We returned to working in silence. I swept up earth and deposited it back in the big plants' plastic surrounds. Elly finished putting away her first batch of music. I went back to the corner by the window to take care of her philodendrons. Most people prefer one to a pot. Elly had six, trained around a pipe organ-like set of bamboo poles. The arrangement leaned against the armoire, which had prevented it from toppling completely. Getting behind to set it straight, I lost sight of Elly. When I came out, she'd gone over to her desk, taking a break. I sat on the piano bench and pulled out my cigarettes. She waggled a warning finger.

"So, what do you think?" I asked, putting them back.

She gave me a blank look.

"The *Liederkreis*. Is it connected with this?"

She nodded slowly, heavily. She'd been expecting me ask. "What I don't understand, though, is why wasn't it stolen? And why the break-in? If the police are right and someone came here planning on murder, doesn't that imply it was someone who knew Dieter or Laura? In which case, couldn't he or she have just knocked and come in?"

As if in response to her question, someone tapped on the studio door. Elly got up to answer. "Inspector March," she said, louder than necessary so I'd be warned. "This is a surprise."

"Miss Gardiner. I see you've started already. I thought maybe you could use a hand."

"How kind. I never realized that 'to serve and protect' included cleaning detail."

"It doesn't, but for you, I'm making an exception." He entered in a suit and tie and nodded in my direction. "Vikkan."

"Well," Elly said, "we could use an extra pair of hands. You can start by getting this fingerprint powder off everything." She pointed at the bucket of Pine Sol and the scrub brush.

March picked them up and carried them to her desk without comment. I wasn't sure whom I admired more: Elly for taking him at his word, or March for playing along. He shrugged off his jacket and rolled up his sleeves, but instead of going at black smudges, he crouched down and begin tearing up the taped outline where Laura had fallen.

By some sort of unspoken consent, Elly and I dropped the subject of the *Liederkreis,* as if March had broken in on a conversation that was none of his business. I watched him a moment, then went over to the desk myself and began wiping it down. When it was gleaming, I looked for the things that went on it: the leather pencil holder, the onyx and brass letter opener, the metal flip-up phone directory, the Rolodex. All were on the floor, treated for fingerprints but left there. "We do that sometimes," March said when I asked. Helpful.

The only thing I couldn't find was Elly's big glass paperweight. Since she was down on the floor again gathering music, I asked her if she could see it under the furniture.

"You won't find it," March answered. "We took it away."

Elly stared at him, distraught. "You don't mean that was what was used to..."

March shook his head. "No. According to the coroner, the weapon was something heavier. But of all the things that got knocked off your desk, only the paperweight was clean of prints. You didn't polish it recently, did you?"

"I don't believe so."

He sat back on his heels and let the scrub brush he'd been

using on the floor drip into the bucket. "The only other place we couldn't raise latents was outside the window. Meaning," he said, standing up in a single, easy motion, "that the murderer wasn't too worried about leaving prints inside."

Elly rose at the same time and put away some music, then turned to face him, arms crossed. "Inspector March," she said, "if you're implying that whoever did this was a regular to the studio, you should just come out and say it. There's no need for sinister insinuations."

"Who does use the studio?" March asked blandly.

"Any number of people. Students, other teachers. When I'm not here, the Conservatory rents it to whomever they please. Some teachers don't allow that, but I'm not one of them."

"That certainly narrows the field."

"Don't be sarcastic," she shot back, only just leaving out a schoolmarmish "young man!"

"What has your investigation turned up?" I put in. "That is," I appended, equally guilty of sarcasm, "if you feel you can tell us."

He flashed us an angry look. "What's the matter with you two? I'm not the enemy, you know."

It was Elly who spoke up. "I'm sorry," she said, not sounding in the least contrite. "We're both on edge with you here. I'd have thought you understood people get that way when the police are around. Childish, to be sure, but there it is."

The two of them locked eyes. March looked away after only a few seconds: two hundred pounds of law-enforcement outstared by five-feet-one of rumpled tweed. "Time out?" he suggested, more chastened than conciliatory.

Elly frowned, not quite ready to back down. She walked over to her club chair. "Help me get this thing up," she directed. "Off the rug."

He complied without a word and took the trouble to brush off the seat. After Elly was ensconced, he perched on the edge of the *récamier*, hunched forward, elbows planted on his knees.

"We don't know much, yet," he said, addressing us both. "Our scene-of-crime technicians and forensics have come up with next to nothing. It's this dirt that's the problem." He scuffed some potting soil with his toe. "It acts like a sponge. There should be spatter patterns, signs of struggle, but this stuff just sucks up everything.

"What we've pieced together comes mostly from testimony. Vikkan's already heard some of it. Mann left the studio around eight o'clock. We talked to the janitor here, Walter Kurek. He says he was loading cleaning equipment onto the elevator and saw Mann exchange a few words with one of the teachers, Mr. Bryce, just outside the washroom on this floor. We checked with Bryce. He confirms using the washroom around that time."

"Has the men's been out that long?" I asked Elly. March looked puzzled, so I explained. "The men's washroom for this wing is actually on the third floor, same as Bryce's studio. The women's is down on this floor. They're both singles, so when one's on the fritz, the other turns coed."

March nodded, as if the information made a huge difference to his case. Elly really had put the fear of God into him. "At eight-fifteen," he went on, "your friends had a visitor. The teacher across the hall—"

"Mrs. Wigrell," Elly interjected.

"—happened to be looking out of her studio, and saw someone at your door. Russell Spiers?" He glanced at Elly and me to make sure we knew who he was talking about. "She couldn't see who he was talking to."

"I wonder what he was doing here?" Elly said.

"Is that unusual?" March asked.

"Spiers is Head of Performance at the University," I told him. "The Edward Johnson Building is more his domain. But if he wanted to see Laura, there's no reason he wouldn't come over."

"I've spoken with him already," March said. "He says he was confirming an appointment."

"How did he know she'd be here?"

"They met earlier in the day. Apparently, she told him then. Anyway, Mrs. Wigrell says she watched Spiers leave, and then, at eight-thirty, she let in her last student of the day. She says she heard singing from over here, and someone playing the piano.

"Laura went out for coffee a little after that, as I already told Vikkan. Most likely, Mann made another trip to the washroom at the same time. Judging from the teas in his jacket and the number of bags we found in the garbage, it makes sense.

"The break-in had to have taken place during that time. When Mann came back, he saw the broken window and went to investigate. We found his prints on the latch and the lower part of the frame, and one of the things forensics turned up there were traces of dried vegetable matter—herbs, like his teas—on the ledge outside, meaning he leaned out. Lucky the rain didn't wash them away.

"The intruder probably hid behind those plants—" he nodded at Elly's philodendrons "—and waited till Mann stepped away from the window so there'd be room to take a good swing with whatever killed him."

"What about Laura?" I asked.

"I'd say when she came back and saw Mann's body, she tried to phone for help. The receiver was off the hook, with her prints on it. There were partial indexes on the nine and one as well. She never got through. Nine-one-one has no record. If the killer had hidden in that corner again—"

"But this is all conjecture," Elly interrupted. "You really have no idea what happened."

March sucked in a breath. "Yes and no, Miss Gardiner. We ran a computer model. Based on the data we have—placement and position of the bodies, prints, the layout of the room—the scenario works. But you're right, it's conjecture.

"One thing is certain, though. Mann and Laura were dead by nine o'clock. That's when Mrs. Wigrell left her studio. She swears the lights were off over here."

He looked from Elly to me, as if he hoped we could add something. I shook my head. His version of events sounded like Colonel-Mustard-in-the-library-with-a-candlestick. Surely the police could do better.

"But why all this?" Elly waved her hand around. "It feels so...personal. As if someone wanted to attack me, too."

March shook his head. "I don't think so. It's more likely an attempt at misdirection. Or to obscure the evidence. Frankly, I was hoping you'd spot something while you were cleaning up."

"I have noticed something." Elly said, twisting around. "My antimacassar. You know, the doily that goes on the back of my chair. It's missing."

March pursed his lips. "It could be what the killer used to wipe prints off the paperweight." He mulled it over, then stood up, flexing his shoulders. "We should get back to work. You might still see something."

We started by joining forces to roll up the rug. "I hope Janssen will pay to have this cleaned," Elly grunted as we leaned it beside the door. Afterward, I went back to wiping up the fingerprint powder, making my way clockwise around the room. By the time I reached the glassed-in display of music's greats and not-so-greats, March had finished by the desk and started ripping up the taped outline in front of the piano. I could see Elly's reflection behind me, busying herself with the last of her music. Her serried ranks of bronze heads looked on. If only they could talk...

It was 9.45 PM when I checked my watch, fifteen minutes before I had to be at Evelyn. I made hasty apologies and prepared to leave.

"Vikkan," March called out when I was at the door, "would you mind coming by Fifty-two Division tomorrow?"

"What for?"

"A few questions, that's all." *Don't ask, just do it.*

"What time?"

"Morning would be best."

I said I'd be there, but not until afternoon.

ꢲ   ꢲ   ꢲ

As if to apologize for Thursday night's Bay Street buffoons, Evelyn's Sunday clients were well-behaved—a little too well, for my taste.

I started off the night with a moody rendition of "Spring in Manhattan" that sounded like Bach cross-pollinated with Gene Puerling. A smattering of applause followed. Next, I moved into a gently lilting version of Johnny Mercer's "Early Autumn". Some chord changes in the song recall the theme from "A Man and a Woman". I snuck in a reference to the movie soundtrack, and someone chuckled. Staying in a seasonal theme, I played some angular variations on "Summertime". A woman hummed along quietly. I finished up with "Let It Snow", and began again: "April in Paris", *"Les Feuilles Mortes"*, "Summer of '42", "Winter Wonderland".

As the set progressed, the patrons grew noticeably quiet. Warm applause followed hard on each number. Appreciative murmurs rose from the banquettes. It was every lounge pianist's dream, except that, perversely, I found myself wishing they'd stop paying so much attention. In a venue like Evelyn, music should be an adjunct, not the main attraction.

"Nice playing," Toby Ryan, the bartender, commented afterward.

"Thanks."

He cracked a bottle of Naya and pushed it across the bar. "There's a guy asked for you," he said, nodding in the direction of the piano. "He had someone else with him, but he's gone now."

I looked over, and immediately wished I hadn't. Russell Spiers, alone with a martini, raised his arm and gestured for me to join him.

"Gee thanks, Toby."

"Not a friend?"

"You could say."

I could have ignored Spiers' summons, but there were some things I wanted to ask him. At least, that's what I told myself. The truth is, I have trouble being impolite. Churchill said a gentleman is never *unintentionally* rude, but I still hadn't mastered the art of the calculated slight.

Spiers' eyes drifted from my lapels to my shoes. "Apparently you haven't lost your charms," he said, sliding over and patting the seat.

"Meaning?"

"I was just talking to John Sanger. He seemed quite smitten with you."

"John who?"

"Of course, I forget, you're above such things." He sipped at his drink. "John Sanger. An agent. An important one. You should be flattered. Then again, it could have been more than your playing that took his fancy. You do look ever-so-manly in a tux."

He drained his martini. To judge from his breath, it wasn't the first. I hoped he wasn't going to make Evelyn his regular watering hole. Showing up twice in less than a week was already twice too often.

"Terrible about Laura," he said, switching subjects the way people do when they've crossed the line from a few social drinks to the start of a bender. "She had such a career ahead of her. I got her started singing, you know. Without me, she'd have graduated with a so-so degree in piano and wound up teaching schoolkiddies out in Bumfucks, North Toronto. Do you know how many of those we crank out every year? It's depressing."

"I understand you saw Laura Thursday evening."

"Where'd you hear that?"

"From Inspector March. The detective in charge of the investigation."

"Been getting palsy-walsy with the fuzz, have we? Funny, I never picked you as the type to go for butch."

"What were you seeing her about?"

If the question sounded out of place, he didn't seem to notice. "We'd had a meeting that afternoon. Howard Snelling called just after she left. His agency had decided to represent her. He wanted to discuss a contract. I passed on the message."

"Was Mann in the studio when you saw her?"

"We only talked at the door. I couldn't see in. Awful to think she was going to be murdered just after that." He picked up his glass, discovered it was empty and raised it to a passing waiter.

Spending time with Spiers was bad enough without watching him get drunk, so I cut to the one thing in particular he might shed some light on. "You don't happen to know what Professor Morris-Jones' problem with Mann was, do you? I hear you two had an argument the day after his master class."

"Is that something else you brown-nosed from your hunky police detective?"

"Forget I asked." I got up to leave.

"Oh, no—don't go rushing off." He put a heavy hand on my arm. "You want to hear about dear little Bernice?" Her name came out *Berneesh,* wreathed in gin. "I'll tell you. Her first quarrel with Mann was just that: he was a man. I used to think she was a dyke, but I've heard not. Must be sending roses to her vibrator, then, because no male's getting in that box, let me tell you." He snickered. "Her second problem," he said, lowering his voice, "was she thought Mann was hiding something." He tried for a significant look, but his eyes kept slewing off.

"Something to do with a certain song cycle?" I hazarded.

"You know about it?"

"I've played it."

"For someone who supposedly turned his talented little backside on music, you do get around."

I was beginning to think that if I wanted to find out what had brought on Morris-Jones' outburst at Mann's class, I could have spared myself some abuse and asked her directly. Then again, maybe not. "How do you know about the *Liederkreis?*" I asked.

"The Dean told us on Wednesday. Apparently, Mann was planning to donate it to the Faculty library. God, what a coup that would have been. Imagine the publicity. The Great Mann honouring us..." His eyes glistened.

"Morris-Jones?" I prompted.

"Oh, yes. You're going to enjoy this. So-o-o like Bernice. From somewhere—don't ask me where—she got this idea into her progesterone-addled brain that these unknown songs weren't composed by Schumann at all, but by his devoted wife." His martini arrived. He tested it with his tongue, pursed his lips, then downed half. "Did I say devoted? Aren't there rumours about her and Brahms, after Schumann threw himself in the Rhine? Imagine, there he was, suicidal, locked in the nuthouse, and the two of them—"

"Why did she think the songs weren't written by Schumann?" I had a hard time making the question sound offhand.

"Who knows? I told her what a rude bitch she was at Mann's class, and she started in on how this *Liederkreis* wasn't Schumann's, how Mann was sitting on evidence that his wife had composed it, and on and on and on. I haven't a clue where she came up with the idea. PMS, most likely."

"Did she say what proof he was withholding?"

"I was too pissed to ask. Mann donating those proofs was just what we needed to lure Doug Rawlings away from the Con. You don't kick a gift horse in the teeth." He drained his martini. "Might not have been such a good thing, as it turns out, but still..."

"What do you mean?"

He sucked the olive from his skewer. "What I mean is, we aren't getting it. That's all. And anyway, what do you care?" He aimed the little plastic spear and threw it at his glass. It landed wide and skittered across the table.

I looked at my watch. "I've got to get going."

"So soon? And here we were, just starting to get friendly. Well, if you must, be a sweetie and order me another." He waved his hand in the direction of the bar. "Beefeater, extra dry. Oh, and Vikkan—that hunky detective? Don't be fooled by all the muscles. You know what they say: Man of steel, heels of helium."

He leered, what I think was supposed to be a knowing look—a hard one to get right when you're three or four martinis on.

Back at the bar, I gave his order, then sat at the piano and started noodling, one of those aimless introductions that could lead into anything.

If what Spiers had said was true, not only was the *Liederkreis* less a of secret than I'd been led to believe, but the work's real composer, which for some reason Mann hadn't seen fit to tell me, was also, if not exactly general knowledge, at least a circulating rumour. And everyone, including Janssen at the Conservatory, had heard about his intention to donate the proofs to the Faculty.

What had Mann been up to, dissembling the authorship of the work? And how had Morris-Jones found out? I couldn't imagine him telling her. And what had she planned to do? Confront him? Call him out?

Some morbid subconscious prompting led me from improvising freely into playing Ellington's "Mood Indigo". I didn't realize what I'd done until I found myself humming: *When I get that mood indigo / I could lay me down and die.* I segued into something livelier, with no references to death or dying. "Gonna Sit Right Down and Write Myself a Letter", I think.

Nine

Groß ist der Männer Trug und List.
("Vast are the cunning lies men tell.")
  — *Liederkreis*, Opus 39, II

"Do you recognize this?" March asked.

I was in his bare-bones office at Fifty-two Division and it was starting to feel as if someone had turned up the air-conditioning. On the desk between us lay Mann's briefcase. The *Liederkreis* title page stared up at me: *Als Geschenk seiner geliebten Braut zugeeignet...*

"Yes."

"So you've seen it before?"

I nodded.

"And would you care to tell me why it hasn't come up in any of our previous discussions?"

"I didn't think it was relevant. Not at first, anyway."

"That decision was not yours to make."

"I'm sorry. I may have been mistaken."

"May have?"

"I was going to bring it up today."

Oil-on-troubled-waters didn't work. His eyes brewed up winter clouds. "Let's get one thing straight. You tell me what you know, *I* decide what's important. Is that clear?"

I raised my hand smartly two inches in front of my forehead. "Yes, sir!"

His look turned dangerous. Massing thunderheads, rumbling volcanoes, the sizzle of a fuse toward dynamite...

"Has Elly said anything?" I asked, pretending not to notice.

"No, Vikkan," he landed hard on my name, "she hasn't. What is it with you two? Did you think a cop wouldn't understand the value of this?" He jerked his head toward the briefcase. "In a *murder* investigation? Jesus Christ, we're not morons. Some of us did get past grade two."

"Look, I said I was sorry, okay? And for whatever it's worth, I did notice you pronounce German rather well."

"What the hell has that got to do with anything?"

"Leads me to think you made it past grade two."

As quickly as it came up, his anger blew over. "You'd make a lousy fucking detective, you know that? I grew up in Kitchener. Heard German every Saturday at the market. Gave me a taste for learning it. Now, tell me what you know about this. Assume for the time being I can follow you."

I took him at his word. "What you're looking at are pre-publication proofs for a previously unknown group of lieder which, according to the title page, were composed by Robert Schumann. Dieter Mann's daughter discovered them last year, and, from what I've heard, he brought them to Toronto to discuss housing them in the Faculty of Music Library at U of T. Mann also wanted to establish whether Ulrike Vogel—a long-time acquaintance of his, you've already spoken to her—would be a suitable candidate to premiere the songs.

"Their value as such is more historical than monetary. Originally, I was under the impression their importance lay in the date at the bottom of the title page: 1839. Schumann is not supposed to have written lieder of any significance until 1840, making a find like this more or less equivalent to unearthing a dozen phthalo and aquamarine canvasses by Picasso all signed a year earlier than his Blue Period. However, I now have reason to believe that their real worth lies in the fact that the songs were not composed by Schumann at all, but by Clara Wieck—"

"—his wife, the famous nineteenth-century virtuoso." A corner of his mouth twitched while he watched my reaction. "Like I said, Vikkan—past grade two. Now do me a favour. Check it over."

"For...?"

I got another just-do-it look, like the one he'd given me the night before.

I pulled Mann's briefcase over. March busied himself with papers, then swiveled to his computer. I leafed through the songs, humming occasional snippets of melody. After a few minutes, I said everything looked just as I remembered it.

"All there?" he asked, eyes glued to the screen.

"Yes."

"Nothing missing?"

"That's what I said. You hardly need me to check page numbers."

He two-finger typed a string of characters, punched Enter, and turned around. "I phoned Anna Mann on Friday, in Vienna. Miss Gardiner gave me her name. She was pretty broken up, but luckily, she's some kind of lawyer. Dealing with her father's death on foreign soil gave her something to hold on to.

"Saturday, she called back and asked about Mann's effects. She knew he had this *Liederkreis* with him, and unlike you, she thought it might be important. She gave me the low-down, including the part about it being by Schumann's wife."

"Fiancée. They didn't get married until 1840."

He disregarded the correction. "She was worried the proofs

might have been stolen. After she told me what to look for, I went hunting."

"And found them, so why ask me to check them over?"

He searched my face. I wasn't sure what he was looking for, and his gaze was difficult to hold. "Something's missing."

"What?"

"The document proving the songs were composed by Clara Wieck." He studied my expression a few seconds longer. "You didn't know, then?" he asked.

That phrase again. "No, I didn't." I said irritably. "Up till now, I've only heard that Schumann didn't write them. If there's proof, I certainly haven't seen it."

He nodded, satisfied. "According to Anna, there's a letter from the publishers, addressed to Schumann. It identifies the songs as Clara's and asks Schumann to proofread them. The publication was going to be a surprise, a present of some sort, otherwise I guess she would have done it herself."

"Are there copies of this letter?"

"Anna says no."

"You think it was stolen?"

He shrugged. "It's not in Mann's briefcase. It's not in Miss Gardiner's studio. It's not at Mann's hotel."

"He was close to Ulrike Vogel. Could he have left it with her?"

"I already checked. Negative."

It came to me abruptly that if he'd spoken to Anna on Saturday and had already investigated the missing letter with Ulrike, he'd known about the *Liederkreis* when he dropped in at Elly's studio on Sunday. His *Do you recognize this?* bit, and the anger that went with it, had been a sham.

"Do you enjoy playing games with people, Inspector March?" I asked.

He gave me a blank stare. "Do you enjoy non-sequiturs?"

"You knew about this when you came by Elly's studio last night. Was it fun waiting to see if we'd say anything? Acting pissed off just now?"

"You want me to apologize?"

"You asked for my cooperation. You have a shitty way of eliciting it."

"Nobody's saying you have to like me."

"You got that right."

Something went on behind his eyes. For a split second, they looked like February ice on Lake Ontario. He looked down. "Can we just get on with this?"

I'd originally figured on having to tell him about the *Liederkreis* itself before explaining how it might connect with the murders, but since he was already up to speed, I jumped straight to Ulrike, her expectations of premiering it, Mann's reservations.

He took notes, frowning when I finished. "Ulrike doesn't have a strong alibi. She says she left the Conservatory at seven-thirty, right after you saw her, and drove straight home. A neighbour saw her car pull in at eight o'clock. She took a phone call shortly afterwards, which we've confirmed, but it doesn't mean much. She could have gone out again."

For some reason, I found myself wanting to defend Ulrike. "But you understand, she's only a suspect if she knew that Mann was having second thoughts. That he'd been auditioning Laura. I asked her, and she said no."

"You asked? When?"

"Yesterday."

"You're telling me that even then, you knew this music might be important?"

"I was only trying to help. 'Cooperate.'"

He looked as if he wished he'd never used the word. "In future, let me handle the questions. What else can you tell me?"

I told him what I'd heard about Mann's intention to donate the proofs to the Faculty, and Janssen's ever-so-polite directive that I keep my mouth shut. March looked grim. Doug Rawlings' money and the competition between the Faculty and the Conservatory were news to him. I guess I hadn't been the only one who'd neglected to tell him things.

Finally, I brought up the subject of Morris-Jones.

"Already talked to her," he said.

"About what?" I asked, surprised. He'd only found out about the *Liederkreis* on Saturday. He couldn't possibly have investigated Mann's peculiar silence about its real composer and Morris-Jones' academic *idée-fixe* already.

"Her name came up when I spoke to Ulrike Vogel. The call Ulrike received on Thursday night? The one proving she was at home? It came from Morris-Jones. She was trying to locate Mann."

※　　※　　※

It was one-thirty when I left Fifty-two Division. I didn't stand a chance of getting a table at one of the crowded restaurants on Queen Street, so I purchased Japanese take-out from Village by the Grange and went across the road to AGO—the Art Gallery of Ontario. The Henry Moore in the courtyard looks like a mouth biting someone's ass. I sat on the lower mandible and opened up my soba noodles and teriyaki. The weather had gone back into pseudo-summer mode.

The meeting with March had left me with some odd feelings. I'd observed a change in his behaviour the more we talked. While I'm-the-police-and-you're-a-civilian never quite disappeared, a different side of him started to emerge. Familiar, almost. Buddy-buddy. *Let's work on this together.* It was as if he were playing a solo variation on good-cop/bad-cop. And it worked. I enjoyed earning good-cop's approval. Worse, a devil at my shoulder started whispering Spiers' drunken comments in my ear.

March and I had discussed Morris-Jones. He'd already heard about her antics at Mann's class, but wanted my version anyway. I told him what I'd learned from Spiers, that she knew the *Liederkreis* had been composed by Clara Wieck. He nodded: *That's the kind of thing I need from you.* I couldn't help wondering again how she'd found out. Surely not from Mann. Ulrike? I didn't think so. If Mann wanted the composer of the *Liederkreis* kept secret, Ulrike would have played along. And I couldn't see her deigning to confide in Morris-Jones.

March wanted my opinion: Her public baiting of Mann notwithstanding, was Morris-Jones a likely suspect? The one thing she could be expected not to do was steal and thus further obscure the fact that Clara Wieck had composed the *Liederkreis*.

Next, he asked for my thoughts on why Mann hadn't told me—or the Dean of the school to which he was planning to donate the proofs—that the work was misattributed. "Could it be a fake? Publisher's letter and all?"

I shook my head. "Mann's teaching was unorthodox, he liked poking fun at the musical establishment, but I can't see him perpetrating a hoax."

"An eccentric, in other words."

"More like 'unconventional.'"

"What about those teas he carried around with him?"

It seemed a particularly banal example from which to infer

eccentricity. "He was concerned about his health, that's all. The man *was* over eighty."

March picked up a folder. *"Betula, agropyron, veronica officianalis, cichorium."* From the halting way he read, I guessed no one at the Kitchener market spoke Latin. "The herbs forensics identified on the window ledge."

"Birch, couch grass, speedwell, chicory," I translated.

He whistled. "Impressive."

"Past grade two, you know."

"I have no doubt."

He kept on with questions about Mann, asking almost nothing about Laura, a clear indication of where he intended to focus his investigative efforts. I told him if he wanted to know Mann better, he should pump Elly. He winced and said he'd tried that, last night at the studio. She must have rapped his knuckles a few more times after I'd left.

Toward the end of the interview, he leaned back in his chair and clasped his hands behind his head. The posture looked stagey, like something Humphrey Bogart or Dana Andrews would do before dropping a bombshell. "There's one more thing. Mann and Laura had a visitor inside the studio prior to the break-in."

"How do you know?"

"Mrs. Wigrell, the teacher across the hall. She heard Laura singing at eight-thirty."

"So you said yesterday."

"She also heard someone at the piano."

He prompted me with his eyes, as if he'd made a point I wasn't getting. I shook my head. "Sorry, I'm not following you."

"Mann's left hand was crippled. So who was playing? And why haven't they spoken up?"

203

Never ridicule ignorance, Uncle Charles used to say. *Ignorance signifies lack of knowledge, not lack of intelligence.* "He was missing two fingers," I said, keeping a perfectly straight face, "not five. He was more than capable of sketching in a left-hand part. Sorry. No mysterious visitor."

March sat forward, deflated. "Oh, well. Live and learn."

We seemed to be finished. March stood up and offered his hand. The grip was firm, surprisingly warm, and caught me off guard. Was he saying thanks, or had his usual lack of manners merely slipped?

✄   ✄   ✄

I fed the last of my soba noodles to a couple of pesky gulls, then drove over to the university to pay a visit to Professor Morris-Jones.

As a student, I'd never been inside her office. Given her garish taste in clothing, I imagined a room similarly bedizened. I was wrong. Neatly ordered white melamine bookshelves stretched the length of one wall. An uncluttered desk and Kawai upright occupied the one facing. A floor-to-ceiling window at the end gave onto Philosopher's Walk. Even the poster over her desk came as a surprise. Instead of a labial lily by Georgia O'Keefe or one of Tamara de Lempicka's monumental nudes, an ink sketch of Beethoven scowled forth majestically.

The woman herself, however, was *comme d'habitude.* Today's poncho was fuchsia—a lovely match for her orange hair—and her fragrance smelled like patchouli cut with turpentine.

"Wot the 'ell do you want?" she asked, glowering out of the doorway.

"May I come in?"

"I'm busy."

"This won't take long."

She marched into the room, but since she didn't slam the door, I followed her in. She whirled around. "Well? Wot is it?"

"You've heard about Dieter Mann, I imagine," I began lamely.

"'Course I 'ave. Don't be daft." Her North English vowels scraped the air like fingernails on slate. "I read the papers, don't I? And I've already been 'arassed by the police. Get to the point."

"I couldn't help noticing you were out to get him last Wednesday."

"So what? Fuckin' bastard deserved it."

"Did your...feelings...by any chance have anything to do with a certain piece of music that's recently come to light? One you felt wasn't quite what it's being made out to be?"

She glared, not saying a word—all the confirmation I needed.

"I was wondering how you found out."

"What are you, a bleedin' detective all of a sudden?" She sat down heavily in front of the Kawai. "'E waltzes in 'ere, shows the Dean some music, says 'e wants to see it 'oused in our library. Dean tells us on Wednesday: an unknown work by Schumann, very important, significant acquisition, blah, blah, blah. First I've 'eard about it, isn't it? So I asks 'is 'ighness, 'When did Mann discover it?' 'Last year sometime,' 'e says. Roight. Nobody sits on a thing like that for a year. So I did a little research, didn't I? Called everybody I knew to find out if they'd 'eard anything. Nothing. Nobody's seen it. Nobody's 'eard about it. Finally, Dennis Bouchard in London says, 'Why not call Mann's daughter?' So I did. Introduced myself. Asked her what the bloody 'ell was going on."

"Not in those words, I hope."

"Don't be a prig. Daughter tells me she's the one 'oo found

it. Says no, she doesn't think 'er father's shown it to anyone. But 'e's the Great Mann, isn't 'e, so the thing must be legit if 'e says so, right? Then she tells me, like I already know, about some letter 'e 'as sent off for authentication. Definitely the goods, she says. Paper, watermark, ink...the whole kit and caboodle. I ask her, 'What letter?' 'Why,' she says, 'the one that proves this *Liederkreis* is by Clara Wieck.'"

"So it was Anna who told you?"

"Wot's it to you?"

"I got the impression Mann didn't want the information to be general knowledge—"

"Too bloody roight 'e didn't."

"—but Russell Spiers said you knew somehow."

She nearly spat. "Slimy ponce. Bleedin' sod thought it was a big joke. First 'e asks what proof I 'ave, then 'e says: 'What's the difference? If Mann wants us to 'ave it, 'oo cares 'oo wrote it? The publicity's great.'"

She stood up and stomped over to the window. "You've 'eard about that pig Rawlings, 'aven't you?" she asked, addressing the view outside.

"Yes."

She was oddly quiet a moment. "I'd like to see us to get 'is endowment," she said finally, "same as everybody else. Wot do I care if the money comes from a muck-for-brains 'oo only wants 'is name in lights? An' it's true, if Dieter-fuckin'-Mann gave us those proofs, it'd be in all the papers. Sure to catch Rawlings' eye. Spiers was right. I could see 'is point." The admission didn't come easily. She faced me again, her face hard. "But there's no fuckin' way I could just sit tight and let Mann make fast and loose with 'istory. Even if it served our interests."

"You're sure he intended to conceal the truth?"

Her expression could have curdled milk.

"But a lot of Clara's music's been published," I pointed out, "with her name on it. Why would he do that?"

"You're a fuckin' expert all of a sudden?"

"I've been told he brought the letter to Toronto. That he kept it with the proofs. It's missing now."

"Sod probably flushed it down the loo."

Her patchouli was starting to make me woozy, but I had one more question. March had no doubt already asked, but I wanted to hear her answer myself.

"Why were you trying to locate Dieter Mann on Thursday night?"

Right away, I knew I'd stepped over the information-fishing line. "None o' your fuckin' business, Lantry," she growled, advancing on me, her perfume acting like a riot shield. "None o' your goddamn fuckin' business."

❧   ❧   ❧

I went home to work on scales. And clean out my ears. Hollywood's version of a musician is one who never practises. He or she can play anything at the drop of a hat. A saxophonist jams soulfully on a tune he's never heard. A violinist performs Mendelssohn after a week-long amorous interlude during which she hasn't so much as resined her bow.

Conversely, in films about athletes, much is made of the training before the big match, the big fight, the big game. The tedium of finger exercises obviously doesn't hold a candle to the sex appeal of grimacing faces and sweating bodies. Just the same, real musicians practise, for hours every day, to stay in shape. To some, it's a grind, a necessary adjunct to the high of performing. For me, it's an end in itself: part physical activity; part meditation; part, if one is predisposed to think that way, worship or prayer.

Musicians tend to store up stress in funny places. For me, it's usually the thumbs. I didn't realize how much strain I'd been under until I started practising contrary motion scales. Beginning at the middle of the piano, the right hand flies up the keyboard while the left plummets down. If the thumbs, which cross under the other fingers, aren't perfectly supple, the hands go out of sync. That day, what should have resembled the furling and unfurling of eagles' wings sounded more like two crabs scuttling in opposite directions. On crutches. It was going to take a lot of time to work out the kinks.

Time I wasn't going to get. The phone rang. Elly, of course. "I'm not disturbing you, am I? I have a favour to ask." *What else is new?* "I need you to do some coaching. Now, don't say anything—I know you don't like it, and normally I wouldn't ask, but I have a load of students preparing for exams right now. Laura was helping out—"

"Can't you find someone at the Con?"

I took her silence as mute esteem for my talents. Or my suckerdom. Voice teachers are gods. They perform the magic, unlocking the gold imprisoned in their students' throats. Vocal coaches, on the other hand, are behind-the-scenes lackeys. With their usually underpaid help, singers practise entries, get used to accompaniments, and have hammered into them that *Fräulein* rhymes with "oil-line", not "how fine".

"How many students are we talking about?" I asked.

"Just one, really. She's Grade Eight. I've arranged to accommodate all the others. Her name is Janice Cleary."

"Soprano, painfully shy, frizzy brown hair?"

"You know her?"

"She was with Laura last week, at your studio. A friend of Siobhan Rawlings."

"Yes, well, I didn't want to burden you with that one. Not

the way Janssen keeps tabs on anything that has Rawlings' name attached."

"A wise decision." *Faded-denim eyes inspecting me like a side of beef...*

Janssen's preoccupation with Rawlings reminded me of something I'd been meaning to ask. "Elly, you don't happen to know why Mann wanted the *Liederkreis* proofs housed at the Faculty, do you? Janssen was the one who told me about it first, on Saturday. He was worried Rawlings would find out. He thought I already knew."

"He spoke to you, too, did he?" Elly clucked. "I thought it was ghoulish, worrying about something like that so soon after what happened. I told him as much."

Bravo, Elly. "So why did Mann want the Faculty to have the proofs? Not to cast aspersions, but aren't there dozens of more suitable institutions?"

She sighed. "I was wondering if you'd ask."

"You know, then?"

"I think so. It was because of my father. To make a long story short, the accident that injured Dieter's hand happened when the Allies occupied Vienna. Sanitary conditions were appalling. People died from paper cuts and hangnails. Penicillin was extremely scarce. Father managed to get it for Dieter."

"Not by way of Harry Lime, I hope."

"I don't find that amusing."

"Sorry."

"Father was just one of hundreds of Canadian soldiers in Vienna. I have no idea how he came to befriend Dieter. Unlike a lot of men his age, he never talked about the war.

"At any rate, when the Allies pulled out, the two of them lost contact. When I first met Dieter in New York, he commented on my name, and told me about the Corporal

Gardiner who, for all intents and purposes, had saved his life. It turned out to have been Father. That was the first I ever knew of it."

"You alluded once to you and Mann having 'something in common.' Was that it?"

"It was."

"You think Mann chose a Canadian university by way of saying thank you?"

"I can't say for sure. It seemed unsuitable to pry."

"As unsuitable as inquiring why he didn't want anyone to know his thank-you present wasn't exactly as advertized?"

She didn't answer. I knew better than to ask again. "I'll take Janice. What's the music?"

Elly recited the list, sounding relieved. "I've got copies of anything you don't have. I can give them to Janice."

"No. I'll come by and pick them up. Are you at the studio?"

"Yes, until seven."

❧   ❧   ❧

I drove over half an hour later. Elly handed me the music through the door, busy with a lesson. I really should have checked first, since the main reason I'd gone to the Con was to carry on our conversation.

I justified the wasted trip by giving in to an urge for jelly doughnuts at the Con's unofficial purveyor of caffeine and carbohydrates on Bedford Road.

With three blueberry-filleds and a large coffee in hand, I took a table near the window and amused myself watching people come and go from the St. George subway station across the street.

There'd been a time when my every day started and finished at St. George. Mornings, I emerged for rounds of classes and rehearsals at the Faculty. Nights, I got sucked into its bowels again and whisked back to my apartment on the Danforth. I tried imagining myself amongst the periodic crowds that issued from the station half a decade later while I hunted out the scant filling in my doughnuts and chased powdered sugar coating with not-half-bad coffee.

A Hammond-organ grin and boyish thatch of blond hair interrupted my reverie: David Bryce, inches from my table, shucking off his expensive leather knapsack. "Hey, Vikkan," he said. "You looked lost."

"It happens sometimes."

"Can I join you?"

I moved Janice's music wordlessly to one side. He set down his pack and started rummaging inside. "Looking for my wallet," he apologized. As if I cared.

"Why not keep it in your back pocket like everyone else?"

"Doesn't look good. Breaks the line." He extracted an Eddie Bauer billfold and picked off a piece of lint. "I'll be right back."

He returned with coffee. "Terrible about what happened," he said, ripping open sugar packets. "I heard you were with Elly Gardiner when she found the bodies. How's she taking it?"

"Like a trooper."

"She would." He shook his head in contrived amazement. "An incredible woman. I really admire her."

I wondered how he'd react if I said the feeling was less than mutual.

"Her connection with Dieter Mann was kind of odd, though, don't you think?" he asked.

"Meaning?"

"Don't get me wrong. Elly's one of the best we have. But let's face it—she's not in the same league as Mann."

The assessment got my back up. So did the proprietorial we. "None of us is," I replied tartly.

"What was he like to work with?"

"I enjoyed it." I wasn't about to share the full extent of my pleasure, not with Bryce.

"You're so lucky." He shook his head again. "I was really looking forward to rehearsing with him."

"Ulrike tells me she'll be going ahead with the *Liederkreis* premiere."

He sipped his coffee. "That's right. She wasn't going to, not at first, anyway. She said she could never do it, not without Mann. I convinced her to think it over. I mean, what better tribute could she give him than to sing his great discovery?" He leaned closer. "I feel so bad for her. I mean, there's so much tragedy in her life already. And with all that talent. You've played for her, you must have some idea." Wide, green eyes begged me to agree.

"You'll be accompanying for her, of course," I said.

He looked down. "She's come to rely on me."

"Teaching history and theory not enough for you any more?"

"I'd like to think I've paid my dues."

"You've done a good job. Your name's on a lot of the Conservatory books now." Alongside Molly Peterson's, the brilliant, lonely woman he'd exploited to get it there.

"It helps to keep a high profile." His quick smile showed fewer teeth than usual. "Say, look, I really should thank you again for filling in last week. I hated to miss that concert."

"What was the problem?"

He made a face. "Stones. Can you imagine? It sounds so old-fashioned. Like gout or dropsy. But they're gone now.

Past." The pun came off smoothly. He'd used it before.

"I enjoyed working with Ulrike," I white-lied. "And it did get me a preview of the *Liederkreis.*"

"Beautiful, isn't it? Those songs..." Words deserted him. "What did Laura think of them? I couldn't believe Mann's generosity in sharing them..." Speechless again. "Mind you, Ulrike didn't think it was such a good idea."

A warning bell went off inside my head. "Say again?"

Bryce frowned. "I said, Ulrike didn't like the idea. You understand, she's come to think of those songs as—"

"No, not that," I interrupted. "Are you telling me Ulrike knew Laura had sung through the *Liederkreis*?"

"I mentioned it to her. Why?"

"She told me she didn't know."

"You *asked* her?" He didn't pretend not to see the implications. "Come on, Vikkan, you can't be thinking she's involved in Mann's death."

"Mann's *and* Laura's."

"When did you talk to her?"

"Sunday."

"Two days afterward? She'd still be upset, forgot I told her, that's all. When I said she didn't like Mann showing the work around, I only meant in a general kind of way." The backpedalling was smooth; it might even have been the truth.

"Do you mind if I ask you something?"

He shrugged. "Sure."

"What did you think when you interrupted Laura and me going over the *Liederkreis* with Mann?"

"Think? I don't know. Generosity, like I said—"

"I hate to burst your bubble, but it was more than artistic largesse. Mann wasn't satisfied with Ulrike's singing. He was looking for someone else to premiere the work."

Bryce's face went blank. "No way," he said flatly. "He would never have done that."

"You'll have to take my word for it."

"But he wanted Ulrike to sing the *Liederkreis*. He and his daughter both wanted it."

"Funny, that's more or less how Ulrike put it, too."

ズ ズ ズ

I tried not to lose myself in speculation after Bryce left. Ulrike's denying that she knew Mann had asked Laura to sing through the *Liederkreis* might have been nothing more than Bryce claimed: the oversight of a grief-stricken woman. The best thing for me to do would be to pass what I'd just learned on to March and leave it at that. Let him deal with what could be an understandable and innocuous deviation from the truth.

I polished off my last doughnut and had a look through Janice's music—generic Grade Eight material: a couple of Italian art songs, a Baroque recitative, a Fauré I didn't know, a Schubert I did. The requisite twentieth-century song was by Peter Warlock, a spirited little ditty called "Robin Goodfellow". The botanical refrain appealed to me: *"...with lily, germander, and sops in wine..."*

There were two other customers in the shop: a grey-haired woman whose gaunt features and ramrod posture could have stemmed from iron-willed Rosedale breeding or a life on the streets, and a student with books spread in front of her. Behind the counter, a goateed teenager was shooting the breeze with a lookalike friend in a Raptors cap.

"...so I says, yeah, I remember her. He didn't have a picture, nothing like that, but he described her, you know, like they do on TV? Coulda been anyone. So I says, 'Who is she?' and that's when he tells me. I says, 'Oh, yeah, I know her. She used to come in maybe like maybe two, three times a week.'"

"What was she like?"

"A couple of years older than me, but, you know, good-looking. We used to kid around. I asked her name once. Anyway, this cop says, real serious, 'Did she come in last night?' and I says 'Yeah, she was in here around eight-thirty maybe, buying a couple of coffees to go.' Then he says can I be more specific about the time? I'm thinking to myself, 'This is weird, man,' you know, like those lame reruns of *Dragnet* on DejaVu. I can't believe he's serious, but I say, 'Yeah, well, it was about twenty to nine.'"

"He didn't say why he wanted to know?"

"Not right off. He's just standing there asking all these questions with this chick beside him—fuck, man, I hate women cops, they're worse than men—and she's making these notes while I talk. There's customers coming in, so I says, 'Look. I gotta job to do. What's this all about?' And he says, 'Murder.'"

"No shit!"

"Yeah. Turns out this girl he's asking about got killed. Just after she left here. Can you believe it?"

"No way."

"Yeah. I coulda been the last person to see her alive."

I judged the talker to be about seventeen, an age when the male ego knows nothing of compassion and seeks only to fill every available space with its inflated self-worth. His connection with Laura, however tenuous or accidental, had become a trophy, something to make him look good in the eyes of his buddy.

I drank up the last of my coffee and approached the counter. Mr. I-hate-women-cops turned wary when I said I'd overheard him, defensive at having someone draw attention to the attention he'd been drawing to himself, but relaxed ("No shit, man!") after I said I knew the woman the police had been enquiring about. When I asked him to repeat something he'd said, he turned suspicious again, but complied, albeit sullenly. No, I hadn't heard wrong; no, he hadn't made a mistake; yes, he was sure. What, did I think he'd make something like that up?

I left the shop curiously elated. I now had not one, but two significant pieces of information to pass on to March.

Ten

Um die halbversunkenen Mauern.
(" 'Round old walls, decayed and half-sinking")
    —*Liederkreis*, Opus 39, VI

I called Fifty-two Division early on Tuesday. A male operator informed me Detective Inspector Andrew March was "unavailable."

"Do you know when can I reach him?"

"I'm sorry, sir," came the smooth, field-all-calls reply. "He's in a meeting."

I stifled an urge to pout, Hollywood starlet-style—*But I just want to know if I got the big part*—and left a message, saying I'd call back.

I'd scarcely cradled the receiver when the phone chirped back.

"Mr. Lantry?" The voice on the other end was timid and uncertain.

"Speaking."

"My name is Janice? Janice Cleary? Miss Gardiner said I should call?"

"That's right. To arrange a time together. When's good for you?"

"Miss Gardiner says she won't be in her studio? After four o'clock?" Janice had trouble forming declarative sentences.

"You're saying you want to meet at the Conservatory. For an hour?"

There was a long pause. "With Miss Erskine, it was only half an hour." You'd think I'd suggested she take off her clothes.

"Four-thirty, then?"

Four-thirty was "okay." I asked her to sign out Elly's key if she got there early.

I had two choices of what to do with the next few hours: study Janice's music or go outside and work. Léo wanted a retaining wall in front of the main house rebuilt. To my mind, the sagging fieldstones looked cap-R Romantic, but he maintained that for the rent he charged the boutique-owner couple upstairs and the media consultant bachelor downstairs, ruins were out. I decided to get started on the wall. Anything was better than contemplating coaching a shy sixteen-year-old through the sophisticated passions of Schubert and Fauré.

After two hours with a crowbar and spade, I'd prised most of the stones out of the ground, accidentally killing a few salamanders along the way. The stones were bigger than they looked—only a small part of them actually protruded from the slope they held up—and much heavier. I lugged-kicked-dragged-cajoled them over near the driveway, arranging them precisely in order of removal. Some people have the knack for building stone walls, fitting them together like two-ton jigsaw puzzles. Not me. Better to take advantage of someone else's spatial-orientation cleverness now and save myself some trouble later on.

At eleven-thirty, I broke off and went inside for some apple juice. I tried March again, and this time got through.

"Vikkan. What can I do you for?"

"Are you busy?"

He just grunted.

"I've discovered something concerning Ulrike Vogel. I can't swear it's relevant to the murders, but—"

"Do you like Vietnamese?" he interrupted.

Huh? I held the receiver away from my face and stared at the earpiece. A silly gesture when you're all alone. I put it back.

"Are you saying you want to talk over lunch?"

"Call it community liaison. The new face of homicide. Do you know Saigon Maxima, over near Bay Street?"

"The place with that disgusting durian-fruit drink?"

"That's the one. Can you meet me in forty-five minutes?"

I looked down at my muddy jeans and passed an exploratory hand over my unshaven jaw. "Better make it an hour."

꙳ ꙳ ꙳

I arrived a bit late, hair still shower-damp, but clean and presentable in pressed jeans and a fresh shirt. A plate of shrimp chips sat on the Formica table. March munched through them while we waited to place our orders: flank steak soup with tripe and tendons for me, sugarcane crab for him.

"So?" he asked, pouring tea from a dented chrome pot. "What have you got?"

"You remember I told you I'd talked to Ulrike Vogel? That she denied knowing Laura had sung the *Liederkreis* for Mann?"

He nodded.

"I ran into David Bryce yesterday. According to him, it isn't true."

"Bryce—that's the teacher who was seen talking to Mann outside the washroom on the second floor Thursday night?"

"Right. He's also Ulrike's accompanist."

"Accompanist? I thought she didn't perform anymore."

"He plays for her students' lessons, so she doesn't have to teach from the piano. Anyway, Bryce interrupted Laura and me Thursday afternoon, going over the songs with Mann. He claims he told Ulrike."

"And you think that might be significant?" He didn't sound impressed.

"As I recall, you said I was to tell you what I know, and you'd decide whether it was important."

Good-cop liked the answer. He smiled and blew on his tea. "But you suspect she lied to cover up a motive?"

"Premiering these songs would be a major step toward re-establishing her concert career. She used to be quite famous, in Europe anyway. If she thought she was going to lose the opportunity...well, let's just say she'd be unhappy."

"To the point of committing murder?"

"How much has anyone told you about *das Vöglein?*"

Not much, apparently. Even the nickname was news. I started recounting everything Mann had told me. Our orders arrived, but my soup was too hot, so I kept on while March dug in: Ulrike's former career, the accolades, the anticipation over singing her accompanist/lover's new work, the betrayal, the suicide attempt...

"On stage?" March interrupted, a stick of crab-encrusted sugarcane halfway to his mouth. "Now that's truly wacko."

"You'd be amazed how many neuroses go into the making of a musician."

He looked up, one eyebrow raised. I tested my soup. Perfect. "The parallel between Ulrike's humiliation in Vienna and what was going on with Mann, the *Liederkreis* and Laura is hard to ignore," I said, fishing a honeycomb of tripe out of the broth.

"Agreed. But let me tell you something about this case." He took a napkin to his mouth and signalled for more tea. "In most homicides—let's leave out drive-bys, serial killings and domestic disputes—there's usually a single detail in the victim's life—a hiccough, if you will, a glitch—that points toward a motive. It could be anything: a new insurance policy, a mistress, a sudden attack of conscience. Nine times out of ten, when you find the glitch, it's gold, because only one other person is threatened by it. It takes some creativity to get yourself killed, you know. Not many people's lives are so interesting that they can spawn a whole host of would-be murderers."

"*Cherchez la femme,* in other words."

"With motive, I'm on solid ground. I know where to look for evidence."

"Sounds dangerously close to inductive reasoning. I thought you people were supposed to avoid that."

"Don't tell anyone, okay? My problem here is, if this *Liederkreis* is involved, it generates too many motives." He ticked off on his fingers. "Nils Janssen, who doesn't want the Faculty of Music getting the proofs. Ulrike Vogel, who doesn't want Laura Erskine singing it. Morris-Jones, who wants to keep Dieter Mann from rewriting history."

"Wish you could apply Occam's Razor? Trim off the fat to narrow the field?"

"The hand that rocked the cradle kicked the bucket?"

"Sorry?"

"Something my father says when he hears a mixed metaphor. But you're right. There's too much going on here."

He turned silent. I got started on my soup in earnest, aware of him watching me closely. When I asked what he found so fascinating, he looked away.

I picked up my bowl for a final slurp, then set it down. "There's something else. You know your theory that someone visited Mann and Laura prior to the murders?"

"Yes?"

"You may have been right after all. The bag you found in the studio, the one from the doughnut shop—how many coffees were in it?"

"Two. Large."

"That's what the guy at the doughnut shop said."

"Been investigating on your own again?"

"Just a coincidence. I overheard him boasting to a buddy."

"What's your point?"

I waited a second or two, just as he'd done prior to putting forth his "mysterious visitor" theory the day before. "Dieter Mann never drank coffee."

Whatever reaction I was expecting, it wasn't the one I got. March looked sideways with that appeal-to-the-wings expression stand-up comics reserve for stupid comments from the audience. "That," he said, looking back, "is supposed to prove someone else was in the studio? Both coffees were black, Vikkan. Double sugar. How many people do you know drink coffee that way? Laura had been singing for nearly two hours. Chances are, she and Dieter Mann were going to keep working until the Conservatory closed down. The toxicology report showed significant levels of caffeine in her system—a real java addict. She bought two coffees to save going out again. You need to be careful about jumping to conclusions."

I restrained myself from pointing out that he'd jumped to conclusions, too, when he proposed there'd been a visitor to the studio in the first place.

"And speaking of medical reports," he went on, "there's something else you should know." He hesitated, weighing some pros and cons. "The way Laura died—it isn't what it looked like."

Dark hair matted with congealing blood... "What do you mean?"

"You remember Miss Gardiner's paperweight? The one wiped clean of prints?"

"You said it wasn't the murder weapon."

"It wasn't. But it was used in the attack. The coroner found a subdural haematoma on the side of Laura's skull opposite to the one where the obvious damage was done. The bruise is consistent with an object the size and shape of the paperweight." He waited to see if this made any sense. I shook my head. He went on. "This isn't pleasant, but I'll spell it out. Whoever murdered Laura knocked her unconscious and killed her afterwards. And not by beating her head in."

"How, then?"

"She was suffocated."

"Suffocated?!"

"It showed up in the postmortem. Cerebral anoxia from blockage to the airway. We found wool fibres in her mouth and nose. Forensics matched them to the roll cushion on Miss Gardiner's fainting couch."

"So what did Mann die of? Poison? Drowning?"

He wasn't in the mood for humour. "He died of just what it looked like: severe repeated trauma to the head. I've asked for a second examination, but there won't be any surprises."

"Why not?"

"The object used to inflict the head injuries on both of them didn't come from the studio. Whoever killed them brought something along, and not just to do a little cranial readjustment after they were dead."

"But why not strike Laura with whatever it was, instead of knocking her out with the paperweight? It doesn't make sense. And why kill her so differently afterward?"

He shrugged, palms up.

"You still think Mann was killed before Laura?"

"Fits what we've got."

"You said his prints were on the window frame and the latch, and there were traces of herbal tea on the ledge outside.

Couldn't he have come into the studio, seen Laura and the broken window, and gone over to investigate?"

He shook his head. "You saw where she fell—right in front of the desk. Evidence suggests she was calling for help."

"You mean the prints on the phone? That doesn't mean very much. She wasn't exactly a stranger to the studio."

"We only found prints on nine and one. And my instincts say the killer wasn't after her. The way she died was just too...unplanned."

"But if what Bryce said about Ulrike—"

"Is true? We don't know that it is."

"You think he lied?"

"In a homicide investigation, everyone lies." He caught our waiter's eye and made scribbling motions in the air. "I appreciate your telling me, though."

"You're welcome, I think."

The waiter tallied our bills and laid them on the table. I reached for mine, but March put out his hand—a big mitt, like a farmboy's, but with no dirt under the blunt nails.

"I'll get it, Vikkan," he said. "My treat."

༄   ༄   ༄

The coroner's report on Laura must have crossed March's desk well before that morning.

The thought only sprang to mind as I waited for a snarl of traffic to inch me closer to Castle Frank. He had to have seen it at least a day or two ago. So why wait until today to tell me how she died? Surely not to spare my feelings.

A moment before, I'd been feeling good—pleased, even—that he trusted me enough to discuss the case. But with this new realization...

I tried to muster some anger, but found I couldn't. It's hard to get indignant with someone who's just sprung for lunch. *In a homicide investigation, everyone lies.* With that attitude, I suppose he'd always be holding back, looking for contradictions between what people told him and what he actually knew.

It was a little after two when I finally pulled up in front of Ulrike's house. The sun was oppressively bright in a hard blue sky—a good omen, since "things coming to light" was the reason I'd driven over. I'd done my duty telling March what I'd learned from Bryce, but somehow it wasn't enough. Ulrike had lied to me, personally, and I couldn't let it pass.

I went round to the back yard, thinking the French doors off the patio would allow me to see if she were teaching. If she were, I'd skulk around until she finished.

The sounds of singing came dimly through the glass, but when I peered through the bevelled panes, there was only Ulrike, alone at the piano. Some intuition must have warned her of my presence. She looked up before I knocked and rose with a puzzled expression. Perhaps the light outside kept her from seeing who it was. She opened the door partway. "Yes?"

"I hope I'm not disturbing you," I said, sounding like Elly. "I was afraid you'd be teaching."

She glanced at a thin gold watch on her wrist. "There is a pupil coming shortly."

"I won't be long."

As on my previous visit, when I'd posed the same question I'd come to ask now, I wasn't sure how to proceed. *"Fräulein Vogel,"* I tried, *"es gibt etwas, was ich Ihnen vorher gefragt habe..."* For some reason, I felt safer speaking German. Maybe it was the stiff formality of *Sie, Ihnen,* and *Ihr*—they'd make calling her a liar seem less personal. "There's something I've been wondering about. Concerning the *Liederkreis.* As you recall, I asked before if you knew that Herr Mann had shown it to Laura Erskine. You said no. Forgive me for asking again. Are you sure?"

I suppose she could have said it was none of my business, but instead she looked down and fiddled with the clasp of her watch. *"Ja,"* she said, *"ich habe gewußt.* I did know. I should not have said otherwise." Her voice was soft but held only the barest hint of contrition.

"Warum haben Sie mich angelügt?" Why did you lie to me?

She responded in English. "I am sorry. I do not wish to talk further on this subject."

Decades of musicianship went into the sentence, giving it the implacable weight of a closing cadence.

"Did you by any chance suspect Herr Mann was auditioning Laura?" I persisted. "To premiere the *Liederkreis*?"

She glanced up sharply. "No. I do not *choose* to think so. Not now." It took a moment to realize that her odd phrasing—do not choose to think—didn't stem from any difficulty with English. She meant it literally. "Ever since Dieter discovered the *Liederkreis,"* she said, "I was his choice to sing it. When I heard that he and my former pupil..." She cast about for words, took a deep breath, then drew herself up. "I felt *verraten*—betrayed— like a lover. You understand? But I have paid for this, with days and nights of humiliation. Doubting Dieter...*that* was betrayal."

"You're saying that when I spoke to you before, you were denying your own feelings? Out of respect for Herr Mann?"

"Precisely." She relaxed. "You are most understanding."

But not gullible. "The police may not be so sympathetic," I said. "They believe the killings of Herr Mann and Laura Erskine are connected with the *Liederkreis*. If you lied to them—"

"But it is only you who asked if I knew," she interrupted impatiently. "The police have not questioned me on this."

"But they have questioned me about it," I said, not quite accurately, since it was I who'd brought the matter to March's attention.

She tossed her head. *"Die Polizei kann denken, was sie will."* The police can think what they will. "It would be *lächerlich* to suspect me in the death of Dieter. Absurd. They have already spoken to me about last Thursday. I told them what they needed to know."

"Which was?"

Her chin went up a hair's breadth. "That I was at home all evening. That I left the Conservatory at seven-thirty and arrived here at eight. My neighbours have been questioned and have told the police they saw me driving in. I did not leave the house afterward. There is a phone call to prove I was here."

"The one from Professor Morris-Jones?"

"You know of this?"

"May I ask what she wanted?"

"To find Dieter. I do not like the woman—I have heard about her *unentschuldbare Unhöflichkeit* last Wednesday—but she said she wished to speak with him, to apologize."

"And you told her where he was?"

"I said only that he was at the Conservatory, and suggested she call him later at his hotel. I gave her the name."

"Was that all she wanted?"

I'd asked one question too many. "It is not for you to concern yourself with these things. It is for the police." She went to close the door, then thought better of it and stepped forward, appealing. "Understand, Vikkan, I, too, would like to know what happened. It would be...*bequem*...handy?...to suspect Fräulein Professor Morris-Jones of some involvement. Anna has told me she made enquiries about the *Liederkreis*. However, Anna also told me that the document proving Frau

Schumann composed it has been stolen. You have studied with Fräulein Professor, I imagine?"

"Yes."

"Then you know of her *Vorliebe*. Her..."

"...predilections? Naturally."

"Es ist unwahrscheinlich, sie stehle das genaue Ding, das ihre Theorien rechtfertigt." It is unlikely she'd steal the very thing that vindicates her theories.

"True."

"So you see? I have given the matter some thought. You must believe me. Fräulein Professor merely said she wished to apologize to Dieter. That is all. We did not talk of other things."

A doorbell chimed distantly inside the house. "My student," she said. "You will excuse me now."

The door was shut before I had a chance to say goodbye.

I let myself out of the yard and through the narrow passage between houses to the street. As I was getting into the Rover, a classic Honda CRX pulled up. I didn't recognise the driver until he stepped out: Bryce. Of course—he'd be playing for Ulrike's pupil. He raised his hand and flashed some teeth. I nodded, trying to get the motor started, but the Honda's puppy-dog sex appeal had made the jeep bashful. Bryce was up the front steps and through the door before it finally found the confidence to turn over.

꙾   ꙾   ꙾

"All I wanna do is have some fun / Till the sun comes up / On the Santa Monica Boulevard..."

Sheryl Crow's paean to California hedonism came through the door a quarter-tone sharp, accompanied by banging triads.

I couldn't see in because Elly's coat-tree, a jacket draped over its arms, had been pushed in front of the window. Most Conservatory students—and not a few teachers—are neurotic about being observed in the pants-down business of practising.

I knocked. The singing choked off mid-phrase. A moment later, the coat-tree moved aside, and a flustered Janice Cleary let me in.

It seemed like a good idea to gain her confidence before we started, so I casually mentioned the blocked window. "You don't have to do that, you know. No one can see you from the hall if you're over by the piano. Miss Gardiner's been very clever about that."

Janice's cheeks flushed scarlet—so much for winning her trust. How long had Elly said until her exam?

I took my seat and suggested we start with some vocalises. In thirty seconds, I knew I'd made a mistake. The exercises' demands battled with Janice's shyness, and won. Her high notes came out strained and seriously under pitch. Her low ones were so breathy it was hard to hear a pitch at all. Singers can't afford to be timid—about their emotions, about their bodies, or about the sounds that come out of them. How this one could even utter a peep was beyond me.

I cut the vocalises short and said maybe she'd like to familiarize herself with her accompaniments. She ducked her head and began retrieving music from her satchel, setting it on the music stand, almost but not quite catching a volume of Fauré before it fell to the floor. After making a stab at drawing herself up into a singerly pose, she tore into her examination list, anxiously pushing the tempi of the languid Italian songs into the realms *presto agitato,* making Schubert's babbling brooks sound like white-water rapids and turning the Warlock piece into a day at the races. What should have used up the

229

rest of our half hour left us with five minutes to kill, a yawning chasm three hundred seconds wide.

Janice stood awkwardly, one foot planted atop the other, chewing her lower lip. I wished I could think of something to say, something to put her at ease. Under her frizzy hair and teenage-baggy clothing was a pretty sixteen-year-old who wanted badly to sing, if only the turmoil of adolescence would let her.

"I guess it must feel strange, working with me rather than Miss Erskine," I said.

She blushed.

"Did you like her?"

"She was all right."

"Just 'all right'?"

"We laughed a lot."

"You enjoyed working with her?"

A vigorous nod, but no eye contact.

A brisk tap on the door interrupted the one-sided conversation. Elly bustled in, loaded down with two cartons of Mason jars.

"For my sister," she explained. "They're on sale at Canadian Tire. She wants to make jam of last year's strawberries so there'll be room in her freezer when the new ones come in."

She put the cartons down and sat at her desk. Janice sidled over, as if Elly offered some kind of protection.

"How did it go today?" Elly asked.

When Janice didn't answer, I replied, non-committally: "All right." Janice shot me a pained look.

"It's only three weeks till the exam," Elly said. "I want you two to get together every couple of days before then. You're available, aren't you, Vikkan? And if you don't mind, can you work at home? I'm very busy. The studio will be hard to get."

My life, as directed by Elly Gardiner. I told Janice to call and we'd set up a schedule. She mumbled something like "Okay," crammed music into her purple satchel, grabbed her jacket and bolted out of the studio.

I got up and shut the door, then went over to the *récamier.* "Fainting couch" March had called it. I liked that.

"You have charms," Elly commented as I tried to sit upright on a piece of furniture suited only to graceful supinity. "But not to soothe the savage beast. Or breast. Whichever it is."

"You mean Janice?"

"Indeed."

"It's hardly my fault."

"I wouldn't be so sure. Look in the mirror sometime."

"Is that some sort of compliment?"

"It's perfectly understandable you'd make a sixteen-year-old bashful."

"Why, Elly, I thought you'd never noticed."

She tsk-ed.

"Tell her I'm gay," I said.

"I doubt it would do any good."

"How am I supposed to coach her if she has a crush on me? She's so uptight she can hardly sing a note."

"Don't worry. It'll be over in a few weeks." I didn't get a chance to ask her whether she meant Janice's infatuation or the upcoming exam because she changed the subject. "Janssen read me the riot act today," she said, pulling her Rolodex forward on the desk.

"What for?"

"Thursday night. You remember I signed out at the front desk but left my key with Dieter and Laura?"

"I'm not likely to forget anything about that evening."

"Somehow, he knew. You'd think in light of what happened,

he'd ignore it, but instead, he gave me sh—" Elly caught herself "—he dressed me down for not following the new rules." She turned the Rolodex's knob and extracted a card.

"But the studio was broken into. It wouldn't have made a particle of difference if you'd returned the key."

"That wasn't Janssen's point. 'Once procedure's established, it must be followed.'" She made a notation on the card and put it back. "I'm starting to have second thoughts about that man. You know I was on the committee that elected him?"

"I think you told me."

"He seemed so right at the time: former registrar, knowledgeable, efficient, diplomatic. And with a vision of the Conservatory as a real player in the international music world. It's a lofty ideal, Vikkan, but you know? I think it's gone to his head. Would you believe he even had the temerity to suggest the murders might generate some useful publicity?"

"He said as much to me. It could just be the times we live in. Spin is everything. Some people might congratulate him on his marketing savvy."

Elly shook her head and began flipping through her file again.

"There's something about Janssen that's bothering me, too," I said.

"Oh, what's that?" she asked distractedly.

"This idea of his that I should come on staff. I know he consulted you about it."

"He did."

"Then maybe you can tell me: why does he want me? There must be dozens more suitable who could fill the post."

"He wants the best. He believes you're it. And whatever else I may think of him," she said darkly, "he's right about that."

It sounded like a prelude to one of her usual reproaches for everything I'm not doing with my life, so I answered back lightly: "Let's not go there today," or some similarly overused phrase.

She stopped fiddling with her Rolodex and turned around. "And why not?" Her look was not the one of good-humoured exasperation I expected. "Isn't it about time we had this out? What's the matter with you, Vikkan? Don't you realize most people would kill for what you have?"

I could see in her face that she regretted the choice of words, but she wasn't ready to back down.

"Dare I say I never asked for it?" I asked, startled.

"That's a stupid, wilful comment, and you know it, like saying you didn't ask to be born. You have talent, and like it or not, that entails responsibility."

"Maybe in *your* books."

"Well, if not in yours, then all I can say is you must have a library full of very selfish literature. As long as I've known you, you've been dickering around, avoiding your obligations, waffling over opportunities like this one, distancing yourself from people who are trying to help. What do you intend to do? Go back to your little cabin in the woods and play Chopin at the chipmunks for the rest of your life? What's the good of playing the piano if you won't share it with anyone? That's not being a musician. It's—"

"Onanism?"

She slammed her hand on the desk. "Why, do you have to do that? Always look for something clever to say? Do you like keeping people at arm's length, or is it something you developed to protect yourself from Berényi?"

"That's way below the belt, Elly."

"And I hope it hurt! Or at least got your attention!"

Why was she doing this? And why now? We'd always only danced around the subject of my future in music, or at least negotiated a way to keep the issue alive without ever coming to blows.

I looked off to my right, at the window with plywood still in the frame, the sill with circular stains where Elly's flowerpots had sat for years. With nothing to brighten the space where Mildred and Chastity and their floral friends used to sit, the room had a transient, unwelcoming feel, like an apartment before moving day with all the pictures taken down. The bare linoleum tiles, minus the Turkish rug, added to the coldness.

A movement at the desk caused me to look back. Elly was pulling a hankie from her sleeve. She sniffled into the balled-up cotton, her eyes strained and bright. "I'm sorry, Vikkan. Really. Forgive me. I didn't mean it to come out that way."

It felt as if someone had just stabbed me in the chest. *Mais, mais, voir un ami pleurer...* The Jacques Brel refrain surfaced unbidden. *To see a friend cry...* Worse than the tears was the apology. "Elly—"

"It's all right." She wiped her nose. "I'll be fine. Just give me a moment."

I stayed put while she drew herself together, dabbing at her eyes. Finally, she stuffed the hankie back into her sleeve. "I'm so sorry," she said. "I don't know what came over me." A rueful smile accompanied the time-honoured cliché.

To discuss it further, or not? To make comforting noises about the emotional toll of the past week? To excuse, pretend, talk away the last few minutes?

"You know, Elly," I said carefully, "I think I liked it better when we left these things unsaid."

Her response was a wry look that made me want to get up and hug her.

"Me, too," she said. "Me, too."

The elevator beckoned with gaping doors at the end of Elly's hall. Hard to tell if it was stuck, or merely catching its breath before heaving off elsewhere. I took a chance and stepped inside.

In the time it took to ride down one floor, I could have served a formal supper—and cleaned up afterward. The cabin's scarred wooden floor needed work, though. Definitely not suitable for dining. A little Indian Sand and some paste wax, maybe?

I should probably have used the slow descent to think over Elly's outburst. In a way, I suppose I did, by displacing my feelings onto Janssen. Who did he think he was, chastising her about her key as if she were a junior member of staff? And how had he known she'd left it with Mann and Laura? Was it from things the police had told him, or had he taken to spot-checking the key sheet to find out who was disobeying his edict?

My churlish thoughts must have worked some kind of voodoo, because when the elevator's long double-doors finally slid back, the man himself stood before me, in double-breasted blue today instead of grey. Perhaps his dry cleaners hadn't come through on time.

"Have you got a minute?" I asked.

He looked mildly surprised. "Yes, I think so. I'm just on my way up to the office. Would you like to talk there?" He made to get on the elevator.

"Going down," I said. "We'd better take the stairs."

He frowned. I wondered if the sluggish behemoth was on his to-do list of Conservatory reforms.

Inside his office, I got straight to the point. "It's about Thursday night. I understand you chastised Elly for leaving her key with Mann and Laura."

His eyebrows went up. "That's not at all what I expected. I

was hoping you'd reconsidered my offer to work here."

"Not if it means being called on the carpet for petty infractions."

"Miss Gardiner is not the only one I've spoken to," he said stiffly.

"I have no doubt, but in her case, your timing was lousy."

He looked amused. "I had no idea she had such a loyal champion. But perhaps you're right; it could have waited. Was that all?"

"No, there's something else. Did you happen to know specifically who was in Elly's studio that night?"

"Doing a little amateur sleuthing?" he inquired, studying his nails. The sarcasm was polite, carefully modulated, and landed right where he meant it to. Asking questions about the murders, I felt like a character in Agatha Christie. "Laura Erskine was my friend," I said evenly. "I'd like to find out what happened."

"I see." He leaned back in his chair, elbows on the arms, fingers steepled in front of him. "Russell Spiers dropped by shortly after seven. We had scheduling conflicts to resolve. As you know, some teachers do double duty here and over at the Faculty. Spiers mentioned something about going to see Laura Erskine and Dieter Mann afterward, in Miss Gardiner's studio. So, yes, I did know they were there. And I suspected—quite rightly, as it turned out—that Miss Gardiner had left them her key."

"Which you found out by...?"

"Checking the key sheet. It wouldn't have done to barge in on Herr Professor Mann for something like that. Understand, it isn't that I don't trust Miss Gardiner. I'd merely been expecting some staff to have difficulty adjusting to the new precautions. Security is no longer something about which we can afford to be lax."

"Indeed. First petty vandalism, and now murder. Very bad for the image." Two could play this game of genteel sarcasm.

There was nothing more I wanted, so I glanced at my watch. Janssen accepted the gambit and rose. "Please," he said, showing me out, "if you're talking to Miss Gardiner, explain what I've just said. I wouldn't want her to think my reprimand was personal."

He shut the door and left me in the company of his predecessors, ranged in frames up and down the hall. Their expressions were benign, if a little smug and stuffy. Janssen's keen gaze would look out of place here. These principals had governed a staid institution, but one whose influence reached across the country. There were branches in nearly every major city. Its graded exam system allowed teachers in communities as remote as Glace Bay and Puvungnituk to lead their students from musical infancy to full-blown Conservatory Associateship. One didn't even have to enter the building to be granted that honour. Statistics alone ensured that a good percentage of the country's gifted studied, if not at, at least through the Conservatory. Had any of these men felt that wasn't enough?

I decided not to get the Rover when I left the building, but to walk a few blocks west, over to Spadina. There was a good florist there managed by a voluble Hungarian—Rose, appropriately enough—and I wanted to see what she had by way of potted plants, violets in particular.

Something began to niggle in my brain on the way over, a mental itch I couldn't quite scratch away. It grew as I walked by the brick-walled estate of the St. George Club, and became unbearable by the time I hit Huron Street. I stopped across from the David A. Croll Apartments and tried to figure it out. Was it something I'd just heard? From Janssen? Elly?

I watched a squirrel lurch down the sidewalk. The scraggly-tailed critter had something in its mouth—last year's acorn?—and was headed for a big maple, stopping every few feet, looking around. When it got to the tree, it scampered up partway, then fled behind the trunk with its prize. Something carried, something moved, something removed...

The penny dropped. Elly's key. Of course.

If Mann and Laura had died in her studio, who had returned the key I'd watched her sign out on Friday morning?

Eleven

So stumm und verschwiegen sind
Die Sterne nicht in der Höh'
Als meine Gedanken sind.
("Not nearly so speechless
Are the stars that glitter above
As my startled, spellbound thoughts.")
— *Liederkreis*, Opus 39, IV

I tried to reach March as soon as I got home, my second call to Fifty-two Division that day. At this rate, I'd have to enter the number in memory-dial. A different voice from this morning's answered, but with the same cagey, "Inspector March is unavailable." I left my name once more and said I'd call back.

It was now six-thirty, three and a half hours before work. I hadn't been spending much time at the carriage house recently, except to practise and sleep, and the place seemed somehow different. In the past months, I'd gotten used to the unpacked boxes against the walls, the open crates of wiring and electrical fixtures underneath the piano. Now it struck me how temporary they made the place look. Why put so much effort into renovation, then refuse to make it home? This wasn't a stopover; there'd be no return to Caledon.

I changed into a pair of cut-offs and started in on unpacking boxes, alternating "Now where should this go?" with tidy-up work on Evelyn's book. I'd taken a staggering number of pictures on Léo's property. Mostly, they were in pretty good order—vetch with vetch, spurge with spurge, mallow with mallow—but there were some mix-ups. One showed up that evening. The shot I'd wanted for the chicory page, but thought I'd lost, had snuck in with the mertensia. I located the protective envelope labelled "chicory" in the filing cabinet, shook out the accompanying transparency, and extracted the calligraphed sheet. *Cichorium intybus.* Cholagogue...digestive ...diuretic... Chicory, I recalled, was one of the herb traces police forensics had turned up on the ledge outside Elly's window. It seemed March's reconstruction of Thursday night had been right about at least one thing: if Mann had been drinking a tisane with *C. intybus,* he might well have left the studio more than once to use the washroom. I replaced the old photograph with the one I'd just found and refiled the envelope.

Unpacking boxes went slower than I'd expected. Almost every one held some reminder of Christian: a kerosene lamp from camp-outs by the river, a pair of grass-stained work gloves, the secateurs Léo had bought for him (at the Museum of Modern Art, of all places)...little landmines of recall I hadn't realized I'd planted. Love, it seemed, had a will of its own when it came to hanging on.

By nine-thirty, I'd emptied four boxes, and finished up picture-filing for Evelyn's book, feeling oddly energized. I hunted around for a clean ruffled shirt, gave my tuxedo a good brushing, checked my hair—behaving itself for once—and hopped in the Rover. The contrast of bow tie and tails with scruffy Naugahyde had me humming "That's Why the Lady Is a Tramp" as I pulled out of the driveway.

I got to Evelyn a few minutes early. Rosemary Dickens was at one of the banquettes, looking elegantly sexy and anything but managerial in strapless sea-green. The thirtysomething natty-suit-and-tortoiseshell-glasses beside her was vaguely familiar. I tried to think if I'd seen them together before. Rosemary sometimes uses her tiny office as a changing room, emerging dressed so there's no doubt she's off on a date—nor how the date will end—but she rarely engages in preliminaries upstairs in the lounge.

I sketched a wave and made for Léo's office. I hadn't seen him since Saturday and wanted to check in. He was on the phone. "Evelyn," he mouthed, hand over the receiver, pointing me to an armchair. I shook my head and signalled I'd come back later. Might as well start my set early.

For reasons I don't understand, it happens sometimes that playing comes easily, as if my brain and body have had a lube and oil change. I think a musical thought, and out it pops, right there at the ends of my fingers, no effort involved. It was one of those nights. I played Burt Bacharach for nearly an hour, something I wouldn't normally do for fear of scaring off the sixties-and-seventies-shy, convincing myself, if no one else, that it was high time the composer of "I Say a Little Prayer for You" and "What's It All About, Alfie?" got accorded his rightful place in the pantheon of great American songwriters.

When I finished the set, Rosemary beckoned me over, squeezed my hand, and gave me an affectionate kiss that somehow left her lipstick intact. Her gentleman friend turned out to be none other than John Sanger, Russell Spiers' music-agent companion from Sunday.

"Rosemary wasn't lying," he said after introductions. "You're better than most."

"Most what?"

"Lounge lizards."

I turned to Rosemary. "You said that?"

"No. John's in professionally judicious mode. It means he's impressed."

"She's been telling me for months I should give you a listen. My roster's full, but she's very—"

"—persuasive—"

"—insistent. I happened to be here Sunday—" he shot her a quick, intimate glance; I didn't want to know how the rest of that evening had gone "—and came up. Now I'm back. She's right. I'm impressed."

"Russell Spiers said you'd been around," I said.

He looked pained, as if he'd just bitten a piece of aluminum foil. "Does he always drink like that?"

"Luckily, I wouldn't know."

"He kept saying I shouldn't waste my time on you, or words to that effect."

"Professionally speaking, you probably shouldn't."

"Are you signed on with anyone?"

"Just the union."

"You like this sort of venue?"

"It's the only one of its kind I've played."

"Do you have a contract?"

"Just an arrangement with the owner."

"What kind of music do you play? I mean, when you're not here?"

"Good music, of course."

"I should have expected that. What I mean is, do you have a particular style? How do you call it?"

"Person-to-person when I'm flush, collect when I'm not."

He hadn't heard that one before. He winced and turned to Rosemary. "Hard to get a straight answer out of this one."

"He's just trying to be modest, dear."

Rosemary, the great male mediator. I stuck my tongue out at her and felt around for a cigarette. Sanger offered me a light from a monogrammed Zippo. "Seriously," he said, "I'd like to hear what you can do. Could we get together sometime? I represent some big names."

He rattled off a few, and, yes, they were big. If I were anyone else, I'd have been thrilled. Instead, I felt myself backing away.

Rosemary sensed my discomfort. "John's not name-dropping," she said, laying her hand on my arm. "It's his agent version of a résumé."

"I'm aware."

"Do you sing?" he asked.

"Yes, but not here. Not usually."

"Your own material?"

"Generally."

"Do you take requests?"

"Depends who's asking."

"I'd like to hear something you've written. Something with words."

I couldn't very well refuse, not with Rosemary sending looks my way. "All right. Stick around. I'll try to work something in."

Over at the bar, Toby had a Naya waiting. I would have preferred Scotch. Evelyn was my haven away from professional eyes and ears. Sanger's presence begged something stronger than mineral water.

"You know that guy with Rosemary?" I asked.

Toby nodded. "They've been seeing each other for a couple of months."

"You know why he's here?"

"Checking you out. Rosemary told me. He's an agent. Great idea."

"Is this a conspiracy?"

He gave me a shitkicker grin.

"Bastards," I said. "All of you."

He chuckled and started wiping down the bar.

With a lot of people rooting for you, it's pure grinchiness not to give them what they want. The lounge wasn't crowded—Tuesday night is the off-night par excellence—and I doubted the patrons would object to a little showing off. I sat at the piano, thought for a minute, then started in on a song I'd written years before but never played for anyone. The D-flat major introduction rolled like a hymn through the big Yamaha, bringing conversation to a halt. *Very bad form for a lounge pianist.* Even the highball glasses stopped tinkling. I held the fermata as long as I could—a single unresolved chord hanging over an abyss of promise—then started:

> *The crazy things we do here in this city*
> *The hours of our lives we waste away*
> *Caught between survival and self-pity*
> *Hopes and dreams have somehow gone astray*
>
> *Morning fades to nighttime disillusion*
> *Looking for the stars that don't appear*
> *Longing to escape from the confusion*
> *North is any place that gets me out of here...*

It was a terrific song: lush harmonies, an engaging tune, plenty of room for pianistic swaggering. Nobody seemed to mind the downer subject. The applause afterward sounded as if I'd just executed a solo run-through of "Rhapsody in Blue". I followed it with another "down" song *("...'cause if I didn't know this was loss, I'd've said it was love..."),* chased it with a dash of be-bop, moved into one or two wordless ballads, a couple of jazz studies à la Gershwin, and a few more songs of my own.

I stayed rooted to the bench during the ovation that

followed, feeling as if maybe I had stepped over some kind of propriety line. When the clapping finally spent itself, I headed straight for Léo's office.

I made it as far as the bar.

"Nice playing. If this is the Tuesday show, what's it like on Saturdays?"

The voice came from behind. "I wouldn't know, Inspector," I replied, turning around. "I'm off on weekends."

"It can't get much better than this." He was standing very close, wearing his police-detective's dark suit. The tie was loose, and I could smell that he'd ordered a drink during my set.

"Compliment noted. I'm glad you enjoyed it. And I hope this doesn't sound unappreciative, but what are you doing here?"

"Unwinding."

"Out of all the bars in Toronto, you chose this one?"

"I wanted to hear you."

I didn't bother to hide my skepticism.

"And you left me a message," he added.

"Saying I'd call back. I'm working now, you know."

"I'm not."

The corners of his mouth twitched, as if he'd said something funny. More than one drink, I thought. Not many, just enough for the smell on his breath to seem—for lack of a better word—deliberate.

"Look," I said, "if you want to talk, we can use Léo's office. As long as you don't mind his being there."

"No need. I'll stick around." Still that look, as if he were enjoying a private joke. "What are you doing when you finish?"

"What do you think?" I said irritably. "Going home. Really—can't this wait till tomorrow?"

He pursed his lips. "I don't think so."

What's wrong with this picture?

It was early Wednesday morning. Robins chirruped mightily on the dew-damp lawn around the main house. Squirrels chased and nattered at each other in the maples by the driveway. The sunlight coming in my window was golden-green through a tracery of sumac leaves. In my hands was a tray of toast and steaming coffee. And over on my couch, his hand shoved indolently under the elastic of his briefs, lay Detective Inspector Andrew March of the Metropolitan Toronto Police Force.

"Breakfast," I said.

I climbed over him, balancing the tray between the back of the sofa and the window sill. He reached up and put a big hand on my neck, drawing my head down. Our lips brushed. The sensation was as tantalizing as a too-small sip of water on a dusty summer day. The odour of him sparked a feeling that shot from my solar plexus to my groin and back up to my throat. I returned the kiss with force. Toast and coffee teetered and crashed behind the couch, forgotten.

How did it happen?

I finished work shortly after one-thirty, having taken John Sanger's card and gone back to my usual don't-scare-the-natives repertoire. March—Andrew—had stayed and walked with me to the Rover. On the way, I kept expecting him to ask why I'd called—the business concerning Elly's key—but he stuck to compliments on my playing. I told him not to quit his day job if he wanted to be a music critic.

We walked the last block and a half in silence. At the jeep, I asked where his car was. He said he'd come by subway. I found that hard to believe—he struck me as the type who'd never use public transit—but I offered him a ride anyway.

The Rover liked him as soon as we got in. I had no problems with doors, or windows, or ignition. Over the roar of a well-behaved engine, I asked, "Where to?"

He looked straight ahead and enunciated—very clearly, and in a tone there was no mistaking—my own address.

The motor didn't stall just then because of mechanical problems; my foot had slipped off the clutch. In the charged silence, he added: "Take the backstreets."

Passion drags foolishness in its wake. The winds to which lust throws caution have a habit of changing. The disorder they blow back makes one wonder if the surge of liberation is worth the clean-up afterward.

I wasn't, however, thinking that morning about the drive home that ended in a shirt minus several buttons and a bow tie tangled in the accelerator.

Nor was I thinking about pillow cases used later as towels when we were too spent to climb down from the loft.

I wasn't even thinking about the sweet, second-time-around taste of a man whose skin smelled like honey and fresh laundry flapping in the breeze, or the third time oh-what-the-hell-let's-do-it-again saltiness.

I was thinking about the spilled coffee and soggy toast behind the couch.

So was Andrew. He started chuckling. The sound was low and dirty, with more than a hint of little-boy wickedness. "We'll have to do something about that mess. But not—" he made motions in the air with his tongue a millimetre above my skin "—like this."

I put my hands on either side of his head. His short, blond hair had a nap like thick carpet. I lifted his face. His grey eyes made me think of rainy Saturdays, warm and safe inside my

247

bedroom, looking out at Uncle Charles' garden, the foggy landscape ripe for dreaming in...

"Last night," I said, "how did you know I wouldn't throw you out of the car?"

"Because you didn't."

"My Uncle Charles had a name for that kind of logic."

"I'm sure he did."

"What if I had?"

"Kicked me out? I'd have walked home, I guess."

"Have you ever done this before?"

In answer, he slid his hand to the place god-fearing people don't go and started doing expert things with his fingers. I cuffed him on the side of the head. "That's not what I mean."

The hand withdrew. He laid his cheek on my abdomen. "Not since I joined the force."

"Before then?"

"A friend in high school, and...someone I knew at university."

The sweatshirt he'd worn on Saturday. "Waterloo?"

"Kinesiology. I thought about teaching PhysEd."

"And that someone..."

"Is married. I'm godfather to his girl. She's seven. They live in Elora."

"Why me? Why now?"

At first, I thought he hadn't heard me. "Do you know Milton Acorn?" he asked finally. "Canadian poet. He wrote something, I can't remember all of it... 'I spun you out of my eye's fire / It wasn't you, but my own desire / For the pure vein of silver running there.'"

I felt something go through, out of me, as if someone had cranked open a hot-water valve. I blew out a long breath.

He looked up. "I figured you'd understand."

"A cop who quotes poetry," I said, trying to lighten the mood.

"Past grade two," he said lazily. "And now," he sat up, "breakfast."

"Clean-up first."

Instead of helping, he tried to enact something you'd see on a Greek urn while I was bent over behind the couch mopping up. I slapped him away, muttering Uncle Charles' favoured response to spills of all kinds: *Who'd've thought the old man had so much blood in 'im?* When I turned around, he mugged a wounded puppy expression.

I told him to shower while I made another stab at breakfast. He emerged wrapped in a towel. The bulge underneath it grew as he watched me pour coffee into mugs, receded when we sat at opposite ends of the couch to eat, legs up, facing each other.

"'S good," he muttered through a mouthful of toast.

"Homemade."

He nodded, sucking butter from the space between his thumb and forefinger. No expressions of surprise. No compliments. Just the nod and some serious, ruminant-style chewing. My own arousal barometer rose a kilopascal or two.

"You wanted to tell me something yesterday?" he said finally, brushing crumbs off his chest, reaching down to the floor for his coffee. "You left a message."

"I'm surprised you remember."

"What was it?"

"Two things. One is that you can add Nils Janssen's name to the list of people who knew Mann and Laura were in Elly's studio."

"It's always been there."

"Because he's president?"

"Yes."

"I guess that makes sense, but you have to understand: Mann's visits to Toronto were completely unconnected with the Con. Elly arranged everything for him, privately. She didn't keep Janssen posted on his whereabouts. Mann's being in the building at all was unusual. Janssen shouldn't have known."

"So how did he?"

"Russell Spiers. The two had a meeting earlier, before Spiers dropped by the studio to see Laura. He told him then."

"That's funny. Neither of them said anything about a meeting."

"You think it's significant?"

"I can't see them both forgetting."

"The other thing is Elly's studio key. Did she happen to mention she left it with Laura and Mann on Thursday?"

"No." He drew out the syllable, as if he'd have a few choice words for her later on.

I jumped to her defence. "Now don't go getting pissed off. It's an easy enough thing to have forgotten."

He tweaked one of my toes. "You really like her, don't you?"

"I could throttle her sometimes."

"What did she do to get you so devoted?"

"Left me no choice."

"Was she your teacher?"

I shook my head. "She's voice only. Long story, and I'm not getting into it now. The thing about her key is that someone returned it to the front desk Thursday evening. I know because I watched her sign it out on Friday. Has anyone explained to you how the Con closes down at night?"

"Yes. Karen Jacobs, the night girl at the front desk. She buzzes the studios at a quarter to ten so everyone knows it's time to clear out. When the keys come in, she files them in a drawer underneath the counter of the front desk. The janitor checks any studios whose keys are missing at ten."

"Which means Elly's key had to have been in place by then, or the janitor would have gone up. Talk to Karen. See what she remembers. I doubt she took the key directly; it was more likely left on the counter. People do that all the time. Whoever's minding the front desk usually lets the keys pile up before getting around to them. Alternatively, whoever brought it back could have leaned over the counter and dropped it into its slot in the drawer if Karen had been distracted for a moment. One way or the other, he or she had to have come by the front desk. You need to get Karen to remember who she saw leaving after eight forty-five."

He took a sip of coffee and looked out the window. I couldn't tell whether he was pleased or miffed because he hadn't cottoned on to the returned key himself. I stroked his calf. He frowned, staring through the leaves.

I got off the couch and went over to the piano. The keenness of passion attenuated, our conversation back to the murders, the August-Förster seemed to offer a kind of solid familiarity.

"I also saw Ulrike Vogel yesterday," I said.

He looked over. "You've been busy."

"Bryce was right—she did know Mann had had Laura sing through the *Liederkreis*. And she suspected why."

"Did she give any reason for lying before?"

"Respect for the dead. Shame. Denial. All very dramatic. It might even have been genuine."

"Do you think she'd kill to hang on to the premiere?"

"You asked me that before. I really don't know. It's a question you're better equipped to answer than I. My experience at sussing out murderous intent isn't quite what yours must be."

I meant it lightly, but his face clouded over. "It's no joke."

The spectre of Detective Inspector March slipped into the room, the first I'd seen of him since Andrew had undressed me the night before. I didn't know whether to apologize or let it ride, so I compromised, picking out the tune of "Sorry Seems To Be the Hardest Word" with one finger. He smiled, but it didn't last very long.

I got up and started collecting dishes. He took it as some sort of cue and went hunting for his clothes. His towel slipped, then last night's lover disappeared inside shirt and pants. He wound a tie through his collar, knotted a quick four-in-hand and shrugged into his jacket.

"You got a brush?"

"In the bathroom."

I followed him to the back and watched him run bristles through his hair. It was short enough that I couldn't see why he bothered.

"One more thing," he said, studying himself in the mirror. "David Bryce. He says he hardly knew Dieter Mann. Is that true?"

"Yes. Why?"

"He was seen talking to him around eight o'clock."

"I remember, you said. Outside the washroom."

"Aside from Spiers, that makes him the last person to see Dieter Mann alive." He turned around. "I wondered if it was something I should follow up."

"Where was Bryce at the time of the murders?"

"In his studio."

"With anyone?"

"He says not."

"Not much of an alibi, then."

"It checks out. The janitor saw him go upstairs after talking with Mann. His studio's on the third floor."

"I know. Far end of the south wing."

"The janitor went up right afterward. Spent the next hour in the hallway, polishing the floor. He says Bryce was in his studio the whole time. Couldn't have missed it if he left."

"Then why ask about him?"

"No stone unturned."

At the front door, he turned down my offer of a ride downtown. "It's okay," he said, "I'll grab a cab on Queen Street." He reached for the doorknob.

"I'm going to visit the Dean today," I said, sensing he didn't want a return to intimacy for goodbyes.

"Dean?"

"Simmons. At the Faculty. Mann met with him about the *Liederkreis* proofs. I want to find out exactly what was said."

"Right." He touched my arm, a curiously impersonal parting gesture. "Let me know if you learn anything."

He went briskly down the driveway and turned left at the sidewalk—no hesitation, no backward glance. I waved anyway, then went inside and phoned the Faculty of Music, setting up an eleven-thirty appointment to see the Dean.

I didn't feel like doing much of anything in the vacuum left by his departure, so I puttered around, carrying on yesterday's task of unpacking. I found three sketches for a kite I'd never built and tacked them to a post supporting the loft. A maple chess-clock went beside the stove as a timer. Some matted watercolours I'd done of Léo's house and the surrounding hills hid a drywall seam in the room at the back. Six origami grasshoppers in colours of the rainbow found their way to the top of the filing cabinet. *More than hobbies, less than vocations*—reminders of transitory interests that compelled my full attention for a period of time, then faded. Only music seemed to have the power to hang on.

While I was in the back, I cleaned my Pentax and all its lenses, then, around ten-thirty, made coffee and sat at the piano. Christian stared out from the framed photograph beside the music rack. Dark hair so much like my own, blue eyes... I stared back, my thoughts not on him, but March. Andrew. I felt traitorous, but what could I do? The kinaesthetic memory of last night ran roughshod over any notion of fidelity to the dead. Were my feelings about Christian going to go the way of kite-building and watercolours then? Was that all it took? A romp in the hay?

Was that all it had been?

The re-emergence of March-the-detective, the coolness of his farewell, left me wondering. Worrying. Why had he slept with me? For all he knew, I could have been a murderer. My involvement with the case was surely enough to make me a suspect, even if he claimed otherwise.

And why had I slept with him? I'd told Léo I couldn't trust anyone who'd even want to be a policeman. Now I'd made love to one. Several times. Which of us was guilty of violating ethics? And which of us had possibly invested more in what had happened than was there?

The hardness between my legs provided an answer, and I didn't like it. I got up from the piano and headed for the shower.

꙰   ꙰   ꙰

"I doubt the Faculty will get the proofs now."

Dean Simmons settled his genial bulk into a worn armchair. Between us was a low table with a plate of Peak

Freens and a steaming mug of tea. The Dean took a biscuit and bit in. A few crumbs fell to the front of his turtleneck and onto his corduroys. He brushed them away and picked up his mug. "Mann said the donation was against his daughter's wishes. She feels the proofs should remain in Germany, part of the national heritage. So I assume that unless he made specific provisions in his will, they'll go to her."

"That'll certainly come as a relief to Nils Janssen."

The Dean blew on his tea and looked at me inquiringly.

"The Rawlings endowment," I explained. "He was worried about the publicity you'd get."

"Humph." He took a swallow and put down his mug. "Do you want to know what I really think of Rawlings' endowment? I wish he'd just give his money to the Con and be done with it."

"Janssen's not quite so phlegmatic."

"I'm sure he's not. Question of seeing things as they are, Vikkan. The Faculty's doing a fine job. We have excellent teachers. Our orchestral programme's providing the country with half its symphony players. History's got some good people in it. Education's swamped with students. Things are tight—where aren't they?—but Rawlings' money isn't going to make that much of a difference."

"Not all your department heads agree."

His eyebrows went up. "Spiers?"

I nodded.

"Russell Spiers is a pain in the ass. He's been sucking up to Rawlings behind my back for months now. He refuses to understand that even if we do get the money, it'll be disbursed equally throughout the Faculty. If this were the military, I'd have him drummed out for insubordination."

"Not much you can do, then?"

"He has tenure. But," he added darkly, "his term as Head

of Performance is coming up for review." He picked up another Peak Freen and dunked it in his tea.

"Did Mann actually show you the *Liederkreis* proofs?" I asked.

"Yes. Surprised me, actually. Seemed to me they weren't something you just carried around in a briefcase."

"Mann was accused more than once of not having enough respect for the printed page," I said. "For what the musicology set likes to call 'historicity'."

"Ah, yes. 'The concert hall is becoming a museum, and interpreters slaves to history.' It was his father who said that first, wasn't it? Romantic, really, when you think about it. Makes sense he'd be more concerned with the music itself than the paper it was printed on."

"I'm sure he knew its value."

"No doubt. A very peculiar man."

"When he spoke to you, what exactly did he say?"

"He described the work, explained how it came into his possession. Said that for personal reasons, he wanted to see it housed in the library here."

"Nothing else?"

"Not that I can recall."

"Nothing about the composer?"

"Schumann? No. Why would he?"

So Mann hadn't told the Dean. And Morris-Jones hadn't shared her intelligence either. "Schumann didn't write it," I said. "It was composed by Clara Wieck."

The Dean's big, grey eyebrows shot mid-forehead and stayed there while I related what I knew.

"Clara Wieck," he muttered. "Well, that certainly changes the nature of the thing, doesn't it?" He shook his head slowly. "What do you suppose he was up to?"

The question seemed to be rhetorical. I shrugged. The Dean got up, brushing off more biscuit crumbs, and went to his window. "A great man, Vikkan," he said, peering through two slats of the horizontal blind. "Legendary, really, in his own way. I wish now I'd had the chance to meet him more than once."

He stayed by the window, peering outside, seemingly lost in thought. Presently, to my surprise, he began to chuckle.

❧   ❧   ❧

It was near lunchtime when I left the Faculty. I'd read somewhere that the Intercontinental Hotel across from the Con had a new chef, another young Turk hell bent on reinventing *haute cuisine*. I decided to find out what the fuss was about but regretted my curiosity as soon as I entered the restaurant. Not only did the room smell more of money than culinary excellence, I found I was seriously underdressed, even for lunch.

Worse, a brash voice hailed me as I was being shown to my table.

"Vik! Hey! You by yourself?"

Doug Rawlings sat two tables away. Across from him was the model-redhead I'd seen the week before with Janice Cleary. It appeared both had reached the dessert and coffee stage. He waved me over expansively and stuck out a damp hand.

"Mr. Rawlings," I said. "A pleasure to meet you again."

"It's Doug. No need for last names. Sit?"

I looked wistfully at the table that should have been mine. "Thanks."

Rawlings introduced me to his daughter while the *maître d'* pulled out my chair and fussed with my napkin.

"How do you do, Mr. Lantry?" Siobhan asked very properly,

extending a slender arm across the table. Her pale blue eyes gave me a rapid vertical stare that didn't go with her girls' school manners.

"You're a friend of Janice Cleary's," I said. "I saw the two of you together last week."

"Yes, I remember. Over at McDonald's." She turned to her father. "Mr. Lantry's helping Janice get ready for her exam."

"That so? Janssen finally get you?"

"Not yet. I'm helping Siobhan's teacher out a bit. She's got a lot on her plate right now."

"Because of Miss Erskine, Daddy," Siobhan explained. "My lessons with Miss Gardiner are an hour now, remember? Janice still gets only a half hour and goes to Mr. Lantry the rest of the time. Like I was doing with Miss Erskine."

She made it sound as if she were getting preferential treatment. Rawlings beamed, but some reflexive insecurity made him ask if she liked the arrangement. "The president thinks Vik here's pretty hot stuff, you know," he added.

Siobhan's eyes darted to me and back. "Janice thinks so, too. But I like it the way things are."

Rawlings put an arm around Siobhan's shoulders and squeezed. "That's good, honey. As long as you're happy."

A waiter materialized for my order, reciting today's "creations", a schizophrenic list of veal stuffed with Roquefort and mango slices, quenelles in anisette with onion marmalade and prune purée, and venison with lingonberry coulis. Siobhan examined me covertly from the confines of her father's heavy embrace while I made a decision.

"You know what my wife says, Vik?" Rawlings asked after I'd settled on quenelles. "She says I spoil Siobhan. Can you believe that?" He held up a hand as if he thought I'd actually reply. "Okay, okay—maybe sometimes. But I've got the money, and she's my little girl. And look at her. Does she look spoiled to you?"

This time, he wanted an answer. "Not at all," I said.

"Of course not. If anything, I'm too strict. We're churchgoers, you know. Baptist."

"Oh, Daddy," Siobhan put in, "you're not too strict."

Rawlings beamed again.

"I was just talking to Dean Simmons," I said, changing subjects. "Over at the Faculty. Your name came up."

"That so? What did he say?"

I hesitated. Rawlings spotted it right away. "Go on," he prodded. "Tell me the truth."

I shrugged, apologizing in advance. "He said he'd just as soon you gave your money to the Conservatory and left him out of it."

Rawlings' face went blank. A low burble started in his throat, and I was wondering if I'd given him a coronary when the sound suddenly burst forth as loud, braying laughter. Heads turned. Rawlings carried on, dabbing the corners of his eyes with his napkin. "What a riot," he gasped. "I knew I liked you, Vik. Don't beat around the bush, do you? He actually said that?"

"I'm afraid so."

"Wouldn't say it to my face, though, would he? But at least he admits it." His whole body shook.

Siobhan, filial devotion slipping, looked away.

"Don't think I don't know what's going on," Rawlings said, his mirth petering out. "Janssen trying to impress me when all he ever wants to do is take a bath when I leave the room. The Dean wishing I'd just disappear. And that fag—what's his name? Spiers—sucking up all the time.

"You know what my father did for a living, Vik? He was a honey dipper. A sewer cleaner. The guy who goes around emptying your septic tank. Types like Janssen and Spiers have had their noses in the air since the day I was born. But now I've got something they want, and suddenly I'm the rat's ass. It's great. Like holding a bone between two hungry dogs." He dabbed at his eyes some more.

My order arrived—hard on the hungry-dog simile—but I found my appetite slipping as Rawlings expounded on his theme like a demagogue who can't see that he's lost his audience. Fortunately, the quenelles' presentation was more artful than generous.

"Daddy," Siobhan piped in when I was about halfway through, "I have to go now. My lesson with Mr. Bryce is in five minutes."

He broke off. "Of course, sweetheart. You run along now. I'll keep Vik here company."

She gave him a kiss, which he returned with a proprietary peck on the forehead. Then she held out her hand to me. "Goodbye, Mr. Lantry." Her middle finger rubbed provocatively against my palm while she smiled sweetly at her father.

"My little girl," Rawlings said, watching her leave.

"Not so little. She's what? Sixteen?"

"Seventeen. I know, I know. Kids grow up too fast these days, Vik. Way too fast. Comes from having parents who don't care. Me," he announced, tapping his chest with a thick forefinger, "I care. And Siobhan's better for it. I look at the other girls from her school, and I think to myself: Thank God she's not like that. You know what I mean. She's sweet. Innocent. Just what I'd want a daughter of mine to be."

There's none so blind, I thought, unable to find a suitable response to his unwitting avowal of parental cecity.

"Siobhan's seeing Bryce for theory and history, then?" I asked, figuring her musical training made for a safer topic than her moral education.

"You know him?"

"We graduated together."

"Is he any good? Janssen says he is. I see his name on all the books Siobhan uses."

"He's certainly high-profile."

He smelled equivocation. "You don't think he's good?"

"Oh, no, I'm sure he's excellent."

I turned my attention to my plate. Rawlings went back to holding forth about himself, which encouraged me to finish up quickly. As soon as decently possible, I called for the bill, which Rawlings insisted on paying.

☙ ☙ ☙

"Surprise!"

Elly looked at the florist's crate I was holding. "What's all this?"

"Replacements. Begonias, violets, even a Christmas cactus. They say the best thing when a pet dies is to get another right away. Well, say hello to Fido."

She eased the studio door wider, letting me in. "This isn't necessary."

"Of course not. And I understand. You don't want to feel disloyal to Mildred and Chastity. Still, trust me, it's the best thing."

I carried the crate to the piano and set it on the bench. The glaziers had been in. A new window with its little sticker still in the bottom corner admitted late afternoon light across the plants.

"What's gotten into you, Vikkan?"

"What do you mean?"

"You're not usually this chipper."

There was a funny little catch in her voice—fatigue, maybe, or something deeper.

"I'm sorry, Elly. I thought the sooner things in here got back to normal..."

"No, Vikkan," she backtracked. "I should thank you. It's terribly considerate."

She sat in her club chair and began massaging her arms as if she had a chill.

"Is everything okay?" I asked. "I can put the flowers in a corner and get to them later, if you like."

"I'm fine. Really. And I do appreciate this. I'm just a bit tired, that's all."

It wasn't fatigue troubling her. "It's hit home, hasn't it?" I asked. "The murders."

I knew what she was feeling. After leaving Rawlings, I'd wandered over to Queen's Park and sat for a while, thinking over the past few days. There had been, I realized, something almost pleasant about them, a feeling of being uprooted, of being accorded special status in the universe because of grief. Now the emotional upheaval was ebbing, and things were returning to normal. For Elly, who had known Mann better and Laura longer than I, normal would mean a lengthy period of enduring the banal, with a constant adjunct of remembrance and loss.

" 'The Hour of Lead'," I said.

"I beg your pardon?"

"Emily Dickinson. *This is the Hour of Lead— / Remembered, if outlived, / as Freezing persons recollect the Snow— / First— Chill—then Stupor—then letting go—.*"

"That's it exactly."

I started taking flowers out of the crate and placing them on the window sill.

"I saw Inspector March downstairs earlier today," Elly said, watching me work.

"Talking to Karen Jacobs," I said over my shoulder

"Are you turning psychic, or have you taken to trailing the police?"

"Neither." I told her about the key. "It may not lead to much, but if Karen remembers anything—"

"She isn't always at her post," Elly interrupted. "It isn't a job that pays well. I think sometimes employers don't realize how taxing it is to sit around doing nothing. Clever of you to have thought of it, though. I gather you've seen Inspector March since Sunday?"

"Several times."

"Has he told you anything?"

"Only that Laura didn't die the way it looked."

"I know." She pointed to her *récamier*. I noticed for the first time that the roll cushion was missing. "The police were very polite. They actually apologized for taking the cushion away."

I finished setting out the flowers—pride of place going to two extravagantly efflorescent violets, *Saint-paulia ionantha*—and watered them from the kettle on the desk. Afterward, I wandered around, idly straightening things. Elly remained where she was.

"You know what the worst of this is?" I said, pulling some yellowing leaves off the philodendrons by the window. "The more I talk to March, the more it sinks in that someone you and I both know did this. I feel uncomfortable saying: 'These are the people I suspect,' but that's exactly what we need to do."

"Ulrike," Elly said, without hesitation. "Janssen. Possibly Morris-Jones. Maybe Russell Spiers. He was seen outside the studio."

"It feels strange saying it out loud, doesn't it?"

"Yes. It's one thing to ascribe motive, or means, or opportunity, like in a book, but quite another to imagine someone you know committing murder."

"Motive. Means. Opportunity. You're starting to sound like March."

"Marsh, actually."

"As in Ngaio?"

She nodded. "It's easier to think about if I pretend it's a murder mystery."

"You've given the matter some thought, though."

"Of course. And I spoke with Inspector March yesterday. He dropped by in the morning."

"Oh? What did he want?"

"I'm not entirely sure. He had a lot of questions about you."

"Really?"

The murders may have knocked Elly for a loop, but her gossip-nose might still pick up a scent. I was close to the big bookcase with its five glass-fronted tiers of bronze busts, so I pretended to inspect Brahms' beard.

"Yes, it was most peculiar. He seemed to be fishing for something." *Oh-oh.* "I couldn't quite see where he was going. I'm sure he doesn't suspect..."

I studied the names impressed on the square bases: Chopin, Bach, Purcell, Rimsky-Korsakoff. Mann had stood beside me Thursday night, looking at this same display. What was it he'd said? *"...some of these lesser composers were talented. I would miss them if they were not here."*

Suddenly, I wasn't listening to Elly anymore. Schubert, Elgar, Haydn, d'Indy... The busts were in no particular order, neither alphabetical nor historical. Wagner, Beethoven, Spohr...

"Elly," I interrupted, "have you looked at these recently? I think one of them's missing."

"Missing?" She got up. "Which one?"

"I'm not sure."

She came over and started looking. Handel, Verdi, Hummel, Rameau...

"Delius," she said. "He was right here on the end, beside Haydn. The others have been scooted over to fill in the hole."

We looked at each other. There was no need to state the obvious.

"You should call Inspector March," Elly said.

"Right."

She went to her chair and sank down. "This is too awful, Vikkan. Attacking Dieter and Laura with..." She let out a shaky sigh. Her head fell back against the chair. "And they knew what they were doing, didn't they?" she said to the ceiling. "I mean, whoever would notice a missing bust of *Delius?*"

⚹   ⚹   ⚹

Elly's six o'clock pupil showed up before I could call. I said I'd drive by Fifty-two Division on my way home.

In the hall outside, Mrs. Wigrell was hunched down, hugging one of her pupils goodbye. The boy—Asian, about seven—smiled happily from the folds of her flowered dress. I waited until she stood up and shooed him off, then asked if she were busy.

"My next student isn't till six-thirty."

"May I talk to you for a minute?"

She gave me a noncommittal look, the one people use with suspected Jehovah's Witnesses. I realized she didn't know who I was, even though we'd spoken briefly the week before. "I'm a friend of Miss Gardiner's," I said. "Vikkan Lantry."

"Yes. I saw you two together last Friday." *In the teachers' lounge, waiting to be questioned.* "Come in."

Her studio was Elly's in mirror image, but furnished more sparsely. Posters of kittens adorned the walls, along with Crayola drawings—presumably her students'—and a paint-by-numbers portrait of Schubert.

"I'd like to ask you something about last Thursday night," I said, standing just inside the door. "I hope that's all right."

Teaching children must have immunized her to requests that came out of the blue. "What do you want to know?" she asked placidly.

"I understand you told the police you heard singing coming from Miss Gardiner's studio at eight-thirty."

"That's correct."

"And that when you left here at nine o'clock, the lights were off."

"Yes."

"You heard and saw nothing else in the intervening half hour?"

"I was teaching."

"But you did see someone outside the studio at a quarter after eight."

"Yes. Russell Spiers from the University. I happened to be standing where I could see through my door across the hall."

"Could you see who he was talking to?"

"No. I only saw him briefly. He seemed to be saying goodbye. The studio door closed, and he left."

"Could he have returned?"

"It's entirely possible. I said so to the police. May I ask why you're interested?"

"Laura Erskine was a friend."

A look of concern crossed her face. "Oh, I'm so sorry."

266

Given a chance, she'd surely have come over and hugged me.

"Did you know Laura?" I asked.

"Not well. We chatted sometimes in the hallway. I know she sang beautifully. As you pointed out, I heard her on Thursday night. It was only a snippet, but it was lovely. Mahler. The last song of the *Kindertotenlieder.*"

That would be right—Laura had said she'd brought it along, hoping to tempt me into staying with her and Mann. A good choice. On any other night, it would have worked.

I wasn't sure what I was hoping to get from Mrs. Wigrell. Asking questions was just an excuse. I'd seen her in the hallway and felt the need to establish a connection. She'd heard Laura singing only minutes before she died. It seemed the right thing to do. I couldn't think of anything else to say, so I thanked her for her time and left.

Halfway downstairs, I turned around and went back. Mrs. Wigrell had started playing Mozart's "Ah, vous dirai-je maman". I knocked and poked my head inside.

She broke off mid-phrase. "Yes?"

"I'm sorry to disturb you again. Something just occurred to me. You said you heard Laura singing the *Kindertotenlieder.*"

"That's right. The final song."

"I believe you also heard someone at the piano, accompanying her?"

"Yes."

"How did the playing sound? Odd, in any way?"

"I don't think so. Why? I know the accompaniment's fiendishly difficult, but it sounded fine to me."

"Complete, would you say?"

Her former look of maternal warmth got replaced by something faintly quizzical, as if she were starting to suspect I wasn't quite right in the head. "I'm not sure what you mean," she said. "I only heard it briefly, through the door, but it seemed to be all there."

I said a second quick thanks and closed her door before she could call the white-coats.

The *Kindertotenlieder.* Songs on the Death of Children. How many hours had I spent learning it? Mahler had written it for full orchestra, never intending it to be accompanied by a single pianist. The last song in particular was a killer. The whole first half depicts a hellish storm, complete with crackling lightning and buffeting winds. Bass and tenor instruments fuel the gale, blustering around in double thirds and octaves, the upper notes all studded with gusting trills. What probably isn't too taxing for an orchestra—the cellists play the unornamented notes while the violists toil at the busy-work—is a virtuoso feat on the piano. The ring and little finger of the left hand have to pick out the fast-moving bass, while the rest of the hand shakes out rapid-fire trills.

Trills that Dieter Mann, minus a left thumb and index, could not possibly have played.

Twelve

Manches geht in Nacht verloren.
("Much is lost 'twixt night and morning.")
    —*Liederkreis*, Opus 39, X

Y ou're sure about this?"

"Absolutely," I said. "There's no way Mann was playing."

"It's what I said in the first place."

"You didn't ask Mrs. Wigrell what Laura was singing."

"And she couldn't have been playing for herself?"

"Not likely."

"Explain."

The curt request didn't come from the same man who'd spent last night with me. His desk at Fifty-two Division looked wider than before.

"The accompaniment's too physically demanding," I said. "You couldn't play it and sing at the same time. Not well, anyway."

"So you'd have to be good to play it at all?"

"Yes, don't expect that to tell you much. Nearly everyone you've talked to could manage it. Except maybe Morris-Jones. I have no idea what her pianistic skills are like."

"And this missing bust?"

"You've seen the display in Elly's studio. There must be thirty or forty of the things. No wonder she didn't spot it right away."

He sank his chin into his palm and drummed the desk with

his other hand. I couldn't get him to look at me directly.

"So, it looks like the murderer didn't come in with a weapon after all," I said.

More drumming. "Is anything wrong?" I asked.

He frowned.

"Andrew?"

He swivelled around, opened a drawer in the filing cabinet, and passed me a dark blue folder. "Read this." Not a request; an order. Uncle-Charles-in-my-head whispered: *Love is not love which alters when it alteration finds...* I doubted Shakespeare meant his sonnet to cover the present situation. But if he did, Andrew March was certainly in love, because his behaviour toward me hadn't altered in the least, professionally at any rate.

I opened the folder. Inside were several fax sheets, the top one typed, the others handwritten.

"I spoke with Mann's daughter again," he said. "She sent me these."

The typed sheet was a short cover letter in English. The handwritten ones were in German. An extravagant crest surmounted the first—Gottlieb & Schranz, Verlag—dated August 17, 1839. The next, in a different handwriting, had only *Toronto* at the top. *"Meine liebste Anna,"* it began, *"Manches Mal haben wir über das Schicksal dieser herrlichen Entdeckung geredet. Ich weiß, Du bist mit mir nicht einverstanden..."*

I looked up.

"Go on. Read it."

Dear Anna,

Many times have we spoken about the fate of this marvelous discovery. I know you do not agree with me, but really, when you think on it, what difference does it make whether this library or that university holds the thing? Music lives in its performance. The printed page is merely a guide, infinitely reproducible. It has no value in itself.

Of course, this *Liederkreis* being by Clara Wieck gives it uncommon significance, especially to those who must know a work's provenance before consenting to its genius. It is on this account that I am writing.

I have conceived an idea. Forgive your father for not discussing it with you. The thought has been in my mind for some time—since first you found the proofs waiting patiently in the attic at Piedmont, in fact.

I am overcome with the urge to play a joke, what may be perhaps an old man's last chance at prankstering. I have decided that this work shall come to light *exactly as intended:* that is, I shall donate the proofs to the University here just as if they are the work of Robert Schumann. I have no doubt historians will gather round to debate their authenticity. Ink and paper and dry analysis mean so much more to them than ears and heart. But such is the nature of the work that in the end they must concur: a masterpiece by Schumann.

Only *after* this, and after the songs have been premiered, will I reveal the truth that only you, and I, and little Ulrike know.

Your grandfather had his fun with a joke of this kind when for years he played Beethoven *Bagatelles* that he'd written himself. Perhaps it's in the blood, this urge to prick the balloon of learning.

Indulge me, my dear, and say nothing of this. I am sending Jakob Schranz's note back with this letter.

Keep it safe until I return. The proofs I will leave here in Toronto, as planned.

Your loving Father

"When did Anna get this?" I asked.

"Yesterday. With the time difference between here and Vienna, she waited till today to call. Read the rest."

I turned my attention to the other sheets. The fax machine had had a hard time with the handwriting. The bowls of the letters were clear enough, but the old-fashioned ascenders and descenders trailed off to jagged connect-the-dots. I struggled through, filling in what was missing, mentally changing some of the unfamiliar spelling. Luckily, the publisher's insignia and the date had clued me in on what to expect.

I finished reading and laid the folder on the desk, leaving it open. "So there it is," I said. "Proof the *Liederkreis* wasn't composed by Schumann."

"Proof?" He spun the folder around and read out loud: " '*dieses liebliche Werk von Ihrer Braut*'...this lovely work by your fiancée...as much skill in composition as in playing...a noble and generous gift to have it published for her...' I don't think so. Proof would be the music itself, written in Clara's hand."

"Sorry. Should I have said 'secondary source indications'? You'll make a wicked history teacher if you ever decide to leave homicide."

A warning look: Don't get cute.

"At least we know the letter wasn't stolen," I said.

"Which is going to make a lot of people very happy, but right now, it's a complication I don't need."

"How so?"

"That professor with a mouth like a pimp? Morris-Jones?

She suspected Mann wasn't going to reveal the truth about the *Liederkreis,* right? The way she acted on Wednesday put her on the suspect list, but we figured she wouldn't kill him and steal the letter. It didn't make sense. Now that we know it wasn't stolen..."

"You think she went looking for it and got carried away?" I shook my head. "I don't know. I can't see Morris-Jones as the murdering type. A lot of bark, sure, but—"

The dark line of his eyebrows rose a fraction at the bridge of his nose. "I see—you can recognize the murdering type? Care to tell me how?"

Okay, okay, I get the point. "Does she have an alibi?" I asked.

"She was with a grad student between eight and eight-thirty. That's been confirmed. We know she tried to locate Mann just before that, because of her call to Ulrike Vogel. The story, by the way, is that she wanted to apologize."

"I know. Ulrike told me. Hard to believe. Easier to imagine a certain former prime minister admitting he received kickbacks on an airplane deal than believing Morris-Jones wanted to say she was sorry."

Something like a smile broke through, but only for a second. "She walked over to the Conservatory afterwards— Ulrike had told her Mann was there—but she only checked the key sheet. Since Miss Gardiner had already signed out, it looked like there was nobody in the studio. Morris-Jones left and went home."

"Any way to check that?"

"She says she phoned Mann's hotel later on from her apartment. The receptionist remembers a woman calling around nine, with, I quote, an 'excoriating' accent. I think we can assume it was her."

"Literate receptionist. Must have made it past grade two."

Hook threaded, bait not taken. He straightened up the faxes and closed the folder. "Did you get anything useful from Dean Simmons?" he asked.

"Only that Mann didn't tell him the *Liederkreis* was by Clara Wieck."

"At least now we know why."

"The Dean wasn't too upset when I told him. Surprised, yes, but I got the impression he found the whole thing rather amusing."

"Strange reaction. Mann's little joke wouldn't have done his faculty much good."

"The Dean's very easy-going, not at all like Janssen. And quick, which always catches his staff off guard. I wouldn't be surprised if he intuited what Mann was up to. If he did, I'm sure he'd see the humour in it. What about you? Any luck at the Con?"

"With Karen Jacobs? She says she went to the washroom at nine. When she got back, Janssen was at the front desk, looking over the key sheet. If he's telling the truth, that was just to check up on Miss Gardiner.

"Some people had dropped their keys on the counter while Karen was gone, but she didn't get around to them till nine-thirty, when David Bryce showed up and asked her to check for a book another teacher was supposed to have left him. She couldn't find it and told him to check the mail room, then came over to the counter and started on the keys. She can't remember whether Miss Gardiner's was among them."

"No help there, then. Anyone could have returned it, including Bryce, while Karen was looking around for his book."

"I also called on Russell Spiers at the Faculty to ask about his Thursday night meeting with Janssen. He says he simply forgot to mention it when I spoke to him before."

"You'll have to talk to him again. If Mrs. Wigrell saw him outside Elly's studio at eight-fifteen, and someone was in the studio with Laura and Mann at eight-thirty—"

"—he might have seen whoever it was and 'forgotten' that, too? I know. Hell, maybe he was the one she heard playing."

He stood up and started pacing, massaging the back of his neck. "I don't like this. I really do not like it. If someone was in the studio at eight-thirty and hasn't come forward, you'd have reason to think that person's the killer. But it doesn't work. The studio was broken into. The killer didn't knock and get invited in. And, no," he cut me off before I could say anything, "he or she did not go out through the window, then break it so it looked like he came in that way. They'd have had to jump to the roof, and we found no indication of that. There was a fresh coat of tar down there, remember? A descent from that height would have left an impression. So what was the mysterious piano player doing? Sitting around while somebody smashed the window and climbed in?"

His office wasn't big enough to contain his frustration. He gave up pacing and parked himself against the desk.

"He or she could have killed Mann and Laura, then left the building and gone around and climbed up," I said.

"Why?" He asked out of reflex; he hadn't really heard.

"To make it appear the studio was broken into. Same reason they faked the vandalism inside. So the whole thing would look random."

I might as well have spoken to the wall. Grey eyes I'd seen such promise in that morning looked but saw no farther than the puzzle turning round behind them. He straightened up. "This is going nowhere. I'm out of here. I need some rest." He swung his jacket off the back of his chair. "Maybe something will come up."

"Concerning the case, you mean."

He registered the humour with a twist of the mouth that didn't quite make it to his eyes.

"I wish I weren't working tonight," I said.

"It's just as well. I'm beat."

⚘ ⚘ ⚘

Outside Fifty-two Division, I couldn't think where I'd left the Rover. When I did remember, I stood patiently at the corner and waited for a green light to turn red before stepping into the street. A minivan honked and swerved. I gave the driver the finger before realizing it was me who'd made the mistake.

Like the man whose day-after remoteness had me distracted, I, too, was exhausted. Unlike him, though, I had to be at work in a few hours. To go home, or not to go home? Perchance to sleep? I decided to tough it out.

Food was becoming a priority. I hadn't eaten since my lunch with Rawlings, and it was now after seven. There was a Portuguese fish market on Baldwin Street over in Kensington Market with a terrace out back. It wasn't too far from Fifty-two Division. A walk there and back with grilled sardines in between might do me good. It would only kill an hour or so, but I'd figure out what to do afterward.

What to do came to me as I was mopping up the oily remains of supper with Portuguese cornbread. The scheme Mann had outlined in his letter to Anna would only work if no one knew that Schumann hadn't composed the *Liederkreis*. That information, as I'd discovered over the past couple of days, was less of a secret than he'd supposed. What were the chances that his "old-man's prank" was less of a secret as well?

He hadn't discussed it with Elly. I knew that. For all her

closed-mouthedness at times, she'd have said something by now. What about Ulrike? He'd have had to tell her sometime. She couldn't very well give a concert of songs by Clara Wieck without noticing that the program said Robert Schumann.

I called her from a pay phone, but all I got was the answering machine. I couldn't think how to ask what I wanted via a message, so I hung up.

On the way back to Dundas Street—a pleasant enough walk through the evening-lit avenues bordering Kensington Market—it dawned on me that if Mann had spoken to Ulrike, she might have said something to David Bryce. He was, after all, one of the people Mann had overlooked when, in his letter, he had incompletely listed the cabal who knew the identity of the *Liederkreis's* composer.

On the off-chance Bryce would still be at the Conservatory, I drove over, pondering the potential consequences of Mann's prank. A single question fueled my speculations: would anyone feel so threatened that they'd kill to prevent his plan being carried out?

By the time I pulled into the Conservatory parking lot, I had an answer.

☙ ☙ ☙

The view into Bryce's studio was obscured by a coat-tree, the same kind as in Elly's studio. Someone must have gotten a deal on them a few decades back. I couldn't hear anything inside, which meant Bryce wasn't practising—unless it was his smile in front of a mirror. I knocked.

A shuffle of coat-tree moving aside, a quizzical look through the little glass pane, and *Vikkan—what are you doing here?* left unasked when he opened up.

"Hi," I said. "Can I bother you for a minute?"

"Sure. Come on in. Have a seat." He cleared music from an orange-and-brown seventies-style daybed in one corner.

"I'm not disturbing you?"

"Just finishing up." To prove the point, he squared some student papers and slid them into his leather knapsack. Company for his wallet, I guess.

"Working hard?" I asked.

He rolled his eyes. "You don't know the half of it. Between my own students and playing for Ulrike..." He shook his head.

"She's keeping you busy?"

He shrugged. "What can I say? She needs me. And, frankly, she's more important than all this." He waved a hand, dismissing the studio, his desk, the row of textbooks between metal bookends.

"You must know her pretty well by now," I said. "You're one of the chosen few."

"It's true—she doesn't open up to people easily."

"But she does trust you."

Mahatma Gandhi couldn't have replied "yes" more humbly.

"You have quite the history of gaining people's trust," I said.

His eyes flickered over to the books on his desk, the official Conservatory imprimatur on the covers, Molly Peterson's well-known name in big print beside his own. "You don't think that's wrong, do you?"

"Wrong? No."

"It's how you get ahead."

" 'Ambition succeeds where talent fails'?"

His show of teeth came a split second late. "A question of getting ahead when ahead is where you want to be. There's no harm in making the most of opportunities."

"Like cozying up to Ulrike?"

"I wouldn't be playing the *Liederkreis* premiere otherwise."

"Just getting ahead," I said.

"It's what you've got to do, Vikkan. I never understood that about you. Back at school, you were the best. Everybody knew it. You had Spiers on your side. You could have taken advantage of that, but you didn't. And now this *Liederkreis*. How could you turn down a chance to play it? I don't get it. It would have been the opportunity of a lifetime."

"Maybe," I said. "Just not my lifetime." I didn't want to get into this, not with Bryce. Luckily, his mentioning my turning down Laura provided a lead-in for the reason I'd come. "You know the police think it may be involved in the murders?"

"What? The Schumann?"

"I'll assume you know he's not the composer."

His eyes went hard a moment, like bits of green ice. "Of course."

"What's been puzzling them is that the letter proving Clara Wieck composed it has been missing for a couple of days."

"Was it stolen?"

"As it turns out, no. Mann had sent it back to Vienna, to his daughter. Apparently, he was up to something."

The eyes went wide. "Oh?"

"I wondered if you knew anything about it."

"Me?"

"I thought perhaps he might have discussed it with Ulrike, and she'd said something to you."

"Shouldn't you be asking her, then?" The eyes still guilelessly wide.

"Look," I said, annoyed, "do you know what I'm talking about or not?"

He dropped the pretense. "Mann's little joke?"

"Did Ulrike tell you about it?"

"Yes, last week. Mann discussed it with her on Wednesday. I didn't want to say anything just now because—well, because it's what she wanted. She thought the idea was amusing, might even bring some extra publicity. But after he died, she started worrying how it would make him look. She idolized him, you know, like a father. The thought of him looking foolish... She didn't come right out and say it, but I knew she was asking me to keep quiet."

"And, of course, she'd be able to rely on your discretion."

"We've become close. She counts on me. A talent like hers..."

I could feel another of his dithyrambs coming on: Ulrike the *artiste,* Ulrike the fragile little bird. The one at the doughnut shop had been enough. I made noises about seeing a man about a dog, and left.

❧   ❧   ❧

"Well," Léo said to me later that evening, "at least you don't have to ask yourself the morning-after question."

I raised my eyebrows over a glass of Scotch.

" 'Will I ever see him again?' " Léo said. "The investigation should take care of that."

"Ha-ha."

It was nearly two in the morning. The last of Evelyn's patrons had left twenty minutes ago. Léo and I were alone on stools at the bar.

"You're not feeling guilty, are you?" he asked.

"Guilty about not feeling guilty, maybe. But I don't think it's that."

"What then?"

I drained my Scotch and went behind the bar for another. "I think, Dr. St-Onge," I said, "that I'm not very good at distinguishing deep emotion from summary concupiscence."

He smiled at being called doctor. "Take a piece of free medical advice—don't hide behind four-dollar words."

"Sorry, can't help it. Uncle Charles' doing. The stronger the feeling, the bigger the word."

"Stick to one or two syllables."

"All right. How's this?" I dropped some ice in my glass. "Last night I fucked a man who's acting *reeaalll* cool today."

"I didn't say your grammar had to slip."

"Here's to sloppy English," I toasted. "It sounds so convincing." I came around and sat down again. "Who knows, Léo? Maybe I'm just a fringe benefit of his job."

"That kind of self-deprecation doesn't suit you."

"It's two in the morning. We're sitting in an empty bar. I'm allowed."

"That only works in black-and-white movies."

I sloshed my ice cubes around. They made a nice, comforting sound. "He says he's never done this before."

"In that case," Léo mused, "and given the unusualness of the circumstances, I think we can assume he's influenced by something more than casual lust."

"Which is precisely what I don't want to hear."

"You're concerned where it might lead?"

"That's a bit premature, don't you think?"

"It's what's bothering you."

"I wish you wouldn't get in my head that way."

"Doesn't take a genius."

I toyed with my glass a bit longer, then dipped a finger in and licked it off. "What if, Léo? What if?"

He knew what I was talking about. "Andrew March is not Christian," he said. "Christian was unique. He wasn't meant for this world."

"How terribly operatic."

Léo's eyes flickered, but he wasn't about to be cowed by sarcasm. "Do you blame yourself somehow?" he asked. "For what you didn't see?"

"I saw, all right. I just didn't know what it was."

"Would you have not loved Christian if you had? Would his illness have scared you off?"

"It's what drew me to him in the first place."

"And you're worried something similar could happen again?"

"Or that it won't."

I took a big swallow of Scotch and got off my stool. A cigarette I'd left in an ashtray on the piano had gone out. I relit it and took a drag, then noodled a few bars of "One for My Baby".

"This is all your fault, Léo. If you hadn't encouraged me to cooperate with him—"

"—you wouldn't have slept with a man who, by your own account, leaves nothing to be desired. In the bed department, at any rate. *Mea culpa.*"

I played the pianistic equivalent of a raspberry and turned around. He was grinning, the crowsfeet behind his glasses crinkling back into his hairline.

"How is the investigation going?" he asked. "Have you been able to help him out?"

"I've talked to some people, made a few suggestions, that's about it. The physical evidence points to Mann dying first and Laura surprising the killer."

"So you're concentrating on who'd have a reason to kill Mann?"

"Right. You remember that music I told you about?" He

nodded. "It's almost certainly at the heart of things. The problem is, instead of reducing the list of suspects, it keeps generating more."

"Like a detective novel."

"Exactly. I keep thinking reality ought to be different."

Léo chuckled. "For you? I don't think so." He stood up. "You finishing this?" he asked, holding up my glass. "We really should clear out."

"Pass it over." I drank up while he locked his office and turned off all but a few security lights.

The air outside felt good, but hit me like a soporific. A Peter Warlock song popped into my head: "Come, sleep, and with thy sweet deceiving, lock me in delight awhile..." Text by John Fletcher, 1579 to 1625. Léo gave me a funny look when I started singing.

"Goodnight," I yawned. "See you tomorrow."

"Take care, Vikkan." He gave me a hug and Gallic kisses on both cheeks. "Sleep in. I think you need it."

❧   ❧   ❧

Which advice I would have followed, if the phone hadn't woken me. I let the machine answer; I was learning.

"This is Ulrike Vogel. It is nine-oh-five, Thursday morning. Please return my call."

Later, I thought and rolled over, snuggling into unchanged sheets laced with pheromones. My body responded in a way not conducive to slumber. After fifteen minutes, I gave up and climbed down from the loft.

I was finishing a third coffee when Ulrike called again.

"Guten Morgen, Fräulein Vogel," I said. *"Sie haben vorher telefoniert.* What can I do for you?"

"Would you be free to come by this morning? There is something I wish to discuss with you."

"When were you thinking?"

"In an hour, say?"

"I can be there. May I ask what it's about?"

"We will discuss it when you arrive. *Bis später.*"

That was interesting. There were things I wanted to ask her, but I couldn't imagine why she wanted to see me. I puzzled over it while getting ready to leave and was still mystified about it when I pulled into her street an hour later.

She opened her door before I reached the front steps. "Vikkan," she said, holding out her hand. I wondered if I was supposed to kiss it. "Thank you for coming." Thank you? From Ulrike? "This way, please."

She led me through her long hallway down into the teaching room. Late morning light poured in through the French windows, making the piano look freshly polished.

"Coffee?" She gestured to an end table holding a small porcelain pot, a creamer of steaming milk and a single cup.

"Thank you."

She sat on the sofa and poured, adding the milk without asking. I took the cup and settled into the Biedermeier chair.

"I will come directly to the point," she said, watching me sample the coffee. "What is your impression of David Bryce?"

"Do you mean his talent, or personally?"

"His musicianship."

"He plays well enough. An excellent sightreader, technically proficient."

It was a cagey answer. Ulrike picked up on it right away. "Then you feel he is not...*ein echter Künstler?* A true artist?"

"I'm in no position to judge. I haven't heard him since we graduated. That was over six years ago. Why?"

She stood and went to the piano. The backlighting put her face in darkness and made a soft aureole around her hair.

"I have a very special request. The reason why I asked you here." She paused. "Would you consider playing for me when I sing Frau Schumann's *Liederkreis?*"

The penny dropped—Ulrike waiting by the door, the gracious manners, hot milk for my coffee. I should have known she wanted something. "You have reservations about Bryce?" I asked.

"No, no. He is a fine studio accompanist. Always so...available. I have no complaints. But for something this important..."

She left the piano and sat down next to me. Her face no longer in shadow, I could see she'd gone to some trouble to make herself up. Nothing overdone—just a suggestion of blush, some flattering colour around her eyes—the whole skilfully applied, the effect nearly subliminal.

"You see," she said, leaning close. "Dieter never heard him play." A whiff of lily-of-the-valley came off her blouse. "But he did hear you. I could always sense when Dieter felt he was in the presence of great talent." She leaned a millimetre closer. "A talent such as yours, for example."

Bryce had said there was no harm in making the most of opportunities. I wondered how he'd feel if I took his advice now. "I'm sorry," I said. "I don't think I can do it."

Bryce had also said he couldn't understand why I'd turned down Laura's similar request to accompany the *Liederkreis*. Once again, just as on that long first day after the murders, I found myself wondering how things would have been different if I'd agreed. If I'd stayed on Thursday evening and made a commitment to the future, instead of heading off for a communion with the past.

Ulrike's voice cut through my thoughts. "But I do not understand," she said impatiently. "We have worked together. Like Dieter, I can tell that you are *außergewöhnlich*...extraordinary."

"I'm very flattered, and I thank you, but the answer's still no."

She wasn't used to being refused. Not much practice, I guess. She looked down, hiding her expression.

"It's because of Bryce," I said, calling on ethics to which I felt no real allegiance. "He's said more than once how much he values working with you. I wouldn't feel right taking over from him."

It was the right thing to say. Ulrike tilted her head and nodded. *"Natürlich.* This I understand completely. But I ask you, please—think on it."

For courtesy's sake, I assured her I would.

Presently, she rose and moved back to the piano, to the keyboard itself this time. As if unable to stop herself, she let her hand wander over a few notes, then started singing:

> *Deine Lippen selbst mir sprachen*
> *Wörter, die ich kaum verstand.*
> *Strahlen hell die Nebel stachen*
> *Ungewißheit rasch verschwand.*

The third verse of the seventh song: With thine own lips thou hadst spoken / Words of portent yet unclear / All around bright rays had broken / Through the mists of doubt and fear. Beautiful. Ulrike was in fine voice.

She stopped singing but remained by the piano, gazing outside. Was she trying to tempt me? Some sort of musical seduction? If I hadn't had other things on my mind, the strategy might have worked.

286

"Fräulein Vogel," I said, shattering the silence left in the song's wake, "I know about Herr Mann's little intrigue."

She stood very still, scarcely breathing, as if she were posing for a portrait. I wasn't sure she'd heard me. "I was afraid of that," she said finally.

"You didn't approve?"

"On the contrary. Dieter talked about it with great delight. Such pleasure it would have given him. Alive, he could have—how do you say?—brought it off. But now?" She shook her head. "How did you find out?"

"Indirectly, through a fax Anna sent to the police. The plan was ill-conceived, you know. Too many people knew the work was Clara's."

She turned toward me, suddenly animated. "You will not speak of this," she said sharply. "I will not have Dieter's memory ridiculed. No one is to know what he was planning."

"It's bound to come out, one way or the other."

She made no effort to conceal her annoyance this time.

"Ulrike," I said, risking her first name, "I have to ask—did you yourself discuss Herr Mann's scheme with anyone? Prior to his death?"

I thought at first she wouldn't answer. The view through the French windows held her attention again. She moved closer to the glass, twisting a ring on her right hand, looking down to inspect it, up again. When her words came, they were toneless, an admission of something I could only guess at.

"David Bryce," she said, exhaling softly, "and Russell Spiers."

※　　※　　※

Ulrike's little neighbour, Tessa, was squatting in front of the Rover when I came outside, poking her finger through a dime-sized hole in the bumper. The hem of her school tunic trailed on the pavement. The green uniform didn't suggest the kind of place that sends its kids home for lunch. Maybe Mr.-and-Mrs. Tessa had a housekeeper.

"What's this for?" she asked, turning her finger around experimentally.

"The crank."

"What's a crank?"

"A great big long metal rod with a handle on it. You put it in there and turn hard when the motor won't start."

"Can I see?"

"It's in the back. Maybe some other time."

She got up and adjusted herself under the tunic. "Were you visiting your friend again?"

"Yes."

"She has a *nice* car."

Shattered by a child's honesty. "Is that so?" I asked. "What kind?"

"A red one," came the solemn reply.

"Impressive."

"But she doesn't use it much."

I crouched down and looked her straight in the eye. "And how do you know? Do you spy on her, dogging her every movement so she never has a moment's rest from your cunning observation?"

Tessa giggled. "You talk funny."

I straightened up. She followed me around the jeep. "She talks funny, too. And she likes to go out in the rain."

"Really?"

"Yes. I saw her once."

"You did?" I asked, fiddling with the door latch.

"Yes. I was up in my bedroom. I couldn't sleep because we

were going on a field trip the next day. At school. We went to the zoo. Did you know they have a white tiger there? It's awesome. I want one."

I banged the door with the heel of my hand. Tessa didn't seem to notice that I wasn't paying much attention.

"So I sat up in bed and looked out my window. I'm not supposed to do that. Daddy gets mad when he looks in and sees I'm not sleeping. But it was raining. I like the way things get all shiny in the rain, don't you? That's my bedroom over there." She pointed straight-armed at a dormer in the house beside Ulrike's.

"Mmm." I banged again.

"And that's when I saw her drive her car into the garage and come out the front door and go walking down the street. She didn't have an umbrella or anything, but she wasn't running, and she was getting all wet, so that's how come I know she likes going out in the rain."

The latch came unstuck. At the same instant, a little *frisson* ran up the back of my neck. I turned around.

"When did you see this?" I asked.

"Last Thursday."

"Are you sure?"

"We were going to the zoo the next day."

Ulrike had said she'd been at home all Thursday night.

"Tessa, this is very important—you don't tell lies, do you?"

She shook her head solemnly.

"Never?"

"Never."

"What time do you usually go to bed?"

"Seven-thirty. Except I get to stay up on weekends. Why?"

Thirteen

Meine Liebste auf mich warten.
("And my darling there attends me.")
    —*Liederkreis*, Opus 39

I used a phone at the Edward Johnson Building to call Fifty-two Division. For once, I made it past the operator.

"Two things," I said in reply to a very brusque *Yes?* "First of all, it turns out Mann's little joke with the *Liederkreis* wasn't exactly a secret. He'd discussed it with Ulrike. She told David Bryce. There's no surprise there; he'd have had to know since he'd be involved. However, what is surprising is that she also told Russell Spiers."

"Spiers? Why?"

"I don't know. I was lucky enough to get that much out of her. The ice wall came down when I started asking questions."

"Did she want to stop Mann from going through with it?"

"No, she was prepared to go along. And in any case, she'd tell the Dean if she wanted to stop him, not Spiers. I'm at the EJB right now. I want to find out what Spiers has to say."

There was a long pause. "I think perhaps you'd better leave that for us." Us? As in we, the police? More silence. "Further involvement at this point on your part could jeopardize our investigation."

The careful phrasing sounded like the close of a Royal Commission report. Or a Dear John letter. Smart rejoinders flashed through my head like dialogue cards in a silent movie:

Direct: "Are you speaking personally or professionally?"

Sarcastic: "Does this mean I can expect a cheque in the mail?"

Cliché: "But, Inspector, you can't take me off the case. Not now. Not when I'm so close."

Off-colour: "You want me to pull out? Now?!"

"I'm going to talk to Spiers," I said evenly.

And what came back, equally controlled but chillier was: "You had something else to tell me?"

"Yes. You may want to talk to Ulrike again about her alibi."

A shuffling of papers and something like the click of a ballpoint. "Go on. I'm listening." Note-taking and curt questions on the other end while I recounted what Tessa had seen through her rainy window on Thursday night. "Thanks," he said when I finished. "We'll get on it right away."

He hung up. I frowned at the receiver. It felt as if I'd just talked to Crimestoppers, not a man who quoted Milton Acorn and had licked me in places probably still illegal in parts of the world. There must have been someone in the office with him.

With that thought in mind, I went upstairs to the second floor to pay a visit to Russell Spiers.

* * *

As Head of Performance, Spiers had earned the privilege of an office with an antechamber, the latter staffed by an iron-haired woman who'd clearly attended the withering "What? No appointment?" school of secretarial arts. I was trying without much luck to get past her when Spiers himself poked his head out the door—probably to ask for a fresh pot of coffee.

"Can I see you a minute?" I asked over Dragon Lady's head. Her eyes narrowed. Spiers' went wide. "My, my," he said.

"Will wonders never cease? If it isn't the lovely Vikkan Lantry come a-calling. Far be it for me to refuse."

I eased past the cold Mrs. Danvers gaze and into Spiers' office. He held the door just wide enough for me to have to brush against him as I entered.

"And to what higher powers should I burn incense for this unexpected visit?" he asked, going around his desk and sitting down.

"Try the gods of curiosity," I said, staying close to the door. "I'm here about the *Liederkreis* Mann discovered."

"Oh? And what's your interest?"

"Its connection to the murders."

"Playing policeman, are we? After some brownie points with that delectable detective?"

I held my peace. Responding to Spiers' insinuations was like feeding him a single potato chip then setting the bowl within easy reach.

"Well, are you just going to stand there?" he demanded.

I stayed where I was. "Last Sunday at Evelyn, you implied you didn't know very much about the *Liederkreis.*"

"I was drinking. I don't remember what I said."

"I bet that's what you say to all the boys."

"Oooh," he mugged, "set out the cream. Curiosity certainly hasn't killed this kitty."

"Let me refresh your memory. You inferred you didn't believe Morris-Jones when she told you the songs were by Clara Wieck."

"Did I? Well, you know what a hysterical bitch—"

"Cut the shit, Spiers. I talked to Ulrike Vogel this morning."

"Is that supposed to mean something?"

For a second, I wondered how Andrew would deal with Spiers' evasiveness. Probably a lot more aggressively than I. Telling Spiers to cut the shit had just about exhausted my tough-guy repertoire.

"She says you knew Clara Wieck wrote the songs," I said. "She also says you knew the conditions under which Mann wanted the information to come out. Why did you try to make me think otherwise?"

"Because, Vikkan, dear," he sighed, like an actor playing to the gallery, "I didn't think it was any of your business. What Mann was planning would have exposed this Faculty to ridicule. And as I recall, you wanted to get away from here fast enough after you graduated. Why would I think you'd even care?"

"It wasn't Mann's intention to ridicule the Faculty."

"No? Then tell me, how do you think we'd have looked? Recipients of a highly publicized donation that turned out to be a fraud?"

"I wouldn't call it a fraud."

"Come off it. How many people even know who Clara Wieck is? Once it got out our Schumann was written by his wife, most people would have read 'fraud'."

"Most people? I think you mean Doug Rawlings."

Bulls eye. The day before, driving to the Con, when I'd tried to figure out who stood to lose the most if Mann went through with his prank, Spiers had been my number one choice.

"Rawlings is an asshole," he spat.

"Who'd think twice about giving money to a school that looked as if it didn't know its ass from its elbow. Or should I say its brass from its oboe? Hope you don't mind my asking, but just how far are you willing to go to secure that endowment?"

Spiers rose. "That's enough. You can leave."

"Not so fast. Did you by any chance tell Morris-Jones what Mann was up to?"

"What? And miss the fun of watching her stew over the misattribution? You've got to be kidding."

I put my hand on the doorknob. "One more question.

Who did you see in Elly Gardiner's studio with Laura and Mann when you called on them Thursday night?"

The Dragon Lady's eyes glittered, pitiless and triumphant, as Spiers' "Get the fuck out of here" followed me from his office.

⚜ ⚜ ⚜

I wrapped a rag around the end of a flyswatter and pushed it under the August Förster's strings. I hadn't cleaned my piano in months, and dust bunnies were breeding on the soundboard.

Janice Cleary was due to come by at five-thirty. I'd tried practising to clear my head of the confrontation with Spiers, but my heart wasn't in it. I didn't have the time to start making bread, although I needed to, since all that was left of my last batch was one slice and a crust. And the urge to unpack boxes had deserted me.

I plugged in my ShopVac and passed the brush attachment over the tuning pins. Cigarette ash and eraser shavings skittered amongst the chromium nubs and disappeared into the machine's greedy little trunk.

Treating the August-Förster like a piece of fine furniture (instead of the maintenance-free musical tool it really is) produced an effect similar to raking leaves or washing a car. Thoughts began drifting in and out of focus without regard to order or sense...

Spiers feared Mann's Liederkreis *prank would discredit the Faculty and thereby ruin its chances for Rawlings' money...*

Nils Janssen saw the Faculty getting the proofs as honey that would lure Rawlings away from the Conservatory...

Morris-Jones suspected Mann would never reveal the truth about the songs...

Ulrike Vogel had lied, repeatedly, to dissemble an obvious threat to her career plans...

I unhooked the keyboard cover and vacuumed the raw-looking levers of wood, felt and metal inside. Exposed this way, my king of instruments looked like the emperor with no clothes.

Mann, his skull smashed...Laura, knocked unconscious, suffocated, bludgeoned...a broken pane of glass...Elly's key...Mann at the window...Laura calling 911...someone else in the studio before the break-in...two cups of coffee...a paperweight wiped clean of prints...

I cleared the music rack of books and pencils, set the framed photograph of Christian on the bench, retrieved lemon oil and cheesecloth from the kitchen and went to work polishing the case. The song Ulrike had sung a snippet of earlier began running through my head:

> *Deine Lippen selbst mir sprachen*
> *Wörter, die ich kaum verstand...*

I started humming. With thine own lips thou hadst spoken/ Words of portent yet unclear... The list of herb traces found on Elly's window ledge floated up to consciousness: *cichorium, agropyron, betula, veronica.* The Latin syllables fit the rhythm of the song. *CI-cho-RI-um, A-gro-PY-ron...*

I was down on my knees polishing the pedal lyre when Janice Cleary knocked. I backed out from under the piano but misjudged the distance to the bench behind me. My ankle struck one of the legs and jostled the lemon oil I'd set beside Christian's picture. I reached out too quickly to steady it and ended up knocking the photograph to the floor. I cursed succinctly, let Janice in, and went back to inspect the damage.

The photo had landed face down. I squatted and picked it up gingerly. Bits of broken glass fell from the frame to the floor. All of a sudden, a wave of déjà-vu descended, one so strong that I stopped dead and stared off into space. What was so familiar about this? I stayed crouched down and tried to pinpoint the paramnesia, aware of Janice standing awkwardly nearby.

Then it came to me: Sunday night—cleaning up in Elly's studio, picking glass shards off the flowers beneath her window sill. But why had that memory been lurking so close to the surface? The moment I posed the question, I had the answer.

The order of events in Elly's studio—*we'd gotten it all wrong.*

"Are you all right, Mr. Lantry?"

Janice's voice brought me back. I shook my head and straightened up, apologizing.

"It's okay," she said, slinging off her satchel. "I do that, too, sometimes."

If the comment indicated she might be feeling less shy than last time, I killed the possibility by asking her to call me Vikkan. She blushed and buried her nose in her bag, rooting out music. I flipped on the ShopVac and sucked up the broken glass, trying to decide whether to call Andrew or wait until we'd finished.

"I saw your friend Siobhan yesterday," I said, switching off the machine, having reached a decision.

"I'm not speaking to Siobhan anymore."

"Really? Why's that?"

I should have known better than to ask. "Forget it," Janice muttered.

I shrugged and sat at the piano. If she didn't want to tell me, I wasn't that interested. "Shall we get down to it, then?"

This session went no better than the last one. What is it that gives people the urge to sing, then fills them with dread at the thought of opening their mouths? Squeezing toothpaste from a frozen tube would have been easier than getting Janice to free up her voice. As before, I focused on details strictly mechanical—entries and diction—and left psychological and vocal problems up to Elly.

At ten to six, the phone rang. I welcomed the reprieve and took the call. The voice at the other end sounded a lot less chilly than last time.

"I'm just back from Ulrike's. Her story's changed for Thursday night." What? Mr. No-Further-Involvement volunteering information?

"Hold on a sec," I said and covered the mouthpiece, making apologies to Janice. She hoisted her shoulders in a show of indifference and began inspecting the kite sketches I'd hung next to the kitchen.

"So, what did Ulrike say?" I said into the receiver.

"You want the short or expanded version?"

"What's the difference?"

"Histrionics, tragedy, breakdown, pleas for understanding."

"Shorter, please."

"She got home at eight, just like she said before. And she did get a call from Morris-Jones. But then things start to change." He took a breath and mimicked the Texaco Opera Broadcast announcer. "Distraught because she knew Mann and Laura were together, and surmising they were looking at the *Liederkreis,* she decided to take a walk in the rain—tragically, like a jilted lover. Unable to master her jealous suspicions, she ended up on Bloor Street, where she caught a cab to the Conservatory. There, she stood alone in the parking lot, gazing up at the lighted window of Miss Gardiner's studio."

"That's concise, all right. Where'd you learn to do that?"

"First-year creative writing at the police academy."

"And here I thought all they taught you was how to shoot guns and harass people."

"Oh, no. We had weekly seminars on getting in touch with our inner bully, too."

"Very enlightened. I had no idea." I felt heartened by the apparent *volte-face* from his earlier stiffness and would have liked to continue the badinage, but I felt constrained with Janice hovering nearby. "What time was Ulrike doing her doppelgänger number?" I asked instead.

"Excuse me?"

"*Doppelgänger,* as in the Schubert song. The one about the man who sees a ghost of himself gazing up at the window of his faithless beloved."

"Around eight forty-five. Eventually, she found the courage to confront Mann and Laura directly, but when she got to the studio, the lights were already off."

"After nine, then."

"Would have to be. But there's something else. While she was in the parking lot, she claims she saw someone lurking on the fire escape at the south end of east wing."

"Someone on the fire escape?"

"That's what she says."

"Surely she's not suggesting she saw the murderer? That fire escape doesn't pass anywhere near Elly's window."

"I know. I thought it was strange, her mentioning it."

"Maybe she was adding colour to her story. She didn't by any chance say anything about the window itself, did she?"

"No. It's why I'm having trouble believing her. If she really was in the parking lot between eight forty-five and nine, she had a clear view of the window. She'd have noticed if it was smashed. Unless she did it herself. Or the studio got broken into in the time it took her to enter the building and reach the

298

second floor, which isn't very likely."

"Actually, she may be telling the truth. There's a third possibility, something that just came to me a little while ago."

"Oh?"

Over by the kitchen, Janice had lost interest in the sketches and was pushing experimentally against the loft's support posts, checking to see if they were as strong they looked.

"Look," I said. "I have someone here right now. Could we get together later? I need to see photographs of the crime scene to check out my idea. I could tell you what I'm talking about then."

"We videotape crime scenes now."

"Whatever."

"Anyway, I can't do it. Not tonight. I'm leaving for Hamilton in half an hour. I have to be in court tomorrow morning."

I tried not to let my disappointment show. He could have at least acknowledged that my invitation encompassed more than looking at pictures. "One more thing, then," I said. "Did you get a chance to ask Ulrike about Mann's scheme involving the misattribution of the *Liederkreis?* Specifically, why she told Russell Spiers about it?"

"I did, and I have an answer."

"How did you get her to tell you?"

"Threatened her with a rubber hose."

"Your inner bully coming out. What did she say?"

"Spiers called her Thursday afternoon after Morris-Jones told him the songs were being wrongly attributed. He wanted to know if it was true, and figured Ulrike would be the one to know. Thanks to Bryce, she knew by then that Mann was auditioning Laura to sing the work. She told him about Mann's plan out of spite."

"Another excellent synopsis. You have a talent for narrative summary."

"It's a gift."

Janice was growing restive. I wished I were alone. I really wanted to know whether his deadpanning was a defence against Tuesday night or an oblique reminder of it. "When can I see you, then?" I asked, adding: "To look at the videotape."

"Tomorrow. Later in the afternoon. I should be back by then. Call me here."

I had trouble returning to Janice's lesson. Even at the other end of the phone, the good Detective Inspector's voice had set up a low-level hum in my groin, but his banter, poised between invitation and distance, had left me confused.

Janice seemed distracted, too, as if she couldn't adjust to having my full attention again. I played the introduction to "Caro Mio Ben'," and she came in with the words to "Lungi Dal Caro Bene". An entire verse of Schubert got waylaid. Some mixed-up syllables in Fauré produced a lewd French spoonerism. At the end of fifteen minutes, we called it quits. I made encouraging noises about her upcoming exam, set a time to see her again and watched her scoot out of the carriage house.

Ten minutes later, she returned.

I'd gone to the back room to work on Evelyn's book and gotten sidetracked by a Museum of Natural Sciences publication called *Edible Garden Weeds of Canada*. At first, I thought her knock was a squirrel outside up front, but when it came again, I put down a recipe for bull-thistle stew and went to see who it was.

"I forgot something," she said in the doorway, talking to her feet. "Some music."

I glanced at the stand she'd been singing from. "I don't see it."

"Maybe it's on the piano?"

I went over and looked through the photocopies. "Not here, either. What was it?"

"My...my Warlock."

"Do you want to check your bag again?"

She came in and set it on the bench, pawing through the contents. "Oh," she said lamely, "here it is." She took hold of the strap. The door stood open, but she made no move to leave. "Mr. Lantry?" she said, looking down again.

"Yes?"

"I heard you just now. On the phone. It was about last Thursday, wasn't it? The night Miss Erskine..."

I nodded. "That was the police."

"I think I know..." She faltered, twisting the strap through her fingers. "I think I know who was there."

"There?"

"On the fire escape. You said somebody was on it."

"Who?"

She mumbled something I didn't quite catch.

"I'm sorry?" I asked.

"Siobhan," she said, not much louder. "I think it was Siobhan."

"Really? What makes you think that?"

"Because I met her afterwards. At McDonald's."

"Afterwards?"

"After seeing Mr. Bryce."

She seemed not to be giving me all the information I needed. "You're saying Siobhan had a lesson with Mr. Bryce and left by the fire escape?" His studio was at the end of a hallway, next to a metal door with an EMERGENCY EXIT ONLY sign hung enticingly on the latch bar.

"Yes. No. It's...she was...she wasn't...she wasn't having a lesson with Mr. Bryce."

"But you just said..."

She looked up imploringly. All at once, I understood what

this was all about—the embarrassment, the difficulty with words, the hoping I'd understand.

"You're not saying Siobhan and Mr. Bryce—?"

Her cheeks flushed a painful shade of red.

"Janice," I said quietly, "why are you telling me this?"

"You said you didn't believe there was somebody on the fire escape." Her voice rose, as if I'd accused her of something, or somehow let her down.

"Did Siobhan see something?"

"No! You don't understand!"

"You're right. I don't. Perhaps if you explained?"

I tried to sound reassuring, the way psychologists in movies do. I guess it didn't come off that way. Janice stayed rooted to her spot by the piano bench. Her chin went down, concealing her face behind a tangle of hair. I remembered what she'd said earlier, about not speaking to Siobhan.

"Why aren't you talking to Siobhan?"

This time, I got the question and the inflections right. She let go of her satchel and sank onto the bench.

"It's because of Miss Erskine."

I waited.

"I liked her, you know. I really liked her. She was my friend. She listened. We talked. About a lot of stuff."

"Like Siobhan and Mr. Bryce?"

She nodded, her lower lip trembling.

"There's really nothing wrong with it, you know" I said quietly, carefully. "Mr. Bryce isn't that much older. If Siobhan wanted—"

"It's not that! You don't get it!"

"What, then?"

"It's what she was doing it for. He was helping her cheat. On her exams."

"You mean her history and theory exams?" The ones Bryce would be preparing her for?

"He was...he was giving her the questions. She wanted me to have them, too. I told her I didn't want them. It wasn't right. She said I was being a wimp. And now she says it's my fault she can't cheat anymore." Her voice took on an edge of desperation. "She says if I hadn't talked to Miss Erskine, she could have kept on doing it. She called Miss Erskine a bitch. And she wasn't! She *wasn't!* God, I hate her!"

Suddenly, Janice was in tears. I wanted to do something—go over to her, put my arm around her shoulders—but instinct told me not to. I went to the kitchen for a box of Kleenex and set it down beside her. She grabbed a handful and turned away.

Long minutes later, the sobbing eased up. She blew her nose wetly.

"When did you talk to Miss Erskine?"

She sniffed hard. "Last week."

"Did you tell Siobhan?"

"That I talked to Miss Erskine? No."

"How did Siobhan find out, then?"

"From Mr. Bryce. That's what she said. He told her. She said he's way more of a friend than I'll ever be." She turned to face me. Tears welled up again on her lower lashes.

"It's all right," I said, really wishing I could give her a hug. "I'm sure you did the right thing."

She looked at me uncertainly.

"Do you want to use the bathroom?" I asked. "Splash some cold water on your face?"

She swallowed and nodded. I showed her to the back and gave her a handtowel, then went up front and disposed of soggy Kleenexes. When she reappeared, the hair at her forehead was slack with damp, but her eyes were clear. I handed her her satchel and confirmed the time of our next session as if nothing had happened. She smiled weakly.

As soon as she was out the door, I telephoned Fifty-two Division.

"Detective Inspector March isn't in."

"Is there a number where I can reach him?"

"I'm sorry, sir. We can't give out that information."

"But he'll be back tomorrow afternoon, is that right?"

A disconcerted pause, as if I'd enquired about a state-level secret.

"Yes, sir. You could try then."

≫   ≫   ≫

I climbed the Conservatory main staircase to the second floor, passed by Janssen's office, turned right, then left, then right-left-right again, past the elevator and through the doors at the end of Elly's hallway. It was eight-thirty. I'd called earlier to find out when she finished teaching. I hadn't said much, only that I wanted to talk.

"Tea?" she asked, letting me in.

"Please."

"I've only got orange pekoe left."

"No problem."

I snaffled her club chair while she busied herself with the electric kettle and Styrofoam cups. She seemed more herself than the day before, comfortable again in the familiar surroundings of the studio. Replacing her flowers had been a good idea, after all.

She handed me my tea and went back to her desk to doctor her own with sugar and creamer.

"Well?" she asked.

"Things are getting complicated."

"So I gathered. Do you want to fill me in?"

"I'm not sure where to start. A lot has come up in the past twenty-four hours."

"Try the beginning," she said drily.

She listened with her head to one side, saying nothing while I talked, taking occasional sips of tea.

She'd known nothing of Mann's prank involving the *Liederkreis;* her expression convinced me of that. She looked miffed that she hadn't been privy to the intrigue. The possibility of Morris-Jones as a suspect, now that the proof of Clara Wieck's authorship had shown up, received a slow assessing nod. Ulrike's multiple deceptions brought forth an exasperated sigh. What she thought of my suspicions about Spiers was hard to tell, except that when I related his parting comment, the corners of her mouth tightened. When I explained why I was sure Mrs. Wigrell across the hall had heard someone in the studio with Laura and Mann, she glanced involuntarily toward her door.

"And now," I finished up, "something's come to light that makes me wonder if we haven't been barking up the wrong tree altogether."

"What's that?" she asked, her first words in fifteen minutes.

"David Bryce has been sleeping with Siobhan Rawlings."

Elly set her cup abruptly on the desk's edge. The pity of Styrofoam—it doesn't convey astonishment like the hard clink of china. "You're not serious!"

"I'm afraid so."

"How on earth did you discover that?"

I recounted my conversation with Janice that afternoon, watching Elly's reaction closely. I hated to admit it, but one of my reasons for coming to see her was to find out if she'd known about Siobhan and Bryce. It was just possible that Laura had told her, and she'd chosen not to say anything. Doug Rawlings' endowment, if the Conservatory got it, could make a huge difference to the institution to which she'd devoted her life. She might not be immune to expedient silence where his daughter was concerned.

"That man has the morals of an alley cat," she fumed when I finished. "I don't know how he got on staff here in the first place."

"Good looks and duplicity," I replied. "Some of the teachers think he's great. You've told me so yourself."

"Silly victims of their own vanity when he turns on the charm."

"I gather you didn't know about him and Siobhan, then?"

"I most certainly did not," she said, emphasizing each word. "If I had, I'd have gone straight to Janssen. An affair with a student is one thing—it wouldn't be the first time—but supplying her with exam questions? I can't believe you'd have to ask."

I'd offended her, but there was no taking it back. "Do you think Laura threatened to go to Janssen?"

She didn't answer, caught between indignation and the obvious implication of my question. I got up and went over to inspect her new flowers. She'd misted them recently. Large drops of moisture had collected on the leaves.

"Here we've been thinking that Dieter's discovery was at the heart of this," I heard her say behind me, as if to herself.

"And Andrew keeps glossing over Laura's death as if it's somehow secondary," I said.

"Andrew?" I felt her ears prick up.

"Inspector March." I fixed a strand of Christmas cactus that looked uncomfortably tangled in its pot. "And there's something else we have to consider now, too."

"What?"

I picked a bead of vermiculite off a begonia and turned around, leaning on a free corner of the sill. "I think Mann and Laura were killed before the studio got broken into."

"Before?"

"It came to me this afternoon. Do you remember when we were cleaning up by the window here? All that dirt and pottery and broken glass? Do you recall where most of the glass was?"

She looked at me blankly. "On the floor?"

"Yes, but where in relation to the mess?"

She shook her head. "I'm sorry. I don't follow you."

"I think the glass was mostly on top," I said. "At least, that's how I remember it."

"What's your point?"

"Think about it: you break the upper pane here," I gestured behind me, "and unlock the window. Some of the glass falls onto the sill, but most of it lands on the floor. Then you raise the lower pane and climb in, knocking over the flower pots. They land and break on top of the glass. But that's not how it was. The glass was on top of the mess."

"Which means," Elly said, catching on, "the pots got knocked off the sill before the window was broken."

"Exactly. The killer messed up your studio and came back afterward."

"Why?"

"For your key. We assume it was turned in so the bodies wouldn't be discovered till morning. If the killer left the room, and only thought of that afterward—"

"The only way to get the key would have been to break back in." She nodded, considering. "Does Inspector March know about this?"

"Not yet. I haven't told him about Bryce, either. I was hoping to see him later tonight."

"Tonight? Does he keep such late hours? I thought you played at Evelyn on Thur..." She looked down and started toying with a thread on her cardigan. "Oh. I see. *Andrew.* Well," she said, recovering, "I hope he's pleased by what you've found out." She looked up. "Whenever and however you tell him."

≈ ≈ ≈

We left the studio a few minutes later, Elly claiming a long day.

"I think I'll have a talk with Bryce tomorrow," I said as we walked downstairs.

"Do you think that's wise? Shouldn't you leave that for Inspector March? 'Andrew,'" she added, unable to resist.

"He won't be back till late in the afternoon. I want to find out for myself if Laura threatened to go to Janssen."

"What makes you think Bryce will tell you?"

"Nothing, really. I just want to see his reaction."

"Well, be careful."

We reached the front desk. Elly turned in her key and signed the sheet—in emphatic block letters, I noticed.

"You're not enjoying this by any chance, are you?" she asked, laying the pen down.

The question surprised me. I couldn't come up with an answer. Elly turned around and put her hand on my arm, looking up into my face, studying me with bright, shrewd eyes. "You *are* enjoying it." She nodded. "I think I understand." She took her hand away. "And now, are you going to walk me to my car, or shall we say goodbye here?"

"I'm over the other side of Queen's Park."

"In that case, goodnight. Take care."

"You, too."

I watched her pepperpot silhouette dwindle down the hall toward the parking lot exit, then went outside via the main doors and lit myself a cigarette. I wasn't quite ready to leave yet.

Walter Kurek, the Conservatory janitor, had been interviewed by the police. According to him, Bryce had exchanged a few words with Mann outside the second floor washroom, around eight o'clock. Bryce had gone upstairs immediately afterward, and Walter, polishing the hallways on the third floor, confirmed that Bryce had been in his studio for the next hour.

How closely, I wondered, had Walter been questioned? Bryce had never been a serious suspect; confirming with Walter that he'd been in his studio at the time of the murders might simply have been a matter of form. More important, had the police appreciated what it might mean that Bryce had walked up to the third floor, whereas Walter had taken the slow-as-molasses elevator?

I finished my cigarette and went back inside, up to the second floor, retracing the route I'd taken to get to Elly's studio a half hour earlier. When I got to the elevator, I pushed the button and looked at my watch. The second hand made a full sweep and a half before the doors opened. Walter had been doing floors that night, so he'd have had to load his cleaning cart, mop and pail and most likely a big electric buffer into the cabin. That would take maybe a minute. I held the doors and waited, then stepped inside and pressed "3".

Forty-seven seconds later, with no accompanying sensation of ascent, the doors slid open, presenting me with a view nearly identical to the one I'd just left.

Assuming at this point that Walter would have been unloading equipment, not watching the stairwell ten metres away, I added on another minute. The total, from the moment I'd started timing, came to just over four minutes.

Since I already had the elevator, I let it carry me back to the

309

second floor, then walked over to the women's washroom and checked my watch again. Moving briskly, but not too fast, I entered the stairwell and climbed to the third floor, continuing all the way to Bryce's studio at the far southwest end of the wing. Total time for this trip: forty-five seconds. Just as I expected. Even allowing for Bryce to spend a minute or two in his studio, he'd had more than enough time to go back to the second floor without ever being seen by the janitor.

My next step was to locate Walter Kurek himself.

If once, as a student, I'd known the exact location of his office, I couldn't now remember. Somewhere in the basement, presumably—ground floor, if you happened to enter off Philosopher's Walk. Maybe in the sub-basement beneath that.

I searched the maze of duct- and wiring-infested corridors, through whimsical right-angle turns and up and down unexpected little half-flights of stairs. I finally located a door marked MAINTENANCE, but no one answered when I knocked.

It was Walter who found me.

"Can I help you?"

The voice came from behind, Polish-accented and suspicious. I'd been testing the boiler room door, feeling like a kid playing at Bluebeard's castle. I turned around. "I was trying to locate you," I said.

"It's not that third-floor washroom again?"

"No, it's not that. I have a couple of questions I'd like to ask about last Thursday night."

"Are you police?"

"No."

He looked as if he didn't quite believe me. "I have already spoken to them."

"I know. I'd just like to verify what you said."

"For what reason?"

"I have a personal interest. I knew the two people who were killed."

He scanned my face a moment longer, then pursed his lips and nodded. "What do you want to know?"

"The police asked you about David Bryce, is that right?"

"Yes. I saw him talking to the man who got killed."

"And you confirmed that Mr. Bryce was in his studio from shortly after eight until past nine o'clock?"

"That's right. I was in the hallway. I would have seen if he left."

"I hope you don't mind my asking, but are you sure it was Mr. Bryce in his studio? Did you actually see him go in?"

The wariness returned his expression. "I saw him go up to the third floor. He was in his studio when I got there."

"You're certain? Did you look inside?"

"Why would I do that?" Walter folded burly arms across his chest. "I could see that Mr. Bryce was inside. He'd put his coat-tree in front of the window."

I could tell I'd be making a mistake if I pushed him further. I thanked him and started to walk away, feeling his eyes on my back. He waited till I'd nearly reached the end of the hallway, then called out, sounding defensive: "How else could it have got there?"

Fourteen

Und eh' ich's gedacht, war alles verhallt.
("Ere I did think it, deception it proved.")
—*Liederkreis,* Opus 39, III

The run of attentive listeners at Evelyn ended Thursday night.

When I arrived there after my chat with Walter Kurek, I walked into a lounge three-quarters full of patrons nursing the how-can-it-just-be-Thursday blues, clearly needing a booster shot of soothing sounds to ease them into the long day before Saturday. I noodled my way through three sets of what the doctor ordered—Lloyd-Webber showtunes and Streisand hits—nearly sedating myself in the process. The clients paid little notice, conversed quietly, and kept Toby Ryan busier than usual with vodka martinis and Chardonnay.

The snorefest gave me time to consider what I'd learned from Walter. It proved nothing, really. If what Janice had told me was true, Bryce and Siobhan had been together the night of the murders. Of course they'd blocked the view into his studio. Bryce did that anyway, as I'd noticed when I called on him to ask about Mann's *Liederkreis* prank.

The tranquillizing effects of "Don't Cry for Me, Argentina" and "Evergreen" didn't help me sleep when I got home. The odour of lust still lurked in the loft, and when I tried to ignore it, I started worrying about Bryce again. It had been a mistake telling Elly I was going to talk to him. The smart thing would be to leave it for the police. Fishing for information about the *Liederkreis* was one thing; confronting Bryce came under a different heading altogether, tantamount to an accusation of murder. I could still back out, but I knew I wouldn't. Couldn't. I rolled over, stared at the ceiling, and pondered why.

Murder had cut short a nascent friendship. Two friendships, really, because who knew how close Mann and I might have become had Laura and I started working with him in earnest?

I might have prevented Thursday night's events if I'd remained at the studio. I didn't have to go running off. I could have stayed with Laura and Mann. If I had, they might still be alive. I needed to atone, to take some sort of decisive action to compensate for what had proved to be a fatal truancy.

I wanted to solve the puzzle. "You're enjoying this, aren't you?" Elly had asked. She didn't disapprove. She understood. In a funny sort of way, she'd given me her blessing, whatever her reservations.

All good reasons for confronting Bryce in the morning, and none telling the whole story: that I wanted to prove myself to the man whose scent still lingered up here in the loft. I wanted to show him a trophy, a prize, something to impress him, to invite his praise. The trouble was, the trophy I was after more properly belonged to him. He was the detective, not me. Solving murders was his business, not mine.

Since the dawn of time, men have competed against each other to catch the eye of those they desire. Bigger, faster, stronger, smarter... Laudable or catastrophic, the competition makes sense when it's two men fighting to impress a woman. But what happened when the mate one was vying for also happened to be the man one was contending with? The compulsion was absurd, but, it seemed, as impossible to resist as the seasons or the tides.

I drifted off an hour or so later, contemplating what sort of uneasy truce would have to exist between lust and contest in a relationship with Andrew March. Uncle Charles' never-far-off voice murmured stark lines from *Peer Gynt:* "In love, a prophet and a tomcat are the same."

I called Elly early the next morning to see if she knew when Bryce took lunch. She sounded surprised, less by the question than by the hour of the call. She was supposed to be calling me at this time.

"You're still intending to talk to Bryce today?" she asked.

"That's the plan."

"You're opening a can of worms, Vikkan. Bryce's affair with Siobhan already puts the Conservatory in jeopardy with Rawlings, but if on top of that he was leaking exam questions..."

"I know Laura confronted him about it," I said. "I have to find out whether she threatened to go to Janssen as well."

Elly was silent for a moment. "I don't know his schedule," she said finally. "Even if I did, I'm not entirely sure I'd tell you."

"You don't happen to know where he eats?"

"I've seen him at the Swiss Chalet," she admitted.

"The one across from the Conservatory?"

"That's the one."

Even the click when she hung up was full of misgivings.

I stayed in the carriage house for the next couple of hours, practising, trying not to contemplate what I was about to do. Around eleven, I left for downtown. I needed to get a table near the Swiss Chalet entrance so I could snag Bryce when he came in, and that meant getting there before the restaurant filled up for lunch.

It was nearly one o'clock before he finally showed up. I caught his eye and waved him over. The hostess who brought him to my table looked as if she just might just forgive me for hogging a prime booth during lunch with nothing more than a salad for company.

"This is great, Vikkan," he enthused, slipping off his ever-present leather knapsack. Dressed in khaki slacks and a wool shirt, he looked as if he'd just come from a photo shoot for the Gap. "I hate the line-ups here. The food's pretty good, though, as long as you stay away from the barbecue sauce. Tastes like detergent." He caught a dirndled waitress's eye, flashed some teeth, and ordered a quarter chicken—white, no sauce—without consulting the menu.

"Funny how we keep running into each other," he said after she left. "You disappeared—what? five years ago?—and now everywhere I go... What happened to you, anyway? How come you dropped out of sight?"

"Tired of city life," I said.

"Pressure too much?" he asked, ignoring what was obviously a drop-the-subject answer. "I know, it's true. Once your name gets around, it never stops." He put on a sympathetic face. "I understand, believe me."

"It wasn't that."

"No? Personal stuff?"

"In a way."

"Well, whatever," he said, finally getting the hint, "it looks like you're back in circulation now."

"I wouldn't put it that way. People just keep roping me into things. Like Ulrike. Would you believe she even asked me to accompany the *Liederkreis* premiere?"

His imitation of innocence was pretty good. "Really?" he said. "You refused, of course."

"Why 'of course'?"

"Leopards and spots. You already turned down the chance to play it once."

The waitress came back with his chicken and a small bowl of salad. Bryce busied himself with the plastic container of dressing.

"It's not news to you, is it?" I asked. "Ulrike wanting me to play for her."

He speared a chunk of iceberg lettuce and gave an aw-shucks-you-caught-me-out grin. "She started pumping me about you," he said. "I put two and two together. Can't say I was happy about it, but I did tell her the truth." He popped the lettuce in his mouth.

"Which was?"

He swallowed. "That you're a better pianist than me." He shrugged, as if the admission hadn't cost him anything at all.

"You weren't worried we'd be in competition for accompanying the *Liederkreis* premiere?"

"Competition? From you? I don't think so."

He shook his head and went back to his salad, polishing it off in rhythmic forkfuls, as if by rote. For the next few minutes, I might as well not have been there. He pushed the bowl aside and started cutting his chicken into neat, bite-sized pieces. The meat went into a tidy pile in one third of his plate, his fries into another, the halves of what looked like a toasted hamburger bun completed the arrangement. The operation was mesmerizing.

"You weren't fond of Laura Erskine, were you?" I asked.

"Huh?" He looked up, his fork poised over the plate. "Where'd that come from?"

"Just an observation."

He looked puzzled. "What do you mean?"

"I couldn't help noticing. Last week, when you dropped in on our lesson with Mann. You totally ignored her. I wondered if there was bad blood between you."

He stabbed a fry and brought it to his mouth. "You're imagining things."

"That's good," I said, watching him chew. "I was afraid it might have had something to do with what she knew about you and Siobhan Rawlings."

His jaw froze. I couldn't hear a pin drop only because the restaurant was crowded. He swallowed. "What, exactly," he said, recovering, "is Laura supposed to have known about me and Siobhan Rawlings?"

"I was hoping you might tell me."

He made to take another fry. "Siobhan's a student of mine. What else is there to tell?"

"How about that you were balling her?"

He blinked. "Where'd you hear that?"

"From Siobhan's ex-best-friend, Janice Cleary. Who also maintains there was some quid pro quo going on. A little matter of you leaking exam questions?"

He set his fork down and looked at me with hard green eyes, his face as still and unrevealing as a store mannequin's.

"Laura knew, didn't she?" I asked.

I got the distinct impression that behind his eyes, he was scanning for the right choice between truth, evasion and outright denial. Without looking down, he picked up a napkin and blotted the corners of his mouth. "Janice Cleary," he enunciated very clearly, "is a stupid little teenager, and Laura Erskine was a tiresome, meddling bitch."

"That's funny. 'Bitch' is exactly how Janice said Siobhan characterized Laura, too. She must have scared you bad."

"Meaning what?"

"Where were you when Laura was murdered?"

He exhaled sharply, derisively. "Is that some sort of accusation? You think I had something to do with the murders? For your information—and it's none of your fucking business—I was with Siobhan Rawlings that night. In my studio. 'Balling', as you so quaintly put it. If you don't believe me, ask her."

"It won't be me asking."

"You shit. You told the police? It's not something they needed to know."

"No? You don't think they'll be interested that Laura knew what was going on between you and Siobhan? That she threatened to tell Janssen? That is what she said she was going to do, isn't it?"

Bryce didn't answer. In the silence, I realized what I'd said. *You don't think they'll be interested.* Future tense. He looked past my shoulder, as if seeking inspiration in the view outside on Bloor Street. Then he glanced down. A water glass took his attention. He put his fingers on the rim and started turning it in little half-circles. An expression of private amusement came over his face. "You haven't told them yet, have you?" he asked.

It was my turn to look for inspiration. None came.

"You know, Vikkan," he said slowly, looking up, "I used to wonder how you could possibly play the piano as well as you do. I think I know now. You're some kind of idiot-savant. You really don't have a clue about anything."

I couldn't figure out what he was driving at. He noticed and shook his head as if he felt sorry for me. "Of course Laura said she'd report me. What would you expect her to do? But here's the catch: she did tell Janssen. And guess what? He wasn't going to do anything about it. Nothing. Nothing at all. *Rien. Nada. Nichts.*"

※　　※　　※

I left the restaurant shaken and not a little humiliated. Without thinking, I crossed Bloor Street and made for Philosopher's Walk, heading for the grass at the back of the ROM—the same spot where Laura and I had shared lunch a week and a half ago.

Across the way, a number of the Con's windows were thrown open, letting out a cacophony of pianos, violins, trumpets, voices and flutes. The whole building sounded like an orchestra tuning up.

I sat down and hugged my knees close to my chest. Why hadn't I seen it coming? Of course Laura reporting Bryce to Janssen had posed no threat to him. He'd probably laughed in her face. He might have been less sanguine if his misdeeds had involved anyone other than Siobhan, but with the Rawlings endowment still undecided, he knew Janssen wouldn't risk a scandal by taking any action.

I closed my eyes and hugged myself closer. Swirling orange patterns danced across my eyelids. The sun felt summer-hot through my jeans, but did nothing to dispel the nasty chill forming in my stomach. *What if Laura had disapproved of Janssen's politic silence?* What if she'd threatened to expose Bryce by going to Rawlings directly? If Janssen even suspected...

I'd made a mistake, and I knew it. I should have listened to Elly and gone straight to the police. Why did Andrew have to be out of town right now? Bryce would almost certainly tell Janssen about our lunchtime encounter, giving Janssen plenty of time to polish whatever lies he'd need. And there were still the crime-scene photos I wanted to look at. If they confirmed that the studio had been broken into after the murders...

A thought suddenly occurred to me: did Janssen have access to copies of the studio keys? The way I figured it, the killer had broken into Elly's studio in order to retrieve her key. But if Janssen had duplicates, or could get one without attracting attention, why would he bother? He could simply go up to the studio, unlock it, and retrieve the original.

The memory of Bryce's scorn still stung. I needed to do a little checking before I saw Andrew. I didn't feel like having my conjectures ridiculed twice in one day. I stood up, brushed myself off, and crossed Philosopher's Walk to the Conservatory.

❧   ❧   ❧

Had I the authority of the Metropolitan Toronto Police Force, I could probably have gone up to the front desk and simply asked about duplicate keys. Figuring a civilian enquiry would be met with suspicion, or at least require an explanation, I decided to rent a studio instead and deliberately lock the key inside.

The studio I got was way up on the fourth floor, an airy, garret-type room with a pretty good Bechstein. I had to kill time before going back downstairs, so I practised Bach Suites for half an hour. The piano was turned to face the door, and I noticed several pairs of curious eyes peering in. When my memory for Bach's counterpoint gave out, I left—keyless— and went down to the front desk.

"Could you just give me a spare?" I asked, apologizing for my fictive absentmindedness. "I'll come right back."

The woman in charge—not Karen Jacobs, but Mrs. Hewson, an imposing woman who probably didn't know she'd been nicknamed "Cow"—looked me up and down. "You'll have to go to maintenance," she said curtly, giving no indication that she recognized me from my student days.

"But I've done this before," I said. "They usually just give me a copy right here."

She gave me a look that spoke volumes about what she thought of people who locked their keys inside the studios more than once. "Not anymore. All the duplicates are with the janitor."

I found Walter Kurek lunching on sausage and rye bread in his basement office. I wondered if he lived there. His shift didn't end until the building closed at night.

"Yes," he said, between mouthfuls, his eyes roving over my face, "I have all the extra keys. Since last week. The locks are being changed."

"That would be because of the vandalism on Tuesday? Not because of what happened Thursday night?"

"Yes."

"So until they're changed, you have the old spares?"

It took a long while for him to nod and say yes. My second appearance in two days had made him doubly suspicious.

Upstairs, as he let me into the studio, I asked if he'd made a lot of trips like this since being given charge of the duplicate keys. "It must get really annoying," I added sympathetically.

"It hasn't happened. Until now."

"I guess no one else has a set of spare keys? The president, for example?"

It didn't matter that I tried to sound offhand. Walter's eyes narrowed. "No," he said, "even if Mr. Janssen did something like this,"—something *stupid* like this—"he would have to come to me."

I could see there wasn't much point in asking whether Janssen, in fact, ever had.

Instead of going straight back to the front desk afterward, I made a detour to Elly's studio. From inside, a tenor strangled out a few phrases of Handel's *Ombra mai fu'* and stopped. A moment later, he started again. It didn't sound like the same voice. This time it was rich, confident, supremely legato. Elly working her magic. I left her to it and went downstairs.

As I was signing out, it occurred to me that not once had I been asked to show a student card. Surely that formed part of the new security precautions. Changing locks and tracking keys wouldn't go very far if a stranger could walk in off the street and rent a studio.

I was wondering about that when I turned and came face to face with the man for whom, in his own words, "security is no longer something about which we can afford to be lax."

"Vikkan," Janssen said, "would you come upstairs a moment? I'd like to have a word with you." His tone was polite, but there was no mistaking the steel in it.

Nils Janssen may well have been president of the Royal Conservatory of Music, but I was no longer a student. I could have told him to take a hike. Instead, I followed him up to his office, my heart racing.

"I've just spoken with David Bryce," he said, closing the door.

"That's interesting," I said, trying to sound calm. "So have I."

He went to his desk and sat down. "It seems I misjudged you."

"And I you."

"I asked for your discretion. This is hardly what I expected."

"As I recall, your concern was about Mann's gift to the Faculty."

He picked up a slender gold pen and began tapping it on the desktop. "You've been enquiring into affairs that don't concern you."

"Pardon me if I don't agree. The murders that occurred here concern me quite a lot."

"Looking into them is a matter strictly for the police."

"Whom I intend to assist as far as I can."

The clicking of pen on wood continued. "You will not go to them."

"I beg your pardon?"

"You heard me. You will not go to the police. Mr. Bryce's misconduct with Siobhan Rawlings has no bearing on their investigation"

"I beg to differ."

The pen-tapping stopped. Janssen spoke quietly. "Under no circumstances will I allow this to get back to Doug Rawlings."

"Is that what you told Laura Erskine?"

He drew in a sharp breath. "I assured Miss Erskine the situation would be dealt with."

"As apparently it was."

A muscle twitched beneath his right eye. "This is none of your concern."

"Forgive me if I don't agree."

His voice rose a fraction. "Stay out of this."

"No." The refusal came out sounding less confident than I wanted. Janssen picked up on it.

"Try to understand," he said. "I had to make a decision based on what's best for the Conservatory. Unless you hold a position like mine, you can't begin to know how hard such decisions can be. I'm asking for your cooperation."

"And I'm not giving it." This time it came out firmly. "Not as long as the possibility exists that Laura Erskine died to protect your interests with Doug Rawlings."

Janssen glanced down, toying with his pen again, rolling it delicately between his thumb and index finger. "That supposition," he said, "is dangerously inaccurate."

"I don't happen to think so."

"What do you intend to do?"

"I believe you already know."

He began inspecting the backs of his hands, as if looking for flaws in his manicure. "It will be a mistake if you go to the police."

"Are you threatening me?"

"No, Vikkan, I'm telling you. Your accusation is absurd."

"Let's let the police determine that, shall we?"

He looked up, his eyes flashing. "Let it be, Vikkan," he said, his voice perilously quiet. "An investigation into Mr. Bryce's misconduct will have disastrous consequences for the Conservatory."

"Why? Because Rawlings will find out Bryce has been fucking his not-so-innocent little daughter?" Janssen flinched at the obscenity. "Somehow, I doubt the police will care. And it won't be Bryce's affair that interests them. It'll be your silence."

He half rose. "Which has nothing to do with the murders!"

Only one word seemed adequate to the situation, and I used it as I made for the door.

"Bullshit."

⚸   ⚸   ⚸

Rudeness, however justified, never comes easily to me. Call it a bourgeois hang-up, call it fear of conflict, call it what you will; I left the Conservatory with my heart pumping and palms sweating.

My first thought, when I reached the Rover, was to get in touch with Andrew. He'd said he'd be in later that afternoon. How late was later? I looked at my watch: three o'clock. He might be back now. I jammed the key in the ignition and floored two tons of bolted steel and dented aluminum into traffic.

There was no need to rush. Detective Inspector Andrew March hadn't yet returned to Fifty-two Division.

"Tell him to call Vikkan Lantry as soon as he gets in," I said, giving my number. "Do you have any idea when he'll be back?"

"I'm sorry, sir. If it's urgent, we can relay a message."

My first instinct was to say yes, do that, but then I thought about it. How urgent was urgent? Urgent was saving somebody's life, not knowing who'd killed them after the fact. I said "No, just have the inspector call me," and left.

Standing outside, waiting to cross Dundas, I felt in my pocket for my keys and discovered I didn't have them. Had I taken them into the police station? I didn't think so. That meant I'd left them in the Rover. Not the brightest thing to do, since the doors have no locks.

When I got into the cab, I discovered something worse. In my agitation upon leaving the Conservatory, I had somehow managed to shove the key into the ignition upside down. I wouldn't have thought it possible, but there it was, teeth up. I swore aloud, figuring I'd never be able to get it out. I was wrong. It pulled out easily. The real problem came when I tried to start the engine. Instead of the roar of V-8 kicking over, all I got was the dispirited clicking of a dead solenoid. The inverted key must have kept the ignition circuit open all the time I was driving to Fifty-two Division. The starter would be fried.

I groaned. On top of everything else that day, the last thing I needed was the aggravation of compressing the jeep's heavy motor by hand. I should have been grateful that I at least had that option, but I'd used the crank before and knew what lay ahead.

A few minutes later, panting with effort, smiling grimly at intrigued passersby and wincing from where the crank had smacked me on the wrist, I had the motor up and running.

I wondered where I'd find a new starter. Rovers have an affinity for Jaguar parts, but I didn't want to pay the price. Thinking about starters kept me occupied while I headed along Dundas to Beverley, down Beverley to Queen, then along Queen toward High Park. The mental distraction proved temporary. Soon enough, my thoughts returned to Janssen.

What exactly had happened Thursday night?

I knew Spiers had told Janssen, during the meeting they'd both neglected to mention, that Laura and Mann were in Elly's studio. Had he gone there afterward, knocking politely on the door, come to pay his respects to the Great Mann?

Laura had brought Mahler's *Kindertotenlieder* with her, a special treat to work on when she and Mann finished the *Liederkreis*. Had they already reached the fiendishly difficult fifth song when Janssen showed up? If so, it wasn't unreasonable to imagine Mann inviting Janssen to take over at the piano. Laura would have gone along—regardless of ill-will between her and Janssen—out of respect for Mann.

At eight-fifteen, Russell Spiers had shown up, wanting to talk to Laura about her appointment the next day with music agent Howard Snelling. Spiers must have seen Janssen in the studio at that time. Why was he denying it? Did he think Janssen had done him a favour by preventing Mann from embarrassing the Faculty with his Schumann-Clara prank?

At eight-thirty, Laura had gone out for coffee. Whose idea had that been? Janssen's? A strategy to let him deal with his victims one at a time?

While Laura was out, Mann had gone over to the window. Elly had warned me earlier against opening it, but clearly, that's what Mann had done. His fingerprints were on the lock and frame, and traces of the herbal teas in his jacket had fallen to the ledge outside. Perhaps he needed the air. He hadn't looked well the day before, and I remembered that the studio had been getting pretty stuffy even before I left.

What then? Had Janssen taken advantage of Mann leaning out the window to remove the bust of Delius from Elly's bookcase? After Mann closed and relocked the window, had Janssen shown it to him, pretending to admire it, then simply waited for an opportunity to strike him?

When Laura returned, Janssen had probably been kneeling beside the body, concealing the battered skull. What had he said to her? *Mann's collapsed—call an ambulance?* She'd have gone immediately to the desk, and Janssen—appearing helpful in that ineffectual way people have during an emergency—would have gotten up and come over. With her attention focused on the phone, Laura might not have even seen him pick up the paperweight he'd used to knock her unconscious.

But why then not kill her with the bronze bust? Why suffocate her, then conceal the means of her death with the same object he could have used to kill her in the first place? It made no sense. Just the same, that's what he'd done, thoroughly ransacking the studio afterward and confusing things even further.

It must have annoyed him to discover he'd left the key inside the studio, especially since he was the one responsible for the security measures that prevented him from getting a copy without drawing attention to himself.

My guess was he'd dealt with his oversight immediately. At that time of night, most people going in and out of the Conservatory would be using the front entrance. He could risk a trip down the northeast staircase to the Philosopher's Walk exit. The bust was only twenty centimetres tall, about the size of a litre of milk, easy enough to conceal under a jacket folded over his arm. Once outside, it was just a short stroll to the rear of the building. Hoisting himself up onto the odd little half-floor rise of basement at the back wouldn't have presented much difficulty, and he must have suspected, if not known, that with the roofing repairs going on there, he'd find a ladder with which to reach Elly's window.

A less coolly efficient person might not have thought of breaking only the upper part of the window in order to unlock and raise the lower pane. Equally, a less punctilious person might not have bothered to reclose it. But Janssen was exactly the sort of person who would think of both.

The traffic on Queen Street came to a sudden halt near

Dufferin. A streetcar had come unmoored from its wires. It took the driver only a few minutes to reseat the aerial, but in that time, I considered my reconstruction of Janssen's movements and arrived at the frustrating conclusion that no matter how accurate my suppositions, no matter how compelling his motives for murder, nothing by way of proof had yet showed up to place him in the studio on Thursday night.

※　　※　　※

My answering machine was blinking when I got home. I got a beer from the fridge and listened to the message.

"Vikkan, it's Andrew March. I'll be staying in Hamilton tonight. I'll try to catch you later."

I punched the off button and stared at the machine. A lot of good that did, leaving a message without a number. Some indication of what was keeping him wouldn't have been out of line, either. Well, at least he'd said he'd call back.

I needed something to occupy me until then. A portion of the retaining wall I was repairing still needed dismantling, so I donned a pair of cut-offs and went outside to work, leaving the door open in case the phone rang.

I jimmied out the last stones and laid them carefully alongside the others, then started digging back the low embankment—the first step toward deepening the bed, installing drainage tile and putting the whole thing back together. I probably wouldn't finish until some time next week.

I worked solidly for two hours, listening at first for the phone, then losing myself in the rhythm of digging. Around six o'clock, at the insistence of my stomach, I broke off, returning my shovel and crowbar to the small toolshed behind the carriage house. On the way, I noticed that the sumacs up front had proliferated well past the point of looking merely unpruned. I made a mental note to attack them the next day.

Andrew didn't call while I was making supper. Neither did he call while I was eating. Nor afterward, while I was washing up.

Only a few of the boxes stacked against the wall remained to be unpacked. I opened them up, thinking to kill time, and found they contained only music, most of it unorganized. I didn't feel like playing librarian just then, so I sat at the piano and tried practising. After a few listless scales, I gave up.

A session of bread making didn't appeal either, but my last batch was finished, and a certain ever-present stickler for discipline wasn't going to accept my buying bakery bread just because I wasn't in the mood to make my own. I assembled the ingredients for a molasses-graham loaf—no kneading required—and set it to rise.

Why was Andrew staying in Hamilton? It couldn't be for another day in court; tomorrow was Saturday. Why wasn't he back, sifting through evidence, checking leads, questioning suspects?

And wanting to be with me?

I went to the back of the carriage house and sat at my draughting table. Rows of books stared down from the pressboard shelves. I picked one at random, a text on modern naturopathy, and started flipping pages. Vermifuge, aperient, sialagogue, antilithic... On any other day, I'd have found it fascinating.

Half an hour later, I checked my batter and transferred it to loaf pans. Still no word from Andrew. The bread would take forty-five minutes to proof. Time enough to stroll over to High Park, wander around, and prove to myself I wasn't waiting for a call.

☙　☙　☙

Somewhere around Grenadier Pond, I started humming the seventh *Liederkreis* song, the one Ulrike had sung a fragment of the day before. *Deine Lippen selbst mir sprachen / Wörter, die ich kaum verstand...* With thine own lips thou hadst spoken / Words of portent yet unclear...

By the time I returned home, the melody was well and truly stuck in my head. The silly concatenation of botanical nomenclature that scanned with it was there, too: *cichorium, agropyron, betula, veronica*—the herbs found on the ledge outside Elly's window.

I was still singing when I put my loaves in the oven and forty minutes later when I took them out. The tune wouldn't go away, even when I went back to the draughting table with the firm resolution to work on Evelyn's book. I'd scarcely started when I found myself staring off into space again.

Deine Lippen selbst mir sprachen...Janssen...*Wörter, die ich kaum verstand...* I knew he'd been in the studio, killed Laura and Mann, but what proof was there?... Cichorium, agropyron... Would police forensics turn up something once they knew where to look?... Betula, veronica... Could anyone spend time in a room, commit murder, and leave no trace?... *Strahlen hell die Nebel stachen...* All around bright rays had broken...

I shook my head to clear it. The naturopathy text I'd put aside earlier lay open on the table. I started leafing through again. The boldface plant names and precise line drawings still didn't grab my attention. Alfalfa, anise, barberry, couch grass, dandelion...

I turned to some glossy photos in the middle of the book. The switch from black-and-white to colour seemed to furnish the distraction I needed. The tune inside my head began to fade.

The silence proved shortlived. The instant that I registered the absence of the German words and Latin syllables, the reason for them having been there floated up to consciousness. I stared in disbelief at the book in front of me.

Proof—*my brain had been telling me I had it all along.* I knew exactly what had happened in the studio that night.

I laughed out loud. Despite the enormity of what I'd just realized, how could anyone ignore that the epiphany had come wrapped in poetic lines about sunlight breaking through the mist?

I needed to confirm just two things. The first I found without getting up from the draughting table. The second required a quick call to Elly.

No, she said in reply to the single question I asked, she hadn't mentioned it. Not a word. Not to anyone.

ᘔ   ᘔ   ᘔ

"Vikkan! I've been wondering when I'd hear from you."

The warmth of Evelyn St-Onge's voice travelled down the wires. In the background, I could hear a dishwasher. She'd be in the big slate-floored kitchen, windows open, letting in the cedary Caledon night air.

"I was planning on coming up last weekend..."

"But there's been some trouble. I know. Léo filled me in. How are you holding up?"

"Well, let's just say it's been an intense week. I'll tell you about it when I see you. How are you doing?"

She hesitated. "I was over at the Pan-Abode today, airing it out. I wish you'd been here. It wasn't easy, all alone."

"Léo's not there? I thought he'd gone up for the weekend."

"No, he had to fly to Montreal. Family business. He should be back in Toronto by now if you need to reach him."

"No, I just called to see if it was okay if I came up tonight."

"Tonight? That would be wonderful. When are you leaving?"

"Soon, I think, but don't wait up. I have a key to the cabin. I'll sleep there."

"Are you sure? If you're only here for a short visit, I want you staying in the main house. There's plenty of time to make up a room."

"Save it for tomorrow. It won't be like it's the first night I've slept alone in the cabin."

She caught something in my voice. "You're sure you're all right?"

"Can't hide anything from you, can I?" I teased. "It's nothing. *Une affaire de coeur.*"

"The detective?"

I couldn't hold back a smile. "Léo *has* kept you informed. Don't worry. I'm letting passion take over from good sense, that's all."

"Well, you can tell me about it tomorrow. How's my book going?"

"Half way there. Would you like to see what I've got so far?"

"I should probably wait till it's finished, but I'm too excited. Bring it along."

I started packing as soon as she rang off—socks, underwear, and T-shirts in an overnight bag; transparencies and vellum pages in a large artist's portfolio. A couple of macro lenses for the Pentax. Hiking boots. A flannel jacket. Toothbrush.

I probably shouldn't be going up to Caledon, but I no longer felt like playing widow to the telephone. If a call were going to come, it would have by now. What I'd pieced together—the evidence the police would need to build a case—wasn't going to change overnight. I'd call Fifty-two Division tomorrow, when Andrew got back.

Or maybe Sunday, when I got back.

I deposited my stuff in the back of the Rover and took out

the crank. The air had turned thickly humid, and the always-temperamental engine proved singularly recalcitrant. After fifteen shoulder-straining revolutions of the metal rod, blisters started forming on my palms. I straightened up, caught my breath and went to the toolshed for a pair of gloves.

There was no light inside, and I jostled a few rakes and things before finding the gloves, lodged between a basket of screwdrivers and a paint can filled with screws. I donned them, went back to the Rover and bent down.

The crank wasn't there.

I experienced a moment of disorientation. I was sure I'd left it hooked up to the engine through the bumper. It couldn't have fallen out. I felt for it on the ground anyway, then looked up.

That was when I noticed the object perched on the hood—a bronze head, about twenty centimetres high, the size of a litre of milk.

I froze. A searing jolt of adrenalin rushed through me. I'd parked at a forty-five degree angle to the carriage house, leaving only a small wedge between the building and the front of the jeep. If someone was behind me, I was trapped. And someone was behind me. I heard a rustling in the sumacs.

Instinct told me not to move. "Bryce?" I said.

The bushes moved again, then came the soft scrunch of shoes on gravel. The skin on my back tingled. If I could just turn around...

I felt cold metal brush my neck. Gently. Then it was gone.

"Bryce?" I asked again.

More footsteps. The steel touched the other side of my neck.

"Gee, Vikkan, how'd you know it was me?"

I put my left hand on the hood, meaning only to straighten up, but the metal crank descended brutally on my wrist. For a split second, I felt no pain; then it struck like a bolt of lightning. My eyes flooded with tears.

"How did you know it was me?" he persisted.

"The cheap dramatics," I said weakly, using my head to indicate the bronze bust. The rod came down again, this time closer to the elbow. I gasped and felt my legs go weak.

"Very funny," he said, and landed another blow, this time to the triceps. "How did you know?"

"You told me yourself," I said, sinking to my knees, feeling sick. "Twice. By accident." The words came out sounding hoarse. "I just figured it out."

"Really? What did I say?"

"I turned Laura down...for the premiere."

"You're not making sense."

"I said I wouldn't play...if she sang. The *Liederkreis*. Somehow you knew." I felt as if I were going to throw up. "We only discussed it...in the studio...the four of us. Me, Laura, Mann, Elly." I took a ragged breath, fighting back the nausea. "Elly didn't tell you. So...it had to have come...from the other two. You were there. With them."

The talking was making me dizzy. I let my head fall forward. I felt Bryce poke the crank into the middle of my back. "Aren't you the clever one, noticing something like that?" he taunted, prodding me, making me sway back and forth. The nausea proved too much. I vomited abruptly on the driveway.

Bryce withdrew the crank. "Mann was the one who told me," he said, as conversationally as if he were talking over dinner. "He wanted Laura to give the premiere instead of Ulrike. He asked if I'd be interested in playing for her, since you'd already refused. I knew that bitch would never work with me. But..." he leaned closer, drawing out the syllable, "now that she's dead, and Mann, too, well, let's just say Ulrike will be singing, and I'll be right there, on stage, front and centre."

The taste in my mouth was awful. "Ulrike..." I gasped, spitting, "...asked me...to play."

I felt something on my back again. Not metal this time. Something flat. A shoe. "You think I cared? You're so fucking predictable." He pushed me forward onto the gravel. "Of course you said no. I wasn't worried. At least, not till now. I can't let you go to the police about Siobhan. She's a good liar, but if they start questioning her about Thursday night..."

He held his foot on my back. The side of my face stung with vomit. Sharp stones ground into my cheek. "You left her," I managed to get out, "In your studio. While you were with Laura and Mann."

"Very good."

"You forgot. About the key. Broke in afterward to get it."

"Right again."

I had to think of something to say, something to make him back off. "Too late," I mumbled. "Already told the police. You and Siobhan...Janssen's cover-up..."

He rewarded my lie with a shattering blow to the left shoulder. "I don't think so, Vikkan. You said you just figured it out."

Bright pinpricks began to swim before my eyes. I knew I was going to pass out soon. "Elly," I found the strength to say.

His foot came off my back. Suddenly, he was astride me, forcing the crank against my neck, pushing my face harder into the gravel. "What about Elly?" he demanded.

I couldn't draw a breath to speak.

"What about her?" he hissed, easing up so I could answer.

I gasped. "She knows. You. Siobhan. Going to come out anyway."

The cold steel came off my neck. His weight lifted off my back. I couldn't raise my head to see what he was doing.

"Fucker!" he spat and kicked me between the legs. I felt a

jolt, like going over a pothole, but strangely, no pain. I tried to move my lips, forcing sound from my throat. "Kill her, too?" I managed. "Me, Laura, Mann..."

His answer came back sounding distant, muffled, as if my ears were blocked with cotton wool. It made no sense anyway. "...didn't kill him...stroke...collapsed by the piano..." What was he saying? "...already dead...Laura came back..." He must have bent down; his voice became clear again. "A perfect opportunity. But you wouldn't understand that, now would you? You know, if you'd agreed to play for Laura, none of this might have happened."

I was too far gone to answer. I couldn't move, I couldn't speak. A white haze suddenly filled my vision. I lay there, waiting for another blow, the last.

It never came. Something was seriously wrong with my ears. Everything seemed remote, reverberant, as if I were at the bottom of a well. I thought I heard him walk away, very fast, then stumble and fall. Now he was rolling, gravel crunching underneath him. But that couldn't be, the drive was level. And the sound should be getting fainter.

Suddenly, it stopped. I heard Bryce get up. He was coming back, running this time. His footsteps set up echoes in my head—overlapping, blurring, growing louder. I waited for the cold, hard, final blow.

There was no descent of steel—on my head, on my neck, anywhere. The running stopped. The echoes faded.

A voice, a cry. It sounded like Andrew. "Shit! Jesus motherfucking Christ!"

A hand on my shoulder. The voice close to my ear. "Don't move." Then again: "Don't move."

And faintly: "I'm coming back."

Then darkness.

Fifteen

Der Wald ist lang, du bist allein.
("Alone thou art, the forest long.")
   —*Liederkreis,* Opus 39, II

T he coroner confirmed it. Mann died of a stroke."

"Why didn't they spot it earlier?"

Evelyn and I were finishing up a late breakfast. Crumbs dotted the big pine table between us.

"The damage to his skull was extensive. If Bryce hadn't trashed the studio, spreading dirt around, blood spatters from the attack might have clued them in that Mann died beforehand. As it was, with head injuries concealing the thrombus, and no forensic evidence to point them in the right direction, it didn't show up until they knew what to look for."

One week had passed since an ambulance had sped me to St. Joseph's Hospital for a dose of Demerol, some heavy-duty bone-setting, and an apology that provincial cutbacks prevented my staying overnight for observation. Léo had come to collect me, insisting that I spend the night under his care. The next morning, an implacably professional Detective Inspector Andrew March had shown up at Léo's Glen Road condo, grim-faced and armed with questions.

Evelyn got up to pour coffee. "More toast?" she asked.

"If you don't mind buttering it."

"You're enjoying this," she teased.

"Some things you can't do one-handed."

"Like buttoning up?"

I felt at the neck of my two-sizes-too-large flannel shirt. The left sleeve hung limply over a bulky wrist-to-shoulder cast. Sure enough, I'd misbuttoned by one. "You try it," I said, sticking out my tongue.

Léo had driven me up to Caledon after the debriefing. The first three days had been rough, doing things for myself through a haze of painkillers. After some brook-no-dissent persuasion from Evelyn, I'd given up and let her pamper me.

I hadn't yet heard from the man who'd saved my life, but back in Toronto, Léo had. More than once, I gathered. Léo had phoned the previous night to bring me up to date on the case against Bryce and had exhibited a near-perfect grasp of the whole affair. Evelyn had missed the call—she'd been at a play in Guelph—and wanted all the details. After a week of taking care of me, she knew the players pretty well herself.

"It happened just the way I thought," I explained through a mouthful of toast. "Mann ran into Bryce outside the washroom at eight and invited him to Elly's studio. Bryce went upstairs to tell Siobhan. I don't know whether they'd just finished what they were up to, or were planning to get started, but she said she'd stick around. When he didn't return by nine, she got bored and left, using the fire escape. The janitor, working in the hallway during that time, assumed it was Bryce in the studio because he'd seen him go upstairs."

"The police have talked to Siobhan, then?"

"Yes. Janssen's worst nightmare. I think I'll be staying away from the Con for the next little while. Janssen may not have committed these particular murders, but I'm not betting he won't want to kill me for exposing that whole business.

"The police also talked to Spiers, who now admits to seeing

Bryce in Elly's studio. I'm not sure why he lied about it."

"Maybe he hoped to get something in return. You said he has a taste for pretty boys."

I took a sip of coffee and reached for my cigarettes. Evelyn passed me a book of matches and watched me light up one-handed. "You're getting good at that," she said, smiling.

I blew out the match. "Not a skill I thought I'd ever have to master."

She got up and started clearing dishes.

"According to Léo," I went on, "the police have more than enough evidence to take Bryce to trial. The DNA tests on blood traces in his knapsack came back positive—Mann's and Laura's. They have the bronze bust with the same blood and his fingerprints all over it. And, of course, they have the herbs."

I'd already told Evelyn the story in bits and pieces. Bryce had been suffering from kidney stones when I stepped in for him the night of the Alumni Gallery Concert. Wednesday, the day of my introduction to the *Liederkreis,* Ulrike had mentioned he was no longer ill, and attributed his recovery to Mann. When I asked Mann to explain, he'd brushed it off as nothing more than a bit of amateur naturopathic advice.

Police forensics had turned up traces of medicinal herbs outside Elly's window. The assumption was they'd come from Mann's pocket, since the tisanes he carried around with him contained the same herbs in varying degrees. Sitting at my draughting table, leafing through a book on plant medicine, I'd suddenly made a connection between Bryce's ailment and the specific *materia medica* found on the window ledge: antilithics to dissolve urinary calculi, diuretics, and demulcents to soothe irritated membrane. A remedy for someone passing stones, and the very mixture the police had discovered in a small paper bag taken from Bryce's knapsack following his arrest.

"Siobhan says he took the knapsack with him when he went downstairs. The way I figure it, he stuffed Elly's bronze inside after attacking Laura and Mann, but when he needed something heavy to smash the window, he took it out again. Removing it must have spilled or scattered his prescription on the ledge.

"The list of herbs kept going around in my head to the tune of one of the *Liederkreis* songs. And as if that bit of subconscious prompting weren't obvious enough, the song's own words were trying to tell me something, too.

"The third verse starts off: 'With thine own lips thou hadst spoken, words of portent yet unclear.' What came to me in a flash was that Bryce himself had revealed that he'd visited the studio that night. Twice after the murders, he made reference to the fact that I'd turned down Laura's request to accompany her if she sang the *Liederkreis* premiere. The matter had only come up that evening, so the only way he could have known about it, other than Elly's telling him, was from Laura or Mann. I suppose Mann could have told him when he and Bryce spoke outside the washroom, but the janitor who saw them said they only exhanged a few words. I should have picked up on it sooner."

"It might have saved you some broken bones," Evelyn commented.

"But then you'd have no one to spoil."

"True," she said, "but I'd have preferred it be under different circumstances." She came over and poured me a last bit of coffee.

I took a sip and set down my mug. "When Mann raised the possibility of Laura as an alternative to Ulrike for the *Liederkreis's* first performance, Bryce had no way of knowing how firm Mann's intentions might be or whether he'd mentioned them to anyone else. I'm thinking specifically of

Mann's daughter, Anna. But the one thing he would know was that if Laura sang the premiere, he'd lose his chance to share in the limelight. She'd never agree to work with him. From the way he spoke about her, I gather their confrontation over Siobhan was pretty ugly.

"When Mann collapsed while Laura was out on a caffeine run, Bryce spotted an opportunity to ensure that Ulrike wouldn't lose the *Liederkreis* premiere. Something must have clued him in that Mann had suffered a stroke, not, say, a heart attack. He didn't have much time to think. When Laura returned, he acted fast, knocking her unconscious with the first thing he could lay his hands on—Elly's paperweight. He figured out how to kill her afterward."

"By smothering her with a cushion."

"Then he tried to confuse things by making it look like Mann's death was murder, too. He figured that beating in his skull would conceal the evidence of a stroke. And while he was at it, he came up with the idea of muddling things further by making Laura look as if she'd been killed the same way."

Evelyn shook her head. "Ghastly. Just ghastly." She rinsed the coffee pot. "Let's not talk about it anymore." She came back to the table with a dishrag. "So, do you have any plans for today?"

"R and R. Same as yesterday. You?"

"A collector from Brussels wants to buy the Kelmscott Chaucer I acquired last year," she said, swiping crumbs into her cupped palm. "I'll have to make some overseas calls. Then I'm going into Orangeville. You can come with me if you feel like it."

"We'll see."

"An outing might do you good."

"I'd rather stick around."

"Well, if you're sure. But today's the last day I'm going to let you wander off between meals. After that, I expect you to spend more time with me."

⚹ ⚹ ⚹

A year before we'd met, Christian had constructed a pavilion at the western extremity of Léo's one-hundred-hectare property. Rectangular, entirely black, with a flat roof supported by big square posts, it framed a panorama of the Credit River Valley below. Fore-, middle- and background drew together under its broad lintel in a balanced, ordered way that made the view look painted. I'd spent the last four days taking in the scene—between meals, as Evelyn had pointed out—trying to find some order in my own internal landscape.

Two weeks ago, I'd planned on coming here to take the pulse of grief. Now that I was back, I found it didn't beat as strongly as I'd expected. Christian's hand was everywhere—in a birch copse culled to emphasize the shadows of the trees, in a split-rail fence that drew attention to a sweep of hillock—but the reminders came like fragments from the far side of a dream. A cedar-bordered rock garden to the left of the main house looked smaller than it should. The excavated pond seemed larger. In my mind's eye, there was no stone path leading up to the pavilion.

At first, the altered recollections disturbed me, as if something I'd relied on to help me keep a promise had suddenly turned traitor. I made forays, trekking one-armed around the property, hoping to arouse feelings that seemed to have deserted me. I began to wonder if the codeine for my fractures was numbing more than physical distress. I'd come back to the pavilion tired, but instead of mulling over memories made keen by loss, I'd doze off against a post, aware of little more than sunwarmed wood against my spine.

The past year hadn't been an effort to get over Christian's suicide; it had been a holding on. It was as if I'd made a covenant with grief, agreeing to remember in exchange for love-affirming pain. The steps I'd taken to move past it only reinforced its presence. But the last two weeks had released me from my unadmitted pact with mourning. Recalling suffering requires an act of will, a focused concentration. Investigating Mann and Laura's murder had disrupted it; the assault by Bryce had shattered it completely.

Then there was Andrew.

The morning after my attack, he'd quizzed me dispassionately, posing questions as if following a script. He seldom used my name, and when he did, it came out studiously neutral. Léo, hovering nearby, shot me puzzled glances: "*This* is the man you were talking about?"

A week ago, he'd left a message saying he was out of town. Then, unexpectedly—fortuitously—he'd pulled up outside the carriage house. I still didn't know why. A few days before that, he'd been stretched out on my couch, morning-after horny, but later on, he wouldn't even acknowledge that the night before had happened. His talks with Léo while I convalesced in Caledon might have been oblique attempts to stay in touch, but I wasn't staking too much on it. He was a professional cop. He'd only had one lover. There had to be a story there, but I doubted I'd be hearing it.

Most often, when I surfaced from my naps, I'd experience a moment of euphoria, as if anticipating something I couldn't put my finger on. Shadows in the valley would have grown or shrunk, depending on when I'd drifted off. The river would be glittering, or threading calm sky-blue between the trees. Perhaps some native sensuality, asleep since Christian's death, was

343

waking up and looking forward to the simple transformations.

Around five o'clock that afternoon, I went back to the main house, past the Pan-Abode screened by trees several hundred metres away. I'd visited the cabin the first day I felt up to walking. It, too, had suffered memory's sea-change. The tongue-in-groove cedar walls surrounded a single floor ten by fifteen metres—bigger than an average suburban bungalow, not as intimate as I remembered. Conversely, the veranda looked less spacious. The windows that had lit up Christian's body a year ago loomed less large. Only the chestnut tree, still in bloom, looked right.

Léo had said he'd be driving up for the weekend, and sure enough, as I got near the house, I saw his Lexus coming down the driveway. He tooted when I waved, then disappeared behind a stand of maples. I waited for him outside the kitchen, stooping to pick mint from Evelyn's garden. A minute or two later, I heard footsteps on the flagstone path.

"Hello, Vikkan."

The voice wasn't Léo's. I straightened up and turned around, taking in the University of Waterloo sweatshirt and the grey eyes that went with it.

"I hope you don't mind—I got myself invited for the weekend."

A black gym bag rested on the ground, with a change of socks peeking through the half-closed zipper. Out of nowhere, Evelyn had appeared. I smelled a conspiracy, and couldn't think what to say.

Léo came around the corner of the house a moment later, grinning, and flashed a little thumbs-up sign.

AFTERWORD

What is a work of fiction, if not a delicious blend of what we know and what we imagine?

Most of the settings in this book are real. Toronto is a realcity (a fact its mayors forget in their drive to make it "world class"), the Faculty of Music really does sit halfway up U of T's Philosopher's Walk, and so on. However, the events I have described taking place in these locations— and, to some extent, their architecture and layouts—are either imaginary or a patchwork of the past and present.

My Conservatory, in particular, is a hybrid of the real, the imagined, and the remembered. After nearly a century of staying pretty much the same, the Con has, at the time of this novel's publication, neared completion of a massive restructuring and renovation. The changes are good for the Conservatory, but, alas, not so good for my story. Rooms that once served a particular function have been put to other uses. Internal policies and procedures have been thoroughly updated. But the school's history lingers on, and so, quite shamelessly, I've borrowed portions of its past, as needed, to make my story work.

My characters are fanciful, although two do bear similarities to real people. The model for Elly Gardiner is a former Conservatory teacher who will no doubt be amused by the recalcitrance Vikkan shows at not heeding her well-intentioned and eminently practical advice. The character of Dieter Mann evolved from unforgettable lessons and classes I took with Karl Ulrich Schnabel, son of the great pianist, Arthur Schnabel. The remainder of the characters in the book are as fictional as the human mind can make them.

Rewriting history is not solely the province of novelists. Writers with less ingenuous aims than pure entertainment have been doing it for millenia. Therefore, I make no apologies for concocting events in the nineteenth century that did not take place. At least I have the decency to admit my fabrications.

(continued on the next page)

The texts for Schumann's *Liederkreis*, Opus 39, are by the German poet, Joseph von Eichendorff (1788-1857). My translations at the chapter headings are intentionally liberal.

With the exception of short references to the texts of Richard Strauss's "Zueignung" and to Peter Warlock's "Robin Goodfellow" and "Sleep," all poetry in this book—German and English—is of my own invention.

Lastly, I would like to thank Melanie Fogel, editor of Canada's *Storyteller* magazine, for her part in the writing of *The Schumann Proof*. An early draft was languishing in a drawer when, through a coincidence that makes me wonder whether Charles Dickens and God aren't, perhaps, related, Ms. Fogel dropped into my life. For no other reason than that she believed in my work, she voluntarily critiqued, scoured, and edited the novel, giving up hundreds, if not thousands of hours to become my teacher, my mentor, my goad and my friend.

Words cannot convey my gratitude.